PRAISE

GO YOUR OWN WAY
ZANE RILEY

"4.5 Stars… This is a character driven novel that beautifully shows us the journey of two young men, bad boy Lennox McAvoy and the innocent Will Osborne. It was a pleasure to go along with these two fantastic characters through their first true love experience while they take their first baby steps towards romance."

—*M/M Good Book Reviews*

"Against all YA novel formulae, it is Lennox's beauty that is Will Osborne's window into his better self. Will's intense physical attraction, his own desperate need for love (or, possibly, just hormones) makes him study Lennox so closely that he begins to see light through the darkness; begins to see the sad little boy behind the abrasive exterior. Only Will has the key to Lennox's prison cell."

—*Prism Book Alliance*

"I was shocked to learn this was the author's debut novel. It was well written and held such realism that one felt as if they were transported back to the halls of their high school. The good, the bad, and the ugly of being a high school student are there for everyone to see."

—*Joyfully Jay Book Reviews*

WITH OR WITHOUT YOU

WITH OR WITHOUT YOU

ZANE RILEY

interlude **press** • new york

To JL—You wished for the stars, and the stars spoke through you.

⊙ one ⊙

Will Osborne sat on his back deck and shivered in the dawn light. Tomorrow was Thanksgiving, and yesterday his father had returned home from the hospital. Last week, Lennox had fallen asleep at his house for the first time, but he hadn't stayed. This morning Will had woken up alone once again.

His husky, Oyster, barked as a gust of chilly autumn wind swept the yard. A kaleidoscope of red and yellow leaves filled the air. Will pulled his sweater tighter around his shoulders as Oyster romped through the cascade of leaves, then ran down the steps into the in-ground pool with a splash. The pool wasn't as full as in summer, but a large puddle became a permanent fixture in the fall. Behind Will, the sliding glass door creaked open. His stepmom Karen sat beside him and handed him a steaming mug. She had her hood up, but her brown hair was long enough to show around her neck.

"I *told* you not to let him down there. Oyster! Get out of the pool!"

His white fur sopping and dirty, Oyster trotted up the pool steps into sight. He raced to the far side of the yard and then back. A few rays of sunlight peeked through the bare upper branches of the maples and oaks lining the yard. The mountains glinted in the mist. Their tops were soft and rounded, bright as a canvas splotched with the vibrant colors of a fire. The Appalachians were unlike the jagged points Will always saw in photographs of mountains. As a kid, he'd always argued that the hills around his house weren't mountains at all, but the tops of the heads of giants who had fallen asleep long ago and never been given a haircut.

Will took a sip of hot chocolate and chewed on a marshmallow. "He left again."

"I know."

Karen sighed just as she had yesterday morning. Every morning for a week, Lennox had been gone when they'd woken up. "We just have to be patient with him. This is a lot for him right now."

Will set his mug on the step between his sock-covered feet. "But he's *safe* here. He finally has a home and can figure out his life. How is anything about living here a lot? Living at that stupid motel is a lot, but here is just home."

"For you, honey," Karen said. "This place has always been home to you. This yard and that kitchen and this dopey dog that just ran back into the pool. I swear I'll kill him. Oyster, no!"

"But if it's a home, and he's welcome, then it should be for Lennox, too."

"You have to think about it from his perspective. He's never had much of a home, not since he was a little kid. It's like how you don't remember much about your mom, Will. It took you time to adjust to our relationship, and it'll take Lennox time to get comfortable enough here to stay."

"I guess. I just… want him to be." Will took a sip again and called Oyster. He wished Lennox was a lot of things that he wasn't. Safe. Happy. His boyfriend. For a few days, he'd assumed the last was true, but he wasn't so sure anymore.

"And he will with time." Karen made Oyster sit and offered him a treat from her coat pocket. "I wish it was always this nice in the mornings. Too soon it'll be freezing."

"Then blistering hot and so humid your skin falls off. I hope New York doesn't get so hot," Will said. He rubbed Oyster's ears and kissed his still-dry forehead. "Good boy. Ready to go inside?"

Oyster whined and ducked his head.

"Too bad, buddy." Karen stood up and stretched her arms over her head. Her hood fell back and her brown hair blew into her face as another gust swept through the yard. "Come on. Time for breakfast."

Will stood and cast his eyes up at the mountains one more time. It was always beautiful here this time of year. Most years they took a trip along Skyline Drive, but it hadn't happened this year. His dad's heart had failed the very morning they were going, right before they got into the jeep. Instead, they'd spent the day at the hospital waiting for news, then sitting with his comatose father until visiting hours ended. Now his dad was awake, and so much had changed since that day in early October.

"We should take our trip once Dad's better," Will said as they went inside. "On Skyline Drive, I mean. After winter's over we'll all go. We'll pack a cooler and convince Lennox to—"

Will stopped. Lennox couldn't go. Skyline Drive was miles and miles long; it carried them all the way down the mountains to the southern state line. Lennox's ankle monitor wouldn't allow him to get to the beginning, let alone the southern end, of the trip.

Karen smiled and kissed his cheek. "We'll see," she said, and that was enough for Will. "Now I've got to get your dad up, and then we've got cooking to start after breakfast. And we'll pick up Lennox again, if we can find him. Give Lucy a call, she's probably seen him. And grab your report card—"

"Ugh, fine. Don't lecture me about my math grade."

Will headed downstairs to his bedroom. It was a little messier than he normally kept it. Several of Lennox's school books and his socks were scattered over the floor; one of his shirts clung to the bedside lampshade. Will pulled the shirt free and grabbed his phone to text Lucy. Lennox had spent most of the weekend with her instead of here. Lucy was Lennox's friend, sure, but why would he choose to stay at that horrible motel when he could be safe at Will's house?

Will rummaged through his backpack until he found his report card, along with Lennox's. He'd opened his yesterday at school with his friends, but Lennox had been absent. He'd missed almost all of November, by Will's count. Karen had called in a number of those absences recently, but Will wasn't sure how much good it was doing. Will tucked Lennox's unopened report card into his bag and headed upstairs.

Ben and Karen were eating breakfast in the kitchen when he joined them.

"Morning, Will."

"How are you feeling, Dad?"

"Little worn, little shaky. Nothing unusual these days."

Ben raised his hands to demonstrate. Both trembled, the left worse than the right. Will glanced at the bowls of cereal on the table.

"Toast might have been easier for you," Will said. He picked up Ben's spoon and helped him eat a few bites. If Ben couldn't regain steady control of his hands, he'd have a difficult time returning to work at his engraving store. "That'll go away eventually, right, Karen?"

"Most of it should, yes." Karen took over helping Ben. "So let's see that report card."

Will grimaced but handed it over. Together, Ben and Karen scanned it and smiled.

"Good job, kid."

"But I have a C plus in—"

"Which is better than usual," Karen reminded him. "A's and B's in everything else. That's a great addition to your applications. Have you finished them yet?"

"No, we just turned in our college essays last week, so I'm waiting on that. Mrs. Martinello told me everything looked great when I saw her yesterday."

"Did she give you the admissions pamphlets?"

Will nodded. "Loads. Sarah Lawrence, NYU, and a bunch for in-state schools. I can show you after breakfast."

As Will cleaned up their dishes, Karen and Ben flipped through the pamphlets Will had dumped on the table. Ben kept eyeing several of the local ones and asking questions about them while Karen flipped through NYU's.

"UVA is a good school," Ben said when Will sat back down with them. He passed the pamphlet on to Will. "Have you looked into their English programs?"

"Tuition's just as steep at UVA as out-of-state," Karen said. "If he's going to pay that much he might as well go to his dream school."

"I saved what was left of your mom's life insurance. That'll help quite a bit," Ben said.

"We'll figure that part out once we know what we're paying for," Karen said. "But for *now*, it's the trials of getting in. Sarah Lawrence over NYU?"

"Definitely."

Will shuffled through the pamphlets. Sarah Lawrence's was on top, with a trio of students and a beautiful building in the background. NYU's depicted the city skyline. He flipped to the in-state schools and paused at one with a picture of a boy that looked similar to Lennox. His nose was too big, his skin lighter, but the eyes and face shape were like Lennox's.

Did Lennox have any plans? Staying in Virginia wasn't something Will wanted to do, but was that what Lennox was going to do? New York meant amazing opportunities for Will and his future, but Lennox was a part of that too, now. Will could see them, strolling along a nameless road hand in hand, talking and laughing. But that road wasn't between the towering buildings of New York City.

"Keep a sharp eye on those dreams," Ben said. He flipped through a few more pamphlets and paused on a bright blue one. "Juilliard? Kid, I hate to break it to you, but you're as tone-deaf as an earless elephant."

"Oh, no, that's... It's for Lennox."

Ben grunted and set it aside, but Karen picked it up. So far, the three of them had avoided conversations about Lennox since Ben had come home yesterday morning.

"He's looking into New York City, too?"

"I, well, no. I just thought, I mean, he's so talented. I thought studying music would be a good choice."

Karen nodded, but Ben snorted. Will flinched. Ben picked up the NYU pamphlet as Karen turned their conversation to Thanksgiving.

"Mia should be here early tomorrow morning. Knowing her, she'll drive all night."

"Aunt Mia's coming?"

Karen laughed at Will's wide grin. "Yes, of course. She never misses one, does she?"

"True. Is anyone else—"

"So this Lennox. That, um, kid. He's—" Ben set the pamphlet down and met Will's eyes. Ben's eyes had changed since he'd woken up. They were darker; the irises were dull and faded. "You like him, right?"

Will nodded. *Here we go again.*

"And he likes you?"

"Yes."

"You're absolutely sure?"

"*Yes.* We're," Will hesitated before adding, "we're boyfriends now."

"Really?" Karen peered at him. "I can't believe he—he said yes?"

"It just happened."

It wasn't entirely a lie. He'd thrown the word into their conversation yesterday and Lennox hadn't denied it. But he hadn't said anything else about it either. If anything, he'd been more skittish than usual last night, but surely that had more to do with Will's invitation to Thanksgiving dinner—and to stay for break—than it did with being boyfriends.

"Well, I'm glad," Karen said. "Your first boyfriend, oh, I can't wait to tell Mia. Wish I could say the same for my mom."

Will groaned.

"Oh, hush. I'm not a big fan of her either, but she *is* my mother. Tolerate her for a day and I'll buy you tickets to a Pirates game."

"Deal. Two tickets so I can take Lennox."

But would Lennox be able to go? That ankle monitor kept him confined, so confined that perhaps he hadn't bothered to consider any sort of future for himself—or them—at all. Will's stomach knotted. New York was the only thing he'd wanted for so long, but now he had Lennox, too. Did Lennox have any plans at all after June? Or even beyond tomorrow?

◀ two ▶

SOMETHING COLD DRIPPED ONTO LENNOX'S nose. He flinched, twisted, and his hand caught on something hard. A gush of water hit him in the face. Lennox bolted upright, smacked his face on the bathtub faucet, and fumbled to turn the water off. Drenched and shivering, he climbed out. It was morning. A cold, crisp frost lined the edges of the bathroom window, and a few faint rays of sunlight lit his face.

"Lennox?"

Someone pounded on the motel room door—an echo of the drunks from last night, but a much kinder voice. Lucy was back. No pellet guns or threats of violence accompanied *her*.

"What?"

"Come out, and *don't* say you've already done that! I need to talk to you."

"You need to go to sleep," Lennox said. He shook his head and splattered water all over the mirror. "It's like six in the morning."

Lucy didn't answer. Lennox pulled off his jacket and shirt. Both were soaked, along with his pillow and the blanket he'd placed in the bathtub to make it more comfortable. Laundry it was, then. What better way to start his Thanksgiving break?

The bathroom window suddenly jerked open a crack.

"Give me a few minutes, all right?"

"Nope."

A shoe propped the window open further, and then a sock hit the wall.

"Fuck off! Give me five damn—*gross!*"

A bra hit Lennox's face. The shoulder strap got tangled in his hair, and by the time he was dressed and dragging his own laundry outside, Lennox was still fighting to pull it free.

"Finally. Give me that."

"Ouch!"

Lucy yanked her bra from his hair and set her laundry hamper at his feet. Her hair, free of its usual long braid, was twisted instead into a dark bun hanging over the adjustable strap of her baseball cap. The cap was yellow and black and matched her nail polish.

"That's a nice lock you've got. Did Will do that?"

Lennox looked at his new doorknob, too. Will and Karen had stopped by last Friday to install it. He'd slammed the door in Will's face not long afterward. Having Will here was too difficult after what had happened to his room, with those words still carved into the wall.

"His stepmom did." Lennox scooped up Lucy's heavier hamper and shoved the backpack full of his own laundry into Lucy's arms. "Here, I'll take yours. So what's the crisis?"

"Well, one, you should be with your boyfriend instead of here."

"He's not—well, he is, but shut up."

They set off down the road together, Lennox slowed by the laundry hamper's weight while Lucy shuffled ahead with his backpack over her shoulders. She stopped to wait for him at the corner.

"Slowpoke. So I need your... expertise? Well, opinion, I guess."

"On what? God, did you pack bricks in here too?" Lennox set the hamper down on the curb. "This isn't all going to fit once it's dry and folded, you know."

"My backpack's in there." Lucy kicked at a few rocks on the sidewalk and watched him. In the morning sun her eyes glinted, a bright brown like Karen's. "There's this new girl at work—"

"Ooh, Lucy's got a crush?"

"Kelly—I've never—but she's got this amazing tattoo sleeve she's halfway through getting done, and this like pink stripe through her bangs and she knows everything about every generation of Pokémon—"

"You've got it bad." Lennox heaved her laundry hamper up and continued across the road and around the next corner to the laundromat. "What? You look like you're about to puke."

Lucy bit her lip and adjusted her hat as they crossed the parking lot. "I'm straight, though. How can I like Kelly? But I do. She's so cute when she's trying to remember what's down aisle six."

Lennox shrugged and shouldered the laundromat door open. He set the hamper down next to the first available machine. "So you're bi. What's it matter?"

"Bi?"

"Bisexual. You like guys and girls, so I'd say you're bi. Or she's just really, *really* special."

Lucy popped a few quarters into the washing machine and nodded thoughtfully. "I could be bi. That'd be, yeah. I mean, I might just want to be her instead of be with her, but even you would think she has a cute butt. It's perky like Will's."

"Good enough to nibble, then."

"Eww!"

"What? He's got a wonderful ass."

"But have you really put your, like, mouth there?"

"Not yet." Lennox snickered as she pulled a face. "What? I've put my dick there too. That's sort of how it works for us."

"Then why were you at the house last night instead of with him, enjoying each other?"

Lennox frowned as she began throwing her darks into a washer, then her whites into the one beside it. The laundromat was unusually quiet the morning before Thanksgiving. Only one other person was there, an older man probably around fifty. Will's dad was around his age, though they looked nothing alike. Ben Osborne was more strongly built and taller; he was like an older, whiter version of Otto from school, whereas this man was thin and frail. If Lennox could handle Otto, then he could handle Ben—if he dared to go back to Will's house now that Ben Osborne was home.

"Well, I live there."

Lucy shook her head as she turned the washers on. Then she started one for his pitiful little heap. Most of his clothes had made their way to Will's house or the dumpster. The drunks had ripped up most of what he'd had in his room.

"You don't have to. I won't either, before long. I'll be done with school soon, then I'm moving to Boston. Once winter's over, I'm out of here."

Everyone had plans to leave, didn't they? Will kept mentioning New York City, and Lucy had her sights set on Boston, for its harbor or more college or something. Will's friends probably had plans beyond tomorrow, too. And Lennox was floundering. Just trying to graduate seemed impossible.

"Lennox, you okay?"

"It's nothing. Just thinking about, you know, the future and stuff."

Lucy nodded and pulled him down onto the plastic chairs between the washers and dryers. She lifted her cap and brushed her hair with a comb from her jacket pocket.

"You'll help me braid? A big French braid this time." She continued to watch him while she brushed out her tangles. "So what are your plans? After graduation, I mean. Have you been looking at colleges nearby or—where did you live before?"

"Richmond. Vienna. I dunno. Live life or something. Get a job, I guess. My ankle monitor will be gone by then, unless I get in trouble between now and January."

"It comes off so soon?"

"It's been over a year." Lennox pulled his leg up and twisted it around his calf as he spoke. "They put it on as soon as I left juvie. Beats the hell out of being locked up again."

"So you aren't looking at colleges, then? Is Will?"

"He's set on New York City. Something with writing, I think."

"Are you going to—"

"Are you done brushing so I can braid?"

Lucy twisted and handed her hair off to him. He began to braid carefully while she snapped the hair tie around her wrist.

"It's okay to, like, not know what you want to do yet. I only figured it out a few semesters ago. You should still apply, though, just to see what your options are. Get away from here instead of getting sucked in for the rest of your life."

"Nah, I, no. Hold still."

"But—"

"Look, I can't afford the applications even if I wanted to. Will was filling his out the other day and they're like fifty bucks a pop. I could feed myself for a year with the sort of money he's putting into applying to a bunch of shitty schools. Whatever, okay?"

"Fine."

"So this girl at the store..."

Lucy talked for the better part of an hour about Kelly. Lennox was glad Lucy might have found someone. She deserved that sort of happiness if she wanted it. His laundry finished first, but Lennox stayed put, helping Lucy study for her statistics final and trying to put off the inevitable.

"You don't have to stay. I'm sure Will is—"

"He's fine."

"Your *boyfriend* would be happier with you safe," Lucy said. "You'll have to figure something out. I leave after this."

"Leave?" Lennox sat up as Lucy closed her book.

"It's Thanksgiving, butthead. I'm going home. You should, too."

Lucy's dryer dinged. As she packed away the last of her clean clothes, Lennox plucked at the strap on his backpack. He couldn't go to Will's house. Ben was home. He wasn't welcome now.

"Look, I'm heading past Will's on my way. Do you want a ride?"

"No."

"You'd rather have those drunks pounding on the door all night than be with Will? I don't get you sometimes."

"Let's just go, okay?"

"Fine."

Ten minutes later, both of them heaved Lucy's hamper across the motel's parking lot to her room. His own would be easy enough to put away, but Lucy's would take—

Lucy gasped. Lennox dropped his side of the hamper on his foot.

The doorknob—his brand new doorknob—was gone.

Lennox hurried in and looked all around his room for it. Nothing. No bolts or screws or pieces of doorknob anywhere. Even the extra latch was gone. He headed back outside to check the dumpster, but Lucy stopped him.

"Milton. He must have taken it off," Lucy said as Lennox eyed the dumpster. "Just go to Will's. We can figure this out after Thanksgiving, okay?"

"I'm staying here."

"But—"

"Have a good Thanksgiving, okay? I'll see you later."

Lennox shut himself in his room. He barricaded the door with the broken mini-fridge, packed every heavy object in the room into it, and then made sure it was wedged between the dresser and the door. He grabbed the last of his books and comics, everything he'd managed to salvage from the break-in a few weeks ago.

The only thing left was the photograph on the dresser. Karen and Will had passed it along to him last week. A much larger version of his Polaroid stared at him. It was a little blurry, and a hazy line ran across the middle, but Lennox could see both of their faces better than before. He was tiny. His hair was bigger than his entire head, and so fluffy it looked like a cumulous cloud. His eyes still managed to sparkle despite the grainy quality of the photo, and his smile was identical to his mother's. She looked unfamiliar to him all of a sudden, though, like a fading shadow in his mind. Not like Will. Will's outline was sharp, bold, brighter than the city lights Will gravitated toward.

Lennox tucked the photograph into his jacket.

Will. The boy he might be falling ass over head in love with. Will couldn't be more important than Lennox's mother, couldn't replace her in his memory. They weren't boyfriends, even if Will might think so. Getting involved long-term was worse than maybe being in love.

Don't think about that. You're just kidding yourself if you think you're in love. It's probably just gas. Or heartburn. Or heart gas. Hearts can probably fart. It's nothing.

Will was already out of reach for him—had always been, in so many unexpected ways—but this was the end of a beginning never coming to fruition. He couldn't be in love with a boy who was leaving. Lennox couldn't be anything at all.

⏮ three ⏭

"WILL, YOU *CAN'T GO*."

"Lucy said he's just sitting over there," Will said as he pulled his boots on. "And that stupid landlord took off his new lock, so—"

"She also said he refused a ride here," Karen said. She blocked Will's way to the door. "He'll come over when he's ready. We can't keep forcing him."

"But—"

"You have *two* pies in the oven, William, and I haven't the faintest idea what to do with them. Now *sit*."

Will snarled as he was turned around and frog-marched back into the living room. His dad was asleep on the couch with Oyster curled up at his hip. Karen pushed him down until he sat and then joined him.

"I know you want Lennox safe, so do I, but dragging him here isn't working. He needs to come here on his own, Will." Karen sighed and helped him remove his gloves and hat. "He's got to trust more than you if he's going to live here. I know you hate hearing that, but it's true. This is a lot bigger than just the two of you. A lot bigger than his home being a motel room."

"I know that, this is just… It's hard."

"It's even harder for him, but you have to be patient."

Will nodded and unlaced his boots. Lennox should be here, not just at night but all the time. He should spend tomorrow stuffing himself with a four-course meal and more pies than Will could count. But he didn't want that. Or was scared to try. Will wasn't sure which it was anymore.

"I'm going to shower and then make the green bean casserole," Karen said. "You better be here when I get back."

Will nodded as she left. Oyster whined in his sleep and rolled off the couch. The television—the tail end of some football game—chattered in the corner. The house phone rang, but Will ignored it. If he was quick, he could sneak over and—

"Will, answer that!"

He picked up the phone.

"Hello?"

"Will? Hi, how are you?"

Will groaned. Their closest neighbor, Meredith, was on the line.

"For the last time, you can't hear Oyster from your—"

"I'm well, too, thanks. Listen, I was just driving back from the store, had to do some last minute shopping for Thanksgiving, you know how my Pete loves his sweet potatoes, and I saw this, this man, I suppose, walking along the road. This, you know, *black* man. He turned down your driveway as I was passing by and I wanted to call you to warn you before I call the police and—"

"No, don't. That's Lennox. He's—thank god." Will dropped the phone and hurried to the door.

"Lennox? Lennox!"

Will darted out of the porch light's range and slammed right into Lennox, who fell back on his butt.

"Ouch! What sort of welcome is that?"

"Sorry, here. Come on, it's freezing. Why didn't you just let Lucy drive you? She called and said—what happened to your eye?"

They stepped into the hall together, and Will reached for Lennox's face. His right eye was puffy, bruised, and coated with dried blood. Lennox, if anything, looked sheepish at the question.

"Did those assholes—"

"Did that one myself," Lennox said. "Was, um, trying to get more glass out of my wall and sort of... punched myself in the face. Figured

I'd come here to get some ice for it, you know. Whole town's shut down for tomorrow."

"No, you're st—" Will busied himself with locking up the front door. Karen's words rang in his ears. He couldn't demand that Lennox stay. He needed to give Lennox a choice. "Do you want to stay?"

Lennox shrugged.

Will led Lennox into the living room, but the sight of his dad asleep made Will head downstairs instead. He grabbed a few towels from his bathroom and joined Lennox on his bed. His eye was still open, but it was more swollen. Carefully, Will pressed the wet towel against the dried blood.

"Did you rip your eyebrow ring out, too?"

Lennox didn't answer. Will almost asked for more details, but Lennox was half asleep already, and the absence of his eyebrow ring was answer enough. He'd run into those drunks again and come off much worse than Will had yet seen. Lennox shut his eyes and then yelped when Oyster leapt up onto his stomach.

"Ugh, I don't want to cuddle, Lobster."

"His name's Oyster."

"Right, yeah, the whitest lobster on four legs."

Will laughed as he pressed the dry towel against Lennox's eye. He got Lennox to open his eyes again and waved two fingers at him.

"How many?"

"Four strikes, you're out."

Will snorted and kissed his cheek. "You're so wrong right now it's painful."

"It's not four?"

"Three strikes, you're out. Four balls, you walk."

"I can think of something better to do with four balls. Especially if two of them are mine and the other two are yours."

"That can wait until you aren't bleeding out of your face," Will said.

"I should get going." Lennox yawned and his eyes drifted shut again. "Got, like, a doorknob to... and mail needs to be..."

Will kissed Lennox cheek again as he drifted off. It wasn't ideal, but Lennox was here. For another night, Lennox was safe, and that was all Will could ask of him.

* * *

WAKING UP THE NEXT MORNING was a serene experience for Will. His room was freezing—he could tell by how numb the tip of his nose was—but with Lennox's warmth pressed against him, that was easy to ignore. Overhead, the floorboards creaked and the doorbell chimed. It must still be early, since his room was only a hazy dark gray, but their Thanksgiving turkey cooking always started at dawn. Sometimes, if his dad was involved, it started the night before.

Will yawned and nuzzled Lennox's hair as a pair of heels clicked on the wooden floors above him. Aunt Mia was here. Karen's slippers flumped away toward the hall; the sound was so faint he could only trace it for a few seconds with Lennox's breathing so close to his ear.

His boyfriend. He hoped so, and yet it was so pointless to keep wishing for that without talking to Lennox. Too much else was happening to even bring the subject up, but still Will crossed his fingers. He didn't want much for that word, just the promise of them being together and exclusive: someone to spend time with, to laze around and watch movies with after school, someone with whom he could start out with homework and end up with laughter falling from swollen lips and rumpled shirts. It was a simple vision in his head, of talk and laughter and sharing himself with the hope of another being offered in return.

Aunt Mia's voice carried down the stairs. "Psst, hey, knucklehead. Wakey, wakey, it's time for us to burn a turkey."

Will rubbed his eyes and reached for his phone on the nightstand.

"You're not allowed to touch the turkey," Will said.

Aunt Mia took the steps two at a time; her heels hit the wood like a jackhammer. His aunt was tall and, according to his dad, looked a lot like his mother. Her arms were thick and gangly; her legs were short. With or without heels, she was a head taller than Karen, and at their last meeting this time the previous year, she'd still been taller than Will. Her hair was a vivid red, and her freckles speckled her skin much as Will's did.

"Aw, Karen said you had a little boyfriend, but I didn't expect him to be such a cuddler."

Aunt Mia leaned over to pinch Lennox's cheek, but Will stopped her.

"Don't! He's—he'll try to stab you if you do that."

"Oh, a bitey little Chihuahua, is he? Fine. Either way, time to get up and help me figure out how to cook a turkey. Your dad's not allowed to help this year, so we're either blowing it up in the backyard on our own or trying the oven. Personally, I think the boring oven has a nice, warm ring to it."

Will grunted as he untangled himself from Lennox. It took a few patient minutes of wiggling and tugging and rolling before Lennox was hugging a pillow and Will was sitting up and pulling his socks on.

"I can't believe you sleep with bare feet. You're just like your mother. She used to walk up the drive to get the mail in the snow with no socks on."

Aunt Mia was still taller than him when he stood up to hug her, but as they broke apart she held him in place by his shoulders. Her eyes were only an inch or so above his, and once the heels were removed, Will had no doubt he'd be looking down at his aunt for the first time in his life.

"Hmm, I think you're taller than me now. I'll be keeping the heels on to establish my authority as your favorite aunt."

"You're my only aunt."

"Don't be picky." Aunt Mia hugged him once more and led him upstairs. "So, how's the sex?"

Will only hesitated for a second as his cheeks flared with heat. "Heated. A little rough, but—"

"Not when I'm in the room. There are some things stepmoms don't want or need to know," Karen's voice called. She appeared a moment later, still in her pajamas with a printed sheet of paper in hand. "Some directions for an oven turkey. Good luck."

With that she was gone, and Will was left alone with his aunt to riddle out the mystery of cooking a turkey. His aunt didn't seem to know any more than he did, but she circled the kitchen several times, pulling various utensils from cabinets and drawers as she talked.

"I want all the details from my sex-crazed nephew. I'm a cool aunt, remember? And I know you've probably done things before, but your first boyfriend is different."

"No, um, I haven't." Will grunted as she heaved the turkey, still in its packaging, into his arms. "I mean, around here, he's the first boy I've met who isn't straight."

"Really? I thought at least a few kids around here would be gay."

"Well, they probably are; they just aren't out." Will shrugged as she handed him a knife to cut the netting and plastic wrapped around the turkey. "I was the only one until he showed up."

"Hmm, well, I'm glad he's here. Your mom would have loved to see you with your first boyfriend. Or any cute boy, actually."

"She didn't even know I'm gay."

"Oh, she knew. You might have been three when she died, but she knew. When you went grocery shopping, you kept ripping out all the pictures of Will Smith's kid and those Backseat—"

"Backstreet."

"—boys from magazines and telling her you wanted her to buy them, too."

"I did?"

Aunt Mia laughed. "The number of magazines she used to have to buy because you would toddle off and tear them up before she could get to you! God, I used to love those phone calls. She wanted a kid leash for your birthday that year."

"No kidding."

Inside, Will was buzzing with—he wouldn't call it excitement, but it was something close. Maybe relief. His mother had known he was gay, and she hadn't cared. She'd loved him anyway. His dad had never mentioned those stories. Maybe she'd never told him.

"So what's his name, then? I want details before we roast this dead bird for dinner."

"Lennox. Are we doing the dump and run in the backyard like Dad always does?"

Most years, their Thanksgiving turkey was cooked in the backyard by his dad. Sometimes it was deep fried, and other times his dad used some weird setup that involved sticking a beer can up the turkey's ass. Will had watched from a distance, just long enough to hold the kitchen door open for his dad to run inside before something exploded. Only last year, the turkey had shot off like a rocket, propelled so high in the air that it had looked, for a moment, as if the mountains had turned volcanic and were erupting raw turkey into the sky.

"It's too cold out. Up in Pittsburgh, it was snowing like crazy already. Besides, I don't think we've ever had a turkey that survived that cooking process. Let's keep this thing in one piece so Oyster doesn't get it again."

They set to work preheating the oven and rubbing things on the turkey that Will didn't have names for. Will did most of this while his aunt read the instructions from Karen's paper, and while it all sounded gross, it felt even nastier when he pulled the bag from inside the cavity of the bird. As they worked, Aunt Mia told him about her life in Pittsburgh, from her advertising job to the various men she'd been dating and dumping. Most of them sounded like middle-aged jerks, and the one woman she'd met hadn't come across as much better.

Aunt Mia grabbed a box of cereal from the top of the refrigerator and opened it. "So, this Lennox boy, how'd you meet him? You've been purposefully turning the conversation away from your dorky little romance for almost an hour. Time to spill."

As she spoke, she shoved a fistful of cereal into her mouth; half of it ended up on the floor. Oyster yipped and gobbled up every brightly colored ring before Will could scold either of them.

"He's... We met at school. I, um, slapped him the first day."

"Ooh! He got you all riled up in less than eight hours!"

"He deserved it! And it was in like ten minutes, actually. It was... I don't know. I couldn't stand him, but he was really hot at the same time. I don't know. We just... grew together. We aren't even..." Will paused and rubbed Oyster's head when he dropped his furry chin onto his knee. "How do you know if someone's your boyfriend?"

Aunt Mia gave him a funny, squinty look. "What do you mean?"

"I mean, I want us to be, and I think he kind of does, too, but it's complicated. I called him that the other day and he didn't disagree, so—"

"Nah, nope. Knucklehead, don't be a knucklehead, okay? Sit down and talk with him about it. Communication is the single most important thing in a relationship. That and honesty. Actually, honest communication is rule number one. Don't assume, and don't force each other to be or do something you aren't or can't be. Got it?"

"I *know* that. But I'm not sure Lennox will say yes, and if he doesn't, then—then I don't know what that'll mean for us. Or his living situation."

Aunt Mia snorted and crunched on another fistful of cereal. "Please, he looked more committed to that cuddle you two were rocking downstairs than I'm committed to eating this entire box of Fruity Pebbles alone."

Will rubbed Oyster's ears and didn't meet his aunt's eyes. "When he's asleep, sure, but when he's awake, so much is going on in his life besides us. Most days all he cares about is whether or not he's going to eat. He's failing most of his classes, and his life is a disaster.

I don't think he's had more than a second to even consider it, and he's terrified of, like, connecting himself to other people."

Aunt Mia ate a little more before answering. "You sure know how to pick them. Damn. Karen said to be on my toes around him, but honestly? You know what you want, right?"

Will nodded.

"Well, talk to him and give him a chance to figure out what it is that he wants, and if it's not the same or compatible, and not a compromise either of you are willing to make, then stay friends. There's no shame in a relationship going that route. But I've got to tell you, from my own experience, that trying to date someone who doesn't want the same things doesn't work and it doesn't make you happy." Aunt Mia offered him the box of cereal. Will took it. "Don't forget about yourself, okay?"

"I... Thanks." Will rubbed his eyes and stood. "I should go wake him up before Karen's mom gets here."

"Oh, Karen's mom is coming? Yes! I love getting her to nag them about having a baby."

"I can't believe you look forward to seeing that woman. She's revolting."

"Yeah, but she's a riot if you don't take anything she says seriously." Aunt Mia shooed him toward the living room. "Go get your boy up so we can be properly introduced."

"Fine. But I'm warning you now, he's crude to people he doesn't know. Actually, to people he doesn't like, too. Or people he does... He's just crude, okay?"

"Sounds like a winner."

Will found Lennox sprawled across his bed. It was brighter now, but still a very gray morning. He held one of Lennox's arms up and let it drop. Lennox didn't stir. Leaving him down here would be better than having him sit through dinner with Karen's mom. She was less fun than skinny-dipping with piranhas. She was very old and very set in her ways. Every time she saw Will, she pestered him about whether or not he had a pretty little girlfriend, even when Karen reminded her that he was gay.

"Lennox? Wake up."

Lennox grunted sleepily and shoved Will weakly when he rolled Lennox off his stomach. A pair of hazel eyes squinted up at Will and then snapped shut again.

"Go away."

"Nope. My aunt's already here, and Karen's mom will be here soon."

"Why?" Lennox sat up, suddenly alert and tense.

Will rubbed Lennox's forearm as his stomach tightened. They could talk now, before he chickened out or kept pushing it off day after day. Waiting wasn't doing him any good; it was only making him second-guess everything.

"It's Thanksgiving. They're coming for dinner."

"I'll just hide down here and starve, thanks. Or head home. Thanksgiving's for family, and I'm not—"

"Thanksgiving is about spending the day with the people you care about, and I care about you a lot."

Lennox plucked at his boxers and tousled his curls. They were wilder than Will had ever seen them, so tangled and frizzy they looked like wires. Will took a seat beside him and rested his hand on Lennox's knee.

"I think we should talk alone. Before we deal with upstairs."

Lennox inhaled sharply as his fingers pattered across the bedding. His tongue ring flicked against his teeth.

Click, click, click.

"You're going to ruin your teeth," Will said. Lennox flinched. "What?"

"Nothing."

"So, um, I wanted to ask you w-where we stand. I mean, I know we like each other and we've done a lot of stuff I never imagined doing with someone so quickly, but... are we dating? Or boyfriends?

Because I keep thinking we are and then I'm not sure. I want that with you."

"Why would you want that with anyone?"

Lennox hopped to his feet and grabbed his jacket and boots. Will followed him with his eyes. He'd expected a biting denial, but it still hurt. Without Will chasing after him, Lennox hesitated on the first stair.

"What?"

"I want us to talk about this. Like seriously talk, okay? I want you in my life and I want us to be boyfriends. I do, and I'm not going to lie about that. You're important to me, and having that sort of relationship with you is too."

"I'd rather just fuck." Lennox knocked his boots against the railing. "I like fucking."

"Yeah, I know, but I know I'm more than some fuck to you. I'm not that blind. I want an honest answer, too. Whatever that answer is, I just want it to be honest. If you need to think about it for a little bit then that's fine, too. I know you've got a lot going on."

"No more than you. With, you know, your dad and everything." Lennox pulled his jacket on and sat on the steps holding his boots. "What do you even mean, 'that sort of relationship'? Like, we kiss and fuck and have fun together. Isn't that enough?"

Will twisted his hands in his lap. He wasn't going to get any sort of answer out of Lennox today. He rarely did. But trying to wrangle a commitment was impossible. Lennox was still skittish, too quick to dart aside like a deer at the faintest hint of trouble. Will climbed to his feet and wrapped his arms around his chest.

"I... How about I tell you what boyfriends means to me and if you think that's something you want to share with me, then you can tell me?"

Lennox grimaced as Will joined him on the step, but he squeezed back when Will's hands closed around his. His grip was like a reflex, and Will settled a little in it.

"Boyfriends is a lot of what we're already doing. That's why I'm so confused about it. It's kissing and hand holding and sex. We get to hang out and make out and talk about, well, anything. Our lives, the things we like and don't. We can share secrets we don't tell anyone else and explore new things we've been too scared to try with someone else or by ourselves. We support each other, too. Mostly, it's a name for what we've already been doing so much of, but it's a feeling, too, I think. Something in here," Will said as he placed his palm on Lennox's chest, "that makes you a little more than you were before. It's sharing your life with someone else and having them share theirs in return. Like taking both of our lives and cracking them open and joining them. Like—like a Venn diagram. Parts overlap and other parts don't. How much does is up to us."

Will cleared his throat and tried to hold back the shiver tingling down his spine.

"That's what I think anyway. It's a commitment; I won't lie and say it's not. If you don't want any of that, then just tell me. And we'll figure out what exactly we are. Because I don't want you to agree just for me or just for sex, okay? I don't want our time together to be a chore for you."

"It isn't."

Lennox's thumb stroked the knuckles on Will's hand, traced the dips and curves before settling on his palm like a wave breaking on the shore. For a few minutes, Will let him fold and bend his fingers, let Lennox run his fingertips over every crease and scar and wrinkled knuckle. It was as if he'd found, between the freckles marking Will's skin, a symphony, a silent soaring of tones Will couldn't hear.

"Whatever this is—god, I keep thinking I'm—but I'm only, look, I—I like you, too. And if that's all boyfriends is, then maybe. But I don't do promises. I don't believe in shitty words that are supposed to last longer than either of us will."

"Who says promises live longer than the people who make them? They might end when you shut your eyes at night. It's up to you whether or not to carry them with you into the next day, the minute you open your eyes."

"I *don't* do promises." Lennox's voice was like steel this time, and Will kept silent. "Promises mean someone gets left behind with empty words and nobody to make them true anymore, all right?"

"Okay." Will uncurled his hands to let go, but Lennox's grip didn't loosen.

"But, I think we could try. Nothing forever or crazy, but if you want to call me your boyfriend, then I guess you can."

"Really?"

Lennox shrugged, but he leaned in when Will kissed him. For a long moment they sat there, and despite the lackluster response and the way Lennox tried to brush off his reply, something had shifted between them. It wasn't large or small or any size Will could name, but it was present. They were something more than before, and that was enough. Lennox's lips dipped and parted, then pressed in again.

"First kiss from my boyfriend," Will said, and he grinned as Lennox kissed him a second time. "I could get used to saying that."

Lennox pulled away. "I'm going to clean up a bit. What's for breakfast?"

"Whatever you want."

"You sure about that? Cause I'd prefer to have you naked and alone."

Will shoved him toward the bathroom instead.

⏮ **four** ⏭

AS THEY ALL SAT DOWN to eat, Lennox tried to hold his tongue. Will's aunt was reminiscent of a subway train. Her cadence was even swifter, and her voice was as shrill as squeaky brakes. So far, she was his favorite from Will's extended family, but she was hard to listen to after a while.

Every word drilled into him like the beat of a drum, in a rapid tempo that Lennox found himself tapping against his thigh. It was too fast, really, and his mind was so busy with it that he missed Karen's mother addressing him.

"So, Lennon, you're a friend from school then?"

Will nudged him as the frail woman across from him addressed him again.

"It's Lennox, and he's my boyfriend, Meredith," Will said. Will's hand found his under the table, but Lennox didn't squeeze back. "He's new to town."

"Oh, a good friend then, that's lovely. It's nice to have a best friend."

The pace of the conversation dropped off for a moment and Lennox filled it with a faint click from his tongue ring.

Click, click.

"Mom, Lennox and Will are boyfriends. They're more than friends. We've been through this."

Will's aunt slapped a pile of mashed potatoes onto his plate and leaned over.

"Get ready for the fireworks," she said. "It's a blast to watch Karen's mom go at her."

"Dear, you're talking nonsense. Don't put words in William's mouth."

"I go by Will."

Will's aunt cleared her throat. "So, Ben, Mom found a stash of Beth's old Dead Kennedys records in the attic. She wanted me to ask you if you wanted them. Otherwise, they'll just get tossed."

Lennox's interest was piqued enough to break him out of the tempo around him. The Dead Kennedys were a great band, much older than he was, but he had a patch with their name on it pinned to his jacket for a reason.

"Really? Yeah, we'll take them. I wish I had all the old records she collected, but they all seem to disappear."

Will poked Lennox with his elbow. "That's a band on your jacket, isn't it?"

Lennox grunted and tried to eat. He managed a few spoonfuls of green bean *something* before Karen's mom was after him again. The pace of conversation was jagged after that, between Karen's neat tone and her mother's stern whine. Ben Osborne said a word or two, but his eyes stayed firmly on Lennox, who ate a few more bites and stopped. He couldn't do this. Nobody wanted him here, and everyone kept saying boyfriend as if beating the word into the air would brand it right across Lennox's forehead. Oyster's nails kept clicking under the table, off-tempo with the voices and the clink of silverware on plates. The room was a tornadic catastrophe in his head.

"They're boyfriends, Mom, just drop it."

"Dear, you're being ridiculous with this boyfriend nonsense. You're going to find yourself a sensible young girl to settle down with, William. You've had only men in your life for too long, and a stepmother who won't do her duty as a woman. It's not your fault you haven't had a proper upbringing."

Lennox had never seen anyone go so red, but Karen stood up and led her mother from the room by her arm. They didn't return.

Silence fell at the table, and Will's dad reached for a second slice of turkey that was pulled away.

"You can't have more than one, Dad. We already told you that."

"It's just a slice of turkey, Will."

Will's aunt put a pile of weird green things on Ben's plate instead. Lennox wasn't sure what they were, but they looked like really long green beans with lumpy pyramids all over the sides.

"Have some asparagus instead, Ben. It'll help your wittle heart."

"Shut up, Mia." But Ben ate what she'd put in front of him. "Don't listen to what she says, Will. Karen's mom is just very old school. She doesn't understand."

"Doesn't want to."

Everyone stared at Lennox. It was the first time he'd spoken since he'd come upstairs, and he considered it quite an achievement. More than once he'd had something to say, but every time Will had smiled at him, all hopeful and happy, and he'd stopped himself.

"Meredith is difficult," Ben said. "It's only a few times a year, and at her age—"

"Age isn't an excuse," Lennox said. "My grandfather's an awful shit just like her. But I guess you're on her side, huh? Who cares if she's a bitch to your wife and son? She probably calls us faggots too, but you don't—"

"Do *not* use that language in my house!"

"Dad, don't—your heart—"

"I don't give a damn about my heart if this little thug thinks he can come in here and—"

Lennox shoved his chair back and grabbed his jacket. Will was frantic, trying to call after him and keep his dad in check, but Lennox made it out to the front lawn and down the rocky, muddy driveway. Without Karen backing him up, Will wouldn't do anything. His dad didn't care, and his aunt didn't either. Will would pick his dad and that was it.

Lennox returned to the motel. He was trembling with cold when he arrived. His feet were frozen in his wet sneakers, and his fingers were so stiff he was sure they would break off if he dared to bend them. The back fence shook as a gust of wind blew down the road and, with it, carried the chatter of three voices he wanted nothing to do with: Shrimpy, Crooked Teeth, and Neck Beard, the assholes who hung around the motel and haunted his daily life. Didn't they ever leave? Or have families they could visit today instead of keeping him from going home?

He peered around the corner of the dumpster and grimaced. All three of them, the pellet gun, and that shoddy-ass pick-up truck. Lennox circled to the back of the motel and climbed the fence. His fingers shook, and his grip was weak from the freezing air, but he managed to sling himself over. He found, though, that his window was locked. He tried Lucy's and got the same result.

It started to rain. Lennox sat under his window before the ground became too wet and watched the street beyond the fence. Oil and muck were washed away, some of it swirling in puddles. He plucked at a few strands of dead, icy grass and kept his ears tuned to the front of the building: an engine rumbling, a chorus of laughs, and what sounded like a radio thumping.

They were going to wait then. Lennox rubbed the bandage over his eyebrow as rain soaked through it. That fight had been stupid. The one who lived here, Shrimpy, had been drunk and had gotten after him, and Lennox, sleep-deprived and annoyed, had taken the bait. A black eye and torn-off eyebrow ring for him, and a busted lip, matching eye, and probably concussion for that drunk. Lennox wasn't sure of the damage. He'd left as soon as the man had tripped and knocked himself unconscious on the curb.

Hours went by. Lennox sat and huddled as tightly as he could, but it made no difference. The rain went from speckles in the dirt to a thunderous symphony pounding the ground and the building. As it soaked through his clothes and into his skin, the wind howled through the street. But he sat and waited. He couldn't risk going around the building if they were watching. Even if they weren't, he couldn't begin to guess what his room looked like now. Perhaps they'd left it alone—or they might have ruined everything left in there he could use to block the door.

As the rain slowed, it turned to icy little beads that pierced his chilled skin and clumped in his hair. Lennox held his knees to his chest and pressed his face into the weak warmth the space created. It wasn't much now that it was dark, but it would have to be enough until it was safe.

Because he wasn't going back to Will's house. He wasn't a thug. So what if he'd been in a juvenile detention center for beating up the people who had landed him in the hospital? So what if he'd had an ankle monitor slapped on when he was released? That wasn't all his fault. It wasn't just his own actions that had led him here. His grandfather had paved this path. He'd given up on Lennox long before he'd picked him up from that correctional boarding school and then dumped him out here. Just one kid left on his own, as always. Just a survivor if he made it through the day.

The ice turned to snow: heavy, wet flakes that melted on contact. Lennox kept his eyes on a spot behind the fence; his insides were empty; his skin was like cold steel. A few flakes, bright white and thick, brushed the ground before darkening to mud.

Out front, the truck's engine revved. It echoed around the building, piercing the stillness that had come with the snow. This was ridiculous. He'd just walk back to Will's since they weren't going to leave. That was better than spending all night out here getting frostbite.

Something hit the fence post at the end of the building. Lennox stumbled to his feet as voices swelled like hunched shadows seen down an alley.

"I bet he broke the window or something. She's friends with him. He's probably in her room, bro."

Lennox bolted. He ran away from them, toward the dumpster, but a shout was enough to tell him they'd seen him. A lunging grab, and he was kicking off the side of the dumpster and up over the fence like a feral cat. One short glance back told him they hadn't followed, but he didn't pause to consider what that might mean.

Get away. Get hidden. Find somewhere safe.

He ran down the road, stumbling on stiff, numb legs. Something pinged against a trash can he ran past, and then something hit the sidewalk under his feet. Lennox put on a spurt of speed, but his arms were dead with cold and his legs were cramped and aching from sitting huddled up for so long. He turned off the main road, away from Eastern and toward Will's. Two miles wasn't that far. And it was dark enough to hide once he got beyond the lights of the town. Another two blocks and he wouldn't see any streetlights or porch lights until he was turning down Will's driveway.

The winter air seared his lungs. Lennox's pace dropped to a slow jog as two more pings echoed along the street. The first splashed uselessly in a puddle, but the second clipped his thigh.

Lennox yelped and stumbled. He slipped on the icy street, but righted himself just in time for a third shot to hit his calf. This time, his ankle twisted on the curb and he fell, knees first, into a puddle. Pain shot through his kneecaps and up his thighs like a bolt of lightning.

He could hear footsteps behind him and a cheer full of sick pleasure that ended with a fourth shot, which pinged him in the upper back. Why hadn't he stayed at Will's house? How stupid had he gotten since he'd left juvie? Lennox tried to stand and stumbled a few feet before another shot hit him in the lower back and knocked him down again.

Will's face flickered behind his eyelids as his cheeks hit the road: that soft, freckled beauty that overwhelmed his vision the way stars filled the void of the night sky above. But no stars were shining overhead tonight. Lennox twisted to see as another shot hit his ass.

Was the end of him here, in some dank, freezing, wet street? After all the nights he'd had, was this the one where he finally woke up to see his mother again?

He tried to stand once more, but was hit in the ass by another pellet. Feet splashed toward him and then stopped around him. Lennox raised himself onto his elbows.

"Thought you'd get away, did you?"

It was Shrimpy. Lennox peered up, his vision blurred by the frost in his eyelashes and the dull throbbing along his backside. Snow continued to fall lazily. Shrimpy grimaced, showing his swollen lip and the dull purple bruise that engulfed his eye like a black hole. He spit in Lennox's face.

Another blast of the gun hit Lennox, this time in his other ass cheek. The closer shot was like ice slicing through his skin.

He yelped and bit his lip, tried to think of something to say, something to do to get free enough to hide, but when he tried to stand, one of them kicked him hard in the ribs. With a choked noise, Lennox dropped back down and waited.

Everything might just be over. No more worries or cares or internal debates about whether or not he could manage to be a boyfriend to someone he was in love with. Nothing else could follow tonight, and that would be okay. His sister would never see him again anyway. She might never know he was dead. Will would find someone who could say yes and hang around to give him promises. Nobody else would care.

They shot his ass again, then landed another kick on his ribs. Lennox curled up and tried to block everything out, to just breathe deep and slow, the way he had so many nights when he'd been locked up with worse boys than these men could imagine.

One breath in, another out. Karen's round face swam before him, radiant as she welcomed him.

"Bet you like that, huh? Like being shot in the ass, you stupid faggot."

A second breath. Lucy's face replaced Karen's. Younger, thinner, a little worn, but the very picture of determination and youthful hope.

A third breath for his sister, at his old home in Richmond. She was older, very like their mother in stature and hairstyle; her eyes searched the skyline for something or someone. He hoped her life amounted to more than his own.

The pellet gun shot against his upper back. He cried out, and his breath came rushed and harsh. All three of them kicked him. A burst of panic flickered in him. In his short life, pain had become familiar, but now something was different: serene acceptance. Nothing else was out here for him, nothing he could do or be.

Will flashed into his mind with such a flood of warmth and light that Lennox's arms and legs suddenly felt strong again. The men paused to reload their gun, and Lennox forced himself to his feet. He took two steps before his legs gave out and another shot slammed into his back.

This time he stayed down.

"What? You don't want it in the ass?"

A shoe bore down against the spot they'd shot several times; it pushed and pushed until Lennox squirmed and choked out a groan.

"Queer."

Lennox pressed his face sideways into the shallow puddle under him, and breathed one more time. For Will, for whatever they were or could have been. It didn't matter now. They might have been in love, or maybe he was kidding himself. Maybe love wasn't something he could feel or share, when he was so—

Headlights flooded the street. The foot on his ass disappeared, and the trio retreated. A car door opened, and for once Lennox hoped it was a cop. He might get locked up again, but at least he'd be away from this and from all of the decisions he couldn't make.

Then he heard something worse: the click of a gun being cocked. A real gun, right over his head. He'd only heard that sound once in his life, but he'd never forget it. It was sharper than the plastic ping of the pellet gun that had haunted his footsteps since July, and it was heavier than a sledgehammer falling on his head. A pair of worn brown shoes stopped next to his face. Lennox held his breath as he looked up. But it wasn't a cop and it wasn't someone about to blow his head off, either. A brown woman stood over him with a shotgun aimed at the drunks.

"Leave now. Get away from this boy and don't ever touch him again."

"Oh, whatever. He's only getting what he d—"

A shot went off. Its force made the road vibrate against Lennox's cheek. It ripped up a chunk of the street, too, and made the three men hurry backward.

"What the hell?"

"You outta your mind?"

"That shit isn't a bow and arrow!"

"I'll wound you either way. Leave." Her strong jaw set and her wide shoulders steady, the woman leveled the gun at them once more.

"Leave now."

"Don't be such a bitch—"

"We were only—"

"Leave."

Another shot hit the street, and the men ran. Lennox listened to their footsteps fade with his ear pressed into the road and his breathing still ragged and harsh. He watched his short breaths ripple the puddle like gusts of wind across a sea.

"Rudolph, come over here now."

Or maybe not. If he was hallucinating badly enough to have a gun-wielding Native American woman and a red-nosed reindeer rescue him, then he was probably dead and floating in ghost space. The woman placed her gun on the ground and knelt at his side.

"We'll take you to the hospital," she said. "Rudolph, can you carry him into the car? I'll lower the seats."

She lifted the back of his shirt and jacket as he winced and tried to stand.

"I-I'm fine." Lennox gasped sharply. He looked up at the woman still checking him and spotted the last person he expected to see standing nearby. Otto was staring down at him, his expression both scared and annoyed.

"The fuck you looking at?" Lennox snarled at him and forced himself to his knees. His chest clenched as a frisson of pain ran along his ribs. Nothing broken, at least, or it would feel a lot worse.

"He's fine. He won't hurt you. This is my son, Rudolph. I'm Malia." She placed one gentle hand on his chest to steady him. "Rudolph, get over here. Help him up."

Slowly, Otto approached and squatted. His mother hurried to their truck. Lennox listened to her shift things and heard the thud of stuff being dumped into the bed of the truck. He and Otto stared at each other warily.

"Why the fuck are you named after a reindeer?"

"That shitty deer's named after me, Fruit Loop." Otto knocked his fist against Lennox's shoulder. "Um, you need a hand?"

"No, but once in a while I enjoy Will's instead of my own."

Otto made a face as Lennox took a deep breath and pushed off from the ground. His legs wobbled, and the moment he put weight on his right ankle it crumpled under him. The ground rushed toward his face before Otto managed to catch him.

"Whoa, just... Easy."

"Rudolph, hurry up. Let's lay him down in the back. It might be a tight fit, but—"

A shockwave ran through Lennox. His insides were rumbling, and his spine was melting like a stick of butter. Someone must have caught him, because what seemed like seconds later Lennox was in the backseat of a pickup truck that was bumping along the country road where Will lived.

"It's going to be just fine," Otto's mom said from the front. "We'll be at the hospital in about fifteen minutes—"

"No hospital." Lennox groaned as he sat up. A hand on his back helped him, but he shrugged away from Otto. They eyed each other. "Turn here. Will's house is—"

"Lennox, you need to get those bruises looked at. Your ribs as well."

"Don't have insurance," Lennox said. He watched the dark shadow of the trees flash past, dotted with bright spots of snow. The distant lights of a house caught his eye before it disappeared. "Turn at, at the house... I don't know the number."

"I do." Otto turned around. "Mom, let's just take him to Will's for now. His stepmom's a nurse. She'll take care of him."

"I damn well know Karen's a nurse. I work with her, but she has Ben on her hands as well, and he needs care."

"And when you set off that, that thing on his ankle? Then what?"

"His—fine, but I'm staying until we can look him over and decide what to do."

"Whatever, just turn here. That's Will's house."

The truck veered to the left, jostling Lennox as the gravel under the tires popped and crunched. Otto and his mom got out, and a few shouts followed. Lennox found himself being scooped up and carried inside. A bunch of people swarmed around him as he was laid face down on the couch.

"What happened?"

"Lennox, you're—no, Dad. Let me through." Several women whispered nearby as Will's fingers brushed his cheek. "Lennox? Did they—oh my god."

Someone had ripped open the back of his shirt along his spine. He wasn't sure what had happened to his jacket. The warm air inside the house soothed his wet skin, but the bruises from the pellet gun throbbed like the steady pounding of a flooding river. Lennox gritted his teeth as tears pricked his eyes. His head was spinning. Every time he opened his eyes, he saw four Wills and a dozen other people behind those blurry, beautiful boys. Hands pressed along his back, around the welts rising on his body. They felt like pockets of poison under his skin being released with every brush and press. He squeezed his eyes shut and imagined little black veins sprouting from all sides of the lumps, spreading the pain deeper, into his organs and his brain.

"Lennox, hey, it's Will. You're okay now. Karen and Malia are going to help you."

He squinted to his left as a gust of warm breath dampened his skin. Will was at his side, with one hand running through his hair and the other squeezing Lennox's hand. He squeezed back as Will kissed his forehead. How could he have been so stupid? Leaving here was a relief sometimes, but this was the safest he'd been in years. Welcome or not, this place was going to have to be his home for now.

◀ five ▶

"WILL, BUD, LET'S GET OUT of the way."

"No, Dad, Lennox is—"

"Passed out," Mia said.

Ben nodded at her and kept a firm grip on his walking cane. When the Ottomans had arrived with an unconscious boy in tow, Ben had done his best to get out of the way. He'd done his best to not say any of the things he'd been thinking about this boy since he stormed out earlier. Every other minute, Ben had to remind himself that Lennox was just that—a boy. Very different from his son, but still a teenager.

After Lennox had left, Karen had come back with her mother, and they finished a very rushed and silent dinner. Will had been itching to leave, to run off after Lennox, but Ben hadn't let him. Meredith left not long afterward, and Will had followed, with his aunt in tow, for a winding drive around town and to Lennox's motel. They'd returned empty-handed, but some sort of bond had not so much formed as expanded between his son and sister-in-law. Everyone in Ben's house except himself seemed to be in on that bond, even Oyster. That shedding monster hadn't greeted him once since he came back a few days ago. But he'd charged right up to Lennox this morning and planted himself at his heels, as if guarding him.

"Listen, you're doing him no good by getting in Karen and Malia's way. Come on. Let's go calm down a bit."

As Mia half dragged Will into the kitchen, Ben lingered in the living room. Karen and Malia hadn't spoken to anyone since they'd settled Lennox on the couch and begun to cut his clothes off. Ben could see marks blistering the boy's thin back, and lumps that looked like eggs pushing through his ribs. They cut up along the legs of his jeans and right through several bloodied patches of fabric. His eyes on Lennox's swollen, bruised, and still form, Malia's son shifted in the entryway. It took Ben a moment to recall his name.

"Rudolph, let's give them some privacy to work in, okay?"

"It's Otto."

Malia frowned at Otto. "You should be proud of your name."

"I'm not a reindeer, Mom."

Mia returned and led Ben to a chair in the kitchen. Ben listened to Otto's lumbering steps follow. Will was at the kitchen table, and for some reason he was holding the salt shaker in a death grip. Ben glanced at him and then at Mia as she helped him sit.

"Well, I had to give him something to hold."

Ben grunted and put his walking cane on the table. The cane shook as he set it down. His left arm had been shaking intermittently ever since he woke up. His right hand had been shaking too, though most of those tremors seemed to be over. His doctors said it was a side effect of both his coma and a momentary loss of blood flow to his brain, and that he was lucky he didn't have any more damage to his brain or nervous system.

"He's a tough kid," Mia said. She squeezed Will's shoulder and smoothed his hair. "If it was really serious they'd take him to the hospital, Will. They're both nurses—"

"I *know* that!"

Will slammed the salt shaker on the table and knocked his chair to the floor. Otto circled all of them and opened the refrigerator. While Otto rummaged, Ben watched his son pace. He was almost frantic, in a way Ben had never seen him. Fear was like little spores pushing out of his skin and into the air. But Lennox was just some boy, clearly some stupid guy who went looking for trouble and found more than his fair share of it. Only this time he'd come off worse. Now, somehow, he'd gotten Will on his side, and Ben was getting tired of it.

"This is my fault," Will said as he turned and paced closer to Otto and then back to the table. "If I'd just gone after him like I wanted to when he first left, this never would have happened."

"His choices aren't your fault, Will," Ben said, but Will quickly spun around with the fiercest glare Ben had ever seen. "If he wants to go out and pick fights—"

"He wouldn't do that. Not with all three of them. This isn't his fault, Dad. You think he likes living there? And never sleeping and having to wonder if tonight's the night he's going to have those drunks break in?"

Mia glowered at Ben as she pulled Will back toward the table. Her defense of Lennox surprised Ben as much as Will's reaction. How did she already care about this little punk who had wedged himself into Will's life?

"Ben, stop." Mia rubbed Will's back and held the sliding glass door open. "Go get some fresh air, okay, Will?"

Will nodded and headed into the backyard. Otto shrugged, uncapped a bottle of juice and followed. Mia shut the door and folded her arms.

"I don't care what your opinion is or isn't about Lennox. My nephew, your *son*, is in love with that boy in there. Stop trying to turn Will against him and start trying to give Lennox a chance."

"Will is *not* in love with that kid," Ben said. He righted the salt shaker in the center of the table and stared out at the back deck. "He's got a crush, or the hots for him, or whatever. Nothing's going to come of this. Another few weeks and he'll see right through that punk's little charade."

Mia shook her head and then flicked his nose. "No, you will. Will's already well past that barrier, even Karen is. You're as much of an idiot as you've always been. And for the record? My sister would have loved that kid, both for who he is and for the way he looks at Will. They're both falling into this pretty hard. Don't make it harder for them by making Will choose."

"Choose what?" But Ben already had an inkling.

"This isn't some sort of war for Will's affections between you and Lennox. Don't force Will into a corner just because you aren't ready for him to be in love."

"He's *not.*"

Mia snorted. "God, I wish Beth was still alive. She'd sort you out. Karen's too nice to you."

"There's nothing to—"

"Will? Could you come in here?"

Karen's voice echoed from the living room. Mia called him back in, and he rushed through the kitchen. Not once did he look at Ben. He even knocked Oyster aside as he hurried to Lennox. His chest coiling tighter, Ben watched him go. Mia was wrong. Of course she was. Will wasn't in love. He was too young, too naïve about romance and relationships to even be close.

Will's quick footsteps headed downstairs and then back up. He didn't return to the kitchen. Ben tried not to imagine the scene on the other side of the wall: Will, worried and anxious, sitting beside that wild head of curls; Karen and Malia tending to all the bruises on Lennox's body; and that boy, passed out, but with some unnamable hold over his son. He'd lured Will into his arms somehow, had tempted him with things Ben didn't want to picture. But Will wouldn't want a relationship with that kid, not once he saw him for who he really was. Lennox didn't care about his son.

That night was the quietest Ben had had in a long time, but he couldn't sleep. Otto and Malia left once Lennox was cleaned up. Karen helped Will make a bed on the other part of their sectional couch, so his head rested beside Lennox's in the corner. Oyster curled up on the floor beside them, and Karen sat up in bed until after midnight trying to find a doctor or Urgent Care where they could bring Lennox in the morning. Nobody spoke to Ben. Karen was up every few hours to check on Lennox and to rub aloe vera on his back. Ben wasn't sure what good that would do for bruises instead of sunburn, but he didn't say anything. By dawn, Karen looked worried.

"Ben? Hey, we're going to head out now. Urgent Care opens at seven, and he's getting worse. The pain's making him sick, and he needs to get his ankle checked. Will you be all right on your own for a few hours? I can ask Mia if she can stay. She slept in Will's room last night."

"Sure."

"I love you."

Karen kissed him and left. He dozed off and on afterward, but woke up to Mia's fiery hair and her arms tugging him upright.

"Come on, you lug. Time for breakfast."

The doorbell rang, followed by several pounding knocks. Mia helped him stand and hurried off to answer it. In the living room, Ben found a pair of police officers: his old friend and frequent customer, Jim Ferguson, with a second, much younger officer at his side.

"Ben, how're you doing?"

"Fine, better now that I'm home. What can we help you with?"

"We're looking for Lennox McAvoy."

I knew it. That thug's nothing but trouble.

Mia spoke first. "What's wrong? He didn't do anything, he's been here all night."

Jim nodded, but his partner began to circle the room as if searching for something. Or someone.

"His ankle monitor went out of range about two hours ago, and we believe this was his last known location," Jim said.

"He's not here. Karen and Will took him to the Urgent Care."

Ben sat as the second officer circled into the kitchen and Mia talked Jim through yesterday and this morning. It was exhausting just to listen to it, and Ben wished none of it was involved with his life or his family. That punk was only going to bring more of this to his doorstep, and eventually Will would get tangled up in his problems and ruin his chances of getting into a good college.

Jim's partner reappeared and stood beside the couch.

"Let me go call this in, let them know what's going on. He should be fine. I don't know how they missed giving him somewhere to go for a medical emergency in his inclusion zone in the first place. Hold tight, okay? Jack, wait here."

Jim left, and Ben took a good look at the second officer. He was young, probably only a few years older than Will. From what Ben could tell, he was a pulled-together young man, held himself well with his back straight and his shoulders back. Mia took a seat beside Ben and ran a hand through her hair in the same way Beth always had. It was difficult to be around her sometimes. She and Beth had grown up as best friends first and sisters second. They were almost mirror images of each other, could have been twins if they weren't three years apart: same red hair, same cheeky smile that Will had inherited, and that layer of freckles that was a little darker on Mia, but still so much like Beth and Will.

Outside, the gravel driveway crunched under a set of tires. Doors slammed and then the front door opened. Ben half expected another set of police officers or even a patrol officer to take Lennox away. Instead, Karen appeared with Lennox slowly hobbling after her on crutches and Will at his side.

"Dad? What's going on?"

"If those men called the police after what they did to him I'll—"

"Lennox McAvoy?"

The second police officer had stepped forward. Lennox froze in the entryway. His eyes darted down the hall to the door, and Ben was sure that if they'd been able to support him, his legs would have done the same.

"Yeah?"

"I'm going to need you to step outside with Officer Ferguson for a minute."

Will jumped right in the way, blocking the officer's path. Ben sighed. This was getting ridiculous.

"Why? What's going on? He hasn't done anything wrong."

"He went outside of his inclusion zone earlier," the officer said. "Until we get him cleared—"

"But—Dad, tell them not to—"

"Will, let them do their job."

The officer stepped past Will to Lennox. Ben expected him to simply walk Lennox outside, crutches and all, to let him hobble along to talk with Jim and settle all of this in a few minutes. Instead, the officer pulled his handcuffs out and tugged Lennox's arms behind his back. His crutches fell to the floor and he swayed. Only the tug on his wrists seemed to keep him upright.

Will lunged at the officer and Karen just managed to hold him back. Mia got to her feet as well.

"Leave him alone! Lennox didn't do anything!"

"You don't need to handcuff him. The boy's got a busted ankle, it's not like he's running anywhere!"

Ben took it all in, from Mia's fury to Karen's shock to Will's horror and Lennox's panicked defeat. The boy was like a rag doll, all the fight seemed to slip out of him, and part of Ben was glad that something in this world seemed to scare Lennox and show him as more than a crude little asshole. Ben pressed his cane into the carpet and forced himself to his feet. His son's eyes were overwhelmed with a fear Ben couldn't begin to process, but it was enough to get him involved.

"Uncuff him. There's no need for this. If Jim had wanted him cuffed he would have stopped him outside."

"I don't take orders from Officer Ferguson. This man has broken his—"

The front door opened, and Jim's voice carried down the hall. "He's all clear, Ben. And I—what the hell are you doing?"

"He—I figured it was smarter to cuff him until we had an answer back," Jack said. "The guy's got a record, Jim. You never know—"

"He's an injured kid who hasn't broken any laws."

"But his record—"

"Is in the past. You don't handcuff someone over this. Uncuff him *now*."

Jack took his time releasing Lennox, and once he had he made no moves to help him reclaim his crutches. Lennox's ankle crumpled under him, and Will caught his weight and held him upright. Jim snarled and took the cuffs from Jack's hands.

"Go wait outside. I need to finish up here."

"Fine."

Everyone watched him leave. Will helped Lennox to the couch while Karen picked up his crutches.

"I'm sorry about that, Lennox. I can't believe he—"

"The fuck's it matter?" Lennox's voice was a little slurred, but he managed to keep his eyes open and himself upright despite how much he looked as though he wanted to collapse. "They always do that. Nobody bothers to figure shit out before they throw me somewhere."

"That's no excuse. Listen, that Urgent Care was outside of your inclusion zone. We got a call not too long ago, but I've spoken with the center in Vienna and cleared everything up. They're going to expand your zone to include a medical facility, okay? I can't believe they didn't do that in the first place, but people up there have a shopping center on every street corner. They never stop to think about how far away things are out here."

Lennox glowered at him with such distrust even Ben noticed it. And he didn't get it. Jim was a police officer, a wonderful one at that. He was here to serve and protect them, and yet Lennox's expression was clear.

"You should get a letter from them at your residence explaining the changes they're making. If you've got any questions, give us a call and we'll help you out."

"It still comes off in January?"

Jim nodded. "You're all set. Ben, Karen, I'll see you around. Again, I'm sorry about this. He's a new officer, but he should know better. Enjoy the rest of your day."

Karen saw him out. Ben struggled to the lounge chair and sat. It took very little to drain the energy out of him, and the sight of Will and Lennox only made him more exhausted. His son helped Lennox lie down on his stomach, tucked him in with a blanket, and then sat on the floor next to his head. They murmured to each other, Will more than Lennox, as Mia came over to Ben.

"I'm going to head out, I think," she said. "You two have enough going on without me hanging around. I'll see you for Christmas, okay? Call if you need an extra set of hands or any advice. Remember what I said, okay? Be patient with them. They're as new to this as you are."

Mia gave him a kiss and a hug and headed downstairs. Karen handed him the remote, and he flipped on to a movie channel. His eyes stayed on Will and Lennox, though, resting together, talking. Sure, they were new to this entire experience—not that it was love— but *he* wasn't. Ben had been in and out of relationships time and time again, at their age and younger. He'd had a few dates after Will's mother and before he'd met Karen as well. Will hadn't even had a *first* date, and yet—

Ben followed the curve of his son's lips, the way one of his fingers played with a springy curl hanging down in Lennox's eyes. Neither of them seemed aware of the rest of the room, not Oyster panting at their knees or Karen smiling over the back of the couch at them. She smiled at Ben, too, and gave him that little nod that made him roll his eyes. And maybe he could see it, a moment of two boys sharing something.

But nothing good would come from it. Nothing good at all.

THAT NIGHT, SLEEP ELUDED BEN again. He tossed and turned, his mind whirling with everything that had happened in the two days since he'd come home. His arm was in knots from elbow to wrist, and his fingers were numb and shook. Ben rolled to his feet and made his way to the kitchen. Water wouldn't help, but it was a distraction from Karen's snores and the aches prickling up and down his arm.

He nearly tripped over Oyster where he lay in the middle of the hall.

"Damnit, Oyster."

"Woof."

Oyster's nails clicked, and he nipped at Ben's pajama pants. He led Ben down the hall, past the dining room, and to the living room. But he stopped Ben there and let go. As Oyster's nails clicked away into the kitchen, Ben frowned and squinted into the living room. Usually Oyster led him into the kitchen and stopped only when he reached the light switch on the far wall.

He could see a large outline on the couch; it shifted a few times, and then he heard an unfamiliar laugh. Ben couldn't hear most of their words, but the steady flow of the boys' voices was soothing. He wasn't wrong, but maybe he wasn't entirely right either. A tether had pulled these two together, linked them up under Ben's comatose nose, and now his son had a friend, a close one maybe, and possibly someone who was even more than that.

"Better?"

"Yeah, but my thigh—"

"On it."

After Will finished rubbing some ointment onto Lennox's thigh, he settled back down on the couch. They shifted and the blanket swooped up and then fluttered down on top of them. Ben stood in the doorway as Will spoke. "You still haven't finished your story. Why did you climb the fence?"

"It's safer to go in through the window than it is to go around to the front and run into them."

"Not if you break your neck," Will said. He reached over and tugged on Lennox's curls. "That window's really high."

"Still safer." Lennox rolled his head away and then turned to Will. "Anyway, it was locked. I sat there while they horsed around, and eventually they came to check out back, and I ran. They chased me down the street with that stupid pellet gun and cornered me. That's it, really."

They lay back down again, and Ben shivered. He imagined Will, stiff and cold, sitting under a window in a dumpy motel waiting for a chance to go into his own room, his home. The way Lennox spoke made everything about this sound normal, even expected.

"I'm sorry. If I'd gone after you as soon as you left, then—"

"It's not your fault. You shouldn't have to run after me. I can take care of myself."

"Is that why you were almost... God, I can't even say it."

"They're just a bunch of stupid hicks, okay? I'm not, I mean, I have to get my mail and stuff, but I'm not going back there."

Ben's heart sank like a stone. Lennox was going to stay here. Every day, Will and Lennox would spend more time together. Before long, they'd be more involved, and it would be even harder for Will to get free of this boy.

"Listen, about yesterday, with us as boyfriends and everything—"

"Forget it," Will said, but his voice cracked, and Ben felt a part of himself splinter too. His son was giving up what he wanted for this kid, being lured in—

"No. I'm sorry. I, I do want what you talked about, but I'm... this is all really weird for me, you know? I didn't mean to be so, like, cold about it. We're boyfriends, if you'll have me. That's all."

"Really?"

Lennox must have nodded, because Will gave a little squeal, and his feet kicked under the blankets. Lips smacked—an out-of-sight kiss, Ben guessed—and he could hear the grin in his son's voice when he spoke next.

"I can't believe... Thank you."

"Did you just thank me for agreeing to be your boyfriend?"

"Kind of. I mean, yes, but it's more that. I know how hard that is for you, and I'm glad you're giving us a chance."

"Well, that's the secret, I guess."

"What?"

Ben leaned closer as Oyster returned and pawed at his leg.

"I like you enough to take a shot at this."

"I, I lo—"

Ben's cane clattered to the floor. Both boys sat up, and a lamp flickered on. Tousle-haired and bleary-eyed, yet happy, Will and Lennox squinted at Ben. An unmistakable peace seemed to have engulfed them since this morning, and Ben frowned as he picked up his cane.

"Sorry, guys. Just getting a drink of water. Tripped over this dumb dog."

"Woof!"

They dropped back down, but Lennox's eyes met his. No forgiveness rested in that gaze. Trouble wrapped itself around this boy like a blanket, and he wore it well. Perhaps too well, if Karen and Will could both turn a blind eye so easily. Something dark hovered around Lennox, and Ben wouldn't let it contaminate his family.

◀ six ▶

By Monday morning, Lennox was on the mend, and the welts and bruises covering his back had shrunk. The gigantic one on his ass, however, was still as angry as ever, a deep brown, almost black, the way Will imagined a blood boil would look. Karen said it wasn't anything to worry about, considering what had caused it, but she kept Lennox home just the same.

"Don't forget your lunch," Karen said, as Will stuffed a piece of toast in his mouth. "And your bag for practice!"

"I've—oops."

Will jogged downstairs, grabbed his bat bag, and returned to the kitchen. Karen forced a brown lunch bag into his free hand.

"Get going; you're going to be late."

"Right, sorry I overslept again."

Karen shook her head and smiled. "I need to get a stronger backbone and wake you up, but you two are so cute cuddled up together."

"Love you. Bye."

Will passed through the living room and was juggling his backpack when his dad appeared. All weekend he'd hovered around Will and Lennox, and had spent a lot less time talking than usual.

"Morning, Dad."

"Morning." Ben peered over at the couch, where Lennox was snoozing on his stomach. "Aren't you forgetting something?"

Will glanced down. Bat bag, lunch, car keys, wallet and phone in his pockets, backpack.

"Nope. I couldn't hold any more if I tried."

"I meant him."

Will tensed. Had his dad said Lennox's name once since they'd come face to face again? He doubted it. Neither of them had spoken to one another, which had worked fine this weekend with Lennox recovering and his dad still tired and recuperating.

"Karen's letting him stay home today. Maybe tomorrow too because of the, um, on his butt. It's still really bad."

Ben grunted. "Have a good day."

Will piled everything into the icy truck bed. Halfway to school it hit him that Karen worked today, was probably pulling out of the driveway right now, which meant Dad and Lennox would be on their own. Together. He swallowed. Lennox was unraveling for him, becoming a little more communicative with every passing hour, but his dad—

Ben Osborne was turning into a snarling shadow, expanding from floor to ceiling, from one side of the house to the other.

Aaron Saunders was waiting in the parking lot when Will arrived. He was bundled up in a red winter coat, with his bat bag hooked over his shoulder.

"I'll be glad when it's spring. I hate pitching inside."

Will hurried to fit all of his bags onto his arms and nodded. "Are we actually throwing today or doing drills again?"

"*I'm* pitching, don't care what coach says. I'll never get anywhere for the season if he just has us do sprints all winter."

"Seriously."

They headed into Eastern High and paused to kick the ice and snow off their shoes. Otto hovered by the band room door as Aaron said goodbye.

"Later, Will!"

"See you." Will was surprised when Otto pulled the band door open for him. "Um, thanks. You aren't going to hit me in the ass with that, are you?"

"Why would I do that?"

"Why wouldn't you?"

But Will stepped into the band room, Otto right behind him. The room was in the usual controlled chaos, with the percussionists wheeling instruments into each other, dropping sticks and sheet music everywhere, while the rest of the group tried to line up chairs and music stands.

"How's, uh, he doing?"

"What?"

Otto elbowed Will in the back and almost sent him face-first into the bass drum.

"Sorry. I mean Lennox. Mom wants to stop by today or tomorrow. She made some paste for his back. Something her grandmother used to make, I think."

"He's... okay. Can't sit down to save his life, but we took him to Urgent Care and they gave him some medication for the pain and checked his ankle and ribs. No breaks, and just a sprain."

"Good. That's good." Otto took a chair and set it down in Will's spot. "Here. I'll get you a music stand, too."

"Why?"

Otto shrugged, and his face turned red. "I'm just, like, being nice, Osborne. Can't a guy be—"

"No. You're just being, like, weird."

Will set his backpack and lunch bag under his chair and then headed to his instrument locker. He put his bat bag on the floor and took out his trombone case. When he turned around, Otto was watching him from across the room. He returned to his seat and slid away from Otto.

"Seriously what is with you?"

"What? Nothing! Don't look at me like I pissed down your throat, Osborne. Man, fuck off."

Otto stomped off, but the concern that had been in his gaze stayed with Will all day. He didn't think it could possibly be for him, but it seemed even less likely to be for Lennox. Something had changed, but whatever it was he couldn't imagine. The guy had been beating on him for close to ten years. Not so much in the past few years, but he'd certainly never *cared* about Will.

Will slogged his way through baseball practice and then hurried home. All of the ice had melted to slush and puddles. He rumbled into the driveway and heaved his stuff onto the porch.

"Dad? Lennox?"

"In the kitchen!"

Will put his bags down in the hall and stepped into the living room. Lennox was asleep on the couch with the blanket shoved halfway down his back. Bruises covered his skin and rose like lumps of coal all over his back. Will pulled the blanket up to Lennox's neck and swallowed. He was safe now. That was all that mattered. The bruises would fade; everything would heal. He kissed Lennox's cheek before heading into the kitchen to greet his dad.

"Hey, how's your arm?"

Ben raised a cup of juice. His entire arm trembled so badly that juice slopped onto the table. As he wiped it up, he said, "Could be worse."

Will grabbed a box of crackers and examined his dad's arm. "Does it hurt?"

"Sometimes. Usually when I'm trying to sleep. My right arm's almost stopped, but my left seems like it's getting worse."

"I'm sure the doctors can do something about it," Will said. "We'll ask at your next appointment."

Ben gave him a tight smile as Will sat down next to him. He'd found no blood on the floor, no bodies anywhere, and two men who appeared very much alive. That had to be a good sign.

"How was Lennox today?"

Ben articulated something between a snort and a growl. "Slept most of the day. Probably because of those pain pills. Those things always make me drowsy."

"And did you guys talk?"

"About what?"

"Dad, he's my boyfriend and he's living here now."

"That's only temporary." Ben climbed carefully to his feet and set his cup in the sink.

"That doesn't mean you shouldn't get to know him." But the firmness of Ben's words scared him. Lennox had nowhere else to go. If Ben threw him out, then anything might happen to him.

"I've got nothing to say to that kid."

Ben went into the living room. Will followed, his cleats echoing sharply on the floor.

"What is your problem with him?"

Ben lowered himself into the lounge chair and turned the television on. It was the worst angle to watch from, and the enormous sectional couch was two-thirds empty. Will huffed and blocked his view.

"Don't get an attitude with me, William."

"Why shouldn't I? You've been treating him like a criminal since he got here."

"And he is one. What the hell do you think that ankle monitor means? He's not a good person, Will. Why can't you see that?"

"Why can't you see past what you think is there and see what I do?"

"You remember what he said to you in that parking lot at school? I know what he really thinks of you, and you would too if you would just—"

"He said that about me, Dad. Not you. *Me*. And I forgave him. Why can't you?" Will clenched his fists. "God, I thought you *trusted* me. You always say you do, but I guess you're just lying to me, because I *know* Lennox, okay? I know him better than you or anyone else ever will, and if you can't even trust me to—"

"You're never going to know him better than he knows himself. Do *not* trust this kid. He's nothing but a thug who's going to ruin your future."

"What's going on?" Lennox's voice was punctuated by a yawn.

Will spun around to Lennox, who was rubbing his eyes. He ignored the tears filling his own eyes.

"Come on. My bed's more comfortable than this stupid, redneck couch."

"What?"

Will grabbed Lennox's hand, yanked him to his feet, and towed him down the stairs. Lennox was wincing, holding his right leg bent with no weight on it. Some of Will's anger trickled out of him.

"Shit, I'm sorry. Here." Will bent to become an impromptu crutch as they hobbled down the stairs together.

He helped Lennox to the bed and tried to examine his ankle. It looked the same, still wrapped in a tight bandage and a little puffy around the top.

"I didn't make it worse, did I?"

Lennox grimaced and stretched out his legs.

"No. It's just twingy when I put too much weight on it."

"Without warning. Sorry."

"Forget it."

Will kicked his cleats off. The first shoe hit the wall with an echoing boom, and the second landed silently in his bean bag chair. All of his bags were still upstairs, but he wasn't going back up, not with his dad acting like an asshole. Lennox was fine—a little too much and pretty crude most of the time, but he was improving. He was more than what he presented, but Dad was an idiot. A big, fat, redneck idiot who couldn't be bothered to try.

"It's okay that he doesn't like me," Lennox said. He shrugged and lay down. "Most people don't. Don't waste your time getting mad at him about it."

"Why shouldn't I? He's being a... being a... He's being a bigot. Just because you have a record, and you've got a big mouth, and I *like* you and—"

"Because I'm black?"

Will flinched. "No, he's not... That's not what he's—"

"When was the last time someone called you a thug for getting beaten up?"

"I, I don't know. I'm sure it... He's not. Those drunks at your motel are definitely qualified as thugs."

Lennox grinned at the ceiling. It was an unkind smile. "Yeah, but they're still the 'drunks'. They're not thugs first, even with a good reason. It's different."

Will flung himself down on the bed beside Lennox. It sort of made sense, but to think of his dad in that way, to think that part of the reason Ben didn't like Lennox was because he was black, was hard. His dad was kind, a good man. Karen said it, his friends said it, even his teachers thought highly of Dad.

Lennox rolled over on top of him and plucked at his baseball pants. "These are really cute, by the way. Really accentuate all your assets."

"Huh? Oh, most of that's my cup. But yeah, I guess."

A kiss brushed Will's neck, then his earlobe. "Forget it, okay? Let me help you cool off a bit," Lennox murmured.

"My dad's not racist."

He blurted it before he could stop himself, but Lennox's expression didn't change. His smile didn't flicker; his eyes didn't dim from that mischievous sparkle.

"He's still your dad, no matter what," Lennox said. "And I mean, I'm not gonna lie, I don't like him, okay? But you seem like you've always had it good with him. Don't let me get in the way of that. He's your dad. You're lucky you've got a decent dad. Lucky you've got one at all."

No arguments or denials or reassurances. Lennox kissed his neck again; his lips lingered and nipped at his skin. Will shut his eyes and sighed. For too many weeks they'd been without each other. One real night together, and then over two weeks with no contact and too much danger and pain. But his dad still hung in his mind.

"Racists aren't good people, and my dad is. Well, most of the time."

Lennox huffed and sat back. "Racists are racists. That's not the only quality a person can have. Your dad… He can be that and a good guy at the same time. Being awful in one way doesn't make you horrible all over."

Will rose to capture Lennox's lips. Thinking about Dad wasn't helping. It only made his gut hurt and his brain buzz like a hive of bees. Nothing would ever be salvageable between his dad and Lennox. He would have to negotiate their hostilities forever.

"So, I know you're fond of these pants, but would you be fonder of them on the floor?"

"I'm always on board with your pants being on the floor."

Lennox grinned against Will's lips and pressed him down into the bed. They stripped each other's clothes, and Lennox had a good time giggling over Will's jockstrap and cup. He held it up to his face like a mask and then gagged.

"Oh, gross. Stale dick sweat. Ugh, I'm not putting my face down there today. Don't even ask."

"Don't make me rub my dick all over your face."

"You know, normally I'd be up for that, but I'll slap it away if you try it right now." Lennox dropped the cup onto the floor with his face twisted in disgust.

"That face is really *not* turning me on."

Lennox arched his hips to meet Will's so their cocks pressed together. Neither of them were hard, but Will gasped at the contact; his stomach bloomed with heat. Their lips met as Lennox rolled his hips a second time, but then he groaned. Only it wasn't a happy groan. Will grabbed his hips and held him still.

"Are you okay?"

"Shouldn't do that yet. Ugh, flexing your ass shouldn't hurt that much."

Very gently, Will helped Lennox roll over onto his back.

"Oh, ouch. I hate having a sore ass."

"Maybe we shouldn't—"

"Oh, we should. We'll just... change things up a bit."

Will's mind whirled. He could take control, could hold Lennox down and ride him, or fuck him. Lennox would arch up under him, or arch back against him, depending on the position. Will shivered and grabbed his cock as it bobbed against his navel. Getting hard fast was never a problem. Not with the idea of topping Lennox dangled before him. Long before they'd met, the idea had been appealing; before he'd ever had a name or a face to fill in his fantasy.

"I c-could top this time."

A beat, a little slip of the expression on Lennox's face, and Will's hunger for control dropped away too.

"No, I think that'll hurt my ass even more."

Lennox shook his head, but the way he met Will's eyes told him his reasons had nothing to do with being injured. Did Lennox only top? Would he ever be willing to switch for Will, just to give him the experience? And what if Will liked topping as much as he expected to, then what?

"Once you're better, then," Will said, his eyes focused on every little movement Lennox made. His fingers flexed as they did over piano keys, and his teeth dragged his lower lip into his mouth and then let it pop back out. "I really want to top. I want to try everything, actually."

Lennox grunted and raised himself on his elbows. His eyes stayed on his stomach. "Right, sure. Handjobs then?"

Will frowned. "We've done that before. I want to try something new. Like, um, I don't know what it's called, but—can I show you?"

Lennox only hesitated for a fraction of a second. It was so fleeting that Will almost didn't catch it; he hoped that uncertainty would disappear from Lennox's eyes forever.

"Okay."

He held Lennox's right thigh and rolled Lennox toward him. Will went slowly, trying to ease Lennox into the movements so he didn't irritate his injuries. After a few fumbling seconds, Lennox was on his side, chest to chest with Will, with his thigh hooked over Will's legs. Lennox shifted and squirmed a little, even as their cocks rubbed together.

"Rutting," Lennox said. "You want to rut. Not quite as good as fucking, but I doubt you've got condoms and lube anyway."

"I do so!"

"Oh, really?" Lennox tugged Will's right nipple between his lips until he whined. "Prove it."

"I've got condoms in the nightstand and lube in, um, well." Will gave Lennox a small shove and grinned sheepishly. "Shut up. And don't give me that look, McAvoy. You are *not* buttering my ass. I'll get some for us. Somewhere. I've never bought it before."

"It's a fun experience. Just don't get any that are flavored," Lennox said. "Or that warming stuff. Don't do that either."

He pushed his hips forward, and Will gasped. It was awkward, as unusual and strange for Lennox as for Will, but after three weeks spent worrying and stressing it was a relief, too. Lennox sucked his nipple again, a little harder and much more like himself. It wasn't the control Will had experienced before, but it sent a thrill down his spine.

Lennox kissed up his chest and neck, and paused at his jaw. "I've missed you."

"I've missed you too."

Lennox's answering smile was so sweet, so silently happy, that it renewed the ache that kept throbbing in Will's chest. He couldn't lose Lennox, not to the state of Virginia or his dad or anything else. Will accepted Lennox's kiss; his toes curled at the gentle caress of lips and the rhythm of Lennox's movements. Somehow, Lennox was always so sure here. He seemed to understand their physicality without the words Will needed.

"I can't believe we haven't done this since your birthday."

"Maybe I felt like being a tease. Switch things up."

Was that a hint?

Will let himself wonder as Lennox pushed his hips forward and rolled them. Surely, at some time, they would switch. Although to Will, shifting from bottom to top didn't seem that large a leap, more like a bunny hop off the curb and into the road than diving off a cliff. The idea of switching was exciting, and created just enough uncertainty to keep him on his toes every time they were together. It was something new for him, but nothing extravagant; just another way to connect with this boy who was winding himself into Will's heart.

Did Lennox want him to take control of their pace right now?

He swallowed, let his hands settle on Lennox's hips, and felt the bones, solid and hard, pushing back against the dark skin stretched over them. Lennox was so thin, so small, even compared to a few weeks ago. Will held him delicately at first, keeping his fingers away from bruises and bones as much as he could. But Lennox was all over him. Will's touch seemed to ignite his lust, that spark of heat that always expanded in Lennox when Will was close. In a few frantic minutes, they figured out an angle that worked. After breathless laughter and mumbled words against the other's lips to guide, Will had Lennox by the waist and was thrusting slow and gentle.

"Shit, harder. That's perfect." Lennox's hips jerked as he spoke, and he buried his face against Will's neck. His voice faltered. "Could you do that again? Please?"

A surge of excitement ran through Will. He could be more than last time—not that he hadn't enjoyed that—but he could be something active for Lennox that he hadn't been so far, a trail into bliss, purposeful and powerful. Maybe, he could convince Lennox to fall apart as Will had for him.

Will rolled his hips forward again and set a steady rhythm that was faster, but still careful.

"Yeah. Like that. Harder."

But trying to keep up a rhythm was a lot more difficult than he'd expected. Lennox didn't seem to mind, but he did seem to want a rougher experience than their position allowed.

Lennox growled and rolled onto his back, taking Will and his weight with him. He waited for Lennox to hiss in pain, to shove him off and turn onto his stomach. Instead he spread his legs and tugged Will's hips down against him.

"You're not going to fucking break me. Please, just—"

"Harder," Will finished. He nodded slowly and let his back relax, let the full weight of his hips press down against Lennox. "Right. I just... If it hurts—"

Lennox kissed him. A slight hiss pushed into Will's mouth; when Lennox didn't complain, he thrust down harder than before, though still tentative, testing the limits, the boundaries of too much and not enough. Lennox's hands grabbed his ass and forced him down harder. His eyes were angry when Will's met them.

"Don't tease me," Lennox said. "I've seen your ass muscles, so I know you can fuck harder than that."

"And you're okay?"

"Am I complaining?"

"Well, kind of."

Will arched back and then thrust once more, this time as hard as he could. Lennox yelped. His head knocked against the headboard.

"Better?"

"Closer to what I want." Lennox pushed one of Will's arms out from under him so Will tumbled down on top of him. "How about as hard as you can, like this? We'll build up to that other one."

"Maybe I'll be inside of you when we do that."

Lennox kissed him instead of responding. Will found a faster tempo, yet still held himself back. But with each thrust Lennox's breathing sharpened, his voice cracked and panted in Will's ear, his nails split the skin on Will's shoulders. It was carnal, the heady rush that came over Will, and nothing like what he'd come to expect since he'd met Lennox. Lennox was always in control—wild and troublesome, but in control during their time together and in front of most people.

Shifting that dynamic gave Will something he couldn't quite place. Lennox clung to him, held him in a new way that made Will feel needed and not just wanted.

"Fuck, harder. I'm close... God, I can't wait until you really fuck me. I bet you'd love that."

Will groaned. His hips were loose and driving. He'd rutted against his bed before, pressed himself against a pillow and thrust until he was dizzy and dripping sweat, but that had been mellow compared to this. Lennox's heat was soaking into him; his words fueled something almost intoxicating running through Will's blood. So Lennox *did* want that, wanted to have Will work him open, to stretch him with his fingers and cock, to intimately own a part of him.

Lennox arched as he came, his eyes shut tight, his voice strained. Will followed; his hips stuttered to a pause, then jerked as he came. His eyes drifted to Lennox's stomach, and he watched the streaks of come cross until Lennox sank down into the mattress.

"Fuck, that was... Fuck."

Will gave a wobbly nod and dropped down beside him. He lay there with his eyes shut and listened to the uneven rush of their breathing settle. Lennox's thumb rubbed his nipple after a while, and Will squirmed. That was going to be a thing for him. He wouldn't be half hard again from a few brushes if it wasn't.

"You like nipple play. I'm going to have to remember that."

"Only if you do that while riding me."

Lennox shifted beside him. The whole bed creaked and bounced as he flopped away onto his side. Will stared at his back, at the rivets of sweat cooling on his skin and the welts and bruises still burned into him.

"Lennox?"

A rattle echoed upstairs; water rushed through the pipes in the walls and Oyster's nails dragged against his door, begging to be let down. Will leaned away to grab a fistful of tissues and then rolled in behind Lennox.

"Here. Before we dry all over you."

Lennox cleaned his stomach and tossed the wad of tissues to the floor. Will grimaced but didn't snap at him. Something was clearly wrong, and he had a good idea what.

"You said you wanted that. To bottom, I mean, just now when we were—"

"I know what I said. Don't rub it in."

"But if you want that too, then why—"

"Why do you always have to talk everything to death? Can't we just fuck how we fuck and leave it at that?"

Lennox sat up so fast Will could tell he had hurt himself, but he didn't flinch or grimace or cry out in pain. He shoved Will's hand away and tried to stand. Will sat up too.

"If you want my dick in your ass then you do," Will said. "Don't be such a, such a—"

"Such a little bitch? I'm *nobody's* bitch, all right? I don't let— nobody has—"

Lennox pushed off from the bed, which made the entire mattress shift, but he stumbled once he was on his feet. Will scrambled and caught him as he flopped backward onto the bed. They sat there, side by side, with Will's arm resting on Lennox's shoulders.

"You've never bottomed before," Will said.

And though Lennox's words from months ago echoed through him—*"I finger myself all the time"*—he wasn't entirely surprised. Maybe it was just him, but a different trust came with bottoming, an expectation of both patience and control and that, if it hurt, the other person would stop. Surely, Lennox realized that Will would.

"Fuck off. That's not—I, I—"

Lennox dropped his face into his hands. His body was shaking.

"I've never trusted anyone with *that* before, all right? Even when I've wanted to, I'd rather just use my own fingers instead of being some asshole's come bucket."

"Is that what I was? Your little come bucket?"

Will's voice was harsh, but he wasn't angry. Not really. It had taken time to figure out Lennox—not entirely, but enough—and to know that he didn't see Will in that light, that something greater was bringing them together.

"No! No. I mean, it's not like that with you; we're b-boyfriends and it's different."

"Exactly. We aren't just fuck buddies or a one-night stand. I'd take my time and listen, just like you did with me. You mean a lot to me. I'm not just going to use you to get off."

"Right." Lennox jostled his shoulders until Will removed his arms. "I guess I just forget sometimes that it's still going to be you tomorrow."

"It will be. Always."

Lennox's head dropped onto his shoulder as he sighed. "Still weird."

"So I get to fuck you then?"

Lennox snorted and laughed. "Since when do *you* call sex that?"

"I don't know. You use it, and there's just something really hot about it. About pushing into you and putting my hands in your hair..." Will threaded his fingers into Lennox's thick curls and they both groaned. "I can't wait to feel how tight you are around me."

"Pretty tight, considering how big you are."

Will flushed and eyed his lap. His dick was soft now, but didn't seem any different than normal—not too large or too small or any of the other things he'd heard girls and boys whisper about back in middle school. He wasn't veiny or anything, just had a slight curve to the left.

"I'm just normal," Will said. But he let his eyes shift to Lennox. Darker, smaller, uncut. Well, sort of uncut. He could see the tip of his head but not all of it. "We're both just… normal. Bigger when we're turned on and smaller when we're not."

Lennox lay back and grinned. "God, you have no idea. Don't you ever watch porn?"

Will snuggled into Lennox's side. "No. I… no. I mean, I've *looked* at, like, some pictures on the Internet, but never with naked people in them. I was always scared Dad would walk in or I'd get a virus and ruin my laptop. And I'm not… Natasha said porn stars are hung like elephants."

"Well, as someone who has sucked quite a few dicks, yours is both the biggest and the cleanest I have ever encountered."

"I'm not *that* big."

"If porn stars are hung like elephants, then you're hung like a horse."

"Really?"

Lennox's fingers skimmed over Will's cock and then up his belly and chest to his chin. Will shivered as Lennox's fingertips traced his Adam's apple and then his lips. He kissed each finger and then let Lennox dip one in to be sucked.

"We're totally having a boner fight so you'll believe me."

Will spit Lennox's finger out and growled. "I am *not* big."

"You are. I'm glad."

Lennox rolled into his side.

"I'm glad you're here," Will said. He pressed his face into Lennox's hair and sighed. Overhead, he listened to Karen's footsteps and the dull, deep murmur of Ben's voice. Karen would probably take Ben's side, would hear what he had to say first and tell Will he was being rash or too blinded by love or something else equally radical. But he wasn't. His dad was wrong to not care about Lennox, to not trust Will enough to give Lennox all the chances he needed.

◀ seven ▶

Water running elsewhere in the house woke Lennox later that evening. Its drip set a steady tempo around him, soft and dull but still loud enough to give him a groove, mellow and gentle. A slow tune would tame it, wrap it up in delicate, broken fingers and carve a massive, deep river through the world's highs and lows.

He heard a high rumble, a deep growl, and something metal slammed down onto something else. It echoed like a pot on a stove and rattled Lennox's insides. He shuddered and glanced around Will's room. The lights were off, the blinds were shut, and for some reason his crutches were now resting against the wall beside the bed. Karen must have been down here.

Lennox pulled his sweatpants on and grabbed one of his crutches. He made his way up the stairs. To his surprise, the door was still cracked open. He pressed his face against the door frame and peered into the room. Karen stood with her back to him, a dish towel thrown over her shoulder. Ben Osborne, face red, was just visible seated on the couch in the living room.

"He is if this is the kind of people you're going to allow him to hang out with! Will is a good kid. I'm not going to sit around while that stupid pu—"

"Don't you dare!"

Karen snapped her towel at him and hit him in the face with it.

"I cannot believe what a bigot you are. Just because Lennox has been in trouble, because he's not the most noble and righteous teenager you've ever met, you think it's okay to talk about him like he's scum. Like he's an animal. He is a human being. One that *your* son is in love with."

In love?

Karen stepped forward and whipped the towel off of Ben. "Will has every right to be furious with you. We all do when you're acting like a child."

Oyster gave a whiny yawn from somewhere out of sight. Lennox shifted until he could see Ben's face. It was tight, smudged red with anger, but surprised and hurt too. Good.

"I'm doing what's best for Will."

"You aren't. And until you do, you're sleeping alone."

Karen stalked off, and Oyster shoved his head through the door opening to sniff at Lennox's legs. His eyes met Ben's, and he tensed. His crutch slipped down the step, and Lennox almost cascaded back downstairs with it.

"I, um... just wanted some water."

Ben said nothing, but the expression on his face was impossible to forget. How could such an awful man have such a kind son? But as Lennox limped into the kitchen, he remembered his own father and mother. They'd been great as a team, loving and gentle and caring. Mama had been the brightest star in any room, always teaching him something new and smiling. Dad had been the same until she died. Her death had snuffed out every hopeful piece of him. His father had become a drunken recluse, good for nothing but anger and disappointment.

"Here, dear. Why didn't you use your crutch?"

Karen handed him the glass of water he'd asked for and huffed as she stared into the living room.

"It's, um, starting to feel better."

Oyster sniffed all around his legs and then yowled at him.

"Hey, um, doggie."

"He likes you. Seems to be pretty common around here."

Lennox sipped his water and glanced at the living room. "Not common enough."

He finished his glass as Karen stared at him in horror.

"Did you hear—"

"Thanks for the water. And the bed."

Lennox hopped back downstairs, Oyster at his side doing his best to replace Lennox's dropped crutch. Oyster was a surprisingly good guide. He bit Lennox's sweatpants, gave a gentle tug, and then guided him to the basement floor and over to the bed. All the while, his head was steady and high enough for Lennox to press his hand against as he limped along. Oyster nudged him to sit and then pressed his nose against Lennox's knees until Lennox was lying down beside Will once more.

"Thanks."

Oyster gave a cheerful bark and then hopped up onto the end of the bed.

Will jerked awake beside Lennox.

"Stop, Oyster."

"He's fine. My personal guide dog on all staircases."

Will rolled toward him and wrapped himself around Lennox with one leg draped over Lennox's knees and his arm stretched across Lennox's chest. His scrawny thin chest. How much weight had he lost since July? Too much, clearly. All of his ribs were visible. His muscles looked bulgy and like little rocks tucked under his skin, but they were weak too. Will snuggled closer and kissed his neck.

"It's too cold down here without you."

"I wouldn't get too used to it. Not if your dad has anything to say about it."

"Hmm?"

"Nothing. Go back to sleep."

Will dozed off, but Lennox lay awake. It would be another week before he was well enough to be on his own. Lucy might be okay with sharing her room. He didn't mind sleeping on the floor. But staying here with Ben just upstairs was a horrible idea. Will was great, Karen was kind, and Oyster was fun, but this wasn't any safer than the motel with that Neanderthal gunning for him. Will would understand his decision and if he didn't, well, that was one quick way to screw up this boyfriend thing now rather than later.

Lennox shut his eyes and listened. Will's breathing was heavy and even, a little quieter than usual, more soft tenor than snuffling, gurgling bass lines. Oyster panted in sets of three, little triplets to break up Will's rhythm and match the drip still pinging in the wall behind the bed.

Ping. Ping. Pantpantpant. Ping-whoosh.

Lennox counted off the measures in his head and let the rhythm hang in his chest and ease him as he drifted off.

LENNOX STARTLED AWAKE.

Click, click, thud.

All around him, little pops of noise exploded: breaths and creaks, the slap of a shutter hitting the house. A flicker of lightning splintered the sky outside and briefly illuminated Will's room.

Lennox scooped up his jacket and flew up the stairs, through the darkened living room and into the kitchen where he banged his hip on the table and stopped. His ankle throbbed. Oyster barked and, a moment later, he was at Lennox's side, biting down on Lennox's sweatpants and guiding him once more.

"No. I, I don't—"

Oyster dragged him toward the sliding glass door and stopped. For a moment, Lennox only breathed deeply; then he rested his hand on the wall. His fingers clicked on the lights by accident.

"Thanks."

Oyster let go and licked his hand.

Lennox tugged the door open and stepped onto the back deck. It was snowing. Puffy flakes drifted onto his bare feet and stuck to the frozen wood. His jacket slipped around his shoulders as he shuffled farther from the warmth of the house and sat on the steps that led into the yard. Oyster joined him; his head rested in Lennox's lap.

He counted snowflakes for a few seconds, then shut his eyes and breathed deeply. It was only a dream, only a dredged-up nightmare from a swirl of memories. Lennox dug through his pockets until he found his pack of cigarettes. For weeks he'd gone without, had almost forgotten them and been proud whenever he reached into his pocket and realized they were still there, untouched.

The sliding door opened behind him. His tail thumping happily, Oyster twisted around to greet Will.

"Lennox?"

Will's feet appeared at his side, and then his legs and chest. Lennox lit his cigarette and took a long, slow drag. Will set Lennox's boots down in front of him, and Lennox tucked his feet into them.

Lennox shook off Will's arm as it settled around his shoulders. Oyster growled weakly and dropped his head back onto Lennox's lap.

"Your dog's such a goon."

"He's protective of you. Kind of like me."

"I don't need you to hold my hand or whatever. I can protect myself."

"That's not what I mean." Will tried again with an arm, and this time Lennox allowed it. "We can both take care of ourselves. But I guess I want to take care of you sometimes. You can need me to do that when you don't want to anymore. Or when you can't. You've done that for me."

Lennox took another drag on his cigarette and nodded.

"I guess."

Will sat with him, a silent presence at his side. He shivered as Lennox smoked and scolded him for the ashes he got all over the steps. When Lennox finished and stubbed his cigarette out in the snow, Will was laughing.

"What?"

"You look like you've got tufts of Oyster's fur in your hair."

The snow had picked up. Will reached over and brushed the snow out of Lennox's curls; he was still grinning as flakes dotted his eyelashes and blond hair. His freckles had faded a little, dulled by the shorter days and the weak winter sun. One person shouldn't be allowed to be so beautiful—to be so intimate with Lennox's heart.

Suddenly, Karen's words to Ben returned to Lennox. A little jolt ran through him. Will wasn't in love with him. He couldn't be in love, and neither could Will.

"Let's go back to bed before we get frostbite on our toes."

Will stood and knocked the snow off his pajama pants and jacket. He held out his hand to Lennox and then slipped when Lennox used his arm to support his weak ankle. They both laughed and stumbled, bent over on shaking legs. Will's hands grabbed Lennox's shoulders to steady him. Oyster barked and pawed at the door.

"Got it?"

"Yeah, sorry. I almost took you down with me."

"I wouldn't mind that."

"Oh?"

Will's arms looped around his shoulders and tugged him closer. Their chests bumped, and a rush of warmth from Will's body kept the chilly air at bay for a minute. "Are you *flirting* with me, McAvoy?"

"I'm always flirting with you, butthead."

Will kissed him slowly, the cold tip of his nose brushing against Lennox's cheek. Lennox smiled into the kiss and almost berated himself for how often he did that these days. Only Will's kisses made him smile, made him press his grin closer and sigh. Lennox lost track of time while they stood on the back porch and shared kisses, tender and slow brushes of their lips that caught snowflakes on their cheeks and mouths.

"You're going to catch cold."

Oyster's insistent barking had finally brought someone to the door. Ben Osborne stepped aside to let them in and then shut the door. His eyes paused on each of them, but they weren't full of anger, as Lennox was used to seeing. He wasn't sure what that look was.

"Get back to bed."

Will nodded stiffly. Lennox led him out. His ankle still burned, as if someone was holding a lighter against it. They were at the door to Will's room when Will stopped.

"Dad, about earlier—"

"Get some sleep, Will. We'll talk tomorrow."

"Right. That's—okay. Good night."

Will helped him downstairs. They stripped off their jackets and climbed back into bed. Lennox listened to the crinkling crunches of Will's bean bag as Oyster made his bed in it. He meant to ask Will about his dad then, about what he'd said in retaliation earlier, and just how much his presence was ruining their relationship. Only he never got the words out. Will curled into his side, buried his face against Lennox's neck, and held him.

Water still dripped in the wall, and Oyster was panting and letting out whiny yawns every few minutes. But Lennox centered in on the thud of Will's heartbeat where it pressed into his side, and on the little, cut-time tick of the vein on Will's wrist. He rubbed his fingers over Will's pulse and sank down, down, down into it.

＊ ＊ ＊

November's burst of snow carried over into December. Lennox rejoined Will at school by the end of the week, still on his crutches, although he refused to use both once they pulled into the parking lot. All day he was bombarded with packets of homework, whose shifting due dates he'd never kept track of in the first place, and whispers both about his crutch and the fact that Will was holding his hand.

"Could we not do this here?"

Will and Lennox had stopped outside Lennox's second class.

"Huh?"

Michael Patterson and his friends turned the corner and made eye contact. Lennox tugged his hand away, his face flushing.

"The hand-holding. That's what boyfriends do," Lennox said. He shared a glare with each of the boys as they approached.

"We *are* boyfriends."

Will sounded hurt, but he didn't make a grab for Lennox's hand again. Lennox flinched and hobbled into the room, but not before Will caught him for a kiss on the cheek.

"I'll see you after school. I've got another meeting with Mrs. Martinello during chemistry. Will you come by baseball practice? We're in the auxiliary gym today."

Lennox grunted, which seemed to satisfy Will. As he left, Michael Patterson and his friends entered the room. They elbowed Will a few times in the doorway, snorting and muttering slurs as they went. As usual, they took their trio of seats around Lennox and twisted to see him.

"Finally found your way back, I see. Shame. We were hoping you'd taken a dive off a cliff," Michael said. He reached for Lennox's crutch, and Lennox snatched his wrist and bent it back. "Hey, fuck off! I'm only looking, man."

"Yeah, don't be so twitchy. What are you? On drugs now probably. Wouldn't be surprised."

"I bet they stuff that shit up each other's asses."

"What? Dude, that's gross."

They turned away to bicker amongst themselves until Otto arrived with the bell. Today, he'd traded his customary red and orange hoodie for a yellow one. Something about his expression was different, and it wasn't until he sat beside Lennox that he figured it out. Will looked at him like that. Karen too.

"About time you got back."

Lennox grunted and flipped his notebook open. It wasn't even his notebook, actually. Will had given him a few, and so far he'd done nothing but scribble music notes in them, from the harmony of Will's home to the roar of the wind coming down from the mountains that morning. Everything about his life had suddenly become so normal, unbearably, terrifyingly normal: a steady home, three meals a day and snacks if he wanted them (he always did), showers every morning or night, quiet time for studying, and a boyfriend. It was unreal. This life wasn't meant to be his, had never been before.

"My mom's been asking. About your—"

"You looking to turn queer too?"

Michael hit Otto in the face with a paper ball, and the three boys laughed.

Otto flicked them off. "Go grow a pair, you weasel. You've got no idea."

"Of what? What it's like to crave a dick in my ass? Nah, but I guess you do. And here I thought better of you, but I guess with how much he's kicked your ass since he got here it's no surprise. Gotta bow down and let him bend you over like a bitch eventually, right?"

"I bet that ponytail's a good handhold."

The boys jittered as the teacher called for silence. Otto glowered at them and then at Lennox. For his part, Lennox ignored all of them. The boys were idiots, too busy trying to be funny and cool to matter much to him. The world held worse than them.

For the rest of the day, Lennox kept to himself. By the time he got to chemistry, he was exhausted from interacting with so many teachers and ready to skip out if not for his bad ankle and the fact that Will was his ride. He supposed he could grab his other crutch from the back of Will's truck, but he'd get back to Will's house at the same time either way. After the first forty-five minutes, Lennox asked to see the nurse and wandered into the guidance office instead. Will was with Mrs. Martinello, and Lennox went right in, past the secretary who tried to stop him.

"You can't go in there. She's with another student."

Lennox knocked the door open with his crutch. Will and Mrs. Martinello jumped.

"Oh, hello, Lennox. I'll be with you in just a moment, okay?"

"No, it's okay, Mrs. Martinello. I think he's just here to see me."

Will pulled another chair over, and Lennox sat beside him. It wasn't ideal when he'd rather be buried under all the blankets in Will's room, but this was better than the steady stares of classmates and the piles of work.

"If you're sure. Your applications are all ready, and now that you have your essay back from Mr. Lorren I'd say it's time to send them out. If you need anything else, let me know." Mrs. Martinello stood and shook Will's hand. "Good luck, Will. Let me know how it goes, okay?"

"I will. Thank you. And—Lennox, do you want some pamphlets? For schools, I mean. You have some for music schools, right, Mrs. Martinello?"

Lennox blanched and tried to climb to his feet, but he stumbled on his crutch. "No, that's—"

"I have a few here." Mrs. Martinello pulled a few pamphlets out of her desk and sorted through them. "You never came for your follow-up, but Will... Well, he's said quite a bit about your musical talents. Mr. Robinette as well. He's been visiting almost weekly to see if you've been back to talk about musical education."

"Well, I haven't and I'm not—"

Will accepted the pamphlets and handed Lennox his crutch. "Thanks, Mrs. Martinello. He'll look them over and get back to you."

Together, they left the guidance office and headed toward the gym. Will stopped at the main doors.

"I've got to get changed and then get to practice. We're through the main gym, the set of doors on the right side."

Will kissed his cheek and ducked into the boys' locker room. Lennox almost followed him, but he had to change books at his locker. He hobbled to the back of the building, stopped at his locker, and then made his way to the gymnasium. The school's varsity basketball team was warming up already; he saw Otto's bulk among the crowd of boys. Lennox spotted Michael Patterson too and hurried past them both into the auxiliary gym.

He'd never been inside the auxiliary gym. The room was about half the size of the main gym. Instead of bleachers lining opposite walls, huge, rolled-up mats boxed in the center of the room. About twenty boys were stretching their hamstrings and shoulders. Lennox spotted the round curve of Will's ass among the rest of the tight baseball pants. Will offered him a little wave as Lennox found the bench in the corner and took a seat.

Lennox was just starting his calculus homework when Otto dropped down on the floor beside him, still in his basketball uniform and smelling like an unwashed dog.

"You staying for the game?"

"I'd rather take Will home and play one of our own."

Otto wagged his tongue between his teeth. "Will usually stays."

"So?"

Otto shrugged, tugged at his jersey. "Dunno. Figured you two would make a date of it or something."

"We're not dating."

"That's not what Karen told my mom."

"Fuck your mom. I think I know my dating status better than she does."

Otto shoved him hard. Lennox slid sideways; his textbook and notebook fell off his lap. They glowered at each other.

"She gives a shit about you," Otto told him. "A lot more than she should, but when we found you in the road—"

Lennox closed his books and pulled his knees up and rested his forearms on them. Nobody else had really talked about that day since he'd told Will what had occurred. His explanation, however brief, had been enough. Will had met those men, and so had Karen. But Otto and his mother were another story, one he didn't want tangled into his own.

"She made you this paste ointment for those bruises. It's some old recipe her grandmother used to make on the reservation."

Lennox paused at the last word. He'd guessed Otto was Native American, but he'd never asked.

"I can go get it while I've got a break."

"Sure." Lennox tugged at his ankle monitor. It wasn't so tight anymore now that his ankle wasn't swollen. "Thanks. For, you know. Your mom too."

Otto nodded. Neither of them said anything else as Lennox packed up his books, but they'd shifted into new territory. Lennox watched him out of the corner of his eye as Will joined them. Otto wasn't like Will's friends. He wasn't kind or happy or gentle, but decent enough—good enough.

"Hey, you ready?"

Will helped Lennox to his feet; his smile was bright even with Otto next to him. Otto stood as well and adjusted his jersey. Lennox gave Will a quick kiss and then growled when Otto grinned at him.

"Fuck off."

"More like fuck on. Right, Will?" Otto took a few bouncing steps away, back toward the main gym.

His eyebrows raised, Will watched Lennox. "Um, sure?"

Otto left as Will and Lennox pushed through the back door of the school building.

"What was that about?"

Lennox glanced over his shoulder as the door shut. "Nothing. Just guy stuff."

Will snorted. "I'm pretty sure I know more about guy stuff than you do."

"Whatever. Otto's just... I was thanking him. And his mom. That's all."

Will raised his eyebrow. "That's good. You need a friend besides me."

"We aren't... I've got Lucy."

Will only smiled, a pleased sort of smile that lit up his eyes. Lennox shrugged as they climbed into Will's truck and headed home.

Home. How many times had he dreaded that word? And while Ben Osborne was still no fun to be around, he'd found a place to exist, however temporary. The town of Leon, for all its woodsy charm, had felt more like an abandoned mineshaft than a comfortable place to live. His grandfather had dropped him deep down to the bottom, left him there with no lights or ropes to fashion a way out. Neither of them had counted on finding Will biding his time down there. Slowly, they were making their way up to somewhere new.

⏸ eight ▶

"WHAT ABOUT THIS ONE?"

Will offered his dad the jar of barbeque sauce, but was given another head shake. Ben cruised closer in his motorized shopping cart and picked up another flavor of the same brand.

"This is the one I use for the ham glaze. Not a lot, but enough to give it that sweet flavor. Don't tell Karen."

Ben set it in his basket, and Will scanned the list. Christmas was almost here. In another week, he and Lennox would be out of school for a long break. So far, he and his dad hadn't talked much at all about their fight. They'd each apologized, but it had ended at that. He'd never had a fight like this with his dad before, so prolonged and silent that it had become a steady undercurrent in their lives.

"I won't. As long as the jar stays mostly full and in the fridge."

"Wouldn't count on it, with the way that boy eats."

Will turned into the next aisle and watched Ben as he picked out a variety of canned vegetables. That boy. Ben rarely used Lennox's name, and Will didn't get it. He loved Lennox, even if they hadn't said it to each other and probably wouldn't for a while. Yet his dad, his father who had never been anything but kind, was treating Lennox like a monster.

"He *should* eat that much. I do."

Will grabbed a can of corn and scanned the aisle for anything he thought Lennox might enjoy. Of course, with Lennox anything edible or questionably edible was fair game. He tossed a few more cans into the basket. Between the two of them, they'd eat that much in one sitting.

"He's barely had any food to eat for *months*. He's skin and bones."

"And still trouble." Ben grabbed a container of fried onions. "I know you like him, and I get all the stuff you and Karen keep saying about how hard his life has been, but that's no excuse—"

"He's good, Dad. He really is. And you don't get it. You don't even try."

Will turned the corner toward the front of the store; his dad's motorized cart hummed steadily behind him. Was this going to be the rest of his life? Every day was another strand of the same argument, another string of reiterated nonsense from his dad about how he listened when he actually didn't.

"Will. Will!"

He stopped a few aisles from the registers, near the pharmacy. "What?"

"Don't use that tone with me, William. I am still your father."

"And a real jackass." He bit his lip before adding, "Sir."

"William Elliot, you are being disrespectful—"

"So are you!" Will turned to him, his fingers curled into fists. "He's a guest in our house. He's *my* boyfriend. There is so much more to Lennox than you can imagine, and you won't shut up and let him be long enough to see that. He's a great guy, and yeah, he's been in trouble and he's messed up, but who isn't?"

"You aren't."

Will snorted. "Everyone is. Mom died when I was a toddler, I'm openly gay in a small town. That changes people, makes them hurt in ways that... Forget it. This is just how it's going to be, I guess. You're impossible."

He went down one aisle and up another to cool off. Not a single conversation ended happily, and nothing they said made things easy again, as they once had been. Lennox was a chasm between them, and no matter how far across Will dared to travel, Ben never met him.

Will stopped and had to shut his eyes to stop himself from laughing out loud. Condoms, birth control, lubricants. He eyed the front of the store and saw his dad at the registers. If Lennox were here, he'd know what to buy. He'd buy it without blushing or trying to hide it under another purchase.

Will's phone rang in his pocket. He pulled it out and ignored the call from his dad. Instead, he ran his eyes over the different options and tried to recall what little he'd learned and what Lennox had said. The flavored ones were out, and so were the ones with the woman-shaped outlines on them. No warming ones either. Finally, Will picked up a water-based one with a purple label. Water-based was good for anal, right?

He headed up front to the register where his dad was clumsily loading their purchases onto the belt. Will hid the lube behind his back and helped his dad load with his free hand.

His dad bent his head and drove forward to the cashier, but as Will set the lube on the belt amongst the canned vegetables, his dad spotted him.

"Since when do you use hair gel?"

Will swallowed as the cashier greeted them and began ringing up their purchases.

"It's not, um, hair gel."

Ben picked it up and his face hardened. Will readied himself for the explosion, for a new lecture about how Lennox was ruining his life or how he was ruining his own or that he was giving himself to someone he couldn't trust, but it never came. His dad set the bottle back on the belt and took a long, measured breath.

"You're paying for that."

Will dug out his wallet and handed his dad a five-dollar bill. "That should cover it."

Will drove them home. At his side, Ben fiddled with the stations before shutting the radio off.

"So you two are... You and him... You've gotten to the stage where—"

"We're having sex, yeah."

Will kept his eyes on the road and did his best not to look at his dad. Ben had done his best to teach him about sex and what a sexual relationship could and should mean. Still, Will had always thought this would be a long-distance phone conversation, with him sitting in his dorm room in New York while they watched a baseball game together. He couldn't hang up on his dad if this got awkward.

"That's... You're happy? He's not pressuring you?"

"He isn't. And we are happy. Maybe not with everything in our lives, but with us."

Ben cleared his throat and shifted beside him. He didn't speak again until they pulled into the driveway and parked. The sun was just peeking over the house; the rounded mountaintops shone like lights reflecting from a mirror. The dusting of snow would melt, and by midday they'd be back to that dreary place between the colors of fall and hard winter.

"I keep forgetting that whether or not I trust him doesn't change if you do."

"Well, I do. Completely."

Will unbuckled his seatbelt and unlocked the doors, but Ben grabbed his hand before he could get out.

"I'm sorry I keep doing this, Will. I'm not trusting you and you've never given me a reason not to before. Your word should be enough, but this is tough for me, no matter who the guy is. You're my little boy. You're my baby, and I know you hate when I say that, but you're always going to be that tiny, red-faced screamer that the nurses handed me in the hospital. All of this," Ben said as he gestured toward the house, "is more than I think I can deal with right now. I never expected for you to date at home, you know that? You didn't either. I figured I'd get to have a nervous breakdown over it after I hung up with you instead of what I'm doing now."

"It's not that big of a deal, Dad."

"Pretty big one from where I'm sitting, bud." Ben patted him on the shoulder and took a deep breath. "Look, I'll make you a deal."

"I'm listening."

"If he watches his mouth, I'll watch mine. I can't promise it's going to happen right away, but I'll try to see him as you do. Karen's furious with me about what I've been saying about him and she's right. I'm—I guess I'm taking a lot of worries out on him and making him into this big monster that's trying to turn you against me and what's good in the world."

"He is what's good in the world, Dad. Don't give me that look. He is. I don't think he's really figured that out yet, but he's so sweet and kind when he just lets himself be who he is."

"All right, enough chat. Let's get these groceries in before they go bad."

Will helped his dad inside. On the couch, Karen was examining Lennox's bare back. After almost three weeks, the welts and bruises had faded to dull marks, no more than smudges of dark ash on his skin.

"They're almost healed up now. Malia's ointment sure does wonders. Your ankle's finally strong again too."

"Even my ass bruise? That thing was like a volcano rising out of me."

Karen shook her head and smiled ruefully. "Yes, even that one. Go get a shower, sweetheart."

Lennox stood, his eyes darting from Ben to Will. He always hesitated when Ben was in the room, and Will got that glimpse of what was about to happen a split second before Lennox decided which direction he would take. Today, it was the callous boy from the parking lot.

"I thought the trash can was supposed to stay out on the curb," Lennox said to Ben. "Open wide, sunshine. We've got half a dozen empty lube bottles and some used condoms for you."

Karen moved to Lennox and Will moved to Ben. It was becoming instinctive to get between them, to block any attempts at physical violence. At first, Will had guarded Lennox, but now that his dad was a month out of the hospital, he was getting stronger and too much for Karen to hold back on her own if he went off.

Only Ben didn't say anything. He took a seat and chuckled. Will could tell it was forced, but Lennox couldn't.

"You're going to need wit like that to keep up with my son."

Karen and Will watched Lennox, but he only shrugged and headed downstairs. Will returned to the jeep for their groceries, and together he and Karen unpacked them and put them away. The only thing left on the counter was his bottle of lube. Karen handed it to him without a word, and Will flushed red as he pocketed it.

"That was something else," Karen said once they were finished. "Did you and your dad finally talk?"

"Sort of. I don't know. Things are so different with us ever since he woke up. It's weird. It's like he's my dad and he's a friend too, now."

"All part of growing up." Karen offered him a glass of orange juice. "You're both going to change a lot over the next few years. Lennox, too. Even me. Relationships with parents change once you get older. Your dad's going to have a harder time of it than you."

"But I'm an adult now. I'm not going to, like, grow or change much more."

Karen only smiled, her eyes sparkling as they had when he was younger. Not long after they'd met, Will, a tiny boy of nine, had insisted he was all grown up and that nobody was more grown up and mature. She'd taken him out to look at baseball bats for their first outing alone, and while Karen had directed him toward the youth-sized bats, Will had gone right for the biggest, heaviest one hanging on the rack. After several attempts to convince him otherwise, Karen had bought it (and a youth bat in his size). And eventually he'd given up using it—until last year, when it was finally just right.

"You go enjoy your Saturday. Go pick one of your geeky movies and have a date downstairs. Maybe get a little lucky."

"Mom!"

Karen spit her juice onto the table. Will froze. He hadn't thought about it, but there it was. The word fell awkwardly from his tongue, unused and thick, a betrayal of a mother he'd barely known, bringing another woman into her place. It was a word he could not remember calling anyone.

"Will—"

"We'll come up for dinner. Bye."

Will hurried away from Karen's shocked gaze and past his father curled up and sleeping on the couch. He could hear the shower running downstairs. He dropped down in front of his television.

If he didn't say that again, Karen would forget about it. And, god, at least his dad hadn't been in the kitchen to hear him call another woman Mom. Ben would never forgive him for taking the last fragment of his mother and giving it to someone else. Karen had never asked to be called Mom; she'd never asked to be anything other than a friend to him. Did she want that title? Did he want to give it to her if it meant hurting his relationship with his dad further?

The shower cut off. Will picked a movie at random. By the time Lennox entered his bedroom, the DVD menu was shrieking with tinny music. Lennox flopped down on the bed beside Will with one hand holding the towel tied around his waist.

"Hey, baby, I've got a surprise for you." Lennox rolled onto his back and raised his hips. His hand tugged at the towel. "All you have to do is work this knot loose."

Will snorted and pressed Play on the remote. "You're ridiculous."

"Horny. With a cute boyfriend in a locked room. You did shut the door, right?"

Lennox rolled into him so his arm slid under Will's shirt and rubbed over his back. Will laughed as Lennox kissed his neck.

"Yeah, I bought something you're really going to like."

"Oh?"

Will pulled the bottle of lube out of his pocket. "Here. Maybe we could use it today."

"Yeah?"

Lennox flipped it over to read the back label.

"Well, it *is* Saturday. Karen and Dad said they were going to a movie today. So the house should be all ours."

Lennox grinned and kissed him once before unscrewing the cap on the lube. He pulled the seal off and then dotted some on his arm and Will's. Will gave a small yelp at the cold goo. It was much thicker than what Lennox had used.

"Oh, it's really thick. That'll be interesting."

Will rubbed it into his arm and curled his lip. "Eww, that's so weird. Why'd you go and put it on me?"

"Allergies. Unless you'd rather find out by putting it in your ass or on your dick."

"Oh. Right. It is different than what you had? I mean, it *feels* different, but the ingredients—"

"Better safe than sorry. So what's the movie?"

"Umm." Will watched the screen for a few moments before he could place it. "*Silent Hill*. It's a scary one."

"Good. Gives me a reason to hide my head under your shirt."

Before Will could say anything, Lennox had him on his back and had shoved his head under Will's shirt. Lennox pressed his lips to the skin under Will's belly button, trailed down to his jeans, and then came back up with his tongue. Will laughed as Lennox kissed over his stomach, to one hip and then the other, and nudged Will's shirt up until it was bunched in his armpits.

"You always taste so sweet."

Will raised his head just enough to see over his shirt and groaned as Lennox took his left nipple between his lips. Lennox sucked and twisted a little until Will throbbed against the zipper of his jeans. Lennox grinned.

"Your nipples are fantastic."

Lennox circled the same nipple with his tongue before shifting to the other one. Will's head swam. He shut his eyes as he reached down to open his jeans. If he waited much longer, he'd never get them off. After they were open, Lennox shoved them down his hips and straddled him. He planted his hands on either side of Will's head, pressed his ass down against Will's cock, and tossed his head back.

"Bet you'd love to fuck me right now."

Will nodded and reached around to grip Lennox's ass. "Yeah, I... If you want, but I'd—"

Lennox cut him off with a fierce kiss and pressed him down into the bed with his weight. His towel was long gone, probably somewhere on the floor, and his cock brushed against Will's stomach. The warm, thick heat of it rubbed against Will as Lennox rocked his hips down against him. How he wanted him. Wanted Lennox stretched and spread out beneath him, accepting all of him into his body, bowing and bending to the pleasure of being taken completely.

Will arched against him as their tongues brushed and slipped first into his mouth and then into Lennox's. Their tongues twisted together, roughly and then more slowly. Lennox ground down against him; his hips rolled in a dizzying rhythm. Will panted into Lennox's mouth and felt a deep rush of heat flood through his body. They both gasped as Will thrust up.

"Let me take you."

Lennox sat back, breathing hard. Will groaned as Lennox's weight settled fully on his cock; he let his eyes drift shut. What he wouldn't give to be inside Lennox in this position, to feel the glorious heat and clench of his muscles around him! Nothing could compare to watching Lennox fall apart with Will inside him.

"How's your arm?"

"Huh?"

Lennox pulled Will's arm up and examined the spot where he'd dabbed lube. It was still a little slick, but he didn't have a rash. Neither did Lennox.

"Condoms?"

"Top drawer."

Lennox tugged the nightstand drawer open and pulled the box out. He returned his full weight to Will's lap. His lips were parted and his eyes were cloudy. Will rubbed his lower back gently.

"How do you want to do this?"

"This is fine."

Will nodded. Of course Lennox would want to stay on top. Having the option to pull away was a comfort for Lennox, and Will could accept whatever made him most comfortable. He fumbled with the bottle of lube before squirting it onto his fingers.

"Oops."

That was way too much. It squelched onto Will's fingers and palm, even onto his bedding. The lube was warm and he realized it had been pressed up against one of them while they made out.

"Damn it. At least it's not cold?"

"Ah, yes, my worst nightmare. Cold lube."

"Shut up."

Will rubbed it between his fingers, rubbing and rubbing, trying to take enough deep breaths to convince himself that he knew exactly what he was doing. That he'd reach around behind Lennox and effortlessly press his slick fingers against his hole and then in, in and out just as his lungs were doing.

"You chickening out?"

"What? No. I, um—"

"You want to watch, don't you?"

Lennox grinned down at him and then rolled onto his back beside him. Will let out a rush of air. That wasn't it, but at least he'd be able to see what he was doing. He wouldn't seem like a nervous, embarrassed moron who couldn't locate his boyfriend's asshole.

"Come here, slapper."

"Slugger." Will snorted. "You need to stop with the baseball talk because you're really bad at it."

"Am not. I want your balls slapping against my ass, so—"

"God, I can't believe I keep agreeing to have sex with you."

Will shifted down the bed; his feet kicked at his pillows as he settled his upper body between Lennox's thighs. Lennox winked at him. Will stared at Lennox's cock almost in his face, at the way it bobbed softly against his belly and at his balls tight against it. Below that—

He swallowed. "Let me know if I hurt you?"

Lennox nodded. "It's fine. I've fingered myself before, remember?"

That wasn't what Will had meant, but he nodded too. Slowly he pressed his finger against the puckered skin. It was darker than the skin around it and clenched tight at his touch. Lennox groaned above him, and Will arched against the bed. He couldn't wait to feel that around *him*.

Lennox pressed against his nudging fingers, and finally, after another series of deep breaths, Will pushed the first finger in. They both gasped. Lennox's hips lifted a little, and Will's mouth fell open at the heat, at the smooth muscle molding around his finger. He curled his finger deeper and thought back to what Lennox had done when their places had been reversed. Everything had felt so much faster, so much better.

"You okay?"

"Move."

Will thrust his finger in as deep as he could and wiggled it. His prostate must be somewhere around that spot. Lennox had found his so easily and he'd done something similar to this, hadn't he? Lennox moaned for a moment, then snorted and laughed.

"Don't wiggle your fingers." Another laugh rumbled out of Lennox, and his ass clenched tighter around Will's fingers. "Just thrust, okay?"

Lennox giggled again, and Will deflated. He was awful at this. Maybe he should just stick to bottoming instead. Will slipped his finger out and looked up at Lennox.

"Hey, no. Don't stop. What's wrong?"

Will shrugged. "I'm just not... You should top. I'm not—"

Lennox tugged him up for a swift kiss. They kissed until Will relaxed.

"You're doing fine. Just no finger wiggling, okay? It tickles."

"I didn't realize the inside of your ass was ticklish."

"Well, somewhere on me had to be."

Will kissed him again and then settled between Lennox's thighs. He stared at Lennox's hole and a thunderbolt of arousal ran through him. Lennox was slick with lube; his hole was a little more open than before.

"Ready?"

"Hurry up so we can fuck."

After a little fumbling, he slipped his finger back into Lennox. A wide grin spread over Lennox's face, and he groaned with each slow thrust. Will was mesmerized by the sight of Lennox's body engulfing his finger. He pressed a second one in and groaned. Lennox took him so well already, so easily accepted his fingers into his body.

"Man, that feels so much better when you do it."

"Really?"

Lennox groaned; his thighs spread wider as his ass squeezed around Will's fingers.

"Yeah, that's... Wow! You'll have to try it by yourself sometime."

"With you watching, right?"

"You're so kinky, but still a tease. Only you would make me watch and get nothing else."

Will grinned as he thrust a third finger into Lennox. His boyfriend's breath caught. His fingers paused as Lennox's ass clenched around him. It was a different feeling, tighter, almost stiff.

"Still okay?"

Lennox took a deep breath, and his ass clenched and then released. Will ran his eyes up his body.

"Lennox?"

"I'm good. Fine. I've never done three, that's all. And your fingers are fatter than mine."

"They are not!"

"Are so. Like your dick. Time to suit that up, don't you think?"

Will face-planted. He couldn't stop laughing, and the force of it made his fingers slip out of Lennox and the entire bed shake. Lennox took hold of Will's cock and rolled him over. A hand slick with lube stroked him, and then a condom was rolled onto him. Will crinkled his nose. He'd never put one on before and it was tight, like plastic wrap around his cock. Lennox's hand closed around him and coated him in lube again.

"Ready?"

"For you? Always." Lennox flopped down on his back; his cock bounced slightly. "How do you want me?"

"Um, this is fine. I think. I don't know. Whatever you prefer or that's easiest for me to move, I guess."

"Like this then."

Lennox sat up and kissed him, bringing him back down to the bed with him until Will was draped over him. Will could feel the sweat coating his fingers and chest; he shook a little, even though his arms didn't tremble as he held himself up and watched Lennox grasp his cock and guide him to his entrance. He swallowed and met Lennox's eyes. They were scared too. No matter what he said or how cocky or goofy Lennox acted, Will was connected enough to see that uncertainty. The time they'd had penetrative sex before, they'd just been two teenage boys, kind of involved and in over their heads with what the world was placing before them and what they might be together. Now they shared a commitment, a promise.

Will's arms shook a little more, and Lennox grabbed them and squeezed hard.

"You wait much longer and my ass is going to close up."

"Right. Okay."

He took a deep breath and thrust his hips forward slowly. Lennox's hand released his cock as the head of it pushed through Lennox's ring of muscles. Will paused. Below him, Lennox's eyes were shut, and his mouth had dropped open, but he seemed fine. He didn't look or act as if he was in pain. He wasn't *that* big. What did Lennox really know about size?

Will thrust deeper, recalling what Lennox had done their first night together. He sank in, inch by inch. His teeth gritted and his breathing was labored. It was truly the greatest sensation in the world to feel Lennox tight around his cock, to have their pulses hammer out separate rhythms as their skins met and their bodies joined. Will let out a shaky groan, and his hips jerked forward the last few inches.

"Fuck! Stop. Shit, shit, *shit.*"

Lennox's entire body had gone rigid. His grip was so tight on Will's forearms it felt as though splinters were piercing him instead of fingernails. Will started to pull out, but Lennox hissed and grabbed his hips.

"Don't. Just, fuck. Don't move. Let me—"

"No. No, I'm hurting you. I'm sorry, I didn't—"

"Stop moving. That's making it worse."

Will froze. His entire body was on alert. Lennox's ass was clenched around him, not the rhythmic clench his fingers had experienced, but a firm grip that almost hurt him, too.

"I'm sorry."

"You just, ouch, went too fast. That's all. Your dick's longer than your fingers and that deep part didn't get stretched." Lennox took a measured breath and quirked his lips. "I told you you're big."

"I'm *average.*" Will huffed and flicked Lennox's nose. "Do you want me to pull out?"

Lennox flicked him back and exhaled. "Not all the way. Go slow."

Will eased his hips back, watching a few inches of his cock slide out.

"Okay. That's—" Lennox groaned and shut his eyes. His entire body sank into the bed as he exhaled. "That's so much better. No deeper than this right now."

Will nodded and continued to pull out. He moved until his lower back ached and only the head of his cock was holding Lennox open. Then he thrust back in. His breathing stuttered, and sparks danced in front of his eyes.

"W-wow."

Lennox laughed, a squeaky sound that crinkled the corners of his eyes.

"Not bad. Now try to keep going."

"Right. Yeah, okay."

Will pulled back again, enough to feel cool air instead of Lennox's engulfing heat. After a few more jagged thrusts, Will found a slow rhythm. His head was spinning, his stomach was tight, and his cock ached. Lennox was sighing as one hand pumped his own cock and the other curled into the bed sheets.

"Deeper. That's... Fuck, that's amazing. Harder, too."

Will braced himself on his elbows and then picked up his rhythm again. He thrust as deep as he could, until his balls were pressed against Lennox's ass. They both groaned. Will thrust harder; his rhythm grew stronger as he squeezed his eyes shut.

"Fuck, you're so tight. This is—I'm going to—"

Lennox's ass clenched around his next thrust and Will collapsed on top of him as he came. Spots filled his vision. His stomach muscles continued to pulse and twitch even after he had come down. Between them, Lennox's hand was finishing himself off. With a shaky groan, Lennox came and his ass squeezed tighter. Will whined. He wondered if he'd get less sensitive over time.

Will pulled out, and Lennox winced and then slapped his shoulder.

"Wh—oh."

He stared at his bare cock, which was a little slick with lube and come but condomless. Lennox's fingers reached down and pinched the end of it just hanging out of his ass.

"Really? You are... Help me get it out."

"D-do I just pull it?"

"I hope so. I am *not* going upstairs to get your nurse mommy to help me. You'll go get her and explain that you don't know how to pull out while wearing a condom."

Will slowly eased it out of Lennox's ass. They both exhaled when it came out easily. Lennox tied it off and tossed it toward the trash can.

"Butthead."

"Sorry. I'm not very good at topping, I guess."

"It's an art," Lennox said. He rolled over into Will's side and nudged his head under Will's chin. "Don't worry about it. The first time I topped, god, that was awful. I almost broke my dick."

Will laughed, and some of the tension in his chest eased. "That was really amazing. We can do that again, right?"

Lennox nodded and yawned. "I'm planning on it."

Will beamed. Against his side, Lennox sighed and snuggled closer. Will stroked Lennox's hair and found his courage one last time.

"I love you."

The silence was exactly what he'd expected. Lennox breathed against his neck. Once, twice. Will swallowed and held him a little tighter.

"It's okay if you don't—"

"Don't lie. I—it's cool. That you feel that. I, um, I don't know."

Will nodded. It was in Lennox somewhere. That was his only hope. Lennox kissed his neck; his fingers traced a few patterns on Will's chest and then settled over his heart. They tapped out its rhythm, then added new beats until Will could hear the sound in his head. He recognized the synchronization of their heartbeats. Their single pulse was a good enough stand-in for Lennox's truth. Lennox did love him. Will just had to be patient a little while longer.

⏮ nine ⏭

"Is that the last one?"

"Yeah, I didn't mark myself down as a girl or anything, did I?"

Lennox shook his head and slid the laptop across the table to Will. Ben watched them from his corner of the couch. They'd been at it all morning, had skipped lunch despite Lennox's numerous protests, and now Will was finishing his last college application. His son was going to college. The first college student on his side of the family. Beth had gone to college, and Mia too.

"You don't have to mail them?"

Will shrugged. "I could, but it's easier to submit online. I just add a folder with my portfolio and use my bank card to pay for it. I didn't realize it was going to be so expensive. I already cut out a third of them."

"And you keep wondering why I'm not going," Lennox said. He rolled Will's wireless laptop mouse across the table and frowned. "Can we have lunch yet?"

"In a minute. This is my Sarah Lawrence one. It has to be *perfect*."

"It's been perfect since last week. Just submit it already. I've starved enough since I got to Leon. Let's not add today to that list."

"We could order a pizza," Ben suggested. "And don't worry about paying for all of those yourself, Will. I told you I'd help."

Will laughed and ignored his last comment. "Not even in your dreams, Dad. Just because Karen's not around doesn't mean I'm letting you eat whatever you want."

"Fine. As long as we don't have that vegan tofu puffy crap again. That was the nastiest shit I've ever put in my mouth."

Lennox snorted, and Will shoved him.

"It was healthy. And don't blame me. That was Karen's idea. She wanted to try something new. I'd much rather eat twenty Big Macs." Will clicked a few buttons and then took a deep breath. "It's done. They're all out."

Ben smiled at Will's nerves, at the way he ruffled up his hair. He was wearing it differently now. When Ben had gone into his coma, Will's hair had been getting long, but he'd had a fairly standard cut: short up the sides and a little longer on top, fluffed up off his forehead. Now the sides and back of his head had been shaved, and the top was longer than Ben had ever seen it.

"You're going to get into all of them," Ben said as the boys stood up. "You're going to do great things up in New York in the fall. I guarantee it."

Will grinned, and Lennox, clearly not wanting to be outdone, kissed Will's cheek and eyed Ben. Lennox kept giving him that look, almost a challenge. It seemed fierce and possessive and made Ben's skin itch. It wasn't a look he wanted near his son.

"You'll get in. Hell, you'll get into enough schools for both of us."

"Not if you don't actually apply to some. I'll help with the application fees until you get more money from your grandfather. Did you look at the pamphlets Mrs. Martinello gave you?"

Lennox shrugged as they all entered the kitchen. "What's the point? Even if I *did* get in—and I won't—I can't afford it. Forget it. I'll just, I don't know, work in a factory or something. Wherever they let people with records work."

"Just about anywhere. Juvenile records are sealed, kid," Ben said. "What schools are you thinking about?"

"None."

"Music." Will pulled a bag of rice from the pantry and then a few vegetables from the refrigerator. "Well, *I* think you should study music. You should hear him play, Dad. He's incredible."

Lennox's lips curled but he didn't respond. Ben, however, was surprised and pleasantly so. Will had never taken to music. That had been a shock, since he and Beth were both musically inclined, but Will had absolutely no sense of pitch and rhythm.

"Incredible, huh? Not sure I'll take your word on that, Will. You're as tone-deaf as Oyster."

"More so," Lennox said. "Oyster can actually howl a tune if you teach him. I got bored one morning."

As Will cooked, Ben examined Lennox. No calluses on his hands that he could see. His voice was punchy enough to hold a tune, but he didn't seem like a singer. When neither boy seemed ready to offer more, Ben finally caved.

"What do you play, then?"

"Your son's dick."

Ben gritted his teeth.

"He plays piano." Will elbowed Lennox. "And guitar?"

"Yeah, I guess." Lennox flipped the napkin holder on the table and shrugged. "Your dick's more fun."

Ben took a deep breath and tried to keep his temper. It was getting easier, and Lennox's comments were becoming generally less crude and graphic, but his words still pissed him off. Nobody should talk about his son like that.

"Would you stop? Dad doesn't want to hear about our sex life."

Will whacked Lennox with a spatula. Lennox laughed and fended him off, and for a moment, Will smiled too.

They were going to keep reminding him, weren't they? Those words spilled from Will's mouth so naturally. But they shouldn't. Will was eighteen. He was still in high school and had only met this boy four months ago. Will had never even kissed another boy as far as Ben knew. Now his innocence was gone, taken by Lennox in more ways than one.

* * *

FOR THE NEXT WEEK, BEN kept an eye on the boys, trying to spot signs of trouble between them, little nuances he could poke at. They seemed quite content, however, and by the following Sunday he still hadn't found any holes. Will and Lennox watched movies together; they got caught more than once making out on the couch or against a wall or the kitchen counter. More often than not they shut the basement door and retreated downstairs. Ben always hollered down after them, but it made no difference.

His son was in love. Or in love with the idea of being in love. Will had fallen for that idea ever since he'd watched Ben and Karen find each other. Karen had been Will's introduction to romantic movies and books, and his post-Disney understanding of love. Yet Ben couldn't find anything honest or substantial in Lennox. What did a boy from nothing and no family have to offer his son? What did Will see in him that made Will want to keep him?

Will spent most of the time he was not with Lennox talking about him and music. Ben had never heard so many badly pronounced musical terms, but Will's motive was clear. He wanted Ben and Lennox to sit down and play. The very idea of that, however, was nerve-wracking. Even if Lennox was a decent musician, they wouldn't have the same tastes in music. Lennox didn't care about classic rock or punk rock or anything besides that too loud and aggressively bass-driven rap music that always thudded through the streets in the cities.

"You could check out my dad's guitar collection," Will said every other day over dinner. Lennox ignored him and inhaled everything within reach on the table. "Dad, you two can see who can play a better arpenguin solo."

"Arpeggio," Lennox and Ben said together.

Ben glanced at Lennox and was met with an icy glare.

"Yeah, that. You two should still bring them out and play. You're both probably getting rusty."

Karen smiled at Ben. "I think that's a great idea. It'll help some of that trembling in your left hand. The doctors said activity would help."

Ben shoved a forkful of pasta into his mouth and didn't reply.

"When is Aunt Mia getting in?"

"Probably late tomorrow," Karen said. "She's picking up your grandmother on the way down. They're driving, so hopefully the weather holds off."

"Nana's coming?"

Lennox snorted as Will bounced in his chair. Ben had to smile. His son was still his little boy. Will loved Beth's mother more than any of his relatives, except maybe his Aunt Mia.

"She never misses a Christmas," Ben reminded him. "I'm sure she's got something special for you this year, to send you away to college with."

"Nana always has the best presents." Will turned to Lennox. "You're going to *love* her. She's the coolest grandmother ever."

"If you've named her after a banana then she ought to be."

"Shut up. She's awesome. You liked Aunt Mia, too."

Lennox shrugged and went back to eating. After dinner was cleared and cleaned up, they all piled into the living room. It was void of the usual Christmas tree. Will had offered to get one, but Ben stopped him. They were expensive, even here with so many tree farms, and it wasn't necessary. All of them were together and that was enough. Oyster might miss having something new to chew on, but the mess of needles wouldn't be missed.

As Karen attempted to get Lennox to pick something to watch, Will disappeared and returned with one of Ben's acoustic guitars— his second guitar, covered in peeling band stickers and scratches. Ben sat up to take it from him, but Will took it to Lennox instead.

"What're you doing with that?"

"I thought you might want to play." Will offered Lennox the guitar. "I even brought one of these things."

He held up a plastic red pick. Lennox stood up and examined the guitar without touching it, then glanced over his shoulder right at Ben.

"Stop trying to force this," Lennox said to Will. "We aren't going to—"

"Play us something," Karen said. "Maybe it'll convince Ben to get back into it."

Ben grunted and rubbed his left hand. It wasn't twitching right now, but it still spent most of the day shaking. His old guitar was dusty and no doubt horribly out of tune. He rarely played it, preferring his newer models and his old favorite, which Beth had given him shortly after Will's birth. Lennox wouldn't manage much with it; some kid who could strum a few chords for a bland rap song was no musician.

"Please? I know you miss it. And you used to have that guitar in your room, so I know you play." Will offered it to Lennox again. "If you play guitar even close to how well you play piano, then—"

"You're such a nag." Lennox ran a finger over the fret board and stuck his tongue out at Will. "And you've never heard me play. I might be the shittiest guitarist who ever breathed."

Sounded likely to Ben. But Will only smiled and shook his head. "No. I'm *the* worst. Just ask Dad. He tried to teach me, and I broke all the strings in about ten minutes."

"They were old strings," Ben said.

Lennox took the guitar, looped the strap over his shoulder, and untwisted it as if he'd done it a million times. Ben frowned but had to watch. Something seemed to shimmer in the air around the boy once he had that guitar in hand. His fingers ran over the curve of the guitar's body, plucked at a peeling sticker, and knocked some dust off the hollow body. He accepted the pick from Will and strummed once. Everyone except Will cringed.

"Ugh, don't you ever tune these things?"

"Been a bit busy," Ben said, his voice sharp, but he watched the fast flurry of Lennox's fingers plucking the strings and twisting the tuning pegs. He knew what he was doing, that much was clear. Within a minute, Lennox was strumming a few chords—G, D, C—and the guitar was pitch-perfect once more. Lennox tapped the soundboard and sat on the arm of the couch. Will curled up on the couch beside Karen.

A melody, twisted with longing and a spike of hope, filled the room. Ben didn't recognize it; he followed the practiced shifting of Lennox's fingers along the frets and tried to mark the places he went and returned to, but couldn't. Once before, he'd seen someone play like Lennox, all heart and experience—not the rigid experience of practice, but the experience of a life spent struggling and learning and knowing what it meant to feel, to ache. Lennox's movements were fluid, so steady and sure and passionate that the form was unrecognizable. This song could only exist through Lennox.

Ben saw it all in an instantaneous spark: a flash of this Lennox Karen spoke so fondly of and the boy Will's heart was after. Ben breathed deeply as the music changed, moving to a syncopated rhythm and then a slow, harmonic tune. Lennox's face was still, his eyes closed, but Ben felt the radiance when he watched him play, felt the passion of a life spent fighting to do exactly this.

Lennox stopped just as abruptly as he'd begun. He tossed the pick onto Will's lap and didn't look at any of them.

"That was beautiful," Karen said. She nudged Ben and smiled. "I can see what Will means. You really should make a career of it."

Lennox shrugged and eased the guitar from around his shoulders. "I'm nothing special. My mom just started teaching me when I was really little, that's all."

"That's not all." Ben surprised himself with his own words, but after that display it was hard to watch anyone, even Lennox, brush this off. Beth had spent hours playing with Will; she'd sat him down with a little guitar and tried to show him notes and chords. Ben had done the same thing a few years later. Will had tried, of course, but he'd never taken to it, never done much more than slap at the strings and fill the house with echoing clangs when he dropped the guitar on the floor.

"I spent years trying to teach Will to play; so did his mom when he was little. You've got something, kid. Don't belittle that."

"Whatever."

That was the end of it that night. Will picked a movie and the four of them huddled on the couch in their pairs. Ben spent more time watching the boys curled up, with Lennox dozing on Will's shoulder, than he did the movie. Maybe it was the flood of music that had poured out through Lennox, but he looked somehow softer in the firelight and the flicker of the television. Ben caught one brief, glowing smile and a sweet kiss that could only mean one thing. But he still couldn't say it, even when his eyes and his ears and these boys exhibited it all so clearly.

At bedtime, the boys stayed in the living room to fold the blankets and clear the dishes they'd used for popcorn and ice cream. Ben hung back in the hall. How had he missed that smile, that burst of certainty blazing warm and calm in Will's gaze?

"You should play with Dad sometime," Will was saying.

He hung the last blanket over the rack in the corner and then jumped and laughed. Lennox had crept up and grabbed him by the sides. They twisted and wrestled, then stood, Will's arms around Lennox's shoulders and Lennox's arms around Will's hips.

"That wasn't so bad, right?"

"No. It was okay. I'd rather sit downstairs with you. You know, naked and panting."

Will used his height as he stepped forward and pressed Lennox back. "They might hear you. He was impressed, don't ruin that."

"He doesn't care if I can play a donkey's ass like a fiddle." Lennox pulled away, but Will held him and brought him back. "Will, don't—"

His son cut Lennox off with a kiss, not chaste or short, but overwhelming. Ben had to look away. When he turned back to the living room, their foreheads were pressed together and their noses brushed back and forth against each other.

"You've definitely gotten better at that," Lennox said. He laughed as Will tugged him closer. "If you *tickle* me again, I won't touch your dick for a w—*ah!*"

Laughter filled the room. Lennox twisted and turned, with Will laughing right along, until he faced away from Will. After a few more minutes of struggling, he sank back against Will and let his arms pull him in.

"You're cut off for a week," Lennox said between deep breaths. "No, don't kiss my neck to convince me other—"

More laughter poured out of Lennox. They stayed there together, wrapped up in each other's arms, with Will's chin hooked over Lennox's shoulder. Lennox kissed Will's cheek. Will met him for another kiss, and when they broke apart Lennox rested his forehead against Will's temple.

Lennox breathed out against him. "I am so in love with you."

Will's mouth dropped open as Lennox pulled away.

"You're... really?"

"I meant—I didn't say—"

"You're in love with me."

"No, I'm not. I'm—I'm in dove with goo. Duh. I'm not... Don't be ridiculous."

Lennox darted for the open basement door and out of sight. Will stood there, his hands shaking. He shook his arms and followed Lennox down the stairs, grinning from ear to ear.

For the first time, Ben let the idea take hold that maybe, just maybe, this boy might be something special after all. He'd worried that Will was falling in love with ideas, with pieces of Lennox, but he'd never once considered that Lennox balanced Will. The heart of this boy, so beaten down that being anything meaningful scared him, could reach out into the world and find someone to hold on to. Yet if Lennox could admit that, without thinking and in such a gentle moment with his son, there had to be more to him than Ben saw.

◀ ten ▶

Nana May called everybody "honey." She was boisterous and spoke before she thought, tugging on her extravagantly dyed red curls all the while. They were more a deep ruby than the true red Aunt Mia sported, but Lennox didn't say anything about that. With her in the room it was hard to get a word in, and much less fun if he did.

"Honey, don't be absurd. If your mother wants to deny how precious these two are together, then let her. Leave her out of it all," she said to Karen on her first night in Leon. "Will, keep him around. I love seeing you with a handsome boy on your arm. It's about time, too. What I wouldn't *give* to have my youth back and to be out dating pretty young men again."

"Oh please, Mom," Aunt Mia said. "You spend all of your time on Twitter and eBay buying wicker furniture for your sister."

"Well, it isn't going to buy itself, Mia. And Ruby hasn't mastered a keyboard like I have. It's the arthritis that keeps her down. I did look into that school you've talked about, Will, and it seems lovely. Are you planning on studying in New York as well, Lennox?"

He shrugged and then winced. One thing he'd learned in the past hour was that she didn't stand for nonverbal responses.

"Speak up, honey. Don't just shrug like you've got an itch on your shoulder."

"College isn't really my thing."

"It could be," Will said. He pulled that stupid wad of pamphlets out of nowhere and showed them to Lennox for the fifty-seventh time. "He's really great at music, Nana. He plays better than Pop ever did."

"Really? That's something I'd like to hear." Nana May set her plate down on her lap. "Where'd you put his old piano, Ben? I hope you didn't sell it, even if none of you can play it."

Lennox jerked back as she leaned toward him.

"He used to keep it in the basement when Beth first brought it here after the funeral. Only my husband Henry ever played it. He tried to teach the girls, but Beth only wanted to play bass guitar and Mia was our little athlete."

"Right. Um, it's not—"

"Oh hush, honey. Ben, where's it at now?"

"The garage, May. Don't glare at me. It's insulated and heated in there. It's fine."

"Hmm, well, I'm sure Lennox will get some use out of it. Give you an excuse to spend more time over here with my grandson. Now what are these schools you're looking at?"

"I'm not—"

Will fanned the pamphlets out across Lennox's thighs. Lennox glimpsed a few pictures of buildings and headshots of old people before he tuned out. He wasn't going to college. Will was deluding himself.

"Oh, Berklee in Boston. That's a great one. We used to live just outside of Boston when the girls were small. Do you remember that, Mia?"

"I was still filling up diapers and drooling, Mom."

"Right. Beth would have. She had just finished kindergarten when we moved to Pennsylvania."

"I was looking Berklee up," Will said. He nudged Lennox. "It's only a few hours from New York, too. We could visit each other on weekends. And look, they've got all sorts of courses on ear training and composition and performance. You could study everything you'd ever want to know about music."

"Oh, jazz composition. Your pop would have enjoyed that, Will. He always wanted to do more with music than play in our living room, but it wasn't in the cards for him."

Lennox scanned the booklet: nice buildings, a harbor, and a bustling city. Music rooms, lessons, students—they tugged at him almost as if they hoped he'd join them, but his wallet would never be fat enough.

AFTERWARD, LENNOX FOUND THOSE PAMPHLETS everywhere. They were on his clothes in the morning, on the bathroom sink, in Will's hands when he was hoping to find a condom and lube. By New Year's Eve they'd made their way into his backpack, and Will had memorized most of the Berklee one.

He went to his motel room that day, more to get away from Will than from his family. Half the lot was flooded with rainwater, but Lucy's old car was parked by her door and nobody else was around. Lennox checked his own room, gathered more of his old comic books and clothes, checked his mail, and then knocked on her door.

"Lennox! Hey, how've you been?" She welcomed him with a tight hug.

"Fine. Just trying to get away for a while."

"Around Christmas? Oh, is that nasty grandmother of his back in town?"

"No, a different one is visiting. His aunt's back. She's pretty cool, but she keeps trying to catch us fucking. Will's banned boner fights until she leaves. It's pretty depressing."

"Aunts are like that."

Lennox sat down on her bed and looked around. The room was full of cardboard boxes, some taped shut, others half full of clothes and books. A stuffed penguin hung out of the box by the door. Lucy shut her door and went back to placing her things in the open box on the bed.

"Are you going somewhere?"

"Boston. I told you that. This is just a lot earlier than I was planning. Kelly found a job up there, so we're going to live together in an apartment near my campus."

"Your pretty lady?"

"She's gorgeous, actually. Gosh, you've been gone a while. Not that that's a bad thing with these idiots next door. So, um, I asked her out, and we're dating, and I just have to say that sex with a woman is significantly better than with a guy. Like, holy shit, Lennox, I feel so sorry for you and Will. Dicks are so pointless."

"Matter of opinion." Lennox played with the flap on the box and pulled the stuffed penguin out. Lucy had told him its name, once: Pepper or Chrome or something. "Will's is massive. Like, size of your forearm."

"Eww, you're lying."

"Nope. I'll take a picture. And he's still growing, so even if I am lying, he might make it to that size." Lennox sat on the edge of the bed. He was exaggerating a bit. Well, Lucy's forearm was much smaller than his own, so maybe it wasn't that far off.

"Doesn't it hurt if it's bigger? I mean, I know it does with, well, a vagina."

"Nah. Well, only because he didn't believe me. First time, well, he got a little eager about getting balls-deep."

"Ugh, no more dicks for me. Nope. Everyone that has one doesn't know how to use it."

"Only because you're dealing with straight boys."

"Whatever. Help me pack."

Lennox was more of a hindrance than a help, but he did what he could while playing with the stuffed penguin. It was weird watching all of Lucy's belongings disappear into cardboard. From her Wonder Woman socks to her biology textbook, everything fit neatly and was shut away. After an hour of working, Lucy lay down on her bed.

"I hope I like it in Boston. I've still got to find a job, but I applied for the fall semester so I've got time and money saved. Something part-time, like here while I'm in school, you know? Kelly finally found a job related to her degree and she's going to make a killing at it. It's like a biology research thing at one of the universities."

"So am I going to meet this mystery woman before she steals you away from hell?"

"She's coming over here after she gets off her shift." Lucy beamed at him and tugged at her braid. "We're going to eat Chinese and watch the ball drop at midnight. I'm sure she won't mind if you join. I mean, I never shut up about you. You're kind of my only real friend in town besides her now."

"Yeah. Maybe. I wouldn't want to get between you and her p—"

"Pervert." Lucy kicked him in the shoulder. "She's great. You'll like her tattoos."

Lennox shrugged and lay down too. He flipped through the mail he'd collected from his box, but it wasn't much. Water bill, junk mail, a magazine from some local store, and a letter from Vienna. He tossed the others in the trash and ran his fingers over the official police seal on the front. Lucy ran her fingers over it too.

"That isn't a warrant for your arrest, is it?"

"They don't send those in the mail. They'd just show up and slap some cuffs on." Lennox tore it open and unfolded the letter. "It's for my ankle monitor removal. January twenty-sixth."

"Sweet. I'll be gone by then, but you can come visit us now."

"Maybe."

They sat back, and Lucy turned on the television. She flipped mindlessly through the channels and told Lennox a little more about her first date with Kelly, and more about how she looked: short, wide, lots of tattoos, and a wicked smile. They'd gone into the city to a hookah bar not far from Lucy's old campus.

"She was so sweet. I've never been big on smoke, but you'd like hookah. It's better than those cigarettes you won't give up."

"I haven't smoked in a while. I don't do it a lot."

"Is that why you reek of it?"

"Sometimes everything is just too much."

"But it's getting better?"

"Now that I'm not here wondering if I'll make it through the night? Yeah. I also get to wake up in the middle of the night to Will humping the bed. Or me. It's a great trade-off."

"And his dad?"

Lennox hesitated. Ben had been different in recent weeks, still leery and uncaring, but after Will had brought out that guitar, it was as if a light had been switched on. Some days the light flickered and the ground shook with thunder, but more often than not, the weak light stayed steady. It wasn't ideal, but it was progress.

"I'm not sure. He's still—" Lennox crossed his eyes and wagged his tongue. Lucy giggled. "Karen's great, but she's off at work a lot. And—"

But he stopped himself there. He'd betrayed his own heart to Will last week, and while Will hadn't spoken of it or of his denials afterward, Lennox couldn't go more than an hour without it crossing his mind.

I am so in love with you.

Those words had left his mouth and brushed right up against Will's skin, his lips. He'd panicked and fled, taken to the back porch after Will had fallen asleep and smoked four cigarettes before he could convince himself to go back in.

And Will returned his love, maybe in a different form or way, but he'd said it, too, which only made it worse. Will had his commitment and love and plans for a future that involved Lennox—a future he kept sneaking peeks at whenever he thought Will wasn't looking. Berklee looked charming and modern, an expensive home for musicians, virtuosos, and other people he could connect to through music. So far, he'd met nobody like that. Mr. Robinette was the closest thing, but a weird band teacher wasn't a friend.

Will was great, but he wasn't everything. Will couldn't be a group of friends or every aspect of his future. His future. What a thing to imagine after so many years of one day at a time. Yet Will was integral to that future; without him it all collapsed, the foundation rotted out, and Lennox was left in a decrepit room with nothing but his ankle monitor and fading lights.

"I am so in love with you."

"*Excuse you?*"

Lucy stared at him. Then she kicked him in the shin.

"Ouch! What was that for?"

"What do you mean you're in love with me?"

"No. Not *you*. I—forget it. You can't help me."

"Since when?"

Lucy sat up and pulled her stuffed penguin out of Lennox's death grip. "Give me Peppers. You aren't fit for cuddling." She stroked the penguin's belly and hugged it. "So you're in love with Will, then?"

"No! I mean, maybe. I'm so fucked up, and I can't sort out my own head... Have you ever, you know, felt that way?"

"Been in love? I thought I was once, back in high school, but now that I'm older I know I wasn't. I was really into him, swept away or whatever. He ended up being a jerk. Has Will said that he loves you?"

"He might have mentioned it." Lennox shrugged and dug into his backpack for his cigarettes. "I'm gonna have a smoke, okay?"

He got up to open the door, but Lucy stopped him with a hand flat against the wood.

"You need to stop putting that tar shit in your lungs whenever you don't want to feel stuff. I bet Will doesn't care for your kisses tasting like smoke."

"It's my body. Who cares what he thinks."

"You do. Look, he's your boyfriend, and it's okay to be in love with the guy. You're lucky he's in love with you too."

"I never said he was—"

"You don't have to. The look in your eyes says enough." Lucy tugged the cigarettes out of his hand. "No more."

"But—"

"No." Lucy flipped the top open. "You've only got three left anyway, and two of them are turned over."

"My luckies."

"Your what?"

"It's a… One of the guys at boarding school, Daniel, used to do it. Learned it from his dad or uncle or someone. You pick one, by letters. So this slot," Lennox pointed to the top left hole that was empty, "is A. Then you go along the rows until you run out of cigarettes. It's kind of stupid, but you pick a letter for something special, like K for Kelly or C for cock or—"

"W for Will?" Lucy pulled out a cigarette. "And then… Aw, did you flip this for me? Or no. Probably for you, you're so full of yourself sometimes. Oh, or *love*. Seems fitting."

Lennox stared stonily at the second flipped-over cigarette. For his sister. For the Lucy he never expected to see again.

"It's for my sister," Lennox said.

"I didn't know you had a sister. What's her name then? Leneisha?"

"Fuck off. Her name is Lucy."

"Her—"

Someone knocked on the door.

"Lucy? I've got dinner."

"I hope you brought double. Lennox is here, and he could eat the entire menu in one sitting."

A bubbling laugh filtered into the room. Lucy glanced one last time at Lennox and handed him his cigarettes. Kelly was about Lucy's height, with a blocky build and thick arms and legs. She had dark hair and hazel eyes and, much to Lennox's surprise, she wasn't white. Her skin wasn't as dark as his, but she was definitely brown. Hispanic maybe.

"Kelly, this is Lennox. Lennox this is—"

"Your first pussy call. I'd say I've been there, but—"

"You're missing out. Although I hear boner fights are a good time as well." Kelly kissed Lucy on the lips and shut the door. "I don't know why I agreed to take a job in Boston. I can't even stand the winters here." She shook the snowflakes out of her hair and took off her coat.

Lucy and Kelly curled up on the bed with the bag of Chinese food and began to sort it out. Lennox watched from the door. He'd never been a third wheel, but surely he was now. It was time to head back to Will's.

"Get over here, knucklehead. This one can be yours, but that's it."

Kelly handed him a container, and he took it. But he didn't sit and he didn't open it.

"Hey, sit down. What's wrong with you? You're not scared of lesbians, are you?"

"You're bi and no. I just… Will's probably waiting for me."

"Invite him over. We can have a big gay New Year's." Kelly smiled and offered him a carton of rice. "We're going to need more food if he eats like you."

"Um, well, I can't, I don't have—"

Lucy was already ahead of him. She pulled her phone out of her pocket and called Will. Lennox dived to stop her, but—"Hey, Will. How's it hanging? Pretty well from what Lennox says. *Anyway,* he's over here with me and my girlfriend, and we were hoping you'd join us for a big gay New Year's Eve. Yeah? Okay. Awesome. You might want to bring him some tacos or something. He's trying to eat all of our Chinese. See you soon!"

Kelly pulled him down by his jacket sleeve. "Eat."

She shoved a forkful of noodles into his mouth. Lennox ate and sat back with them. Kelly fiddled with his ankle monitor and asked Lucy about dates for moving vans and if it was worthwhile to get one.

"I think we'll be better off in my car or yours. I don't have much to bring."

"They're really expensive. We can drive one of our cars up next weekend and then the other one when we leave. Take a bus back or something. They're pretty cheap."

Lennox swallowed a piece of General Tso's chicken whole and let Lucy twirl one of his curls. She was leaving. The one friend he had who wasn't also his boyfriend was leaving for good. He coughed until the chicken went down. Soon Will would be gone too.

"You okay?"

"What? Yeah. I'd be better if I had Will's dick in my—"

"Stop. Seriously, what's—"

Another hand knocked on the door. Lennox recognized the uneven knocks as Will's. He punched out the same rhythm on the bathroom door whenever Lennox got there first in the mornings.

Knock-ka-knock-knock.

Lennox let him in. Will greeted him with a kiss that mirrored Kelly and Lucy's. Lucy introduced him to Kelly, and they all sat down on the bed together with the television humming behind them. Lennox listened, but rarely spoke. All of them were leaving. Each of them had a plan mapped out and a future they were heading toward. What would his future hold? In a month his ankle monitor would be gone, and then what?

"I didn't know you were looking at Boston, too!"

Lucy slapped his arm so hard she sent him reeling. Lennox put a foot down on the floor to keep himself from tumbling off.

"What?"

"Will said you were thinking about applying to Berklee. That's in *Boston*. You know, where I'm about to move to?"

"I'm not." Lennox gave Will a steely look and rubbed his arm. "I'm not going to college or Boston or whatever."

"He's been looking at the pamphlet for Berklee," Will said, and smiled sheepishly at Lennox. "Literally, just glancing at it when he thinks I'm not awake. He'll probably miss the fall deadline since it's really soon, but I think it's a good fit. I really do. You love to play music, Lennox."

"I do n—"

"You do," Lucy said. "I used to listen to you through the wall. When the dipshits weren't around. He played his guitar all summer when he had the chance. You're really good."

"I'm not." Lennox stood up, but Will, Lucy, and Kelly all grabbed him and kept him from leaving.

"Sit down. It's almost time for the ball to drop."

"I'd rather the ball—"

"Yeah, yeah. Shut up, pervert." Kelly gave a hard tug, and he was back on the bed with a pout firm on his lips. "Aw, look at that pout."

Will's finger plucked at Lennox's lower lip. "Cutie."

"I'm not applying to Berklee."

"Okay. Then I'll just give the pamphlets to Lucy and Kelly to look at."

Will opened Lennox's backpack and pulled them out of the front pocket. Two of them were for Berklee, and Lennox was glad to see them go. It was out of his hands. He couldn't go without money or information or anything else. The women flipped through the little pamphlets as the conversation turned to New Year's resolutions.

"Well, move out of here. So check that off," Lucy said.

"Mine was to find a decent job and actually start paying some of my loans back. Unless something drastic happens between now and the nineteenth, I'll get that one done. I'd like to see the Bruins play once we're in Boston. Or take a road trip around the northeast."

"Oh, that would be fun. Let's do that."

"I'm going to graduate and get into college and see Christmas in New York City next year. And a Mets game."

Lennox fell silent once more as the three of them laughed over random resolutions, silly ideas from skydiving to trying to eat at every McDonald's in the New York City area. Will wrapped his arms around Lennox from behind as the television flashed a picture of the ball in New York City. He didn't know where it was, what building that was, or how so many screaming, snow-covered people could line up for hours to stand out there for such a short countdown.

"What about you?"

"Hmm?"

Lucy and Kelly huddled up together with their eyes as bright as their smiles.

"Your resolutions for next year," Will said. He kissed Lennox's cheek, then his neck. "And don't tell me it's to see if your fist can fit in my ass."

"I bet it could."

"I bet we're not going to find out." Will nipped at his jaw and nuzzled his nose against Lennox's neck. "So?"

"I don't know. I've never actually made any before."

"Well, it could be something really simple like learn a new song on the piano or pierce your ears, not that you need any more piercings. I might need a few, or a tattoo. Oh, I should add that to mine." Will's fingers rubbed Lennox's chest and stomach. "It can be something big, too. Like graduating or moving or getting a driver's license."

"Or college."

"Yeah, or that. It's one of mine. A lot of people just pick stupid stuff they're never going to hold to, like getting in shape and going to the gym however many days a week. I try to be practical. Pick things I've already been working toward that I can finally make happen."

"Right."

"Ten, nine, eight—"

Kelly and Lucy continued to count down as Will gave him a squeeze. "You'll find something."

"—three, two, one!"

They turned to watch Kelly and Lucy giggle and kiss. After a quick peck, they tumbled onto the bed in a deeper kiss. Will grinned and poked Lennox's cheek with his tongue.

"You know, I've never had a New Year's kiss," Will said, his fingers lacing together over Lennox's chest. "Have you?"

"My mom once. That doesn't really count, I guess." Lennox turned his head to Will. "So no. I've never wanted one before."

Will nudged him with his nose and tilted his head to kiss him. Lennox leaned into his lips, breathing in when they pressed against his. They kissed softly at first, and Lennox felt the sharp inhalation of Will's nose next to his and the little huffs of warm air that followed. He broke to breathe, then dove back in, catching Will's lips while they were parted.

A sharp whistle filled the room. Kelly and Lucy laughed as they broke apart and shared another kiss of their own.

"Happy New Year."

"Yeah, Happy New Year."

Lennox kissed Will's cheek and watched the sea of people on television waving their arms as confetti rained down amongst them. Next year, Will would be there, maybe in his dorm room watching live, or maybe out in the crowded streets kissing a stranger.

Or me.

Lennox hummed as Will rested his chin on his shoulder and held him. He pressed his hand into the bed and something crinkled. The Berklee pamphlets were crumpled under him. Lennox tugged one loose and stared at the glossy front, at the brick arches of a building that might hold any possibility in the world.

"You okay?"

"Just thinking." Lennox let the pamphlet fall open on his lap and scanned the lists of majors, minors, and courses. He was smart enough for it. Maybe talented enough too. But—

"It's okay to want it."

Yet it wasn't. How could he want more than he could afford, more than he was worth?

"And it doesn't hurt to at least apply and see."

"But I... You had to write all those essays and articles—"

"You'll only need one. Maybe two. I'm applying for writing, so it's different. We'll look at their admissions process when we get home tonight, okay? You'll probably have to play a piece for them or something. Like an audition."

"Playing is the easy part." But he kept looking, letting himself want it, even if only for one night. "I could play in my sleep. And it's such a long shot. Even if they think I'm good, I've still got this"—Lennox shook his ankle monitor—"and a record, and my grades are complete shit this year."

"Sarah Lawrence is a long shot for me too," Will said. "But if I don't do it, I'll regret not trying. Not knowing if it could have happened. I'd rather know for sure than always wonder."

Lennox swallowed and shut the pamphlet. "I'll look. It's not my resolution though."

"Okay. Resolutions are just a silly tradition anyway. You don't have to make one."

Will stood up and said his goodbyes to Lucy and Kelly. Lennox tucked the pamphlets back into his bag along with the letter about his removal date and took a deep breath. He had a resolution in mind, but telling Will he was in love with him again—saying it and staying to hear it back—was way more complicated than college applications or writing some essay. It was more difficult than anything he'd ever done.

⏮ eleven ⏭

THE NEXT MORNING, WILL AND Lennox slept late. It was midday when Will rolled over and got kneed in the stomach by one of Lennox's stray legs. He grunted and rolled back the other way. As he massaged his stomach, Lennox gave a hefty snore and flopped around until one of his arms dropped onto Will's chest.

Will frowned and wiggled free, climbing out of their blankets and Lennox's limbs and over to his desk chair. Sharing a bed was annoying sometimes, at least with Lennox's limbs flying about like pinwheels. He yawned and opened his laptop to put on some music. On the bed, Lennox tumbled around a little more and then Will heard it: that whine, fearful and low in Lennox's throat.

"No, I'm... *no—*"

Lennox bolted upright; one pillow flew across the room and hit the stair railing. His chest heaved, and he squinted as if a predator was circling him, one pace closer with every breath.

"What time is it?"

Will checked the time on his laptop. "Almost noon. Ready to look?"

Lennox fell back into the pillows and rubbed his eyes. "Look at what?"

"Berklee. We got a little distracted last night."

"Make-outs and boner fights are a good distraction."

Will brought his laptop to the bed. He tucked his legs under the covers and set its warm weight on his thighs.

"We're going to look before you're awake enough to talk me into sex. Come on, up."

"My dick doesn't take commands, sorry." Lennox buried his head under the pillows and rolled onto his side facing Will. "Fine. Can we fuck after?"

"We can have sex. After we check out Berklee for you."

Once the site loaded, Will tugged the pillow off Lennox's head and slid down until he could see the screen too. Lennox said very little as they scrolled through the site, from the student life pages to the admissions section that listed audition locations and dates and then something Will hadn't counted on—an interview.

"An interview? For what?" Lennox leaned in and read the section as well. By the end, he was frowning and jittery. "No. Absolutely not."

"But—"

"Do you know how fast I could fuck up an interview?"

"Before you get through the door. Hey, no. Come on," Will said as Lennox made a move to get out of bed. "Let's see what the application wants and the essay question. Most of them give you an option to write like a personal story or something."

"Personal story?" Lennox lay back against his side and blew out a frustrated breath. "Like, a story about how much I like dick?"

"Better leave that story for me. I wrote one about being out in a small town, and the others all had specific questions. Sarah Lawrence had three. I used the small town one for one of them."

Will smiled a little as Lennox relaxed against him again. It wasn't easy to reel him back in most of the time, but first thing in the morning, Lennox tended to give in faster. He clicked through to the application and started one for Lennox. They bantered through the demographic questions, and a brief argument started over what home address to use. After five minutes, Will had convinced Lennox to use his house instead of the motel, since he spent all of his free time here now.

"Okay, what's your primary instrument?"

"Testicle bongos."

Will rolled his eyes and scrolled through the options until he found "Piano." Then he clicked for a secondary one.

"Piano and what? Guitar? I know you've done percussion too."

"Lemme see." Lennox tugged the screen closer to him and tapped through the list. "Yeah, guitar. I can do a lot of percussion, but I haven't played a set in years and I don't play any percussion instrument as well as guitar."

Will added guitar and then clicked through to a long list of audition locations and dates. He wasn't surprised to find that none of them were nearby. Baltimore was the closest, and then probably Nashville. He selected them and copied the dates into a blank document. Lennox watched him with his lips quirked.

"There's no point in saving those. I'm not going to—"

But they both stopped at the next screen. How were they already at the application fee? Will scrolled through the short page and read it as Lennox got out of bed and found his sweatpants on the floor. For all of Will's applications, paying had been the last step, and none of them had cost—

"One-fifty. Forget it, Will. That's a huge waste of money."

"No, it's not, because you'll get in and—"

"And what? Be six figures in debt for the rest of my life? Just forget it. I can use that money to feed myself *all summer* instead of blowing it on an application to a school that'll probably turn me down anyway."

"You don't know that." Hope seeped out of Will as Lennox continued to dress. He couldn't give up so easily, not with his talent. "Listen, I'll front the cost and—"

"You aren't paying that for me. Forget it."

For a moment, Will almost got sentimental. He almost got cheesy and told Lennox how he had paid him back with his heart and love, and a bunch of other lame attempts at romance. None of that would ever get through to Lennox.

"You'll pay me back," Will said. "No, don't argue. Your first show or gig or whatever. I want the first one-fifty you make to pay me back for the application, okay? I get you're short right now, but you won't always be."

"But I might never—"

"You'll pay me back. Or else. Consider it a loan."

"Even if I got in, I wouldn't *go*. I can't afford it, so you're just wasting money."

Will clicked back to the site's main page and found the list of scholarships he'd skimmed earlier while Lennox had blown spit bubbles at the ceiling. Berklee offered quite a few, and he was sure there were more that Lennox would qualify for. Getting him to apply, however, was another matter.

"They have full scholarships. Lots. Look, and they're based on musical merit and financial need. Maybe you'll get one."

Lennox sat down beside him and skimmed the list too. "Maybe. I just—it's all due in like two weeks, and then there's this audition and an *interview*, and am I even going to be able to go to those? Like, are they after my ankle monitor comes off? Cause if they aren't, then—"

Will flipped back to the list of dates he'd copied and smiled. "They are. They're at the end of February and beginning of March. So?"

"So what?"

"Come on." Will leaned over sideways until he fell on top of Lennox. "Please apply. *Please.*"

"I... Okay, but I still need an essay or whatever."

"Didn't you turn one in for English?" Will asked the question before his memory caught up to him. Lennox rarely turned anything in. "Never mind. I'll help edit it if you want. You've got two weeks. Let me go get my wallet."

"But—"

"We can't see the questions without paying the fee."

Will pulled his pajama pants on and headed upstairs to find his wallet. He found his dad already awake and stretching in the living room.

"Morning. Have you seen my wallet?"

"Afternoon, actually." Ben reached for his toes and grunted. "It's on the counter in the kitchen. You have a good time last night?"

"Yeah. It was great. Lennox is going to apply to Berklee."

"No kidding?" Ben stood up and wiped his forehead. "He plays like he did last week, he'll be a shoo-in. We'll have to bring that piano in for him. Make sure it's tuned or whatever."

Will paused at the entry to the kitchen. "Since when do you care to help Lennox?"

"Well, he's... Kid's talented. That's all. He's going to have to practice and pick a piece to audition with—"

"How do you know all of that? Dad, have you been looking on their site?"

"No! No, Karen just browsed a bit last night and I was just reading over her shoulder."

"Right. Well, we're going to work on his application. Is there anything for breakfast?"

"Cereal."

Will nodded. He grabbed his wallet from the counter and then picked a box of cereal from the pantry. Back downstairs, Lennox was sprawled on the bed with Will's laptop on his chest and music pumping through the speakers. Will stopped to listen and recognized a pop song from his iTunes library before it was cut off by the start of a new song. The next one lasted half a second—a short blast of rock—and then Will heard the soft, melancholy melody of a ballad.

Will got comfortable next to Lennox and offered him the box of cereal as he lifted his laptop onto his thighs. His iTunes library was open. Will scrolled down and picked a new song at random.

"Think you could play this?"

Lennox munched on cereal and tilted his head to listen. His eyes slipped shut and, as always when music was sliding through the air, he looked at peace. They listened for a few seconds before Lennox nodded.

"Yeah, probably. It's just power chords. I didn't think you liked pop punk." Lennox reached over and clicked Shuffle. A harder song started to play. "Wow, Bikini Kill? I'm impressed."

"You can thank my dad for that. Mom loved punk bands. She really liked girl bands and the Ramones. She played bass."

Lennox nodded and hummed along. "Sounds like she was pretty cool. You ever think of trying to play guitar or bass?"

"I can't play anything," Will said. "And I guess she was. What I've heard makes her sound wonderful. You would have liked her, I think."

"I think you could learn. Your hands are big enough, and it's about finger movements and strength instead of holding a tune like with your trombone."

"Maybe. I don't know." Will clicked over to the Berklee application and got his debit card out. "All right, let's do this."

Will clicked through all the steps excitedly, but Lennox fell silent. Just as he was about to click on the pay button, Lennox grabbed his hand.

"Don't. I... Don't."

"Why not? We'll put in your education information and check out the essays, and you can work on it today, and I'll do the rest of our English assignment for *Lord of the Flies.*"

"No, it's not... I mean, you're paying for all of this before it's even finished, and if I... What if I don't go through with it? Or I can't get an audition or whatever?"

"Don't worry about the audition. And you will. You're as smart as me, and I'm sure it's nothing too hard. You can type it up on here while I do my math homework." Will rubbed Lennox's arm. "It's okay. No matter what happens. I just want you to have the chance to try, even if you back out or don't write the essay or whatever else."

Lennox shifted around, one arm around his chest, the other stretched back over his head to scratch his upper back. He squinted at Will and swallowed.

"Okay. I'll try."

Will submitted the payment. Lennox jerked beside him; his face dropped.

"I don't have scores. The SAT or AST or whatever. I never took them and—"

"We'll sign you up," Will said, but his heart faltered. "Maybe Berklee doesn't need them. A lot of schools don't require them anymore."

Lennox tugged at his sweatpants and jerked his head up and down. He already looked regretful, and guilt churned in Will. Was he pushing Lennox too much? Having Lennox go to college and be close by after this year was what he wanted, but that didn't mean it was what Lennox wanted.

"You do want to try, don't you? I mean, I know you've been looking at the pamphlet a lot, but I'm not pushing you into this, am I?"

"Bit late to ask now," Lennox said. He clicked through to the education information. "Where's the question?"

Will spared Lennox one more guilty glance before scrolling through the required educational background list. After clicking through three pages, Will found the question, and it wasn't close to what he'd expected.

"The question is about formal music training," Will read. "Or if you haven't had any, what sort of challenges you've faced."

Lennox snorted. "Got plenty of those under my belt."

Will opened a new blank document and passed his laptop off to Lennox.

"Well, get busy. I'm going to go upstairs and work on math, okay?"

"But I... What am I supposed to write?"

"A story about yourself. Truth. Tell them about your experiences and answer what they're asking." Will stood up and grabbed his backpack. "Be honest and you'll be fine."

Will paused just before the landing blocked his view. Lennox stayed on the bed, almost frozen, with the laptop. He was lost, clearly outside of his comfort zone, but Will hoped he'd write something.

He met his dad in the living room. *I Love Lucy* played on the television. Will set up his book, notebook, and calculator on the table and took a seat next to Ben.

"Since when do you voluntarily spend time away from that boy?"

"He's working on his essay for Berklee. It's all due in like two weeks, so I came up here to work so I don't distract him."

"Hmm, well, that's a change."

"Dad."

"A nice one. I miss sitting around like we used to on the weekends." Ben turned up the volume. "You're going to get real sick of being up here, real fast. *The Brady Bunch* is on after this."

"Ugh, I hate that one. They're all goofy little brats with the most bland problems."

"Should have stayed downstairs."

Will rolled his eyes, but for a moment he was pleased. His dad had been doing his best to keep him upstairs when he could. An hour later, when Will was getting ready to rip his ears off because of the laugh track on the television, Lennox appeared.

"Any luck?"

Lennox shrugged and sat down next to him. "This was a bad idea."

"You'll figure something out."

Oyster jumped up beside Lennox and climbed into his lap.

"See? Oyster believes in you."

"He's just an overgrown baby."

Oyster whined and licked both of their faces.

"Ugh, not now, bud."

Ben shut the television off and stretched. "Better get practicing, huh?"

Lennox stared at him.

"If you're going to audition for Berklee, you need to get going."

"Um, I guess." Lennox scratched Oyster's belly and kept his eyes down. "Can I, um, use—"

"Guitars are all yours. Same with the piano in the garage, but it's probably out of tune."

Will shut his books and rolled Oyster to the floor. "Come on. You've got a piece to pick."

Lennox hurried after him, his hands on Will's hips as they headed down the hall to Ben's home office and music room. Guitars were mounted along the walls, several acoustics sat on stands in the corner, and the closet door was laid flat on top of Will's old crib. A tall desk chair sat in front of it. Papers and bills were organized in short, straight stacks across the top. Karen's handiwork, clearly. In the corner, a bookcase held stacks of sheet music and old records.

Will flipped through the stacks of music books. "Some of this might help you for your audition. Most of it's rock, but I'm not sure what you're going to use. Can you use rock?"

"Probably. It's all music. I can play pretty much anything. But the essay. I'm no good at writing. I just sat there." Lennox dropped down onto an overturned five-gallon paint bucket and buried his face in his hands. "I didn't write anything. Just a paragraph of commas."

"Well, think about how you started playing." Will took a seat at the desk and spun around in circles, waiting for Lennox to speak. "Your mom taught you, didn't she?"

Lennox shrugged and leaned back against the wall. "When I was three? I was really little. Started with piano and then guitar when I was six. It wasn't really formal. She taught me from books and from the lessons she took when she was a kid. I don't know what to call it."

"Talk about your mom a little then, and the gift she gave you. She set you on this path, Lennox."

"But after that I just taught myself new stuff. When Lucy was sleeping or playing, I'd take out Mom's old music books and learn those while Dad—they don't want to hear any of that stuff. They don't need some sob story about the orphaned boy who raised his sister and learned music. Who cares?"

"Don't give them a sad story then. Yours isn't over yet, you know. Tell them a beginning and make them excited for the journey that gets you to the end." Will tossed a music book at him, and Lennox caught it. "That's what I did. A little different, obviously, but you've got to tell them your story."

"And answer the question they want answered," Lennox said.

"Seriously, from someone who wants to write as a career, read the question and write the first piece of your life that comes to mind. You can edit it to fit the question after you get something on the page."

Lennox flipped through the book and snorted. "You would throw a beginner's book at me. Did you use this?"

Will glanced at the white cover with an acoustic guitar on it. "Dad bought it when he first tried to teach me, but my hands were too small, and I got annoyed when I couldn't do it right away. Baseball was much easier."

Lennox grabbed one of the acoustic guitars. "Come here. I'll teach you something."

"I can't play."

"And I don't do boyfriends. Oh, wait."

Will rolled his eyes, but he stood. Lennox showed him how to hold the guitar and then how to hold the pick. When he flipped open the music book, however, Will tried to get away. How many times had he sat like this with his father and only disappointed him? He didn't have his mother's robust passion or his father's delicate fingers on the strings. All he could do was—

CRR-TWANG!

Will winced. "Sorry. I can't. You play something. Get in some practice."

He tried to hand the guitar back, but Lennox pushed it into his chest and lay the music book open on his knees. He pointed to the first quarter note on the page, and, for the first time, Will was glad he'd taken band in middle and high school. At least he understood this much. That was an improvement.

"All right, now I know you suck at blowing on that trombone, and I'm glad the same isn't true for blowjobs—"

"Lennox."

"Do you know what note this is?"

"Um…" Will's face scrunched up. The top space was the last letter of the word *face*. "E?"

"Yup, then F and G. All on the first string. Here, hold on."

Lennox grabbed another guitar. "So E is an open string, no fingers on it."

Will plucked the first string from the top and Lennox grinned and laughed.

"No, I mean that *is* an E, but it's reversed on guitar. Bottom to top." Lennox plucked the thinnest string and counted one, and worked his way up to the sixth string.

Will clumsily plucked the bottom string. Doing anything right-handed was awkward, but the world was generally built that way. "And the F is?"

Lennox reached over and placed the pointer finger of Will's left hand on the string next to one of the silver bar things along the long part. He'd have to look the names up later.

"First fret is an F."

Will strummed again and the guitar made a horrible sound somewhere between a boom and a cat screeching.

"I suck at this."

But Lennox had noticed his clumsy right fingers gripping the plastic pick and the sureness of his left hand. He took the guitar and did something very strange with the knobs at the top. After a few seconds of twisting, one of the strings came loose and Lennox pulled it free.

"W-what are you… Dad'll kill you if you ruin his guitars."

"I'm just flipping the strings around. I forgot you're a lefty. It'll probably be easier for you to play left-handed. Duh, right?"

"But—"

"He's got a dozen other guitars in here."

Will kept an eye on the open door while Lennox worked. Lennox pulled all of the strings off, then replaced them in the opposite order. As he plucked and twisted them into tune, Will smiled at the nimble work of his fingers and how effortless it seemed. Lennox truly was naturally gifted.

Once he was finished, Lennox passed the guitar back to Will and helped him hold it. It was still weird, but he felt much more natural with a pick in his left hand. They ran through names for parts of the guitar and then the first two strings before calling it quits. Will was shocked by how much he had learned and how well he seemed to be doing.

"See? You can learn. I told you."

From the doorway, someone clapped. Ben was standing there watching them.

"Well, I'll be damned. You got more out of him than I did in almost six months."

"Helps if you get in him first, if you know what I mean."

"He doesn't. That would be disgusting." Will set the guitar back on its stand. "You won't be either if—"

Ben cleared his throat and picked up Will's guitar. "Changed the strings around. Never thought of that, but if Hendrix played that way, why not Will."

"Yeah, he's no Hendrix. He might hold a tune on it eventually, but he's too tone-deaf for much else."

"I am not—"

"You are," Lennox and Ben said.

Ben put the guitar down and pulled Will against his side. "Come on, kid. Your friends are here to see you. Seems you've been neglecting them."

Will was steered out into the living room and greeted by a small crowd of people. Aaron, Roxanne, Natasha, and—to his surprise— Otto. All four of them were bundled up in sweaters, scarves, and wooly hats. The girls greeted Will with hugs; Roxanne's was the usual lift hug, and she went out of her way to lean back until his feet were off the ground.

"You never texted me! I sent you a Merry Christmas text and a Happy New Year one *and* one to tell you I got my early acceptance to William and Mary!"

"Really? That's great."

Natasha rolled her eyes, but even she was grinning. "She won't shut up about being the first to get in."

"Well she did apply in, like, September," Aaron said. "I'm finishing mine up still."

Will was hugged by Roxanne again and then set down in favor of Lennox.

"Oh no! You aren't flinging me into the air. Later."

Lennox swooped out of her reach and then spotted Otto. "Since when do you hang out with him?" Lennox mumbled against Will's ear.

As Ben offered the group snacks, Will whispered back, "I'm pretty sure he's here for you."

"That's the gayest thing you've ever said. He's definitely *not*—"

"What's up, dickface?"

Lennox turned around to Otto and punched him in the gut. Otto doubled over for a few seconds and then smacked Lennox on the back. It seemed to be some sort of violent greeting. They smacked hands next and then sat down on the couch away from Roxanne and Natasha. Ben patted Will's shoulder as Aaron appeared with several bowls of popcorn.

"Call me if you need anything," he said. "You kids have fun."

Will nodded and sat down between Lennox and Roxanne.

"Can we play Pictionary?" Roxanne asked. "Please."

"Only if romantic partners aren't allowed on teams," Natasha said. "That means you and Aaron and these two dorks."

"Good thing we're just fuck buddies then, huh, Will?"

"I'll show you fuck buddies," Will said, but he nodded as Roxanne went to grab the game from the hall closet. "We're boyfriends. I'll play with Aaron. You play with Otto."

"I'd rather play video games," Otto said as Roxanne returned. "What systems do you have?"

Will shrugged. "I've got an old Game Boy. That's it."

"Seriously?"

"You came to the wrong house for video games," Aaron said. "He won't even play them at my house."

"Come on," Lennox said. He stood and headed toward the kitchen. "We can play with Oyster or something."

Will had an idea of what something meant if the cigarette packet outlined in Lennox's pocket was anything to go by, but he let it go. Lennox had a friend. One who wasn't older or moving away in only a few short weeks. Otto wasn't ideal for him, but friendships came from odd places sometimes. So did boyfriends.

⊕ twelve ⊕

ANOTHER DAY OF BROKEN BONES, two heart attacks that still rattled her with reminders of Ben back at home, and one hiccupping little girl whose parents had been in a car accident with her asleep in the backseat. After their shift, Karen and Malia headed into the parking lot to Malia's truck, tossed their bags and purses into the back, and grabbed the ice scrapers. So far Malia hadn't said much about her older son's plans after high school, but Otto, like Lennox, hadn't put much thought into it.

"Has Rudolph applied anywhere yet?" Karen asked.

"No. He's been talking about the army. And then community college and then some graphic design degree in Chicago and another one in-state. I've told him to avoid the military. He'd never fit well there. I think he'll end up taking a year off. At least a semester to figure out what path he wants to take. I'm just so relieved he's going to graduate. A few years ago I never thought he would."

"He's a good kid," Karen said. "They all are."

As Malia drove Karen home, Karen looked up movies to see the following week, and they chatted about Doctor Baskin's latest priority task sheets for their shifts and how dysfunctional the new regulations were. By the time Malia pulled in to Karen's driveway, they'd settled on a movie and a trip to Richmond to spend a day go-kart racing.

"You'll love it. I took Rudolph and Abe over the summer. Kicked both of their butts, and I don't think they've quite forgiven me yet. Rudolph made me swear never to mention it in front of his friends."

"I'll see you tomorrow." Karen unbuckled and hugged Malia. "Love you."

"You too."

Karen climbed out, grabbed her bags, and headed up the driveway. An unfamiliar car was parked behind hers, an old Civic, half blue and half rust. She stepped through the front door and was greeted with a round of laughter from the living room. Will's friends must be over. They'd been missing their usual visits to the house. Aaron had been around a few times and Natasha had dropped something off in early September, but after Ben's heart attack, they'd faded like footprints in the sand.

They were all in the living room when she turned the corner. Aaron and Will were on one side of the couch, Natasha and Roxanne on the other. Lennox was absent. Karen watched Aaron draw a card from a little box on the table and then pass it to the girls, who both howled with laughter.

"This is impossible," Aaron said. His lower lip was jutting out and Will's hair was on end from running his hands through it. "We're playing something better after this. Like, Life. Yeah, then Otto and Lennox can get their butts in here and join us."

"Oh, boy," Will said. He handed Aaron a pencil and a pad of paper that had what looked like a giraffe in a top hat drawn on it. Will's artwork. He might not spend much time drawing, but he'd taken enough art classes in middle school for Karen to recognize his style.

"Don't tell Lennox to play that game. The last thing I think he wants to do is take the traditional path to marriage and house payments."

"Well, that's what *you* want, so he better be prepared," Roxanne said. She held up the timer. "Ready?"

"I don't know if I—wait, hey!"

Roxanne plopped the timer down on the table, and Aaron scrambled to draw something. Karen draped her coat over the couch and took the card Natasha handed her.

"What are they on?"

"Person, place, or thing."

Karen smiled as she read the card: Everglades. On the paper, Aaron had scribbled what could only be described as a—

"Why did you draw a dick?" Will ran a hand through his hair as Aaron shook his head vigorously. "What do you mean it's not a dick? It's a *dick*, Aaron. Learn to draw."

Karen watched as Aaron attempted to draw the United States, which ended up looking like a giant sperm with Florida as a tail.

"Sperm? Reproduction? Babies? Sex? Stop shaking your head!"

Karen made her way into the kitchen, where Oyster was lying in front of the sliding glass door. He'd been there a while, it seemed, because only his ears perked up at the sight of her.

"Hey, boy. Is Ben outside?"

She peered outside and instead of Ben's gray hair and tall stature, she spotted Lennox's small figure and Otto's swell of a body seated on the steps. A thin cloud of smoke hung around them. Karen set her bags on the kitchen table and rolled the door open. This wasn't the first time she'd caught Lennox smoking; the smell of smoke clung to his clothes. But Otto was another matter. Malia would kill him.

"Boys, put out the cigarettes."

Otto leapt up, slipped on the step, and fell over on his butt in the snow. Lennox laughed until he choked, and it was real, for once. Lennox's laughs were sharp, either biting or hollow, but they never rang with any sense of enjoyment. As Otto pulled himself out of the snow, Lennox turned to Karen.

"It's just one smoke. Only 'cause Will wouldn't let me suck him off under the table."

"Speak for yourself." Otto's cigarette was still in his hand, but the snow had snuffed it out. "I should go. Um, later. See you at school, man. Mrs. Osborne."

Karen took Otto's seat beside Lennox.

"I told you to put it out. Those are awful for your health. The risks that—"

"You're not my mother." Lennox took a drag and blew it up into the chilly air. It hung above them with the mist of Karen's breath. "The pack's almost empty. Just two more left. Then I'll quit, okay?"

"I'm holding you to that. I'll be counting and watching, because everyone who wants to quit says that and it's never true."

"I'm not everyone. Everyone else can afford to buy more."

"I'll see if I can get you the patch or nicotine gum to help."

Lennox snorted and blew another cloud toward the pool. "Seriously? I have maybe one a week, if that. I'm not addicted. Don't worry about me. Go mother Will. He's your kid, not me."

"I'm not Will's—"

Karen stopped herself. Will was her son, in ways different than Beth and different than Lennox's mother to him, but that didn't change facts. It definitely didn't change Will's own heart. She was and she wasn't, and it was the least comfortable place to be sometimes.

"Course you are."

"There's a lot you don't know about."

Lennox held the smoke in this time and when he breathed out, Karen followed the puffs with her eyes. The smoke was so different from the air in her own lungs, and yet they floated together, mingled and twisted as rejuvenating life and tar-like death. As her breath faded, the smoke lingered.

"I didn't mean to say I wasn't. Will's my son. But it's different than if I'd been his mother." She made a grab for Lennox's cigarette and missed. "Seriously, put it out."

"I'd rather put it in, if you know what I—hey!"

Karen swiped the cigarette this time and smashed it under her shoe. Lennox snarled and tugged the packet out of his pocket, but when he flipped it open he stopped. Only two remained, and something about the sight of them made him snap the lid shut.

"That was such a waste."

"Your lungs will thank me later."

"You're such a *mom*."

"I'm really not," Karen said as she toed the ashes off the step. "Even if Will calls me that."

"He does? Since when?"

Karen swallowed and stared out at the dark yard. "Just once. It was an accident. But this isn't about Will, I'm focusing on you right now. Are you ready to go back to school tomorrow?"

"Fuck school. That place is a shitstorm."

"So are your grades. Have you been doing better since you've been with us? I imagine sleep helps a lot."

Lennox shrugged again. "I guess. Will's been making sure I'm turning stuff in. He's pretty testy about getting homework done before sex. It's a good motivator, I guess, but it's not like it matters anyway."

"Sure it does. I hear you're applying to Berklee—"

"Not you too. I'm not. I can't—I shouldn't have let him."

Karen rubbed his shoulder. "Will wants you to succeed, however you want to. You love to play, from what I've heard from him and Mr. Robinette."

"Why on earth would you be talking to that slick-haired weirdo?"

Karen laughed. "He's a nice man. I stopped in after Thanksgiving when you were still hurt. He said you were a marvelous kid to have in class, an outstanding musician."

"And you think *I* need to stop smoking. He'd have to be higher than a satellite to say that."

"He spoke very highly of you."

"Uh huh, sure." Lennox hugged his knees to his chest. "The fee to apply to Berklee was as much as a car payment," he said after a moment. "Will paid it, and now I've got to write this asshole of an essay and finish the information stuff, but I'm not good at that. He wasted his money, and now... I don't know. What good's applying if I can't pay for it?"

"Will can be very single-minded sometimes. But he won't regret this, Lennox, trust me. He means well."

"He's wasting his time. We both are."

Lennox's words caught her off guard. His tone spoke of much more than college or grades or now.

"Have you ever been... Forget it. I'm going to go in. It's too cold out here without a cigarette."

But Karen understood. Uncertainty had hung around Lennox for weeks now; an unanswered question dimmed his eyes.

"I have. Several times, in fact."

Lennox's hand paused on the sliding glass door. "What? I didn't even—"

"You don't have to ask. It's clear as day that you're both in love, Lennox."

"I'm *not*—"

"Sit, come on. Don't be afraid."

Lennox hesitated and then sat beside her.

"Your secret's safe with me," Karen said and she smiled gently at him. "But yes, I've been in love. They were all very different, too. The first boy was in high school. Jack. I loved him a lot for a short while. Then another man while I was in New York and now Ben."

"What do you mean different? Like it's either love or it's not. It's all the same thing."

"Not quite. I love Will differently than I love Ben. Love my parents in more complicated ways. And my friends. You wouldn't say you love your sister like you love Will, would you?"

"Eww, no. But they're both strong. The feelings or whatever."

"A lot of love is. Sometimes it sweeps in like a feather in the wind." Karen tentatively put her arm around his shoulders and breathed deeply when Lennox didn't pull away. "Love is complicated and changing and different for everyone who feels it. Its meaning isn't the same for you or me or Will. But love is always a promise, Lennox. It's always a commitment."

"I don't do promises." Lennox shoved her arm off. "Promises break like hearts."

Lennox headed back toward the door.

"Sometimes love is heartbreak." Karen watched his hand hesitate on the door handle. "It usually is in some way, no matter how the journey goes. Love is the promise. It's one you share, and the commitment is another promise saying you'll both work to stay together. Committing and pushing through the hard parts is where most people fall apart. Love is work if you want to keep it, Lennox. One day it feels like you'll never stop smiling, and the next you can't remember what a smile looks like."

"I know."

He didn't say anything else, but that was enough. It was more than Will had said. Will was open and inviting, a fresh young home to harbor the beginning of a long-lasting love, but in many ways he was naïve too. Love was a fantasy, a wishful hope Will could discover over the next few years: a wild horse to be tamed and then kept neatly in a barn.

The same wasn't true for Lennox. Every new strand splintered his skin with the force of an earthquake. Every hot pulse ran through him and left its jagged mark deep within him. And he was aware of the hard path they faced and of the many branches that would tempt each of them in diverging directions.

Karen headed in and shut the door. Lennox was at the kitchen table with Oyster's head on his knee and his fingers knotted into the dog's fur. From the living room, shouts of laughter reached her ears.

"No! I wanted the fancy house," Will's voice said. "Damn it. I hate the trailer. At least it's cheap, I guess."

"At least you don't have five kids, like Aaron," Natasha said. "Look at all those pink babies."

"If Lennox doesn't come in soon, I'm taking his car and letting one of my kids drive it—*fuck!*"

Aaron's cuss brought another round of laughter.

"Baby girls for Aaron!"

"No, give me a blue one this time."

"But it says girl—"

"Yeah, and she doesn't like pink. Blue."

Karen smiled as the conversation died down again. But Lennox's face was as tight as his grip. His eyes were on the passageway to the living room.

"Why don't you go play with them? Sounds like they've got you a car already waiting."

"No, I hate that game."

"Lennox? It's your turn again!"

Otto answered for him. "He's probably still out back with Karen. I'll spin for him again."

"No, he's got to pick his own career still."

"But—"

Footsteps grew closer, and then Will appeared with his hair still on end and a bright smile in place.

"Hey, we're playing Life. It's your turn."

He reached for Lennox's hand, but Lennox ran it over Oyster's head instead.

"No thanks."

"Well, come hang out at least." Will wasn't to be deterred. He gave Oyster a few pats on his back, and when Lennox still wouldn't meet his eyes, he cupped his chin and brought his face around. "You don't have to play, okay? We're just having fun. Otto kept spinning for you and he's literally only gotten ones. You're still way back at the start on one of those dumb miss-a-turn spaces. We're still in the early part, well, except Aaron. He kept spinning tens and now he's got a horde of children. I'm still way back in the early part."

"I... Whatever."

Will smiled. "That's the spirit. Come on. We'll finish the game and then they've got to get going, and then you and me, well, you've got enough of an imagination to figure that out."

Yet for once, Lennox didn't seem very interested. He did agree to go into the living room, though, and Karen followed to watch from the doorway. Will's yellow car was just past the house-buying stop. Everyone else was scattered around the beginning of the board except Aaron, and Lennox must be the green one sitting way at the back, but already halfway down the college track.

Lennox picked the car up and set it down firmly on the non-college track. Will opened his mouth, and everyone else watched, but none of them said anything. Will pulled out the little stack of career and salary cards and offered them to Lennox.

"You only get to pick one for each if you don't go the college route."

"That's fine. It's just a game, right?"

⏪ thirteen ⏩

LENNOX SLEPT FITFULLY THAT NIGHT. After tossing and turning and dozing off a few times, he got up early and dressed in the dark. Will didn't stir, but Oyster yawned and stretched in the bean bag in the corner. They climbed the stairs together, and Lennox returned to the backyard with Oyster this time. More and more, he found himself migrating out there in the morning and late in the evening.

"Come on, boy. Here."

He lobbed a stick across the yard, and Oyster took off, yelping as he raced after it. As Oyster disappeared into the dark, Lennox pulled his jacket tighter around himself and shivered. Will hadn't said anything more about college last night. His enthusiasm about it seemed to have deflated, which was for the best, of course. Lennox was smart enough, sure, and maybe he could be good enough to go to a school for music, but he couldn't afford it.

Oyster returned with an enormous tree branch instead of the stick Lennox had thrown. He laughed and tugged at it while Oyster pulled. This was all he really needed. A decent place to live, a few people or dogs to share it with. Nothing more. He could find a place in some city, meet other musicians, start a band, and play shows at little dives around the city. That was how *real* musicians made it. Not by spending hundreds of thousands of dollars on a college degree.

Instead, he could spend his money on new instruments that he could teach himself how to play. He could buy a guitar and a keyboard and even a drum set. Then music books and whatever else he came across in New York. Will might despise all the racket in their little shoebox apartment, but they'd be—

Together.

God, how could he buy into that picture so easily? How could he be planning it in the same way Will was?

Well, perhaps not the same, but the vision was them together, still together years from now.

"You're so lucky you're a dog," Lennox said. "Human life is way too complicated."

"Aroo?"

"Yeah, I know he's great. I wouldn't be... be in love if he wasn't. I still don't like saying that."

Oyster whined as he dropped his tree branch. He sniffed over Lennox's knees and then forced his head in against Lennox's stomach.

"Hey, no! Ha, stop!"

Oyster bumped him until he was on his back and shaking with laughter. They lay there for a few minutes, with Oyster's head on Lennox's stomach and his pale eyes staring right at him.

"What do you think about college?"

Oyster panted and almost smiled at him as he rolled off Lennox and onto his back.

"You won't think that when Will leaves you behind."

A whiny bark and Oyster rolled right back onto him.

"Yeah, that's what I thought." Lennox sighed and rubbed Oyster's cheeks, then scratched his head and ears. "I've never even been to New York. Or Boston. I don't know."

He raised his leg high enough to see the monitor's blips of light. Three more weeks and he'd be reintroduced to the world. A life he'd never bothered to dream of could take shape. So many possibilities were out there. For too many years he'd been submerged, been underground when everyone else and the world had been stamping down on the ceiling above his head.

"Maybe, buddy." Lennox rubbed Oyster's head again. "It might be something special."

Lennox sat out back with Oyster until the sun broke over the mountaintops. It filtered in through the bare tree branches and lit the thin sheet of crunchy ice that still remained from the snow. Birds began their morning symphony, and Lennox listened to their tales, their triumphs, and the majesty of songs that echoed and repeated for miles around.

"Lennox?"

Will poked his tousled head out the sliding glass door. He was still in his pajamas and several ribbed red lines marked his face where he'd slept.

"Morning."

Oyster hurried inside for breakfast, but even as he whined Will stayed where he was.

"How long have you been up?"

"Few hours." Lennox stretched and went inside. "I couldn't sleep."

"Oh." Will poured himself a bowl of cereal while Lennox fed Oyster and then grabbed a bowl for himself. "Listen, about yesterday... I'm sorry."

Lennox dribbled milk and Cocoa Puffs down his front. "What? Why?"

"Don't act brain-dead." Will stirred his cereal before looking up. "I'm pressuring you, aren't I? About college and Berklee. And if you don't want to audition, I won't keep bugging you. It's your choice, and I keep forgetting that just because I want to go to college doesn't mean that *you* do and I'm sorry. That's all. I shouldn't force you to do anything you don't want to. Just let me know when I am, okay?"

"I—I don't know what I want to do," Lennox said. "Sometimes I think it's a great chance, and then other times college is just such a huge hassle. I can learn music anywhere, from anyone. I could be out there playing instead of in some stuffy classroom studying. I just don't know."

Will nodded. "That's fair. I did sort of spring all of this on you. We seem to do that to each other, huh?"

Lennox didn't say anything. What did Will mean by that? Will had sprung all of these college applications and essays on him, sure, but he'd never really sprung anything on Will—except, he had. Hadn't he pushed Will's limits when they first met? Hadn't he ignored Will's inexperience—and, to a degree, his comfort with sex and physical intimacy—for the sake of his own rush back into bliss?

He swallowed and set his spoon down.

"You okay?"

Lennox shrugged. He couldn't bring himself to say it, and yet, hadn't he done so much worse to Will than Will had ever done to him? At least Will's motives were good—selfless. While Will had seemed to enjoy their time together, Lennox had certainly taken advantage of his lust and inexperience.

"Fine. Just thinking about that essay. It doesn't hurt to try and see, I guess. But I'll bomb the interview."

"Well, we can practice! You know, to get all of your rude comments out of your system now."

"Oh, I'll still have some. They never get fully knocked out. Well, they might if you fucked me hard enough."

Will's face flushed a soft pink, just as it did after he came. Lennox started to smile and then stopped. How many times had he talked so roughly that he'd hurt Will? Now it might be okay, even flirty, but it hadn't always been. He was sure of that much right now.

"After school today? I don't have anything I have to stay after for."

"Okay. Or now. We could also skip off to my room and—"

"And what?"

Will's dad appeared in the doorway. "Go to school, boys. Don't make me call them to see if you're there or not."

"Fine."

Will finished his cereal and headed back downstairs. Lennox dumped the rest of his and followed. While Will sorted through his closet, Lennox sat on the bed with the Berklee pamphlet and read through it. His heart skipped to a faster beat as each new sentence gave him another glimpse of a moment he might live as a college student.

It was a pleasant dream, but even now so hard to grasp. The moments were there with a myriad of young faces and new music to learn, but somehow his face was never among them.

Will reappeared in a purple knit sweater and a dark pair of jeans that immediately caught Lennox's interest. It wasn't every day that Will wore skinny jeans—in fact it was a once-every-few-weeks adventure—but it was always a fantastic sight to see.

"Now you're just teasing."

Lennox stood as Will grabbed his backpack and twisted his sweater a little where it was crooked around his shoulders.

"Your dick looks so good in these jeans," Lennox said. He pressed a kiss to Will's neck and ran his fingers over Will's hips. "Good enough to suck off right now."

"What? Can you really see it in these?"

Will pulled away and ran his hands over his thighs, then the bulge of his cock. Lennox let out a weak groan. An untrained or unfamiliar eye wouldn't pick up the details, but Lennox had seen Will naked enough by now to put the full image together. His dick jutted just to the left, thick even now as it stretched the fabric between his zipper and thigh.

"You're bending me over something when we get back."

Lennox cupped Will's cock and then retracted his hand as if he'd been zapped. Will hadn't flinched, hadn't said a word or given him more than a little hopeful smile, but he hadn't always reacted like this. Yet Lennox had always made his moves and asked later, if he ever asked at all.

"Did my zipper catch you?"

"What? No, no. Um, static. Your dick's electric."

Will snorted as he drew Lennox in for a kiss. Their lips met slowly; Will's parted and cupped Lennox's bottom lip. He shivered as Will gave it a small tug and stepped away.

EASTERN'S PARKING LOT WAS FULL of students when they arrived twenty minutes later. Will was almost immediately swept up by his friends. Otto was among them; his face was tight with the same discomfort Lennox felt around them. They were nice people; Roxanne and Natasha went out of their way to try to include him. Aaron tried to talk baseball with him, but Lennox couldn't follow any of it. They were all so nice and all so beyond him. Outside of his own world. Even Will was in some ways, but they were lacing those places together. Otto got all of that, without trying and without an explanation.

"What's up?"

Lennox shrugged and slowed his pace to let Will and his friends move ahead of them.

"Mom says hi. She wants to have you over for dinner or something. I dunno. Something about fattening you up."

"Hey, I've got fat on my ribs now. I'm not all bony anymore."

"If you aren't my size then you're starving. Anyway, I'll see you. I've got to go meet with Coach Davis before band. Later."

They separated at the side entrance. Otto turned right toward the back of the school and the gymnasium. Lennox pulled open the band room door and went right in. It was still empty. Will and the others must have gone to their lockers first, but Lennox didn't mind. The quiet was a balm after all the people who had been invading his life lately.

As he set up a few chairs and went to roll the piano in from the storage room, a pair of khaki-covered legs appeared carrying a swaying stack of sheet music. Mr. Robinette stumbled on one of the chairs and half the stack of paper fluttered to the floor.

"Ouch, what... Oh, hi Lennox."

He set the intact stack on a chair and bent to pick up the rest. Lennox rolled the piano toward him. One sheet caught his eye, a jazz piece for piano that looked very complicated.

"That one's for you," Mr. Robinette said. "Practice for any auditions you might have if you're applying to colleges. Will's mom said you were thinking about it."

"More like Will was thinking about it."

But Lennox scanned the sheet and followed the three-four measures from one repeat and back and then over the dotted lines to the next. It was fast, a jivey tune.

"Go set up and give it a go." Mr. Robinette shifted through the pages on the floor and found a second sheet. "Go ahead. You ever played jazz?"

Lennox pushed the piano to its normal spot and opened the cover. Instead of answering, he played: one major scale up and back, a second minor scale up, and then a third little burst of the pentatonic back down. Then he fell into a rhythm, improvising with chords instead of the straight notes of the pentatonic until Mr. Robinette pulled up a chair.

"You certainly know your scales," he said. "Did you take lessons when you were little?"

Lennox played on and shrugged. Questions like this never led him anywhere good. "My mom started teaching me when I was three."

"No kidding. Well, she's an excellent teacher then. Or got very lucky with a talented student."

Lennox shrugged again and read the keys for the piece before him. Then he dove right in; his fingers were a little clumsy, but still he managed to get every note into place, every accent and repetition, until the end of the second page.

Mr. Robinette smiled when he finished.

"It's almost ridiculous how well you can sight-read. However, you're going to want to alter the rhythm here with this one. The measures don't say it, but it's a swing sort of rhythm. This is jazz, after all. It's never as simple as it looks and it's difficult to teach. Here."

Mr. Robinette tapped out a C, first in four beats of eighth notes and then in the same but syncopated. The tune swung as he'd said, almost as if a breath had been wedged between some of the notes to hold them apart a split second longer. His mother had never taught him jazz , though she'd played many jazz songs for him in the evenings after dinner.

"Think you can do that?"

"Think I can play with my toes, too."

Lennox raised his leg and Mr. Robinette stopped him. "Hands first. You can get fancy with your toes on your own time."

"I've got a lot better things to do during my free time. His name's Will. Pretty sure you've met."

"Just play the song."

So Lennox did. After a few taps of the swing rhythm Mr. Robinette had demonstrated, Lennox returned to the song. He played a little slower, measured the beats with his breath, and let the music swing through him steady and strong. Within the swing beats, the accents popped so much better.

"Great. That was really great. I've got more jazz pieces for you. Some swing music too. Just to see how much your skills can be stretched, what your strengths are. It's good to have an understanding of that heading into college."

Lennox shut the key cover and sighed. "Will's been trying to get me to audition for this school in Boston. And I might want to. Maybe. But I don't have the... Just the application was more money than... It's a waste of time."

"No, it's not. I'm assuming Berklee?" At Lennox's nod, Mr. Robinette continued. "It's a great school. More contemporary than a lot of others, so a good fit for you if all of the bands on your jacket are anything to go by. Do you only listen to rock?"

"I'll listen to just about anything twice."

"Twice?"

"First time just to listen to the music and the melodies, rhythms. What they're doing with the real music. Second time for the words. If I like both I stick around for a third."

"You've got the ear for it. To compose too, I'd say. You ever written your own music?"

Lennox shook his head. "I've messed around with chords and progressions and stuff, but I don't write anything down. I just play."

"Try writing it down sometime. Something you like to play that you've just made up. One of the hardest parts of composing is transcribing, but I know you've got a great ear for creating harmonies. Now, have you thought about what you're going to audition with?"

"No. I haven't. I still have to write some stupid essay for the second part of the application. I'll never finish that in two weeks."

Mr. Robinette hummed. "Well, you are pretty late on deciding to apply, *but* a semester off is an option too. You could apply for the spring if you don't get everything in for fall. Just because everyone tells you to go right away doesn't mean that's what's best for you."

"I can do that?"

"Sure you can. You're young and talented, Lennox. With enough patience and drive you can do practically anything. It won't always be easy, but you can. I'd say try to get that essay in, and then a few days a week we can meet after school and work on an audition piece and whatever else they want. What do you say?"

The warning bell rang. A few kids came in, and a murmur of voices echoed down the hall. Lennox stood up and stretched but, at Mr. Robinette's imploring look, he nodded.

"If I get the essay in, then okay. But I won't, so don't start planning or getting all sorts of music together."

"We can still practice, even if you don't apply for the fall. I'm more than willing to give you a few hours every other day to play after school."

Lennox pulled his chair away from the piano as Will and Natasha entered the room. Mr. Robinette didn't bug him after that, but all class he had Lennox up front on the piano, leading the band through new songs and playing the more complicated versions of pieces. He spent the rest of the day by himself until chemistry, when Will settled beside him at their usual lab table and immediately ran his hand over Lennox's thigh.

"Less than two hours now."

That was all Will said, but all throughout their lab on—well, Lennox couldn't recall what they were supposed to be doing, something with compounds to make a good lube if he was lucky—Will's fingers continued to brush against him: his arms, shoulders, back, and thighs. By the end of the lesson, while everyone was cleaning up their beakers and utensils and Ms. Mentore was reminding them of what was on their test the following week, Will's hand slipped into Lennox's back pocket and squeezed.

"It's too bad you didn't have gym today. I could have met you in the locker room instead of waiting until we got home."

Lennox bit his lip and inhaled sharply through his teeth. He was already getting hard, had been off and on through the day when he'd thought about what he and Will would be doing after school. So far, they hadn't had penetrative sex very often. Twice with Lennox topping, and just the once with Will. It was too much of a hassle when Karen and Ben were upstairs and with Oyster always finding a way to nose the door open.

Maybe it had been awkward because of Will's nerves, their fumbling in the new position, and even the sharp burst of pain at the beginning. Yet Lennox had enjoyed it after that, and he could imagine the bliss he'd find with Will once Will was comfortable with topping and used the confidence he'd begun to show in so many other ways in those moments. He could imagine the pure enjoyment of Will plunging into him, teasing him with changing rhythms and measured, deep thrusts.

Will laughed as the afternoon announcements filtered through the speakers.

"I love making you hard in class."

"I'd love it if you got down on your knees and did more than talk with that mouth."

Will grinned, a sultry little quirk pulling back his lips. "You're still not getting that from me yet. But maybe if you're, um—"

Lennox shut his eyes and groaned, not in excitement but in disbelief.

"I was going somewhere hot with that," Will said. "I, um—"

"Maybe if we fuck more you'll have more ideas to fill in that blank. Come on. Let's go before you goof yourself out of sex."

"I'd rather goof in you and fuck. Put a sock in my mouth, would you?"

Lennox burst out laughing as they half-jogged downstairs to their lockers and then to Will's truck. Will sped them home and threw his truck into park so fast he stalled the engine. Their backpacks left in the truck bed, they raced into the house.

Oyster woofed a greeting and was promptly plowed into as they kissed. Will's hands forced Lennox's jacket off; the sleeves caught on Lennox's gloves. As Lennox fought with the jacket, Will's arms circled his waist and he roughly sucked Lennox's neck.

"You gonna fuck me?"

Will nodded against Lennox's throat, and finally his jacket came free. Oyster yelped as it landed on him and darted out of the hall.

"We'll make it up to him later."

Will's fingers bunched into Lennox's shirt and pulled him downstairs. The door rattled shut behind them. Lennox found himself pressed into the bed with Will's eager mouth coasting over his neck and jaw, then over his collarbone. A hot pulse ran through him. Will normally wasn't so aggressive, so desperate as to push him down and undress him.

"Condom," Lennox managed to say as Will sucked at his throat and then his lower lip. He groaned as Will unzipped his jeans. "Lube too."

Will leapt up, dug both out of his drawer and handed them over. As Lennox undressed and coated his fingers, Will hopped around pulling his socks off. He gave a pained squeak.

"What?"

"I shouldn't have worn these jeans today."

Lennox saw Will, tugging at his jeans and trying to unzip them over his erection. It was pressed tight along his hip, but still thick enough to stretch what little space was left in the crotch.

"Well, shut your eyes then, cause I'm about to finger-fuck myself until you get out of those."

"But I wanted to finger you!"

"Get over here, then." Lennox tossed him the lube bottle and stretched out on his stomach with his cock rubbing against the blankets. "I'll get your stupid pants off."

"How—"

"Stand here."

Lennox grabbed Will's hips and directed him to the side of the bed near his ass. He pressed one hand against Will's stomach and pulled at the button on his jeans with the other. It came open after a few tugs, and the zipper slid halfway down from the strain of Will's cock.

Lennox finished helping him out of his jeans and underwear while Will's fingers dipped between Lennox's cheeks and, after a few slick brushes, the first sunk in. Lennox arched into the stretch; a deep moan left him. He couldn't do without that sensation, without Will wanting to have this part of him. More assured than last time, but still tentative, Will worked a second finger into him.

As Will worked a third finger into Lennox, he rolled a condom on Will's cock and tugged him onto the bed.

"But I've barely got three—"

"Go slow, then."

"I don't want to hurt you again."

Lennox pressed Will down into the pillows and straddled his hips. Beneath him he could feel Will's cock, thick and heavy against his ass. He bit his lip to keep from groaning. Taking Will into him, joining their bodies in this way, was so much better than when he topped—not that he'd ever say such a thing out loud. But Will enjoyed this and that was an easy enough excuse.

"Are you sure you're ready?"

Lennox nodded, took a firm grip on Will's cock as he lined it up with his hole, and sank down. A few inches down, then up, then down a little farther until he'd taken all of Will into himself. He was panting heavily by the time his ass was flush with Will's thighs.

"Holy shit, that's... Fuck, that's so much deeper than that other way."

Will's fingers pinched the flesh of his ass; Will's brow was thick with sweat. Lennox shifted and then pressed his hands against Will's shoulders and lifted his hips. They moaned. Lennox dropped down and then raised himself once again with Will's hands guiding his hips and tugging to get him back down.

"Shit, Lennox. This is... Wow."

Lennox found a slow rhythm. He lifted and sank down and then figured out how to roll his hips faster. It was different than anything he'd ever done, not the jerking power of thrusting into someone, but like the steady revolving of a Ferris wheel. His eyes drifted shut as he rode Will. He felt the stinging, pleasant pricks of Will's nails against his skin and the steady thump of his heart in time with the hot slide of Will inside of him.

"Are you... Oh, god... Why are you humming?"

"Hmm?"

Lennox paused on Will's lap, sinking down his cock slowly. It took him a moment to realize that all the beats of his body, Will's body, and their movements had brought a new song from him.

"Sorry."

Will leaned up on his elbows and wiped his forehead. "No, it's cute."

"I'm really not aiming for cute right now."

To emphasize his point, Lennox lifted his hips and slammed them back down. Will's chin dropped onto his chest as he breathed in sharply. His torso flinched and his muscles tensed beneath Lennox.

Will was close. Much closer than he was, although he couldn't blame Will. Being inside someone almost always meant a faster orgasm.

"You're close," Lennox said. He eased his hips up and then very slowly sank back down.

Will grabbed Lennox's thighs. "Wait. I—I want you to come first."

His words surprised Lennox. In seconds Will had rolled them over and was hovering above him, his cock still halfway in his ass. Will thrust in and Lennox bit his lips, both to stop humming and to quiet the guttural moan lodged in his throat.

Will's hand stroked Lennox's cock once as he thrust back in.

"I want to fuck the breath out of you."

Will's hips jerked forward again and Lennox shut his eyes. He'd been right to think this time would be better. Will had been a little unsure, but that had faded as soon as he'd been fully inside of Lennox without hearing any hisses of pain. The stretch of Will's cock was more bliss than uncomfortable, and the force of his hips—

Lennox whined; the noise whistled right through his clenched teeth.

"Come for me."

Will's hips set a hard rhythm. The bed rocked under them. Lennox's body slid toward the headboard. He clenched the blankets and turned his head into the pillow to muffle himself. But it was hard to be silent, and Will's thrust changed angles in such a blissful way that it was even harder to keep his wits and his sense of self as that heady rush began to trickle from the base of his spine out through his limbs and then back.

"Oh, fuck."

Will's fist squeezed his cock, stroked him once more, and then one electric thrust that finally found his prostate sent Lennox into euphoria. His back arched up; his body went stiff as he came. Will's thrusts stopped abruptly.

Lennox's eyes drifted shut as Will stroked his cock a few more times, bringing more streaks of come onto his chest.

Will leaned down, panting and sweating, to kiss Lennox's neck. Lennox tried to open his eyes, but that was difficult after he came hard, as he always did with Will.

"Is it okay if I keep—?"

Lennox nodded. "Or you can come on me and join the party."

Will hesitated before he pulled out. Lennox shut his eyes. His body grew heavy as Will shifted above him and then straddled his waist. When he opened his eyes he found himself staring at the underside of Will's cock, now free of its condom.

"Okay?"

Lennox forced himself to stay awake. He tilted his head up and ran his tongue along the underside of Will's cock. Will jerked, and his cock smacked Lennox in the forehead, but just the tip of his tongue had been enough after too long. Will came on him, right on his cheeks and his hair and his chin. Lennox grimaced as it dripped through his curls to his scalp. That was going to be such a pain to get out.

"Sorry."

Will sagged above him and then slid down until they were chest to chest. He rested his forehead against Lennox's. Their noses brushed, and Will began to kiss the spots of come on Lennox's face. He sucked and kissed over each one, from Lennox's eyebrows to his chin to the line of his hair. Finally, Will's lips returned to his for a sweet kiss.

"Let's not do that part again for a while."

Lennox didn't say anything. His throat was tight, and the adrenaline was leaking out of his body like water from a busted pipe. Will was so exquisite, so painfully true to himself, that it was impossible not to love him, to be in love and be okay with having him share that bond. Yet saying it again was such a risk.

As Will's lips brushed his and smiled, Lennox breathed deeply and said what he could.

"I love you."

How foolish those words sounded. Short, blunt, and so utterly contrary to his behavior, his actions. Will jolted backward. He stared at Lennox. His eyes looked solid as marbles.

"I mean I—" Lennox swallowed. "I'm *in* love with you and I don't really know what to do with that, but I figured I'd tell you again and not run off, and it'd be really fucking fantastic if you'd say something right now."

Will stared. He stared and stared. He peered right into and through Lennox before he dove right onto him. Will's smile captured his lips and then his hot breath ran over Lennox's lips and chin.

"I love you too."

No earthquake scattered the dust from his insides. His heart didn't collapse or burst; nor did Will fill the cracks left by others. But Will was here with him. He was here and happy to offer Lennox himself in return, to share this new moment for as long as the world stayed beneath their feet.

⏮ fourteen ⏭

"So you love me?"

"Yeah. I already said that."

"We're in love?"

"Unless you're changing your mind."

Will shook his head and rolled into Lennox's side, crushing their textbooks between them on the bed. It was their first weekend after the holiday break, and Will still couldn't stop smiling. No matter how many times he asked, Lennox didn't change what he'd said. His comfort with saying those lovely words definitely fluctuated from hour to hour, but he still said them.

To Will.

Lennox was in love with Will.

"Say it again?"

"I've said it like a hundred times since the other day," Lennox said. He tugged his book from under Will's butt and frowned. "I love you."

"Love you too. Say it—"

"You better hope there isn't a limit on the times I'm capable of saying that to you, because, if there is, you're wasting a massive number of them very quickly."

Will bristled. Surely this bliss would never end. They would be together long after the rush of these first "I love yous" left them and well beyond the future Will foresaw so clearly.

"Come on. You're just stalling on your math homework. I've finished everything—"

"Except your Berklee essay. How's that going?"

"That's not homework." Lennox shut his last notebook and added it to the pile on the floor. "Let's put another movie in. I'm getting sick of listening to this menu screen music, even if it is *Jurassic Park*. Isn't there a sequel?"

"Two, actually. The second one's over there somewhere."

Lennox dug through the shelves of movies while Will propped his book open and tried to remember anything that had happened in yesterday's lesson. He couldn't. Maybe Lennox's warnings were right after all. He should do math homework as soon as he could, preferably the same afternoon while he still retained some part of the lesson in his mind.

The second movie began to play as Lennox rejoined him on the bed. Will passed Lennox his laptop as Lennox handed him the calculator.

"Good luck," they said together.

They both laughed, and though Will began his weekly struggle, Lennox didn't touch the laptop pressed against his side. He flipped open a notebook and began to dot the page with several dozen ink spots.

"At least open a Word document to try."

"I'll start writing when you get the first problem right."

Will snarled. Solve for x. And y. And z. When had math become the alphabet?

"You'll never make the deadline if that's the case. You could fill out the rest of the information."

But Lennox only hit Play on the DVD remote and kept dotting the notebook page. Will tried to focus on his own work, but it was much more fun to watch the little girl with her roast beef sandwich and her stupid rich parents screaming. Beside him, however, Lennox continued to tap away.

Tap. Tap, tap. Tap, tap, tap. Tap.

Will clicked a few buttons on his calculator and leaned closer to Lennox. Music. He was writing out music. Lennox connected some notes into sixteenth notes and then made another into an eighth note. A sharp was added to the C's. Maybe. Or were those D's? Then a flat to the B's; Will was used to seeing that. He tried to imagine the tune, but it was only dots on the page to him, intangible until someone brought life to them.

"Do your math or I won't suck your dick for the next week."

"Good thing I was hoping you'd top today instead. Or tomorrow. Or all week. It's been a while."

"Mmm. You won't get that either."

"I will so. I know how to get you horny."

"Bullshit, I'm always horny."

Will chewed on his pencil and smacked it down against the notebook's spiral wire, which was all bent and smashed. Now was as good a time as any to fix it.

"I can't believe how much you procrastinate. Here." Lennox pulled Will's textbook closer so he could see the problems. "First one. Solve for x, y, and z. What do you do first?"

"Um, panic?"

"No."

"Vomit and hope I ate alphabet and number soup that spells out the answer?"

"You'd probably get a closer answer than you usually do." Lennox forced him to pick up his pencil. "Write out the information it's giving you."

Will pouted but did as he was told. "Okay. Now what?"

"What's it asking you to do?"

"The impossible. Seriously, I can't solve for *any* of these if they don't at least give me the answer for one of them."

"They've given you an equation that equals x, Will. Plug that stuff in and figure out the right order to solve for x, y, and z."

Will set to work. By the time the people had escaped the dinosaur island he'd managed to do four problems, some right and some wrong according to Lennox. Lennox shut the movie off as the credits began and went back to scribbling in his notebook. From upstairs a few pots clanged in their usual landslide out of the cabinet and onto the kitchen floor.

Oyster came yelping down the stairs and shoved himself under his bean bag chair. Will leaned his cheek on Lennox's shoulder and poked him in the ribs.

"Can I take a break for dinner? Math's rotting all the good parts of my brain."

"As long as it stays away from the good parts of your dick."

Will sighed and rubbed his temples. Lennox kept scribbling away, and it took Will a few minutes to realize he was no longer writing music, but words. He caught a glimpse of sentences about his mother and music lessons before the notebook was snapped shut.

He was working on his essay then. Lennox was trying, and that was all he ever asked.

"I hope Dad's making meatballs," Will said to break the silence. "He makes the *best* Swedish meatballs… Stop laughing! I'm serious!"

Lennox continued to chortle; his body shook the bed. Will pinched him on the arm, but snuggled closer.

"If you still had your eyebrow ring I'd give it a good hard tug right now."

Lennox tensed. His laughter stopped, and his tongue ring clicked against his teeth.

Click, click, click.

"Although I do enjoy your tongue ring a lot more."

"I've been thinking about taking it out," Lennox said suddenly even as he clicked it against his teeth again. "It gets in the way too much when I'm eating. It's hard to clean too."

"Oh." Will wilted at the idea of it being missing from their make-outs and blowjobs. "I thought you liked having it."

"I never wanted it."

"Then why—"

"You get a lot of things you don't want in juvie."

Lennox left it at that as he stood up and stretched. "Come on, let's go see what's for dinner. If it's *not* meatballs then I'm sure I can find a replacement for you."

"No, hang on. What do you mean you got it in juvie? I didn't think they offered stuff like that."

"They don't." Lennox shrugged and clicked his tongue ring once more.

Click. Click. Click.

"But—"

"Let's just say I'm lucky I didn't get an infection or have my tongue cut out, okay? It wasn't pleasant."

Will frowned and opened his mouth to question Lennox further, but was instead pushed to sit on the end of the bed. Lennox dropped to his knees and raised Will's shirt. He kissed Will's stomach and then ran his tongue over his belly button. Will tensed at how troubling he found what he usually would have enjoyed. Flickers of danger always seemed to permeate Lennox, but this was so stark he couldn't ignore it.

"No, stop. What are you—I'm trying to understand and you're—I don't want sex right now, I want to talk with you. About what you just said."

"It's not important," Lennox said, but his voice trembled. "If you don't want a blowjob, then let's go get dinner. Blowjobs later, right?"

Lennox was jumpy, wringing his hands and tugging at his curls.

"No. I mean, maybe, but... What's wrong?"

"Nothing. You're the one who doesn't want a blowjob, so that's on you."

"Lennox."

Lennox paused on the bottom step, one hand still in his hair. He seemed even less comfortable, more outside of himself, than he'd been the first time he said that he was in love with Will. He didn't flinch, or blink, or move with his usual fluidity, but stood as if cement was hardening inside of his limbs.

"What?"

"Please sit. I... You're scaring me."

"How am I scary? Do I look like a goblin or a serial killer? Or let me guess, you've finally clicked together how evil I am for having this monitor, right?"

"Lennox—"

"Just fuck off."

Lennox vaulted upstairs, and it said a lot to Will that he would rather be in the kitchen with Ben than down here talking to him.

AFTER DINNER, WILL HELPED WITH the cleanup as Lennox went out onto the back deck. When the dishes were drying in the rack next to the sink, Will grabbed his coat and Lennox's from the hall and headed out there too.

Although December had been unusually snowy this year, January had brought a brief burst of warmth. The crunchy snow piles had melted a few days ago, and, while the breeze that whipped through the backyard was chilly, the air was warm for early winter.

Lennox sat on the back steps with a small cloud of smoke hovering above him. Will sat beside him and managed not to pull his shirt up over his nose.

"I told you his meatballs were good."

Will watched Lennox flip the lid on his cigarette pack. Open, closed. Open again. Only one was left, tucked into the center of the box. If he was lucky, that would be the last one Lennox would ever touch.

"I'm not interested in your dad's balls." Lennox took a drag off his cigarette and exhaled slowly. "Not too keen on yours either, if you won't let me blow you."

"Not everything is about blowjobs." Will ground his teeth and resisted the urge to knock the cigarette out of Lennox's hand.

"Sure it is."

"It isn't. You always do this. Whenever it gets stressed with us you just talk about blowjobs or sex or... I don't get it. Blowjobs don't fix arguments. They don't make me forget what we're talking about, either. I love you. You mean so much to me, and that means I *want* to know the bad things too."

"You don't need to." Lennox stubbed out his cigarette. "It's over. It doesn't matter now."

"It does. If it still means something to you then it does. Whatever happened two years ago or two months ago changes who you are. That's what makes you *you*."

Lennox ignored Will draping his jacket around his shoulders and stared out into the yard. Will looked too, at patches of soggy brown leaves, the drained pool, and the ominous sway of the bare trees.

"My first night, a bunch of the older guys got a hold of me. One of the big gangs in the facility I was at. They thought I was part of a different gang and then realized I was just some dumb little queer."

Will tensed beside Lennox. He saw an even smaller version of Lennox, thin and timid, surrounded by a swell of overgrown teenage bodies. He didn't have to think much harder to get an idea of what could have happened to Lennox, locked away and on his own.

"They didn't do that." Lennox met his eyes with a steely glint in his own. Will exhaled, but his doubts still lingered. Something must have happened. With Lennox it was rarely simple.

"It's different in there. Everyone's different than they would be out here. It's just a bunch of guys and, I—I was a willing mouth, I guess. They liked pierced tongues, and it was either agree to it or end up in a hospital room, if I was lucky."

That didn't sound remotely like willing to Will, but he stayed quiet to see how much more Lennox would give him. Another little piece might be all he would need to unspool everything about Lennox that still didn't add up to a full picture.

"So I let them stick this shitty thing in my tongue. Suck a few dicks when I needed to. Blowjobs make—"

"Everything better?"

"Make people like you."

And that was it. It wasn't everything Will wanted or needed to know, but it was enough to understand something he'd never considered about Lennox. Lennox had always been aggressive in his advances, and Will had always assumed that was out of poorly controlled lust. But what if he'd been so over the top not just to gain Will's attention, but his affection? What if his main goal hadn't been getting Will off, but getting him to like him in the only way he'd ever had a boy like him?

"That's not how you make people like you. Not the kinds of people who stick around or love you for you."

"Made you like me."

Lennox tucked his cigarette box into his pocket and slid his arms into his jacket sleeves.

"You could have been the worst blowjob ever or never given me one at all, but I'd still love you right now because of what you've been for me. You got my life when nobody else did. You were a *friend* when I needed one, gave me hope that maybe I could have all of the life I've always dreamed about. I like you because you let yourself be more than what you think you are, when you're with me. No orgasm could have given us this."

Will reached for Lennox's hand, and Lennox reached back.

"But it helped, right?"

"Considering you shoved me out the door afterward, no. I love you as you are. All the worst and the best and the things you think are meaningless. That's why I like you. You can't make someone like you by pretending to be someone you aren't."

Lennox mulled that over as he squeezed Will's hand. He didn't say anything else until they were downstairs and changing into their pajamas for bed.

"I like you for who you are too, you know. And I'm not just saying that because you've never given me a blowjob and I'm trying to get you to give me—ouch!"

Will snapped the waistband of Lennox's pajama bottoms and grinned.

"Maybe I'd already decided you needed one tonight."

"Really?"

Will snorted. "You sound like I just told you Santa Claus was in the living room."

"I don't think he'd give very good blowjobs. All those scratchy beard hairs."

"Well, fortunately for you, my face is still baby-bottom smooth." Will snapped Lennox's waistband more gently. "Yes?"

Lennox nodded and lay back against the pillows, then lifted his hips enough for Will to push his pants down. As Will stroked Lennox to full hardness, Lennox propped himself up to watch.

"I've never been on this side of it before," he said. He bit his lip to muffle a whimper exactly like the ones from yesterday, when Will had been inside of him, and, god, how Will wished to hear that again, to hear every sound Lennox's body could make without any fear or embarrassment holding his lips closed.

Will kissed the underside of his cock and looked up at him.

"You've never had a blowjob before?"

Lennox shook his head and shrugged. "Come on, it's cold down here."

"Aw, are you going to shrivel up on me?"

"I can get smaller, Will. Just watch me."

Will stroked him a few more times and tried to find a good position. Eventually, he ended up on his stomach with his elbows bracketing Lennox's thighs. He kissed Lennox's stomach and the soft skin that was no longer stretched taut over it. Lennox had gained quite a bit of weight in the past month, enough that only a few of his ribs were now visible.

"Probably for the best that you haven't. I doubt this is going to be anything close to what you give me."

"Just stay away from deep-throating, then."

"Deep what?"

"Don't gag yourself." Lennox ran a hand through Will's hair and rested it on his cheek. "And I'll do my best not to fuck your mouth."

A prickle of nerves ran through Will. He'd thought about it once or twice, thought about taking Lennox into his mouth the way Lennox did him, but suddenly, with Lennox's cock in his hand, it seemed so much more daunting. How long was he? How many inches was it from the front of Will's mouth to his throat? If he hollowed his cheeks, wouldn't his teeth drag on Lennox's skin?

"You don't have to tonight if you don't want."

"I do. I've wanted to suck your dick for a while, but it's so—"

"If you say big, I'm pulling my pants up."

"Well, you aren't *small* either. I don't want to hurt you again and, like, I've got *teeth*."

Lennox sat up and drew him in for a quick, messy kiss.

"Babe, you could literally just run your tongue all over my dick and I'm going to come. It'll be in your hair and your eyes probably, but it's not going to take much as long as I get to watch."

Will nodded and they shared another quick kiss before Lennox leaned back into the pillows. And there he was, at eye level with Lennox's dick once more. It was nice, of course, but being this close was a little strange. Every dark curl of hair was visible at the base, he had a pronounced—well, Will wasn't sure what to call it, but the underside had a thick vertical ridge. Was his like that too? He'd have to stand over a mirror some time to see.

"Um, Will? I'm pretty sure your eyes can't suck a dick."

Will cleared his throat and wrapped his lips around the head of Lennox's cock. Salty, not unpleasant. The scent of Lennox was different here, not peppermint and a little smoke, but a hint of the boys' locker room, only sweeter. He circled his tongue around the head of Lennox's cock and sucked.

Lennox groaned; one hand slid into Will's hair. He was suddenly very glad he'd only shaved the back and sides a few months ago.

"God, you look so good like that."

A shiver ran through Will. He flicked his eyes up to Lennox's as he took him farther into his mouth. Lennox bit his lip, and Will couldn't hear that whimper over the pounding of his own heart, but he could feel it vibrate through Lennox's body and all the way down to his lips. His fingers shook, but Will worked his mouth up and down and found a slow, languid rhythm that didn't gag him and had Lennox's fingers flexing tight against his scalp.

"Harder," Lennox said. That seemed to be a theme with him. "Please, harder."

Will sank down and hollowed his cheeks as much as he dared, and then eased his head back. Lennox's stomach tightened and then relaxed. His hips rose up to chase the heat of Will's mouth, and when Will pushed himself a little farther Lennox cried out. Warm goo hit the back of Will's throat, and he choked and pulled off. Lennox continued to come, on his own stomach and over Will's hands resting on his hips.

"Shit, that was... shit."

"I hope it was better than shit. Like, wow factor brilliant would be a better description."

Will sat up and wiped the come off his chin. Then he licked it and gagged.

"Ugh, that's awful."

"Now that's definitely going to convince me to do this again."

Lennox tried to sit up too, but flopped back down like a gummy worm.

"Sorry, I should have warned you. It's all over you."

"It's not too bad. Next time we'll figure out a warning." Will wiped another string of come off his cheek and grabbed tissues to clean them up. Once he was finished, Will settled down on Lennox's chest. They kissed for a few minutes before Lennox squirmed around beneath him to pull his pants back up. Will rolled off of him and fiddled with his own. He was still a little hard from blowing Lennox, although he'd barely noticed that because he'd been so nervous.

"So we're supposed to share stuff with each other, right?"

Will nodded and plucked at the waistband of his pants with a pointed look at Lennox. For once, Lennox didn't catch on.

"And that goes both ways right?"

"Yeah. Why?"

Will tossed the tissues aside and tried to think of anything he'd neglected to tell Lennox, anything that involved him or them, but nothing came to mind.

"Why didn't you say you'd called Karen 'Mom'?"

"I didn't, I mean, I did, but it was just a mistake," Will said. He shivered; his stomach clenched. He sat up only to be pinned back down by Lennox's weight. "She just caught me off guard, that's all. Do I get a blowjob now?"

"You don't say that without meaning it."

"Sure you do. Kids at school have accidentally called teachers 'Mom' or 'Dad' a dozen times."

"Not you. You've never called anyone 'Mom.' You don't make that mistake because it's not a reflex."

"I... Forget it, okay?"

Lennox sat up and tugged Will to him. They sat, shoulders and knees brushing, and Lennox continued. "She's your mom. Karen, I mean. Maybe not in all the possible ways, but in all the ways that matter."

Will curled his toes into the blankets, and then his fingers. Beside him, Lennox sighed and rested his head on Will's shoulder. Lennox didn't say anything else; it seemed he was waiting for an answer Will didn't care to give. He didn't have any reason to talk about this. His mother was dead, and that was the end of that relationship in his life. Nobody could replace her—not for his dad or his aunt or his grandmother.

"Dad won't see it like that. If I call Karen 'Mom,' then it's like I'm getting rid of my real mom. I can't hurt him like that. He always tries to talk about her, and I always... I don't remember. I've tried and tried and I can't. She's just a story, and if he *knew* that... Just forget it, okay?"

Will knocked away the arm around his waist, but Lennox was always so determined. He got his arm around Will's shoulders and held him close.

"Do you really think your dad never considered that you might see Karen as a mom some day?"

"I—I don't know."

"She'd want you to be happy. Both of you," Lennox said as footsteps clomped overhead. "And I think that if you wanted another mother after she was gone, she'd be okay with that, too."

Will glanced upward. His dad was probably sneaking an evening snack despite their rules against them.

He slid his hand into Lennox's and felt the other close around his palm. Lennox kissed his cheek once more and nudged his nose against his jaw.

"Talk to him. You can't ignore this."

It took everything Will had to not say that Lennox himself bottled his feelings like a steel cork in a glass bottle so dark no eye could see through it. Lennox ignored the most important part of his own world: himself. And if Will kept doing that—even about one small piece—he might hurt himself in the same ways, or in more terrible ones: He might hurt Lennox and Ben and Karen too.

"I'll talk to him. On one condition."

"Name it."

"After the last cigarette in this pack is gone, you'll quit."

Lennox breathed deeply and, very cautiously, nodded. Will guessed that the cigarettes were a crutch for Lennox, but they also seemed to be something more. He'd caught Lennox selecting which one to smoke; he'd seen how carefully Lennox avoided two of them and had realized they were flipped over though why, he couldn't say.

"Deal."

Lennox gave him a weak smile as they got under the blankets and curled up together. Will had almost forgotten his request for a blowjob until Lennox wiggled under the blankets completely. He watched Lennox's head curve toward his hips and then giggled as his pajama pants were pushed down.

"Get to work, McAvoy. This dick doesn't suck itself—ouch! Don't pinch me!"

"Don't get any cockier than you already are." Lennox's head poked out from under the blankets. "My ass aches enough afterward as it is."

"Can I watch?"

"Sure."

⏮ fifteen ⏭

"PUT IT ON."

"No."

"Come on. You've got to put this on before you stick it in."

Lennox batted Otto's hands away and knocked the jockstrap and the protective cup to the damp tiles of the boys' locker room.

"Fuck no. I'm not trying out or playing or anything else. I don't fuck around with sports."

"But lacrosse is—"

"A sport."

Lennox adjusted his backpack on his shoulder and lay back on the bench between the rows of lockers. Otto was staying after school for lacrosse. Will had baseball out on the field today. January had started with ice, then offered a steamy week of chilly showers and bright sun, and now, a few days before Lucy's departure, the temperature was in the seventies with a strong wind swirling up what remained of the dead leaves.

"Fine, piss-baby. I'll go try out by myself."

"I thought you were already on the team."

"I am. Football, basketball, and lacrosse. But we do new tryouts every year just to make sure we've got the best team."

Lennox sat up as Otto finished dressing in his uniform—he assumed it was for lacrosse, though he'd never seen the game played—and laughed. Half of Otto's belly was visible, and his shorts were like very loose boxer-briefs.

"Might want to wear something else. Unless you're aiming for a booty call. Mmm, look at that round ass."

He tried to swat Otto's backside and earned himself a punch to the shoulder.

"Don't let Will hear you worshipping my—"

"You clearly don't know the way Lennox worships an ass, if that's your idea of it."

Will turned the row of lockers and fastened the belt on his baseball pants. Lennox eyed them appreciatively and reached over for Will's ass instead. His boyfriend leaned into the touch and wiggled his eyebrows at Otto as Lennox squeezed.

Otto made a face and looked in his locker for a different shirt. "You two are such perverts."

"Beats masturbation."

"We beat each other instead. Boner fights, Otto, man, you should give those a try sometime."

"Yuck. I'm out." Otto headed for the locker room door.

"Don't sound very out to me!"

Otto left. Will chuckled and sat on the bench beside Lennox.

"You going to come watch practice or stay in here?"

Lennox shrugged. "Might hit the band room. Or work on that essay. It's due Friday."

"You're really going to apply?"

"I'm going to try."

What Lennox didn't say was that he was doing it for Will. Maybe a little for himself—Berklee seemed like a great next phase of life, from the state-of-the-art music rooms to the people his age who shared his passion—but mostly for Will. College was Will's realm, for both of them now, and the least Lennox could do was give it a try.

"Osborne, get a move on!"

"Gotta go. Don't forget to invite Otto tonight!"

Will kissed his cheek and hurried out with his bag of gear. Lucy's going away party was planned for tonight: a small dinner at Will's house. Ben and Karen would go out to dinner and a movie for the night and the house, even on a weeknight, was theirs. So far only

Lucy, Kelly, and the two of them would be there. Will had almost asked his own friends, but then decided against it. None of them had met Lucy.

Instead, Will had suggested inviting Otto, though why was beyond him. Otto didn't know Lucy or Kelly. He didn't seem to know anyone well.

Lennox spent the following hour wandering the school. He checked the band room first, only to find it dark and locked. With his pocketknife at Will's house, he couldn't pick the lock. Nobody else seemed to be around. He took a lap upstairs, ghosting after the janitor, and then a loop through the halls on the main level. Outside his English classroom, a voice stopped him. It was Mr. Lorren.

"You should be at your after-school activity, Lennox."

"I'm waiting on Will. He's got baseball and he's my ride home."

"Well, get back to the gym. After hours or not, you can still get into trouble for walking the halls."

"It's not like I'm dumping gasoline on the floors or something."

Lennox kicked the door frame and turned away before remembering what he'd told Will he was going to do. Mr. Lorren had set an assignment for a college essay. He couldn't recall the requirements, or the due date, but maybe he could help. Lennox had scribbled out some nonsense one day and done nothing else with it since.

"Is there something else I can do for you, Lennox?"

Mr. Lorren had returned to his desk, but he watched Lennox curiously over his glasses. Lennox hesitated in the doorway. Will still had at least an hour of baseball, probably more since they were outside, and this essay was due in only a few days. This might be his only chance to have someone besides Will help with it.

"Lennox?"

"Um, you remember that college essay assignment?"

"Of course. I recall you not handing it in, or the secondary option for anyone not applying to college."

"There were two options? Anyway, Will, um, well, I'm thinking about applying to Berklee. For music, you know, and I... It's all sort of last minute, and I'm a terrible writer—"

Lennox dug his notebook out of his backpack, flipped it open, and set his failed attempt at an essay on Mr. Lorren's desk. He waited, expecting to be turned away or worse. Mr. Lorren, however, pushed up his glasses and picked up the notebook. While he read, Lennox paced the classroom and examined the posters on the walls. In almost five months, he'd never bothered to do more than glance at them. Some had inspiring quotes, others had parts of speech or other grammar components. Will would probably understand it all. Writing had never been Lennox's strongest skill.

"Is all of this is true?"

Lennox shrugged and sat on one of the desks. Roxanne's desk, actually. She always sat up front on the right.

"Yeah, the prompt didn't really call for all the personal stuff Will kept talking about, but I don't know what to do with it now."

Mr. Lorren hummed and scanned the page. "What was the exact question?"

"It asked if I'd had formal music training and what my experiences were from that, and if I hadn't, what kind of challenges that, like, presented."

"You could use most of this then, about your mother and how you've taught yourself since then. And all of these hardships. Good lord, Lennox. This is extensive."

"It's too much. They don't need a sob story."

"Well, once you trim parts of this and expand a little about your musical talents, then it should be a great essay."

"Sounds like a lot of work by Friday."

Mr. Lorren waved him over and, slowly, Lennox walked over and stood beside him. Mr. Lorren began discussing his essay, from the beginning with his mother to the smothered ruins of his family and then his time alone with the piano and guitar his mother had left behind. By the end of an hour, his essay was trimmed down and edited, with red ink on every line. All that was left was—

"I'd use this place to expand on everything you know, what your skills are, from strengths to weaknesses. And that should do it. Just one more thing."

Mr. Lorren leaned over the page with his pen and scribbled something across the top. When he leaned away, a large red B was scrawled at the top. Lennox stared at it as the notebook was handed back to him.

"But I didn't come here for a grade. And it's like three months late."

"Hence the B instead of an A." Mr. Lorren gave him a small smile. "I've always trusted one thing about Will: his judgment. He was in my ninth grade class, and nobody else had an ounce of good sense but him. When the two of you became an item, I knew there had to be something more about you for Will to date you. I never imagined this," he said, gesturing at Lennox's notebook, "but I'm glad to understand more and I thank you for letting me know."

"Umm, sure. I guess. I should go," Lennox said, his gaze on the wall clock. "He's probably waiting for me."

"Good luck. If you need any more help or someone to read it over one final time, let me know. If you want to turn in any of your other old assignments, I'll be willing to work something out now that you've got access to the proper technology."

"Right. Bye then."

Lennox hurried out and downstairs to the boys' locker room. It was empty except for the backpacks and stinky socks. He grabbed Will's backpack and clothes from his locker and headed out the back door to the fields behind the building. From the top of the hill where the school building stood he could just see the baseball field and a group of boys dressed in greens and blues sprinting across the—what had Will called it? A square? Diamond?

He trekked down the hill, past another group of boys returning from another field with netted sticks over their shoulders. Otto was among them, but it wasn't him that Lennox spotted first. Michael Patterson was with them, and a sneer took over his face at the sight of Lennox.

"Does Osborne have you carrying his bags now, like a little bitch? Are you his wife now? You going to start wearing dresses to school?"

Several boys chuckled, and one took a knock at Lennox with his stick. Lennox sidestepped it easily and smacked the boy in the knee with Will's backpack.

"I'd rather be his bitch than be you any day," Lennox said. But Otto stepped in his way. He tensed for the worst. His hands were full of Will's stuff and his notebook, and Otto, no matter how friendly they'd been outside of school or with few people around to see them, was a bully. Will had told him that much and now here was the proof.

"Leave Lennox alone, Michael. Same for you, Henry. You won't be on the team if you pick on people like that. Coach won't allow it."

"Coach doesn't care. What's he going to do if he's not around to see it, anyway?"

"Forget about him," another boy from the pack said. "He's in the same boat. Look at that braid he's growing. You're both freaks."

The group of boys continued up the hill, laughing and talking loudly. His teeth gritted and his netted stick resting on his shoulder, Otto stayed at Lennox's side.

"Sometimes I wish I was… Never mind." Otto slammed one end of his stick into the dirt and then kicked it back up onto his shoulder. "Later."

"Wish you were what?"

Otto stopped on the slope. "Like them, you know. Not personality or anything, just—"

"White? Fuck no. Then we'd be just as stupid as them."

"Or like Will. He's… I always used to rag on him, to make them like me. They never messed with me when I did what they did." Otto hesitated. "See you. I've got to get home before my brother does."

"Wait. Do... Will's having a, like, party sort of thing tonight. At his house. A, um, friend from the motel, she's moving away so we're saying goodbye, I guess. You're invited or whatever. If you want."

"Maybe. Mom works until this evening, but I guess I could stop by or something."

"Sure."

Otto nodded and headed back up to the school. Lennox continued down to the baseball field. He met Will on a bench in the covered thing. Tunnel? Will had named that too, and he hadn't a clue what.

"Hey, I'm almost done." Will wiped his forehead and undid a strap on his leg shield thing. "It's nice to be back on the field."

"Right, yeah. Behind the, uh, plate?"

"Right, plate." Will laughed as he packed up his gear and zipped it away in his bag. "So what did you do? Get in some piano practice?"

"No, worked on my essay."

Lennox held out his arm to accept one of Will's bags, and his knees wobbled under the weight. He really was turning into just a bag carrier, wasn't he? A trophy boyfriend for Will to display, with all of his belongings.

"I can carry all of it myself if you want."

But Lennox shrugged Will off and started up the hill toward the parking lot.

"Think you're ready to turn it in with your application?"

"Uh, almost, I guess."

"That's great. We can finish tomorrow and then submit it. Today's for Lucy. And you. Kelly too. She seems nice."

"Yeah. Guess we both found someone worthwhile in this hick town."

"A boring town doesn't mean worthless people," Will said.

Together they packed all of their bags into the truck bed and piled into the front seat. Will drove them home, with a short stop at the grocery store for more bags of chips than Lennox had ever seen. Half the aisle seemed to be piled into their cart, along with guacamole and a jar of oozy cheese. Will made him push it and then loaded his own arms with cases of soda and hooked the plastic straps of a six-pack to each hand.

"That should be enough, you think?"

Lennox nodded. He didn't have a clue. Not once had he thrown a party. His mother probably had birthday parties for him when he was little; maybe even his father had done that. But his birthdays only stood out as flickering candles at midnight and his mother's glowing face singing him awake.

Back at Will's house, they made several trips in while Ben sat in the living room and watched.

"Not that I'm against all the chips and soda, but I seem to remember parties being very different when I was in high school."

Lennox nodded. His own experiences at Lancaster had been full of alcohol and more marijuana than he'd probably ever see again. Ben's time in high school seemed to have fallen in line with that, but Will, as far as Lennox had seen, had never touched drugs or alcohol. He barely seemed to know they existed.

"Well, I'm throwing this one, not the football team."

"Or the baseball team?"

"That was one party, Dad, when we won state. I haven't gone to another one since because of how insane it got."

Ben smiled. "You're a lot smarter than I was at your age. I was out partying and drinking all weekend. Nearly failed out of school more than once. Almost thought I'd given you an older half-sibling a few times."

"Really? After all the condom talks you've given me?"

"Like I said, wasn't so smart when I was in high school."

Will set everything up while Lennox carried all of their bags downstairs. He stayed down there once he was finished. Lucy was leaving. He'd never see her again, no matter what they each said or what promises she made that he could come visit. Friendships never carried over. They never lasted long enough to mean something when he was involved.

Lennox set his essay down on the bed and put Will's bags away: baseball gear in the corner by the bean bag, backpack on the chair at the desk. He tucked his own backpack against the far side of the bed and lay down beside his notebook. The page was smeared with red, as if he'd torn open a packet of ketchup and tried to finger paint.

It wasn't anything remarkable. The grammar was patchy, and Mr. Lorren had covered the pages with comments about his tenses. But it was true, and that was what Will had said, that honesty was the greatest story he had to give.

"Lennox, Lucy's here!"

Upstairs, Ben and Karen were grabbing their coats as Lucy and Kelly took theirs off. They both looked out of place here at Will's, Kelly with her growing poof of red bangs—hadn't it been a bubblegum pink stripe last time?—and her half-sleeves of tattoos that Ben eyed with interest. Lucy, petite, with her braided brown hair and plain clothing, was easier to fit into the picture.

"Dad, this is Lucy and Kelly."

Ben nodded to them as Karen greeted Lucy as if she was her best friend. Lennox didn't get that; Karen barely knew her. But Lucy turned away pretty quickly and smacked her arms around him and against his back with a loud thud.

"Hey, dork," Lucy said.

They pulled away, and a walnut seemed to become lodged in his throat, not that he liked walnuts or would ever eat one whole. She beamed at him and pulled him over to the couch as Will shooed Karen and Ben off to their evening out on the—well, Lennox didn't think *town*, more like cavern dug somewhere into the mountains.

"We brought some movies," Kelly said. She sat down on Lucy's other side, and Will sat beside Lennox. "*Rocky Horror*, of course, *SLC Punk*, *Tank Girl*, and *Tremors*. My vote's for the last one."

"*Tremors?* Sounds like a vagina earthquake sort of movie—ouch!"

Lucy pinched him again, this time on his neck. "Shh, it's about giant worms *burrowing*."

"So kind of like Will's dick in my—"

"*Tremors* it is!" Kelly leapt up and put the movie in. Then she turned to Will because Lucy had pinned Lennox to the couch and was sitting on his hips. "I hope you're not a geeky pervert too."

"I'm not a geek!" Lennox flicked her off.

Above him, Lucy shrugged. "I am. The next LeakyCon is in Boston and I'm already saving because we're going to be right across town!"

"The what?"

"You are such a geek. A precious little high school nerd with a leather jacket disguise." Kelly held up a finger as he tried to argue. "Nope. I've seen all the comic book pages on your window. Nobody with that kind of collection isn't a nerd, even if that's deep, deep down."

"It's not very deep at all," Will said. He shrugged when Lennox glared at him. "What? You talk in your sleep sometimes. I believe last night you were flirting with Spider-Man."

Lennox felt his cheeks flush. He'd been flirting with *Will*, actually, dressed up in a very tight Spider-Man costume, but that was information for another time.

"I was not."

"Aw, time to search for a Spider-Man outfit, Will," Lucy said. She pinched Lennox's cheek and climbed off of him. "He'd get a kick out of that, I'm sure."

"I, well, I wouldn't object."

"Shh, the movie's starting."

They all curled up on the couch and settled in. For hours, they watched movies and joked around while Lucy made dinner, much to everyone's surprise. Lennox had never seen her cook. Most days she was too lazy to even reheat leftover fast food, but she and Will moved around the kitchen in sync. Will pulled out things she asked for and Lucy went to town.

Kelly and Lennox sat at the table and watched the supposed chicken lasagna being concocted while Kelly explained all of her tattoos.

"This sleeve is going to be a bunch of Eevees and its evolutions. This one is Jolteon."

"Who?"

Kelly slapped the table, her mouth falling open. "How do you *not* know Pokémon? Lucy, how can you be friends with this kid when he doesn't know what Pokémon is?"

Lucy only laughed as she took a glass casserole dish from Will.

"I'm going to send you a card in the mail every week until you understand," Kelly told him. "Once you're up there, too. Aren't you still applying to Berklee?"

Lennox tensed. Two days. He was almost finished, but so much else still had to be navigated. Even if he turned in the application, made the audition, and didn't get arrested for whatever came out of his mouth during the interview, they still had to think he was worth the time.

"It's due on Friday. I'm almost done."

Kelly nodded and smiled. "That's awesome. The application and waiting is the worst part. You've got to audition, right?"

"And interview." Will turned to them and opened the refrigerator. "What does everyone want to drink?"

"Water."

"Orange juice if you've got it."

After that, conversation turned to Will's college applications and his schools of choice. As Kelly questioned him and told him about a trip she'd taken to New York City a few years ago with friends from school, Lucy slid the unbaked lasagna into the oven and took Lennox by the hand.

"What do you say we pick the next movie?"

Lennox followed her into the living room. Several DVD cases were spread out on the table, but Lucy scanned the ones in the stand next to the television and groaned.

"These are all romances. I want action right now."

"Will's got a bunch more downstairs."

Lucy pulled him downstairs. He almost stopped her; this was Will's bedroom and sometimes it felt like his own too, but it was their private space. But Lucy wasn't to be deterred. She paused at the bottom step and whistled.

"This is really nice. I figured you two were like half on top of each other in some dinky twin bed, but this is bigger than any dorm you'll stay in at Berklee."

"If I go."

Lucy hopped down the last step and scanned the DVDs on the shelves. "If?"

"I haven't even turned anything in yet."

Lennox followed and sat on Will's bed. His notebook, still open to his essay, slid toward the dip his weight made in the bed. Lucy pulled out a movie, read the back, and then put it back. She turned around and seemed to be steeling herself for an argument.

"But you're going to, right? Don't let being afraid keep you here."

"I'm not staying."

"Then what's your plan if you don't go to college? Will's going away in August, maybe sooner if he gets into a school in New York. I doubt his parents will want you staying here for long."

Lennox clicked his tongue ring as his head buzzed.

Click, click, click.

"Don't click that tongue ring at me."

"Fuck you."

Lucy sat next to him, and the notebook slid between them. "Look, you can't avoid this much longer. If you don't figure out something else besides college, then you're not going anywhere. You don't have a job or a car or a license or anything right now. Will's probably not even thinking about that," Lucy said with a pointed glance around Will's expansive bedroom, "but I am. I didn't have any plans either, thought once I graduated I was just going to pick up and leave, but it doesn't work like that."

"I—I'll figure something out."

"I think you should try this college. Maybe it'll work out, maybe it won't, but it'll be a great opportunity if it does."

"If. They won't want me, no matter how good I am. I've got a record. I've been locked up, and it doesn't matter if I'm the best."

"It does. Yeah, they'll surely ask about what happened and whatever charges you had against you, but you've got something they want, Lennox."

"A strong thrust?"

"Talent. A practiced and hard-earned ability that they've built a school for."

Lennox shrugged, but for a second he could believe that. He was good, that was true, but so much else stood in his way, as always. His dad never had the money for lessons, his grandfather considered music wasteful, and whenever he'd had a chance to join an after-school music program at school he couldn't. His sister's care had come first, and the brunt of it had fallen on him.

"It doesn't hurt to try," Lucy said. "Just think, if you do get in, you'll be like twenty minutes away from me. We can have dinner, and in a few years I'll take you out and get you hammered on your twenty-first birthday. We could all get an apartment together, too."

Lucy gave him a hug that he tried to return. He managed to get one loose arm around her. Then he was up looking for a movie so he didn't have to talk anymore. All anyone seemed to want lately was to talk to him: about college, his feelings, his future. Sometimes that wasn't so bad. Not when he and Will were lying under the blankets in the darkness of the middle of the night with sweat dotting their skin and sharp puffs of breath punctuating their words.

"Is this your essay?"

He spun around, but Lucy had clearly already read it. The notebook was resting on her thighs and one finger was tracing a line toward the bottom.

"It sucks, I know. Mr. Lorren read it over and marked it all up—"

"Use it. Just trust me."

"It's too much of a sob story. I just had to get it out. It's useless."

"It's really not. I know you, right? And I know a bit of what's happened, but I didn't know most of this. It's sad, sure, but the way you've written it makes it real and honest. It makes me want to see what you're capable of."

"Getting arrested and giving blowjobs."

Lennox pulled a movie from the shelves at random.

"Come on, let's go get this movie started."

But Lucy blocked his path and she wasn't smiling. A deep frown pulled her lips down. A memory popped into his head like a burst of light. His father had given him that same look once before, but for what reason he couldn't say.

"Don't belittle what you can do," Lucy said. "If you do it to yourself, then everyone else is going to say that and worse. You *can* do this."

"Whatever."

"No, not whatever. I want to hear you say it so you'll start believing it."

Lennox tried to sidestep to the right and then the left. Lucy blocked his way, and when he tried to shove her aside she pinched his chest hard. She was wrong. Playing well meant nothing.

"You can do this."

"Lucy, just—"

"You. Can. Do. This."

"Get out of my way."

Lucy pushed him back. "Come on then. If you can't, then tell me that."

"Look, let's just go watch the movie."

"Go tell Will he wasted his money. Go tell him how much you suck. Hell, tell your sister that she should just give up on ever seeing you again because you can't—"

Lennox bared his teeth and pushed her back. She landed on her butt on the bottom step. "I can play circles around anyone else who auditions and make them look like shit on every other instrument in that room. Okay? So fuck off."

"So you can do this?"

Lennox shook his head. "I can't."

And it wasn't for lack of ability or lack of trying. He couldn't, because even if he was the *best*, it would never make up for everything else that he was.

Lucy pushed herself to her feet. Disappointment marked her face, and she reached for him, as if she realized how far was too far to push.

"Lennox?"

"Move."

"I didn't mean to—"

"I'm still applying, so you can shut up and be happy, all right?"

He pushed past her and went back upstairs. Will and Kelly had returned to the living room, and another movie had already started. Lennox joined them on the couch and set the movie he'd brought on the table.

"*Forrest Gump*? Doesn't seem like your kind of movie."

Lennox shrugged and dropped his head onto Will's shoulder. An animated movie was playing, with some magical white-haired frost-making kid. Lucy wedged into her spot between Lennox and Kelly. Nobody spoke until they were back in the kitchen eating. The other three carried on the conversation, and once their plates were cleared and the lasagna was devoured, they returned to the living room.

They finished the movie, interrupted briefly by the return of Ben and Karen, and then Kelly and Lucy said their goodbyes. Lennox swallowed as they spoke with Will first. He stayed on the couch and kept his eyes on the coffee table.

"We'll have you guys up this summer," Kelly said. She leaned down and hugged him. "Or spring break if we're all set up by then. Okay? Bye, Lennox."

He grunted; his throat was tight. Kelly was barely a blip on his radar. She was nice and she seemed to bring happiness into Lucy's life, but she was almost a stranger to him. Lucy, however, stood before him as Will and Kelly shuffled into the hall. The front door opened and closed.

"I'm going to miss you." Lucy sat next to him and raised her hand as if she was about to pat his knee, but she set it on her own instead. "We're still going to be friends. Even if I'm in Boston. And... Listen, about earlier, I just want to help you. For you to want more for yourself than you've had so far. I didn't mean to push—"

Lennox wiped his nose on his sleeve. "You did. You always do. But—"

He hesitated. Lucy wasn't Will. She could see more than college and the standard path to growing up. She'd lived more widely than Will, although perhaps not as widely as Lennox had.

"What if I'm not—what if I get in and then I can't—"

"You can. Hell, after being dumped here and everything else you said in that essay, going to college and being safe and out on your own is going to be easy. It's going to be the best feeling in the world, Lennox. And, if you struggle, I'll be in town. So will Kelly. And Will is only a train ride away."

He took a deep breath and shuddered.

"I'm only a long train ride away right now."

"Yeah. Sure."

Lucy hugged him, and Lennox melted into her embrace. She couldn't leave. So many other people did; some left before he'd realized they were gone, while others left stains that stood forever.

"Can't you stay until summer?"

Lucy's breath puffed hot against his neck. "No. I mean, I could, but if I keep staying I'll never leave."

"I'm—I mean, I'm going to—"

Lennox cleared his throat as she pulled away. Lucy smiled and kissed him on the cheek. "I'm going to miss you too. We'll see each other soon, okay? I pr—"

"Don't. Just get going, okay?"

"Okay. Love you."

Lucy gave him another tight squeeze and stood. Time seemed to speed up as she walked away. Everyone always said it slowed down at the worst moments, but for Lennox that was never true. It flew by so fast he couldn't process it, couldn't breathe one breath before the moment was stolen away.

The front door opened and shut. Will sat beside him a few seconds later, an arm around his back. Everything slowed once more, not quite back to normal, but very close.

"You okay?"

Lennox shrugged. Lucy was gone. Both of them. His sister was maybe sixty miles away, but it was a distance he could never cross. Lucy was leaving for good, to start her own life away from all of this, away from him.

"It's okay." Will kissed his cheek and held him against his chest. "I'm still here."

But for how long?

If Will wasn't here, then what did that mean for him? Where did he want to go on his own? Berklee was one path, placed before him with bullet points, yet no matter how stupendous the outcome was, it wasn't truly his own. Berklee wouldn't be his until he took the reins.

◀ sixteen ▶

WILL CRINKLED HIS NOSE AND snuffled.

"Poke."

"Geroff."

He wiggled and shivered as his feet found a cold patch under the blankets. A warm arm slid under his shirt and tickled his side. Will snorted and laughed; his feet kicked and found something soft.

"Ouch! Fuck—"

After a dull thud, something rolled off his nightstand and plunked to the floor. Will grabbed the end of the blanket and rolled over, wrapping himself up like a burrito until he was on Lennox's side of the bed.

Lennox's face was strained. His teeth were bared, and he was clutching his crotch.

"Thanks for that," Lennox said hoarsely. "Appreciate it."

"I told you to stop trying to wake me up like that. From afar or with belly flops. Take a note from my dad."

Slowly, Lennox sat up. He rubbed himself a few times and rested his head back against the nightstand.

"No. I took a note out of your book instead."

"What do you mean?" Will yawned and stretched out in his blanket burrito.

"I finished my application."

Will bolted upright, tried to untangle himself, and instead flopped over onto the floor with Lennox.

"Really? It's done? Let me read over your—"

"Can't. I submitted it."

"*What?*"

Will tugged himself free of his blanket and looked out the window. It was dawn. The square of sky that was visible was pale gray with a warm pink edging. Why would Lennox get up so early to submit a college application he'd been dragging his feet about?

"Figured I'd get it over with," Lennox said, but his smile didn't reach his eyes. "Get moving on that audition and the interview."

"But I was going to read it over, just to double check typos and stuff."

"It's fine." Lennox got up and headed toward the bathroom. "I get first shower."

Will fixed his bed while the shower ran in the other room. He picked out his clothes and then opened his laptop. As usual, Lennox had only closed it instead of shutting it off. But the application was submitted. He had the confirmation in his email and the screen thanking Lennox for his submission was still open.

What had changed?

It had taken so much effort to convince him to apply, and then even more to get him to scribble out his essay. Maybe Lucy had said something to him last night. That must be it. If anyone else could convince him that this was the right choice, it would be Lucy.

Lennox returned from his shower completely naked and rubbed his towel over his ass.

"So, I did what you wanted," he said without preamble. "Your turn."

Will instinctively reached for Lennox's cock. To his surprise, Lennox batted his hand away and chuckled.

"No, dork. I meant I applied, so now you have to talk to your dad or Karen. About your mom, and her as your mom, and all of that mom drama."

Will snapped his mouth shut and then opened it again to say, "You know, that cock of yours isn't self-sucking."

He reached for Lennox again and missed. Lennox tossed his damp towel on the bed.

"Fine. I'll just refuse to go to my audition then."

"You're going. Don't try to corner me into talking to either of them about her."

"I'm not. I just think you should, but it's your choice." Lennox dug a pair of boxer-briefs out of a drawer, had them all the way on before he realized they were Will's and too loose, and then pushed them back down.

Will left to shower and headed upstairs once he was dressed. Lennox had already made a mountain of toast for breakfast and was tossing pieces to Oyster, who was whining at the back door.

The backyard was brilliant white, and snow was still falling.

"Not today, boy. Just a quick potty break and then back in."

He slid the door open, and Oyster barreled right into the snow piled against the door. Most of it trickled onto the kitchen floor as Oyster leapt across the deck. Lennox handed Will a piece of cinnamon toast.

"Karen left a note. School's canceled."

"We can go sledding!"

"You're like a toddler," Lennox said, but he agreed. He wiped up the snow on the floor and grinned. "He's having fun."

Will watched a tornado of white flurries rising out of the yard. Two ears and a tail appeared above the snow before disappearing again.

"You could talk to your dad and Karen too."

"I don't want to."

Lennox sighed and watched Oyster for another minute. "I'd give just about anything to talk to my mom again. Or to still have my dad, even when he was all fucked up. He was still around, you know? I wasn't some shuffled-around orphan. You've still got yours and you're fucking lucky he's still here after that heart attack. Now you've got this great woman who's a mom for you too. I got one chance at parents. You're getting two. Don't ignore what comes with that."

After grabbing his shoes and coat, Lennox went out back and tromped around the backyard with Oyster. Will watched them from the warm kitchen and debated whether or not he wanted eggs with his toast. Lennox was right, of course. They both seemed to have a knack for being right when the other needed it most.

"I'm thinking about an omelet. You want one, Will?"

Ben shuffled into the kitchen and opened the refrigerator. Will watched him dig out what he needed. Maybe Lennox had a point. But if Karen walked in while they were talking—if he said something that might hurt her if she overheard—he didn't think he could live with himself.

"You okay? He giving you trouble?"

Will shook his head. "I'll have peppers in mine, please."

Ben set to work at the counter as Will mulled over what to say first, or if he should say anything at all. Karen was right down the hall. His dad would be unbelievably hurt by what he had to say, surely, and that left only Lennox on his side in this.

"You sure you're—"

"I don't remember Mom."

Ben continued to chop onions as if Will had just commented on the weather. "I know that. Be hard for anyone to remember stuff from when they were a toddler."

Ben didn't seem mad. He hadn't even flinched.

"Sorry."

"For what? Will, I never expected you to remember her. I mean, I hoped, for a long time, but I've made my peace with it."

"You're not mad at me?"

Ben put down his knife and turned to him. "Why would I ever get mad at you for something completely out of your control?"

"I just... I don't know." Will spun the pepper shaker on the table and didn't meet Ben's eyes. "You didn't seem too happy about me being in love with Lennox."

"He gave me plenty of reasons. I think I've been coming around to him, yeah? That's a different situation. With your mom it's more complicated."

"She's my mom. I *should* remember her and I can't. Even when I was little it all slipped out almost as soon as you said it. And now—"

"Now Karen's your mom. I get it, Will. I wouldn't have kept her in my life and yours if I hadn't thought she could be a mom, or something close, for you."

Lennox had said the same, but Will had never believed it. He was more intuitive than Will cared to admit.

"Something on your mind?"

So much was on his mind. His college applications, which had been sent off and would soon return; Lennox's application and that impending interview and audition; graduation, class assignments and projects; the next edition of the school newspaper he'd barely focused on; his dad's health; the start of baseball season, with several subpar pitchers he had to train; and this. Karen and Beth: two moms, one not even a memory and the other so much more than one simple word. Yet he couldn't bother his dad with all of that right now. Not when his health was still weak.

"No. Just school stuff. Thanks."

"That's what I'm here for."

Ben put his ingredients into the skillet as Will looked out the sliding glass door. Lennox and Oyster were diving about in the snow. Nearly three feet of it seemed to have fallen since last night. He hoped Lucy and Kelly had made it out all right. He'd have to call Lucy to check in later. He and Ben ate their omelets, brought a shivering, soggy Lennox in to eat and tried and failed to keep Oyster from shaking himself dry.

"Oh—ugh!"

Will slipped and teetered backward as Oyster shook the water out of his fur. Towels were useless, but Will tried to capture him and prevent any more splatters. Oyster had other plans. He yipped, leaped at the towel Will tried to cover him with, and then darted away at full speed. Will listened to the thumps of his tail hitting the wall as he went downstairs.

"I hate dogs."

Ben chuckled and continued to watch Lennox add a mountain of cheese to his omelet. Will wiped his face off and grimaced at the grimy towel. Winter was the worst time for keeping Oyster clean. One week it was warmer and muddier than April, and the next a pile of snow blocked the back door. Oyster's white fur never stayed clean for long when he went outside.

"Does that mean you're getting a cat when you move away?"

"No. A frog."

Lennox made a face. "Eww. That's worse. They're all, like, slimy and weird."

"I'm going to go dump this with the laundry."

Will walked down the hall toward the laundry room and ran right into Karen. She was still in her pajamas, but her hair was brushed and neat.

"Morning, Will."

"M-morning, M... Karen."

She didn't smile. Will swallowed. She wanted to be his mother, didn't she? Karen had called him her son for so long now, was a mother in all the ways he considered important.

Karen stepped past him. Will watched her go and suddenly he was nervous again. His dad had been fine, and while he was ready for this, it was almost as though Karen wasn't, as though she wanted to avoid it. He dumped his towel with the laundry, grabbed a new one for Oyster, and sat in the kitchen. Lennox was wolfing down an omelet that looked like an inflated mountain, and Karen was sitting beside him while Ben made hers.

"Bacon?"

"A little bit."

"Peppers? I've got a few left from Will's."

"Are they red?"

"Green."

"Please."

Will joined them and found his eyes drawn to her. She didn't act nervous, but then Karen was well-trained to control her emotions in hyper-stressful situations. Lennox finished his omelet and returned to his stack of toast. Karen shook her head as they watched him inhale six pieces in a matter of minutes.

"You eat more than anyone I've ever met."

"It's the libido. Blame Will."

Ben aimed his spatula at Lennox. "No sex talk over breakfast."

"Yeah, yeah." Lennox shoved the last piece of toast into his mouth whole and swallowed. "I'm gonna go dig up that piano you mentioned. Later."

His pointed look at Ben and Karen wasn't lost on Will. Ben finished Karen's omelet and booked for the door too.

"Hold on! I'll show you where it's at."

It was a mark of how much they both wanted Will and Karen to talk that they'd run off to spend time together. Will hoped it wouldn't end in disaster, but right now he had to walk into one of his own.

"I should go check on them so they don't strangle each other."

"Sounds like a good idea," Karen said.

She didn't look at him as he got up and went into the garage. Lennox and Ben were hidden behind a stack of boxes in the corner. A pair of snow shovels clattered to the cement at Will's feet as he approached. He and Lennox would clear the driveway later.

"You're lucky this isn't water-damaged. It smells like moldy shit out here."

"That's because there is mold out here. I meant to clean it before my trip to the hospital."

Ben appeared over the boxes. He looked like a bust that had been balanced precariously on top. He spotted Will and frowned.

"That was fast."

"Yeah, figured I'd make sure you're both coming out of here alive," Will said without meeting their eyes. "We're going to have enough shoveling on our hands without digging a grave, too."

Lennox, however, saw right through his deflection.

"You chickened out. Did you at least talk to him?" Lennox nodded at Ben, who sighed.

"He did. Did you even mention it, Will?"

"I didn't want to bother her while she's eating. Later, okay?"

"He's lying," Lennox said to Ben. "His eyes are lying."

Will blanched. "I am not!"

"You always sweep your eyes down when you lie," Lennox told him. He sat on the boxes in front of the piano and waved Will away. "Go talk to Karen. This is a Will-hasn't-talked-to-Karen-yet-and-he-needs-to free zone. Out."

"But—"

Ben shrugged; his eyes were darkened by his lowered brow. "Drop it, guys. Go dig out the driveway for her, will you?"

Lennox looped his arm through Will's and led him back into the house to change. Once they were outside, dressed in three layers and with shovels in hand, Will couldn't focus. He kept shoveling the snow Lennox pushed aside, and more than once he flung snow right into Lennox's face. Eventually, Lennox whacked him in the butt and knocked him face first into a snowdrift.

Will came up with a mouth full of freezing fluff and snow in his pants.

"You look like Santa Claus." Lennox roared with laughter and toppled backward beside him. "Come over here and warm me up."

Will sat up and tossed a fistful of snow into Lennox's face.

"Hey!"

Lennox kicked up a cloud of snow at him and a furious snowball fight began. Will won by a mile, pummeling Lennox with snowballs and shovelfuls of snows until they were toppled over and panting against each other. Lennox rubbed their cold noses together and laughed.

"I love you."

Will grinned, his frozen cheeks aching from the stretch. "I love you too. Let's get the rest of the driveway done so—"

"Boys, we said to shovel the driveway, *not* make out."

Karen had appeared, bundled up and furious. She wrapped her scarf tighter around her neck and pulled it over her chin and mouth.

"Get back inside. I'll finish this."

"No, we'll help."

"Get inside, William. Go."

Karen turned her car on and finished clearing off the top and windshield. She pulled out a few minutes later. Will and Lennox watched her from the end of the driveway.

"What's her problem?" Lennox heaved another pile of snow from the driveway to the yard.

"Figured you had an idea."

Lennox shrugged but looked uncomfortable. "Why would I know?"

"You said she talked to you about when I called her Mom," Will reminded him.

"She's just stressed or something. Maybe she's got really bad cramps. That'd irritate me too."

"No, she gets lethargic when she's cramping and wants to watch movies and eat ice cream." Will pulled the shovel from Lennox's hand to keep him from ignoring him. "What'd she say?"

"It's not my place to—"

"Tell me."

Lennox still didn't answer, and Will tossed their shovels aside and headed back toward the house.

"Oh, come on. Don't be like that. It's not—"

"You *know* why she won't talk to me about this and you aren't—"

"She doesn't want to, or she's not sure, I don't know." Lennox crossed his arms. "She said she wasn't sure if she wanted to be your mom. Or be called 'Mom.' That's all, okay?"

Will chest shriveled. He was right, then. He didn't have a mom in Karen either.

"Will?"

"I'm fine. Let's get inside for a while," he said. "This snow isn't stopping any time soon. We'll have to re-shovel later anyway."

"Will, don't just—"

"I'll see you inside."

ⓘ seventeen ⓘ

FOR THE FIRST TIME SINCE his injuries, Lennox slept on the couch. Will hadn't said much to him, but it was uncomfortable to see him so miserable. He stayed upstairs and watched weird sports shows with Ben all evening, shoveled out the driveway again when the snow stopped, and, after Ben went to bed, sat up late thinking until he passed out.

Will greeted him with his usual kiss the next morning.

"We've got a delay," Will told him. "I think they'll probably cancel again before long. Wanna build an igloo?"

Lennox agreed, and they had a big breakfast of oatmeal and strawberries. Will's prediction was right. School was called off once more, and they spent the morning outside building a fort and attempting an igloo with an impressively large skylight.

"We used to collect all of our old orange juice cartons and freeze water in them," Will told him as they lay down under the opening. The sky was a bright, clear blue, and the sun was warm. "They're a lot better for igloos than this kind of snow. It's too powdery."

Lennox stretched out and shook the bunched up snow from his gloves. "Maybe next year."

Will blew a cloud of breath into the air. "Sarah Lawrence's campus is supposed to have a lot of green space. Enough for an igloo at least."

Lennox nodded; his mind drifted farther north to Berklee. He'd seen a few pictures in the pamphlet, but most of those had been inside music halls and classes. Perhaps they had the space too, but with Will in New York City, he'd have nobody to build one with.

Boston certainly had enough snow, although they probably didn't have anywhere for a snowball fight.

"Berklee might."

"We should go up and visit them over spring break," Will said. He tossed a handful of snow up into the air and it showered down like cold sand. "Dad was supposed to take me up, but he probably still shouldn't travel too far. We could spend a few days in New York and then go visit Lucy and Kelly in Boston. They texted me last night to say they made it okay."

Lennox's stomach clenched. "That's great."

"You should give her a call later."

"Maybe."

Will sat up and nudged him with his boot. "Hot chocolate and a movie?"

"Sure." Lennox sat up, but the question he'd mulled over all night finally worked itself out of his mouth. "You're not mad at me about Karen, are you?"

"No. This is between me and Karen. Whatever's going on is for me and her to figure out."

Will shrugged and threw himself through one of the side walls of their igloo. Lennox watched it crumble into a cloud of snow. He followed Will out and helped him kick the rest of it over. From the depths of the snow-filled pool, Oyster howled.

"Come on, boy. It's time to go warm up."

Another howl came, as forlorn as anything Lennox had ever heard.

"Oyster, come."

"Arrooo!"

"Fine. We're going in without you."

They were in the kitchen before Oyster reappeared, yipping and whining at their heels. Lennox brushed some of the snow from his fur, but it matched so well he couldn't tell where to start. The dog was shaking, though, and Lennox doubted it had anything to do with the cold.

"Coward."

After showers and several mugs of hot chocolate, Lennox found himself on the couch again with Will resting on his chest.

"You didn't have to sleep up here last night, you know." Will yawned and stretched.

"It was kind of nice. Not very comfortable, but it was nice to have my own space for a night."

"I know. I got to sprawl out for once."

"And I got to have blankets all night."

Will poked him, but Lennox felt him smile against his shirt. "What movie are we going to watch?"

"I'd rather nap."

"We could nap while it plays."

"Too much effort."

Lennox dozed off to the steady rhythm of Will's breathing on top of him. He woke several hours later in a dark living room with Will's warmth gone and the kitchen light casting shadows on the wall. Something was boiling in the kitchen; he could hear it gurgling. Ben's voice carried in to him.

"—I don't know, okay? Not any more than Lennox or you. She's off tomorrow, so you can ask her then."

Will sighed and something hit the counter. "I guess. She's never been mad at me before. Not *really*. Do you think she—"

"Karen isn't going to stop liking you. She loves you like you're her own, Will."

"But Karen's always said she doesn't want any kids. And I keep thinking maybe that means me too."

The burner clicked as it was turned off. The boiling faded and a cabinet was opened and closed.

"Tomorrow, Bud. And you are her kid, okay? She's called you her son I don't know how many times. This is just a big step to take. You might... I don't know. Go wake him up. Chili's best when it's hot."

Will appeared a few seconds later. He paused when he saw Lennox sitting up.

"Oh, you're awake. Dad made chili. You're going to *love* this. It's really spicy."

Lennox followed him back into the kitchen and was handed a big bowl of chunky chili and an enormous corn muffin. All three of them piled back into the living room and Will groaned as Ben turned on a basketball game. Lennox, however, perked up. He hadn't played since he was little, but he understood the rules for this sport.

"Can't we watch something else?"

"But I *know* this one," Lennox said as Will made a swipe for the remote. "I don't know the teams too well anymore, but I can talk basketball."

Will grumbled, but he let Ben turn the game up. After they had each finished two bowls of chili, Will convinced his dad to turn the game down enough so that they could talk.

"Your... Is it a hearing? Your ankle monitor thing's tomorrow morning."

Lennox gripped the empty bowl on his lap a little tighter and nodded. "Yeah, it's at nine. At the station in town. It should be pretty quick, just turning it off and removing it. Nothing fancy."

"We'll go with you. Karen's got work, but the two of us will drive over and then I'll take you two to school after."

"You aren't supposed to be driving."

"To hell with that, it's been three months since I came home. It's high time I got over to the store to check in and start taking a few short shifts. Spring uniform orders are going to start soon. They can't keep up with all of that much longer."

Will leaned into Lennox's side a little. He frowned but didn't say anything else about it. After the game, Karen came out to get some chili. Her hair was a wild nest on her head and her eyes were still half closed and crusted with sleep.

"Morning."

Ben chortled. "It's night, honey. Chili's on the stove. What time do you work tonight?"

"Eleven. There all night. I'll be back after lunch."

Karen disappeared into the kitchen. Will turned back to Lennox. His fingers now had a death grip on Lennox's forearm.

"Do you have to dress nicely for it?"

"For what? School? Pretty sure they'd only say something if I came in naked."

"No, for the ankle monitor removal."

Ben shut the television off. "You should at least look presentable. Nice slacks, one of Will's good shirts, and a tie if you want."

Lennox shook his head. "Can't tie those. Don't have any of those either. I'll just go naked. Make it easier to spot the ankle monitor."

Will, however, stood up and grabbed Lennox's hands. "Downstairs."

"This is not the time for a booty call," Lennox said as he was hauled to his feet. "I doubt your dad wants to spend the next hour picturing us doing what you're suggesting either."

"No. *You* are going to try on my dress clothes. I've got some older pants that shouldn't be too long on you."

"But what I always wear is fine."

"A jacket that's got patches announcing The Dicks and Pansy Division and... Does that say 'Homo Christmas'?"

"It's a song."

"Come on."

Ben's laughter followed them downstairs. Lennox wasn't sure if it was aimed at them or something the news anchor had just said on the television, but it didn't make him feel any better. Will led him right into his expansive closet and began shifting through everything hanging on the left side.

"My shirts should all fit you. I've got some dress pants from a few years ago that should be okay. Probably a little loose in the waist, but they'll fit everywhere else... Aha!"

Will pulled three pairs of dress pants off hangers and tossed them to Lennox.

"These are ugly."

"They're dress pants. They're almost *all* ugly. Put them on."

After six more pairs, Lennox found one he could stand to wear for a few hours the next morning. As Will drifted off beside him twenty minutes later, Lennox gazed up at the ceiling. He'd put the removal out of his mind since he'd gotten that letter in the mail. The entire event had seemed so improbable a few weeks ago. Something always went wrong for him. Until now. Suddenly so much was going right—or at least in what everyone kept telling him was the right direction.

Lennox rolled over as his stomach did the same. They'd never actually remove it. Tomorrow they'd go down to the station, and Lennox would be turned out, still blipping and jangling. He'd never leave Leon or Virginia or do anything greater than the very little he'd already done in his life.

BEN WOKE WILL AND LENNOX later than usual the next morning. The extra hour of sleep seemed to do Will a lot of good; he was cheery and bright-eyed. For some reason, he seemed to be excited. Lennox's stomach was churning like a tornado swirling toward the ground. He shoved the tail of one of Will's dress shirts into his pants and buckled the belt Will had given him. It wasn't pretty, didn't fit the way a well-made suit would, but it was good enough.

"Do you want a tie? I've got clip-ons and normal ones."

Lennox shrugged and let Will loop a dark blue one around his neck and adjust it. He followed the deft twists of Will's fingers as he knotted it tightly against his throat. Lennox swallowed hard to try to loosen it, but it just grew tighter.

"Let's grab some breakfast, okay?"

Will kissed his cheek, but Lennox ignored his words. He wasn't hungry. His stomach was filled with the disappointment that was only an hour away.

"Hey, it's going to be fine."

Will bumped his elbow against Lennox's side.

"We're wasting our time. We should just go to school."

He tried to head upstairs, but Will blocked him.

"They scheduled this to take it off. How is that a waste of time?"

"It just is."

"Lennox, don't—"

"They aren't going to take it off, all right? We'll get there, and they'll decide not to because that's just how it is. They'll find some bullshit excuse to keep it on for another six months or another year or whatever and it just... It doesn't matter. Forget it. Let's go eat."

He hurried upstairs and into the kitchen without Will. Ben set plates of scrambled eggs and toast on the table as Lennox sat down.

"Looking sharp."

Lennox grunted and pushed a particularly plump ball of egg from one side of his plate to the other. Ben joined him, and a few minutes later Will took a seat too. As Ben tried to make small talk, Lennox stared at his plate and let his mind wander.

The last time he did this—a year and a half ago, when it had first been put on—his grandfather had been there. He'd gotten Lennox released only to take him to a new building, where they made Cameron sign a bunch of papers and then forced Lennox to hold out his ankle while they put it on. Cameron McAvoy had made every choice for Lennox then. He was probably still somewhere tugging on strings to make what should be a happy moment just another day of disappointment.

The drive over was the longest Lennox had taken in months. He watched the green blip of his ankle monitor as Ben drove them away from the mountains, through town, and then beyond. Culpeper. That was what the letter had said. He'd have to go to some station in Culpeper to have it removed and sign some paperwork if he passed everything, which he wouldn't.

"Another half a mile," Will said from the front. "Is it going to go off when you get out of the radius?"

Lennox shrugged. It might. Nothing too noticeable on his end, but the police station would catch on. They'd probably think he was making a run for it and be waiting to arrest him when they arrived.

"Bye bye, five miles."

Will turned around and grinned at him, but Lennox's insides ached with a weird hollowness. One trip and then never again. They'd probably attach a second monitor and maybe handcuffs too.

"Lennox?"

"I'm fine."

Ben and Will exchanged a look, and Lennox found Ben's eyes on him in the rearview mirror. He didn't say anything else, but somehow his gaze said enough. He got it. Maybe not entirely and not in the same way Lennox did, but more than optimistic Will ever could.

His ankle monitor beeped, and the pace of the noise increased like a racing heart. Lennox was sweating by the time they turned into a parking lot by a large brown building. The sign out front identified it as the Culpeper Police Station and Courthouse. Will fixed Lennox's shirt and tie when they got out and smoothed down his shirt collar. He wasn't smiling, but his eyes beamed as they caught the weak morning sunlight.

"Let's go get your freedom back."

But he'd never be free, not really. He might be cut loose from a monitor if he was ludicrously lucky today, but not from his record or his decrepit little life or the future that meant absolute uncertainty no matter what decision he made.

Inside, they were walked through a metal detector and then directed toward a small room furnished with several stiff chairs and a table. It was clean as a hospital, but a sharp smell of paper and perfume filled the room. Ben and Will sat, but Lennox stayed on his feet and forced himself not to pace. His palms were slick and he could feel a bead of sweat work its way through the thick hair of his eyebrows. Will kept trying to start a conversation, but Lennox only managed a few feeble grunts. After ten minutes of waiting and watching the clock on the wall tick right past his appointment time, he saw the door finally open. But it wasn't a judge or a correctional officer or even a police officer to arrest him one more time.

It was his grandfather.

Ben stood to shake his hand, and Will sighed in apparent relief. Clearly, they thought he was some prick judge or whatever here to get this over with.

"What are you doing here?"

"Lennox, don't be rude."

Will gave him a pointed look, then paused. Something about Lennox's expression seemed to click the truth into place.

"How long is this going to take?" Ben asked after giving both of them a firm glare.

Cameron ignored him. Instead, he turned to Lennox and eyed his shirt and tie.

"Been a long time since I've seen you dressed so nicely," he said. "It's a nice change. I see the country's been doing you well."

"Well enough for a handful of beatings and a new fuck-buddy."

Will flinched at Lennox's side. "Boyfriend." He leveled his gaze at Cameron, who hadn't so much as blinked at Lennox's words. "I'm Will. This is my dad, Ben Osborne. And you—"

"My shit-tastic grandfather. If you've come back to apologize or dump me somewhere else, forget it."

"I'm here because my presence is required. I signed for you when your ankle monitor was put on. Even if you aren't a minor now, I'm still needed for paperwork."

"That's bullshit."

"*You're* his grandfather?"

Will was on his feet, his hands curled into fists at his sides.

"You left him at that terrible motel? With those assholes who almost—who tried to—"

A frown crossed Cameron's face as Ben stood and pushed Will down into his seat. Lennox snarled at his grandfather and joined Will.

"Forget him," he said to Will. "This is the last time I'm ever going to see him. Fuck him."

"Don't use that language—"

Ben planted his hefty bulk between them and Cameron. "I think you lost the right to tell Lennox what to do when you dumped him in the middle of nowhere."

Lennox leaned back enough to see his grandfather's sour expression. Nobody had ever defended him to Cameron before. Until a few months ago, he'd never had anyone who would. Well, his sister probably would, but she'd always been kept away from such moments.

"He's my grandson. I'd like to see you do any better with all the nonsense he's gotten himself into since he was little."

"I raised my boy right enough that's he's done a better job with Lennox in a few months than you have in years."

Ben gripped the back of Will's chair, and his hand trembled. Will stood to support him in case he got too weak, but the door opened once more and several official-looking people entered: two women, one in an officer's uniform and another in a sharp pantsuit, and one man with several folders in hand.

The woman in the pantsuit spoke first. "Good morning, everyone. Quite a full room today."

"Cameron McAvoy," his grandfather said. He shook all of their hands and then waved his own toward Lennox. "This is my grandson, Lennox. He's here to have his ankle monitor removed."

"I'm Martha Jordan. We're all set after a few forms," Ms. Jordan said. She smiled at Cameron and then frowned at Will and Ben. "And you are?"

"Will and Ben Osborne. Lennox has been living with us."

A long pause followed. Cameron looked astonished but tried to hide it. The officer and two clerks exchanged glances but said nothing. They sat and began asking Lennox a few questions, mostly demographic confirmations, and then about his current life situation.

"How's school going for you?"

"Okay, I guess." Lennox twisted in his seat. "Applied to college a few weeks ago."

"Oh? Where at?"

"One in Boston. For music."

He met his grandfather's stern gaze and swallowed. Cameron had never considered music a worthwhile endeavor. After Lennox's mother died, he'd berated her career constantly and scolded Lennox's father for allowing him to play. Not that his dad had cared by then; he'd doused himself in alcohol to hide from his depression and ended up with something much worse.

"That's great, Lennox," Ms. Jordan said. "Very impressive. I wish you well. Now, there was just one inquiry while you had your monitor. A few months ago you went out of range for a medical emergency, I believe?"

"Uh, yeah. I got, uh, harassed. It wasn't a big deal."

Ms. Jordan eyed Will, who had jerked in his chair. Lennox shut his eyes and crossed his fingers under the table that Will wouldn't say anything.

Will pushed his chair closer. "He was beaten, by these awful men that lived at the building he resided at. They chased him down the street with their pellet gun and... It was terrible."

Ms. Jordan frowned and scribbled a few notes on the page in front of her.

"Was there a reason for the altercation?"

"They were pissed I wanted to suck Will's dick and not theirs."

"Lennox Jacob—"

Cameron made to grab his arm, but Lennox knocked him away. "Shut up. You weren't even in the same county. I haven't seen *you* since—whatever. Can I just get this off and get out of here please?"

"So they beat you because you're homosexual?"

"Yes."

"And you did nothing verbal or physical to provoke them?"

"*No.*"

Ms. Jordan wrote for a few minutes and then swirled a loopy signature across the bottom of the page.

"Okay, Lennox, I just need you to initial where the red is, and then sign and date at the bottom. Mr. McAvoy, you just need to sign the bottom of that form and then fill out this release form for your grandson."

Lennox did so and in a few minutes his ankle monitor was undone and his right leg was paper light. Will hugged him when he stood up.

"We can go to New York for spring break now. And Boston. It's going to be so much fun!"

And so much money, but Lennox didn't mention that detail. Such things seemed so insignificant to Will.

Cameron finished signing the last form and stood as well.

"Is that everything?"

"Yes, sir. We'll keep an eye on him for another six months. Have an officer check in once in a while with his school to make sure he's having no more problems. If he has any arrests during the next year, however, he'll be back on probation or jailed."

Lennox made for the door. He wouldn't go back, or get that awful device strapped back on either. He was free. His leg felt so light it was difficult to walk; he kept swinging it forward too fast to make up for a weight that was no longer there.

In the hall, Will and then Ben caught up to him.

Will was grinning as he took Lennox's hand.

"Do you want to take a train or bus?"

Lennox shrugged. Right now he honestly just wanted to eat. Ben seemed to tune into that.

"What about lunch instead? You can plan a road trip this weekend."

"Oh, we *could* drive!"

"Do you really want to drive in New York City?" Lennox asked.

They passed through the metal detectors, and this time the guard even smiled at him. Will and Lennox waited for Ben to pass through, and Lennox spotted his grandfather approaching next.

"Is this really necessary? If I didn't carry anything in, then I'm certainly not carrying anything out."

The guard motioned Cameron through behind Ben. "Policy, sir. Plenty here to steal."

Cameron curled his lips and passed through. When he spotted Lennox with Will and Ben, he paused.

"I see you've found other arrangements with the—Oswalds, was it?"

Will's grip tightened on Lennox's hand, but Ben stepped forward again.

"Ben Osborne. I don't want you coming anywhere near him anymore. You've done enough harm already. How could you abandon him like that? Regardless of what he's done—"

"Mr. Osborne, it is none of your business how I raise my grandson. He's done wrong and he had to—"

"Horseshit. Stay away from my son and Lennox. He needs love and acceptance in his life, not whatever else you'll spew. Come on, guys."

Ben turned both of them away by their shoulders and led them out. They were halfway down the steps when Lennox spotted a puff of curly dark hair between two cars. It couldn't be. Cameron would never bring her along. He never wanted them to see each other again.

Lennox glanced at the door as his grandfather pushed it open. Perhaps he'd changed his mind and brought Lucy along as a reward. Maybe even out of guilt.

"Lennox, a word."

Ben made a motion to stop him, but Lennox pulled himself free from Will.

"Give us a minute." His eyes scanned the parking lot and spotted Lucy—surely it must be her, her prosthetic leg glinting in the sun—coming closer. She'd had a prosthetic leg since she was a toddler.

Thanks to their grandparents, they'd always been able to afford it, and Lucy had never batted an eye at the lesser expectations other people set at her feet. She bulldozed through all of them at full speed. Nothing had ever stopped her, and Lennox doubted anything ever would.

Will and Ben went down the steps to the sidewalk and the benches beside the courthouse. Lennox met his grandfather halfway. Cameron looked tired, a little more worn and thinner. His suit was looser around his torso and his pants seemed baggier.

"How've you been?"

Lennox sneered. "Seriously? You *dumped* me in that shithole and want to know how I've been? Just fucking dandy."

"That isn't... Look, I did what I thought was best for all of us. I'm glad you found somewhere better to stay. And, uh... I suppose he is your boyfriend?"

"What's it matter to you?"

Cameron didn't say anything. He reached his hand out for Lennox's shoulder and then seemed to think better of it.

"Lucy wants to see you. I told her I'd talk to you about it today, maybe have you down for a visit over spring break. Or bring her to your graduation in a few months."

"I think she's made the choice for herself."

Lennox had turned around just in time to see Lucy's round, brown face spot him from the bottom of the stairs. She'd grown. Her legs were as long as telephone poles and her shoulders looked bony and stretched the way his had as a preteen. She wore a private school uniform.

"Lennox!"

Lucy raced up the stairs and threw herself at him. Lennox caught her and tried to breathe but found that he couldn't. His baby sister. The girl he'd never expected to see again, not in this life or any other. Yet here she was, in his arms once more.

"I've missed you! Why can't I ever come visit? Grandma says all sorts of bad things about you, and then Grandpa tells me that you're sick, but I called all the hospitals and they say you aren't a patient, and—"

"I'm not sick. I... God, you've gotten tall."

Lucy stood back and planted her hands on her hips as she smiled. "I'm five-foot-one now. I'm going to beat you."

He laughed and tried not to choke from his tight throat. She was so much bigger, so much more grown up than the last time he'd seen her.

"I bet you will." He pressed his palm down against her afro and measured: she was almost at his chin now, and with her hair she was at his eye level. "I've still got about eight inches on you."

"Are you coming home with us today?"

Cameron finally seemed to find his voice. "Lucy Abigail McAvoy, what in the world are you doing here? You're supposed to be at school. How did you even *get* here?"

"I hid in the trunk."

"You did *what?*" Cameron pulled her away from Lennox as Will and Ben came back up the stairs.

"Is that your sister?"

Will reached for his hand once more as Lennox nodded. Lucy rolled her eyes as Cameron's lecture continued. Puberty was going to be a lot earlier for her than it had been for him. That same smartass attitude had already arrived.

"Whatever. You don't let me see Lennox and I'd rather not see *you.*"

"Young lady, you are not going to talk to me like that. You're working yourself for a very long grounding as it is."

"I want to see my brother! That's not a crime."

Cameron opened his mouth again, but Lennox cut him off.

"Five minutes?"

"You both need to be in school."

"I haven't seen my sister in over a year because of *you,*" Lennox said. "I'll probably never see her again if you have any say in it. Give us five damn minutes."

Cameron glared at him, but Lucy tugged at his arm.

"Let me see Lennox. *Please.*"

"Ten minutes. I'll be waiting in the car, and then you and I are going to have a very long discussion about this, Lucy."

Cameron went down the stairs, got into his car, and stared up at them. Lucy beamed at Lennox and hugged him around the middle again.

"This isn't the last time I'm going to see you, is it?"

"I don't know. I hope not."

Her smile faded. "I want to see you all the time again. And for you to come to my soccer games, *and* I'm thinking about trying volleyball next year in middle school. You've gotta be around for that."

"He... Grandma and Grandpa aren't going to let me, Luce. I'm an adult now, so I've got to grow up."

"That doesn't mean you have to leave home."

Lennox guided Lucy over to a bench and sat down with her.

"They don't want me at home, that's the problem. And you know I'd be around for you always if I could. Once you're grown up, we can see each other all the time again."

"But that's so far away. You'll miss *everything.*"

Lennox swallowed. "I don't want to."

"Then don't. Come home."

"Luce, I can't—"

He would have to tell her. Did Lucy even know what gay meant? Would she react the same way his grandparents had? Lucy loved him for everything he was—at least, he thought she did.

"Do you know... Um, you see that boy over there?"

"With the silly hair and the freckles?"

"Don't let him hear that. Will's fond of his new haircut."

Lucy crinkled her nose. "The sides of his head are *bald.*"

"Not entirely. That's Will. He's my... my boyfriend."

"So you, like, kiss each other?"

Lennox held his breath and nodded. Lucy made a face, and then her brow lowered.

"Boys have cooties," she told him. "But... Do cooties still work if you've both got boy cooties?"

"Nah, just like you can't catch them from me."

Lucy nodded and swung her legs. Her shoes were just out of reach of the ground. "I guess that's okay, then. His eyes are sparkly. Is he why you can't see me?"

"No." Lennox put his arm around her quickly, before any jealousy could work its way into her. She had always been mad when he spent time with someone else, as rare as that had been. Lennox had been all she'd had for a number of years. "It's not like that. It's that Grandpa and Grandma think I should like girls, that I shouldn't have a boyfriend. That's why I can't see you or come home anymore. They think that if you see me, I'll make you like me."

"But I am like you." Lucy stood up and kicked his shin. "I like boys too. So I can just come live with you."

"That's... No, Luce. That's not what I mean. I mean, you know how Mom and Dad loved each other and had you and me?"

Lucy frowned as she always did at the mention of their father, but she nodded.

"Well, a lot of people think only a girl and a boy can love each other and get married and have babies. Two boys can't have a baby the same way. Two girls can't either. They think it's wrong if you like someone who's your gender. Does that make sense?"

"No. I mean, yeah, but no. That's stupid. He's cute, and you're pretty okay too, and if he makes you smile and brings you cupcakes for breakfast then that's all that matters."

"Cupcakes?"

"Uh huh. Jimmy *was* bringing me Twinkies but then Micah brought in red velvet cupcakes his mom made, so now I play soccer with him at recess instead. Don't worry," she added when she saw Lennox's expression. "They know all about cooties and just want me to help them catch frogs 'cause they're too slow."

"Right. Well, if they ever try anything you don't like, I want you to aim that striker kick right where I taught you, okay?"

"Right in the balls."

Lucy giggled and then sniffed. She wrapped her arms around him again and didn't let go.

"I don't want to say goodbye."

"We won't, then." Lennox kissed her hair and hugged her tight. "We'll see each other again. I promise I'll find a way, okay? I won't be like Dad. I'll come back—"

"I hate him." Lucy pulled away and stood. Her large hands had curled into fists. "He ruined everything."

"He didn't. Dad was... I got the best of him. Me and Mom. He was just sad, Lucy. So sad he forgot how important we were to him."

"He was stupid like Grandpa."

Lennox swallowed. They'd never agreed about their father, and Lennox had his moments too. But he had memories of bedtime stories and Saturday mornings pretending to be dinosaurs and getting piggyback rides all around the house. Their father had been the best for a short time, and Lucy had missed every minute of it.

"Give me another hug before you go."

"I don't want to." But Lucy hugged him again. "I love you, Lennox."

"I love you too, Luce. I've missed you more than anything."

Will appeared at his side. "We can talk to you online if you have a computer. Facebook or Skype or something like that."

"Oh! I can do that! Grandma and Grandpa got me my own laptop for Christmas. They said it's for school, but I talk to Miranda and Jackie on there every night. Can we?"

Will nodded. "I'll show him how to do it."

Lucy beamed and hugged Will very quickly. "You're awesome." Then she turned back to Lennox. "You better keep him. I like him."

"I'm considering it. Let's go before you get into more trouble."

Lucy rolled her eyes as they headed downstairs. "Whatever. He can't hurt me. I'm their perfect little angel, remember?"

The words were a sudden weight in his stomach that practically pulled him down the stairs. Lucy had always been the better of them, according to their grandparents. Soon that could change. And if they caught her connecting with him online, who knew what might happen. At Cameron's car, Lucy hugged him once more.

"I'm LuckyLucy on Skype, okay?"

She whispered it in his ear as they hugged, and even then Lennox knew he'd never use it. Will might push, and it would break Lucy's heart, but if she got into more trouble because of him, or did something stupid or dangerous to try to see him, he'd never forgive himself.

"Love you. Be safe. Study hard and all of that. Play hard too."

"I will."

She climbed into the backseat and at Lennox's motion buckled up. Cameron rolled down the window as he backed up.

"We'll come down for your graduation in June. Even if... I still love you. Despite all of this. I don't want Lucy to lose her brother any more than I want to lose my grandson."

"You should have done a better job then."

Cameron looked away. He rolled the window up and drove away.

Another Lucy gone from his life, this one more important. An ache filled Lennox's chest. He wasn't going to see Lucy again, not online or at his graduation or any other time after that. No force on earth would ever bring them back together again, no matter what Cameron said.

"Are you okay?"

"I'm fine. Let's get out of here before they slap something else on my ankle."

The entire drive back to Leon was heavy. With the radio turned off, silence filled the truck. Will had joined his dad up front while

Lennox huddled alone in the back. Every street sign seemed to flash with his sister's name, every passenger in a passing car or person on the street was a mirage of her features. No more sister, no more friend, and soon, so terribly soon, no more Will either. Everyone left. Nobody ever knew how to stay behind with him.

Lennox, Will, and Ben stopped to eat at a diner in town before heading back home. Ben drove them right past Eastern, and when Lennox checked the radio clock he realized why. It was early afternoon already. When they pulled up, Karen was going up the steps with the mail and a bag of groceries.

"How'd it go?"

Lennox tugged up the leg of his pants, and she grinned.

"Oh, congratulations, honey. That's great. I bet it feels even better."

"Well, not as good as a blowjob, but I'm not going to complain today."

Karen listened as Will filled her in on their day, and when he got to the part about Lucy he paused.

"Lennox's sister was there too. She sort of snuck her way into the car."

Karen looked up from sorting through the mail. "How is she? Did you get to spend some time with her?"

"Good. A few minutes."

"We're going to get in touch online. I never thought about it before. I didn't think a ten-year-old would have Facebook."

"Eleven. Well, eleven in a few months. Can we go in? It's freezing out here."

Once they were inside, Karen went back to sorting through the mail while they pulled off coats and hats.

"Here's the water bill, Ben. And oh, that's mine. Phone bill. We really need to add a line for you, Lennox."

"No, that's okay. I wouldn't know how to use it any—"

"Oh, my god."

Everyone paused as Karen pulled a large envelope from the wad in her hand. Stamped across the front in big blue letters was one word: Congratulations!

"It's for you," Karen said as she held it out to Will. "From NYU."

Will's hand shook as he slit it open. He read the first page, and when he met Lennox's eyes he had tears in his own.

"I got in. They offered me a scholarship, too. Not much, but it'll probably cover whatever your savings won't, Dad."

Ben wrapped him up a big hug. "Congrats, bud. I'm so proud. My college boy."

"I'm going to New York," Will said with his eyes still on the papers. "I'm really going, even if Sarah Lawrence says no. I'm going!"

Karen hugged Lennox as well, and he took a shaky breath.

"I told you you'd get in. Never doubted you."

"We've got so much planning to do now for our trip," Will said. He hugged Lennox and smiled through his tears. "I've got to go call Roxanne and Aaron and Natasha."

He raced off into the living room, and Lennox stood there, slowly peeling his jacket off while Karen and Ben gushed over the news.

Everyone always left, and when they did they never came back. No matter what they said or did or thought, nobody came back once they were gone. Not even Will.

⏸ eighteen ⏵

Euphoria dominated the next week and a half of Will's life. He talked of little else besides New York, and when he did it was about the other schools in the area he'd applied to. Every lunchtime he gathered around a table with his friends—Lennox at his side every other day when their lunches coincided—while they discussed the letters that were starting to flood their mailboxes.

Aaron had an acceptance letter from the university in Charlottesville, and another from a school out of state that had a fantastic baseball program. Roxanne had the most, at seven. Will wasn't surprised, since she'd applied to almost every school in Virginia, but she was very pleased with her record of acceptance so far. Natasha had gotten three letters back from schools near Washington, DC—one denial, one acceptance, and one offering a place on the wait list.

Otto and Lennox were the only free-floaters left, and it took until the week of Valentine's Day before the two failed to show up for lunch one day. Nobody else noticed, but after Will finished his pizza he stood up and searched the room. No bright red and yellow hoodie, and no head of thick curls that matched Lennox's now shoulder-length tangles.

"Have any of you guys seen Otto and Lennox?"

Roxanne shrugged and continued to eat. Natasha shook her head. "Lennox was in math earlier."

Aaron chewed and swallowed the last of his own pizza. "Isn't that him over there?"

Will turned to where Aaron nodded. Lennox was leaning against the far wall next to the bathroom and Otto's bulk was bent over the water fountain.

"Has Lennox applied anywhere?"

Will turned back to Roxanne.

"Berklee. It's a music school in Boston. I'm really hoping he gets in."

"Oh, he'd be great as a music major," Natasha said. "He plays so beautifully. Does he have to audition?"

"Yeah, in a few weeks. He's been staying after with Mr. Robinette when I have baseball. I forget the name of the piece he picked. Something jazzy, I think."

Will kept watching Lennox and Otto as lunch drew to a close. They stayed near the bathrooms and didn't so much as glance Will's way. Was Otto applying to colleges too? Will had never asked, but now that he thought back over the last few weeks, both boys had slowly been drifting away from them. They showed up late or left early or went to the bathroom for most of their short twenty minutes together. Some days they said the lunch line had taken too long, but the absence of trays in their hands said otherwise. Will was glad Lennox had found another friend besides Lucy, but it worried him too. Otto had never been motivated. He was just there, a fly on the wall that went where it was safest. So much about the next year of Lennox's life was undecided, and Otto didn't seem to be offering any alternative solutions.

Lennox greeted Will at the table when the bell ended lunch.

"Ready for chemistry?"

"Sure. Want to review one more time before the test?"

"Nah, I've got this. I'll quiz you, though."

Will nodded and Lennox ran through his stack of flashcards. They took their test to end the third quarter of the school year and left for home. In his truck, Will blasted the heat and waited for the dusting of snow and ice that had fallen during the day to melt. He didn't know where to start with questions for Lennox. Every time he brought up college, it seemed as though he was shoving Lennox into a superheated, lethal spotlight. College should be wonderful and exciting, but Lennox only seemed to dread it.

"How's your audition piece going?"

Lennox shrugged and bumped elbows with him. "Let's fuck when we get home."

"We can have sex if Dad's not around. Or blowjobs. What are you playing again?"

"It's this jazz song. Took me a while to get the groove of it right, but it's pretty poppy. Something classical too, since that's so easy for me. Mr. Robinette said there would be some sight-reading and a few other tasks they'd run me through before I fuck up the interview."

"You won't. I'll start coaching you this weekend."

"Won't you be busy with your friends again? You know, with all those colleges you guys are going to."

Will bit his lip as he backed out of the parking lot and drove toward his house. Of course Lennox was concerned about that. He hadn't even auditioned, and the rest of them were deciding which school to accept for the next four years.

"No, I'm just waiting for the rest of the responses now. Then I've got to decide which one I'm accepting."

Lennox nodded and remained silent until they were home and in Will's room. By the time their shoes and coats were off and Will was stretched out on his bed, he realized Lennox's jaw was clenched tight and his hands were shoved into his pockets.

"You okay?"

"Fine. Just thinking." Lennox kicked at the end of the bed and sat. "When would you leave? For college, I mean."

"Um, August, I guess. Maybe earlier if I joined, like, the baseball team or something."

Lennox nodded, more to himself than Will, and lay back beside him.

"So Valentine's Day is on Thursday," Will said. "I was thinking we could do dinner. Here or out somewhere since we can go all over town now."

He reached out to rub Lennox's now bare ankle and squeezed air instead.

"Valentine's Day?"

Lennox jumped up and began to pace.

"Yeah, we don't have to do anything big. I mean, so much else has been going on and it's only our first one."

"Right, right." Lennox paced the room once, then twice. "Are we, um, supposed to get each other, like, gifts or something? Does a blowjob count?"

Will sat up too. "I mean, I was hoping for some nudity at some point, but I haven't really thought about presents either. We can just spend time together. Just us. That's a good present, right?"

Lennox's entire body drooped in relief. He rejoined Will on the bed.

"Yeah, that's... I mean, I don't even know what to get you. You've got *everything*."

Lennox gestured around his room and Will followed the movement. Books, more movies than the movies section at Walmart, posters, and gadgets everywhere. He did have a lot, but they were just things. Most of them didn't have any real meaning beyond brief enjoyment. But Will shared Lennox's sentiment. What did you get the boy who'd had so little and wished, more than anything, to see his sister again?

Will had thought about Lucy quite a bit since Lennox's trip to Culpeper. She'd been precious, a lot bigger than Will had expected, but still so much like Lennox. She'd been brought back only to be whisked away for what might really be forever. He couldn't rectify that for Lennox on his own.

"We'll spend the day together, after school I mean. Come home, make dinner, watch a movie. Get a little naked—"

"Or a lot. I'm a fan of a lot."

Will laughed and settled down next to Lennox with his laptop. He opened it to the history paper he'd almost finished yesterday and then clicked over to his iTunes. Having shuffled songs going seemed to calm Lennox enough to work. He'd figured that out since they returned to school after the New Year. It also didn't take Lennox more than one play to figure out half of the lyrics and tunes. His knack to pick up music only seemed to grow the more he listened.

Today his laptop started with a movie score, and Lennox snickered.

"You *would* have the *Jurassic Park* soundtrack."

"It's a good theme song!"

As the music began to swell to the main theme, Lennox kneeled over him and sang, swaying his arms like a drunken conductor.

"Da da daaaaa daaaaa daaaaa! Da da daaaaa—"

Will elbowed him in the stomach, and Lennox toppled over and then tackled him. They wrestled, tickling each other's ribs, laughter catching in their throats. Will was out of breath when they collapsed beside each other. A new song had begun, and Lennox pressed his face into Will's neck.

"Is this a Valentine's Day preview?"

His voice was hopeful, and Will smiled. Enjoyment, even now, seemed so unreasonably rare for Lennox. It flickered more than a candle with a dying wick fighting against a harsh, unceasing wind.

"Maybe." Will ran a teasing finger over Lennox's arm and then settled his laptop back on his lap. "Come on. We've got to get this homework done. Unless you'd rather spend Valentine's Day watching me write papers and fill out worksheets."

Lennox groaned and rolled enough for Will to free his arm. "Ugh, worksheets are such bullshit."

"No more of these in college. That's what Karen said."

"Speaking of Karen—"

"I'm not talking to her."

"Will, she's your m—"

"She isn't my mom." Will shoved Lennox away and started typing gibberish just to look busy.

Lennox hummed as he grabbed his backpack from the floor. "I'm sure your dad's relationships with your mom and Karen are both different, but they've both been his wife."

Will gritted his teeth and didn't say anything else. Beside him, Lennox ran through his calculus, French, and several overdue history worksheets. After almost an hour of silence, and nothing but one badly worded sentence to show for it, Will clicked to his music and scrolled for a better song.

"Aw, I liked that one."

"You don't even know who it's by."

"Doesn't mean I can't like it."

He settled on a pop punk band, a piano version of one of his favorites that he'd discovered yesterday evening while Lennox was in the shower. Lately, Will had made a point of finding piano covers and mixing them into his music for days such as this. Lennox always got a kick out of them, and it was a nice break to sit back against his headboard while Lennox scribbled out the music on a notebook and replayed it until he had the tune transcribed.

"Who's this?"

"Panic! At the Disco. They're really good. Even Dad likes them. Karen too, and she only listens to country."

Lennox tugged the laptop away from him and put the song on repeat. Will breathed a sigh of relief as Lennox went about his transcribing. He shouldn't be so glad to distract him, but talking to Karen seemed every bit as impossible as catching a dream in his hands, evaporating from the moment he was awake enough to remember any part of its existence.

"Stop frowning. You want smile lines when you're old, not frowny ones."

Lennox reached over and pressed his pointer fingers against each end of Will's lips and turned them up.

"Better. Now smile with your eyes too."

Will did smile then. Lennox's dorkiness could be infectious, but with two pencils jabbed into his hair and a wad of bubblegum wedged into his cheek he was beautiful. Will kissed him gently on the lips.

"I love you."

"You too, nerd. Take your laptop away or I'm never getting this other stuff done and I *really* want your dick tonight."

Will snorted and kissed Lennox again.

He saw Karen briefly the next morning as he passed through the living room and into the kitchen. She nodded at him with a bagel in her mouth, but as always these days, her delight didn't reach her eyes. Did she not want him at all anymore? Was he not good enough to be her son?

Will sat down to eat alone. Lennox joined him for a quick stack of toast, and then they returned to school. For the next two days he didn't see Karen. She was working overtime and overnight to get Valentine's Day off. His dad returned to short shifts for the two days leading up to it, and report cards for the third quarter were handed out Thursday morning. Everyone groaned as Mr. Robinette made the announcement at the front of the band room after the morning pledge.

"Oh, hush. They aren't due until Monday when I see you guys again. So you can all still have your romance tonight and then the weekend and ruin your lives on Sunday when it's your last chance to get them signed before we meet again. Okay?"

A few people perked up, and some laughed. Will took his without complaint, but Natasha grimaced and Lennox frowned. Behind them, Otto ripped his open and shrugged.

"Well, I'm not failing anything."

Lennox leaned back to glance at Otto's report card. "Since when is a D minus passing?"

"Whatever. I'm joining the army once I'm eighteen. They won't care as long as I graduate."

"The army?"

An alarm went off in Will's head at the note of interest in Lennox's voice.

"You don't want to do that," he said quickly. "You'd hate the army, Lennox. Otto will, too."

Otto snorted. "Whatever, Osborne. Your *dad* was in the military."

Will tugged Lennox around when Mr. Robinette handed him his report card. Lennox opened it, and, while he didn't smile, his lips quirked as if he wanted to.

"Better?"

Will leaned over and smiled. Four A's, two B's, and two C's. It wasn't as good at his own, but it was a vast improvement. Lennox was going to be all right. He had a home to live in and his sights set on a college of his choice. That was all he'd ever needed, just a little direction to get his life onto a track instead of a stationary platform.

"That's great. Now you can give it to Karen or Dad to sign instead of throwing it away again."

Lennox shrugged and tucked it into his backpack. He turned back to Otto and spent all of band asking him about the army and what he was going to be doing, and then what his mother thought of it. Will listened in as best as he could while Mr. Robinette went over the arrangement for their set list for the spring concert in a few months and took ideas for what everyone had liked from the year so far.

All day, Will wondered how anyone, especially Lennox, could show any interest in the military. Lennox couldn't follow rules for more than five minutes, he rarely did anything he was told that he didn't like, and he was *gay*. Being gay in the military was a terrible idea, but maybe Lennox didn't know that.

After school they skipped baseball and Lennox's piano time with Mr. Robinette and headed home. The house was already empty except for Oyster, who greeted them briefly and then returned to the couch where a large patch of white fur had already been shed from a daylong nap.

"So sex or dinner first?"

"How about sex and then dinner and then more sex?"

Lennox grinned at the suggestion and shrugged his jacket just off his shoulders. He winked and tried to toss his hair but the bloom of curls barely moved.

Will giggled but stepped forward anyway. "Dork."

"Only for you."

Lennox led him downstairs with one hand hooked into the waistband of Will's jeans. As Lennox's kisses along his throat and jaw became more aggressive, Will's thoughts turned to earlier. He couldn't help it, despite the arousal coursing through him and the warm hand rubbing over his cock through his jeans.

"Can we talk about something first? Just real quick?"

Lennox breathed deeply but stepped back. "This conversation isn't going to kill my hard-on, is it? Because that's going to make what I want to do difficult."

"No, it's just earlier. When Otto was talking about the army, you weren't thinking of joining too, were you?"

"What? Why would I want to join the army?"

"You just seemed interested."

"Well, he's my friend, isn't he? Would you rather I tell him he's stupid for living his life how he wants to?"

"No, no. Just... Never mind. I was being stupid. Back to kissing?"

Lennox tackled him to the bed as an answer. They spent over an hour downstairs together, Will stretched out on the bed, with Lennox thrusting into him and gently pressing his legs farther apart just to see how flexible he was and what he enjoyed most. Will shook when he came, and spots blacked out his vision. Lennox's lips trailed over his stomach, up his ribs, wrapped around one nipple until he jerked and then went up to his lips.

"Lovely boy," Lennox said against his lips. "I love watching you fall apart."

Will whimpered and shut his eyes. He woke again when the room was dim, with his favorite fluffy blanket tucked around him and Oyster's snuffling doggy snores at the foot of the bed. The door to the stairs opened just as he sat up to stretch and Lennox appeared with a tray in hand.

"About time. You're such an orgasm addict."

Lennox sat down with him and set the tray on their laps. Breakfast. Scrambled eggs with cheese and what looked like shredded hash browns. "Hope you want breakfast. I checked out that recipe you were going to make, but half of it was gibberish to me, so I made breakfast for dinner. I already taste-tested it, too. Happy Valentine's Day."

Will ate the first bite of eggs Lennox offered him and smiled. They weren't like the eggs Ben made, but they were good.

"Not bad. Dad's are better."

"Well I haven't had access to a stove *and* eggs in about four years, so forgive me if I'm a little rusty."

They continued to eat, but Lennox's words stayed with Will through their eggs and hash browns.

"It must have been awful, being locked up in there with those other guys. And all of the—the things they did to you?"

Lennox shrugged and shoved the last forkful of hash browns into Will's mouth.

"Wasn't pleasant, but whatever. It's over. But you and me, well, I've still got plans tonight for us. Unless you have some that are better."

Will let the subject drop once again, but the more it was brushed off, the more the questions built and lingered. So much must have happened behind those doors and bars, and if Lennox still wasn't willing to speak of that time—after every other thing he'd told Will— then it must have been horrible.

"No, I figured I'd let you lead today. That was my plan."

Lennox grinned and set the tray aside. He nudged Will until he was lying down once more and traced his tongue along his collarbone.

"So I get to decide again?"

"Mmm, yeah. I like giving you the reins."

"Thought you liked fucking me more?"

"Sometimes."

Lennox grinned against his neck and kissed his way down it, then up Will's throat until his toes curled into the blankets. Will shut his eyes and let Lennox move around him, applying kisses to his neck and his chest, then several long languid sucks on his left nipple.

"Keep doing that," Will said. He ran his fingers through Lennox's hair and tried to move him to his other nipple, but Lennox refused. "Both need attention."

"You'll get it." Lennox dragged his teeth over Will's left nipple again. "Your nipples are so sensitive, they deserve more than a few seconds."

"So does my di—oh god!"

His nipple was tugged hard by Lennox's teeth, then soothed briefly with his tongue before being twisted gently to the right and then harder to the left. Will's body throbbed at the burst of heat that blazed under Lennox's mouth.

"See?"

"Get your mouth to the other side and do that again."

Lennox laughed and repeated his actions with more certainty this time. The tugs were sharper, the sucks greedier. Will groaned and shifted beneath him; his cock grew hard against the heat of Lennox's body pressing him down. A finger brushed over his hip and then dipped between his legs to rub his still-slick hole.

"How much do you need?"

Will raised his head to glance down his torso at Lennox. One finger pressed into him with ease. Lennox grinned at him and nodded toward the condoms and lube they'd left on the nightstand. He passed them to Lennox as a second finger pushed into him. With a groan, Will spread his legs and breathed deeply.

"A little bit, then," Lennox said, his breath heating the inside of Will's thighs. "You get so tight so fast."

"Not my fault you would rather—oh god—make breakfast than fuck me."

Lennox laughed and pressed a third finger in. Will arched into the stretch, the slight burn that came with it that still tingled with pleasure. As Lennox crooked his fingers and thrust, Will ripped open a condom. His body shook. Until a few weeks ago, they'd had sex once and gone to sleep or dressed before someone came home. But Ben was at work, and Karen's schedule kept her out most afternoons. Now they could explore more, take a break, and then experience each other in a new way. Or continue in ecstasy all afternoon.

"Ready?"

"Condom?"

"Hand it over, dork."

Lennox snatched it away from him, and soon Will felt Lennox's cock press between his cheeks. He rubbed against Will's hole, and then Will gasped as he thrust in, slowly at first and then hard.

"You're always so... Fuck."

Lennox pulled his hips back and thrust forward. Will was jolted up the bed a bit, one hand closing around his cock, not to stroke himself but to squeeze to keep himself from coming immediately. He was always on edge whenever they went for a second round, particularly if that second round meant he was spread open with Lennox fucking him and holding his thighs apart.

Will panted as Lennox found a steady pace and attempted to coax him down. As thrilling as it was to bottom, sometimes Will couldn't get into it. Lennox distanced himself when he topped, stayed back on his knees or took Will from behind. It was only when Lennox was spread out on the bed beneath Will that he truly came apart, and even then he seemed to hold himself back.

"Kiss me."

Lennox's thrusts slowed and then stopped. Will gripped Lennox's forearms tightly and forced himself not to drag him down to him.

"I can't fuck you as hard down there," Lennox said, with a very hard and pointed thrust. "There's a lot less leverage when we're chest to chest."

"That's fine." Will gave Lennox's arm a gentle pull and after a second Lennox lowered himself down to hover closer. "I'd rather kiss you and go slow this time. You fucked me so hard earlier I could do with some kissing."

Lennox still hesitated, but he tucked his forearms under Will's shoulders and settled his weight onto Will's chest. As Will tilted his head up, Lennox shifted a little and missed the kiss aimed for his lips.

"Sorry. So you want to kiss?"

Will nodded even as he caught sight of the uncertainty in Lennox's eyes. Lennox's lips brushed his. Will smiled and nibbled on Lennox's lip. It took coaxing, but Lennox's body relaxed with every kiss and swipe of their tongues against each other.

"Okay?"

Lennox hummed against his lips and arched his hips back. As he thrust in, Will gasped; his hands clutched Lennox's hair and held him down for a deeper kiss. It wasn't the vocal answer Will had hoped for, but he felt too good to press for more. Lennox kissed him deeply; their noses brushed and their chins bumped. Will shut his eyes as Lennox found a new rhythm, different from any other they'd tried. He could feel all of Lennox's body working to roll his hips, to please him in ways he was still learning to understand and control.

"I love you," Will said against his lips.

Lennox groaned, a deep groan that reverberated throughout his body and rumbled into Will's. He stilled, and, despite the condom, Will could feel him coming. It wasn't like Lennox to lose himself so quickly, not in any position or angle they'd tried. Will reached for his own cock, intent on stroking himself to orgasm because of how strong the tremors were along Lennox's back and arms. But a small hiccup from Lennox stopped him.

"Lennox? What's—"

Lennox raised his head and Will was startled to see what could only be tears in the corners of his eyes. Or sweat. He supposed sweat could find its way there.

"I'm fine," Lennox said, but his voice cracked, and he shook his head vigorously. "Sorry. Let me finish you—"

"No, that's okay. I mean, I came so hard earlier I'd probably go into a coma with this one."

Lennox leaned back and slid out of him. He got up and busied himself with taking the condom off and wiping his face on his forearms. Will watched him pace for a few minutes as he wrapped the sheets around himself.

"Are you okay?"

"Fine." Lennox paced toward the stairs and then back toward the closet. "Just had something in my eye, that's all."

"Right. Sure."

Will snuggled down, and Lennox continued to pace. After several moments he slowed down, his breathing seemed more steady and gentle, and his eyes were clear. Or were they glazed and covered, like so much else about him?

Lennox dropped down next to him, but didn't speak. It was only when Will reached out and took his hand that he seemed to come back to himself.

"Sorry. About *that*. Can we not—"

"Do that again?" Will shrugged weakly. "I liked it. I mean, I want to know what you thought and why you—why you're crying."

"I'm not—I just... It gets to me." Lennox rolled his shoulders. "Being that close. Like when you top... It's overwhelming."

"A good overwhelming or a bad one?"

"Both? Does it matter?"

"Yeah, because I like being that intimate with you. Not *every* time, but sometimes I want to feel so connected with you there's no difference between you and me and where one of us stops and the other begins. It's a little scary, but being vulnerable with you is worth the fear because I know you'll give me something wonderful to make up for it."

Lennox lay back down. Will tossed one of the blankets over him and, after a few moments, he curled up behind Lennox and held him.

"I'm not used to being held," Lennox said. "My parents used to, but I barely remember that. Lucy was, well, she's my baby sister. It was always my job to hold her, not the other way around."

"I want to hold you. Only when you want or need me to, and when you don't that's okay too. You've just got to tell me."

Lennox wiggled and inched back toward him. Will tightened his arm around Lennox's chest and kissed the back of his neck.

"And right now?"

"I'd like it if you held me."

"I'd like it too."

Lennox sighed and shut his eyes, but it didn't end there for Will. So much *was* wrong, would remain wrong for a long while, perhaps forever, in the darkest crevasses of Lennox's life. No matter how well Lennox could fit into the ideal future Will envisioned, much of his past still managed to leak out. He wasn't perfect—and Will would never ask him to be—but he was damaged and refused to talk about all that had gone wrong and made him who he was now. The violence with which Lennox tried to free himself from all connections and emotion, tried not to face what might rupture every dam he'd ever built around himself, frightened Will.

"I love you," Will said, and the only response he got was gentle breathing and the steady beat of Lennox's heart against his palm.

⟨⟩ nineteen ⟨⟩

THE MORNING AFTER VALENTINE'S DAY, it took Karen the better part of an hour to wake the boys. She shook them and the bed, had to shut her eyes as she whipped their blankets off after twenty minutes, and then returned with her hands over her eyes at forty minutes to attempt to pull the mattress right off the bed. All she managed to do was slide it a few feet until it drooped on Will's side, but it was enough to send them rolling toward the floor.

"Up! You've got school in twenty minutes and you both need showers. Get moving!"

Lennox groaned from under the blankets, and Will, half off the bed and snarling, hurled a pillow at her.

"Up or you're both grounded."

Will huffed but started to move. Lennox, however, flopped back down.

"You can't ground me," he said more to his pillow than Karen. "You're Will's mom, not mine."

Karen bristled. She'd be lying to herself if Lennox's words didn't ache all the way from her ears to her chest. What kind of mother could she be, after the experiences her own mother had put her through, especially to a young man who would soon be an adult?

"But I can refuse to let you sleep down here with Will. Ben will be quite thrilled if I started enforcing that rule."

Lennox shot up like a spring. "You wouldn't."

"I would. Test me and find out the hard way. Shower and get to school. If you're late, you're both grounded to separate beds all weekend."

"But—"

"Eighteen minutes."

Will and Lennox bolted into the bathroom. Karen returned to the living room and not five minutes later the boys were dripping wet but dressed and ready. They each grabbed a few pieces of toast from the kitchen and almost flew out of the house. She listened to Will's truck start up and then peel out of the driveway, popping gravel and splashing mud as it went.

Ben sat down beside her. "They finally get up?"

"Yeah, and I already called in to tell the school they'd be late."

"They're going to be so mad at you for that." Ben chuckled and sipped the coffee she'd already poured him. "Mmm, good choice. What flavor was this one?"

"French vanilla dark roast. I added some cinnamon to yours."

"You can't cook, but you make the absolute best coffee."

"That's why you married me."

"Part of the reason. One of many." Ben took another sip and kissed her cheek.

Karen settled in with the television for the morning. Oyster curled up at her feet and, except for one furious text from Will about her calling school without telling them, she had a quiet day. Malia was at work, and her other friends were either sleeping off an overnight shift or spending the day at their jobs. She called her brother, just to check in and see about spending a vacation together in the summer with his kids. Will and Lennox would enjoy having some other teenagers around before they headed off to college, and John's oldest was just finishing her sophomore year at James Madison University. Katie would have a bunch of information for Will—and, she hoped, Lennox—about their first semester in college.

She worked on bills and took Oyster for a walk and was considering a nap when Will and Lennox pulled up. Karen watched them through the living room window. Jackets slung over their shoulders, backpacks still tossed in the truck bed, they were laughing, and Will dove for Lennox and wrapped him up in his arms.

They were so sweet together, yet so much still stood in their way. Colleges and graduation, separation, and a past Lennox kept so mute about. That didn't even cover the most basic relationship problems all couples faced: communication, personal space, and individual growth. Yet they would have those problems too. Perhaps they were already facing them without Karen's knowledge.

As they came tumbling into the hall, still laughing and joking, Karen took her seat on the couch.

"How was school, boys?"

Will glared at her. "It would have been better if you'd mentioned we didn't have to *rush*."

"And give you two a reason to stop for a make-out? I'm not that stupid, Will."

Lennox grinned and kissed Will's cheek. "Come on, babe. It was fun. Like a quickie in the afternoon before anyone gets home."

Will frowned. "We haven't done that yet, but I guarantee it was decidedly less fun."

"Well, maybe Karen should go down the road to, um, talk to that nosy bitch neighbor of yours."

"Nobody ever, willingly, talks to Meredith," Will said. "Even she doesn't want to talk to herself. That's why she's always trying to talk to everyone else."

Karen grimaced at the mention of their closest neighbor.

The boys disappeared into the kitchen. Karen listened to them rummaging around in the pantry and the slice of a knife against the cutting board. She had to do this now, before both of them got too distant from this to ever bring it up again.

"Will?"

Both of them poked their heads in.

"What's up?"

Lennox nudged Will and headed toward Will's bedroom door.

"I'll just go down to your room. You know, have a snack, strip myself naked, rub lube all over my—"

"*Lennox!*"

Karen chuckled as Lennox darted down the stairs. But then she was alone with Will and this chasm that had cracked open between them over the past few months. Will fiddled with the sandwich in his hand.

Karen patted the cushion next to her and, after a little hesitation, Will joined her. Neither of them looked at each other.

"I think you know what this is about," Karen said.

Will twisted his hands and set his sandwich on his thigh. "I'm sorry I called you Mom. I didn't mean to. You're just my stepmom and I know that. That's what you've always been, right?"

Those words were all Karen had wanted to hear. She'd wanted this argument settled for months now, had never expected to have such a conversation with Will at all. As a younger boy, Will had always called her Karen. In the beginning, he'd even made a point of enunciating "Mom" extra clearly whenever he mentioned his mother. That, more than anything, had calmed Karen about meeting Will and spending time with him, about becoming a stepmother to that lanky little nine-year-old.

"Right. That's what we've always been. Karen and Will, and that's good. I don't want to take your mother's place, Will."

"You aren't. You're... we're okay now?"

Even as Karen nodded and watched Will head downstairs, her stomach twisted. After so many months of avoiding the discussion, this didn't feel okay. She didn't want to be a mother—not a real one—but somehow this didn't seem right. Will had seemed okay, but she was also certain she'd disappointed him. Or maybe herself?

An ache filled Karen's chest. As much as she didn't get along with her own mother—as many years as she'd spent despising her while she was in college and then away in New York City—she still couldn't imagine her life without her mother. She might have been terrible most of the time, but she'd had her gentle moments, too, helping with homework and tending cuts and bruises, that long trip to the hospital when Karen had broken her arm falling off the barn roof at a family reunion. Will had had none of that. Not with Beth or her. His earliest moments were only with Ben, and, while that was still wonderful, it left a hole to realize he could have shared so much with another person, too.

Lennox poked his head around Will's still-open bedroom door. "You two have a nice chat finally?"

"We talked. It's fine."

Lennox shrugged and joined her on the couch. "I'm glad you finally talked to him. I've been working at him for weeks, and after that one time he refused to say anything to you."

"Do you think you'll have kids someday? Will said you were really good with your sister."

She said it before she thought her words through. Lennox was the last person to go to for advice on this. He was just a kid, but he must feel the same as she did. Being a parent after having shitty parents wasn't appealing, no matter how wonderful the kids were.

Lennox flinched. "No. I'm not fucking up a kid the same way my parents did."

"You aren't fucked up."

Lennox snorted. "Bullshit. I'm lucky I'm not living on the street and addicted to drugs or booze. If I had a kid, fuck, I'd go the same way as one of them. Maybe both. I'm not doing that shit to a kid."

Another obstacle for Will and Lennox. Judging by the look in his eyes, Lennox would stick to his word. Will had never told her his future parenthood plans, but he'd mentioned how he'd take his kids back to some place they'd visited, or how he'd make his own baby clothes when they were little.

"What happened? With your mother and father, I mean. Will told me a little bit, but you never talk about either of them."

"She died when I was little, slit her own wrists. I found her on their bedroom floor. Dad came home and found me and her, started drinking, and didn't quit until he stopped breathing."

Lennox's bluntness caught her off guard. He'd always been a little over the top, speaking for shock value instead of truth, but Karen had no doubt about the honesty of these words.

"Lennox, I—"

"Forget it. Happened a long time ago. You want me to bully Will into making dinner or order out?"

"It's been his turn to cook all week," Karen said. "We'll get him to make something."

She watched Lennox stand and stretch. A rolled up piece of paper in one of his pockets caught her eye. Musical notes were visible on it.

"Is that for your audition?"

Lennox glanced down and pulled it free.

"Oh, no. Something new for the spring concert or something. I've already got my audition stuff set."

"But you're still practicing, right?"

Lennox shrugged. "I've mastered it. I'm still playing after school. The piano in the garage is out of tune, so I use the one in the band room while Will's at baseball practice."

"Is that something you can fix by, um, ear or do we have to call someone out to look at it?"

"I don't know. I've never tried."

Lennox folded the music and shoved it deeper into his pocket.

"It doesn't matter anyway. No matter how well I play, I'll blow the interview."

"That's not true. What are they going to ask you about? I can help, so can Will."

Lennox didn't seem to be listening. "It doesn't matter how well I prepare or what they ask. I'll still—" He gestured as if projectile vomiting.

"You won't if you really do want this."

That was the real question, one that Karen didn't think Will had bothered to ask. She adored Will, but he was so hyped up about graduating and college that the idea of Lennox taking another path didn't seem to cross his mind. His way was the only direction to take, and Lennox had been corralled into it. Trapped. Lennox never took well to being cornered, and Karen's only hope was that it didn't all blow up in their faces.

"Will's really excited about it."

That was the last answer Karen wanted to hear. Will was why he was applying and why he was going through with this audition. It wasn't for himself. They were already turning down the wrong road, but it wasn't for her to stop them. They had to make their own mistakes.

"It's only a good idea for you to apply if *you're* excited about it too."

"I am! I mean... I don't know. It all sounds like such a dream to study music. College always seemed like another planet... Maybe I won't. But Will's right. It's worth it to try. I should like myself enough to take that chance, shouldn't I?"

His eyes were still uncertain, but a shadow left his face for a moment. Will's influence had done that. Maybe Lennox wouldn't go to Berklee or any college at all. He was trying something new, something to expand his knowledge and future. Karen couldn't fault that.

"Yeah, you should always try new things. It's a good habit to have. But I want you to remember something, okay? And this is important."

"As important as proper lubrication before—"

"Lennox, I need you to be serious for a minute."

Lennox rolled his eyes but he faced her.

"No matter what, you should never give up or change who you are for someone else. Especially someone you love dearly. And I don't mean little changes or compromises like which way the toilet paper roll faces or where to put the shoes by the front door, I mean the core parts of yourself. Don't ever let go of yourself for someone else."

Lennox gave her a quizzical look as he stood up.

"Um, right. I'll keep that in mind. Thanks."

He headed downstairs and Karen was left alone. None of that had gotten through to Lennox, but maybe part of it would linger until he needed it most. She'd have to share that same advice with Will soon. Time would tell how well they would work out together, and, while part of Karen was rooting for *them*, the rest of her was rooting for Will and Lennox as individuals. Lennox, especially, needed a champion for himself.

⏪ twenty ⏩

"COME ON, WILL! KEEP YOUR hands on the—"

"Eye," Otto said with a snort. "Keep your eye on the ball."

"Uh, right."

Lennox turned back to the field and the first pre-season game. That much he was certain about. Everything else was beyond him.

"What's it called when they swing and miss again?"

"A strike." Otto offered him a handful of peanuts. "It's a strike when they don't swing sometimes too."

"That doesn't make *any* sense."

"Sure it does." Otto cracked a few peanuts and tipped the meats into his mouth. "You've just got to understand the rules. That's why *I'm* here. This is just a scrimmage, so it's easier to talk you through this."

"Right. I'd rather be in the band room working on my audition piece."

"That one was a ball," Otto said as a pitch smacked the squatting guy's mitt. He'd have to ask the name for that position again. "See how it went way outside?"

"Outside of what?"

Lennox crossed his arms over his knees and frowned at the little red and white ball the guy on the hill was twiddling between his fingers. Will was at bat, and so far he hadn't done much but stand there and spit.

"When is your audition anyway? Don't you have to, like, teleport yourself away from here to do it?"

"Saturday afternoon. I got the letter last week. Changed my mailing address with the post office, too. Karen made me."

"She's smart like that."

Will swung and the bat cracked loudly. Lennox didn't see the ball fly out to the grass, but one of the guys out there chased it down and threw it back just as Will slid into one of the bases.

Otto whooped. "Good hit, dude!"

"Was that good?"

"It was an opposite field double, so yeah. He's got a good swing, your boy."

Otto went back to his peanuts as the game continued, and Lennox tried to watch and comprehend what was happening. Will ran while the hill guy was throwing, and even though the squatting guy threw, he got to stay at that base. It was all so bizarre, but Will was grinning and wearing tight, dirty pants that kept Lennox's eyes on him. That was enough reason to watch and cheer.

"Mom wants to know when you're coming over."

"Huh?"

"For dinner, remember? We invited you fucking forever ago. She's got a soft spot for you after—you know."

Lennox shrugged. "I should go practice."

"That's what she said."

"Like you would know. You've had how many dates this year? Oh, wait. It's about one hundred with nobody now, right?"

"Fuck off."

Lennox got up and jogged down the bleachers as the guys on the field jogged in. Was it over already? Nothing had really happened except for Will hitting the ball and then standing on a base. He met Will at the fence and crinkled his nose at the tangy scent of way too much sweat.

"Getting bored already?"

"Confused mostly. I was going to go practice a little more before this weekend. Get my last few hours in and stuff."

"Yeah, okay. Go. This isn't even a real game. Go be awesome."

Will waved and headed into the tugout? Dugout? Fuck if he knew. Lennox waved and headed back up the hill to the school. The band room was empty, but the piano was set up as it was almost every afternoon these days. Only Mr. Robinette and a music stand littered with sheet music were absent.

"Hello?"

The silence struck Lennox as odd, but as he sat down he also realized how strange it was to announce himself. So much had changed since the first time he'd snuck in here to play. Now he was auditioning for some college. He still couldn't fathom it.

He was doing it to make Will happy. And maybe a little bit for himself.

"Ah, I wondered if you were going to show up."

Mr. Robinette was behind him; the door to his office was now wide open. He'd taken off his tie and undone a few buttons on his shirt, as he did most afternoons when they practiced.

"You just want to play it through a few times or mess around with something else?"

Lennox took a seat at the piano, but didn't bother opening his bag. He'd memorized the piece he was playing by Valentine's Day and now, almost two weeks later, he could write it out measure for measure on blank sheet music. But playing it was becoming repetitive. He'd spent two hours, three times a week, almost nonstop with the same four pages and nothing else.

"I'd rather try something new. That piece is getting a little old."

Mr. Robinette smiled and pulled up a chair. "I had a nightmare the other night, and it was the theme song playing while I ran around a haunted house Scooby Doo style."

"You didn't catch a ride in the Mystery Machine, did you? I've always wanted that van."

"I've got a lunchbox version of it. It doesn't hold much, though, because it's too narrow. Anyway, play what you want. I'll be here until about four-thirty, so it's all yours."

As Mr. Robinette returned to his office, Lennox pulled what had become his music notebook out of his bag and opened it to the latest page. He'd taken to composing when he should have been taking notes, especially during calculus class, where he had no reason to pay attention anyway.

The latest page was a tune he'd come up with while the other kids had been tapping their pencils and erasing answers. Every moment of his life carried a rhythm, a melody, and an emotion he could create with, and his notebook was becoming a testament to that. He played through everything he'd jotted down over the past few days, but after several rounds he kept coming back to one. It was a piano version of one of the songs Will had played on a loop a few weeks ago that he'd tried, and mostly failed, to create.

"I'm getting ready to lock up!"

Mr. Robinette's voice carried into the band room. A few minutes and several jingles of Mr. Robinette's keys later, the office door was shut and Lennox was closing the cover on the keys.

"That last piece you were playing, was it a cover?"

Lennox shrugged as they headed for the door.

"It was supposed to be. Didn't sound much like the song."

"Well, the others did. They were all really good, even the ones that weren't covers."

"Uh, thanks."

Lennox watched him at the door to the parking lot. He'd been a great help over the last month, all year if Lennox was honest. Mr. Robinette had believed in him in his own way since school had begun, and thanks to him he had a decent shot at this audition.

"Thanks for all of this. I actually feel like... Just, thanks."

Mr. Robinette gave him a genuine smile and patted him on the shoulder.

"You're very welcome. Let me know how it goes when you get back, okay? I'm rooting for you. Got all of my fingers and limbs crossed. You deserve the chance. Don't doubt that or yourself."

"I won't."

It was funny to have so many people believe in him. Happiness was a strange feeling as well. Until he'd let Will into his life, he hadn't been able to capture such a feeling in his chest and keep it there.

The wind had picked up, and a steady drizzle fell. Lennox headed down the hill and met Will and Otto halfway. They were talking and laughing, which was very unlike them. Normally, they glowered and sniped and only made nice for Lennox's sake.

"Hey!" Will greeted him with a sweaty kiss and a hand to hold on the way to the truck. "How was your last practice?"

"Fine. I just played a few pieces I've been writing, nothing fancy."

"I bet you could play with your dick at this point. It's ridiculous."

"What the hell, dude? Why would you even suggest that?"

Aaron had appeared behind them, all lean limbs and muddy jersey. He draped an arm around Otto and Will and grinned.

"He's a pervert, that's why," Lennox said. "And even if I tried I wouldn't put on that kind of show for you. You'd probably feel so emasculated by the sight of another guy's dick that you'd chop mine off."

The other boys grimaced.

"Don't talk like that," Will said as they reached his truck. "I like you with your dick attached."

"Ugh, shut up." Otto pulled a face and flicked Lennox's ear. "You want to come over for dinner tonight? You know, so my mom stops pestering me about it."

"Uh—"

"Go. I'm going to Aaron's. Love you."

Will kissed his cheek and after taking Lennox's bag he got into his truck with Aaron and drove off. Lennox stared after him, suddenly nervous. Did Otto drive or have another way to his house? Did he even want to go to Otto's place? Sure, Otto's mother had saved his life four months ago, but seeing her again would be awkward, and worse, it would remind him of what had happened in that street, of the life he'd left behind without really noticing it. Had it really been months since he'd been back to that dying motel?

"Let's go sit inside. I've gotta call my mom to come get us."

Lennox followed Otto into the band hall, and they took a seat next to the doors by the vending machines. Otto called his mom while Lennox tugged at the rubber sole of his sneaker. It was ripping away from the rest, and his sock was soggy from the rain puddles.

"Hey, I'm ready. Lennox is coming over. Uh huh. No, he's here. Stayed after too. Okay. Tell him to shut up. He's not getting my old... *fine*. Bye."

Otto popped a few coins into the vending machine and sat down with a pack of Pop Tarts. As he munched, Lennox twisted his fingers and pulled at his shoelaces. Right now he could be with Will, on his way to Will's house for a good nap or a dinner he was familiar with. Otto was an okay school friend, but going to his house was getting in over his head. In a few months, he'd never see Otto again. Otto was joining the military and Lennox was, well, he was going to do something with his life.

"Have you talked to your mom about the army yet?"

Otto broke a Pop Tart in half and shoved it into his mouth. "She's not a fan. But I think she'll get it once I sign up. I mean, what else am I going to do? At least in the army I get to do physical stuff and get paid, you know? I'll have to cut most of my hair off, but that's okay. I only keep this because Mom wants me too. Says it's tradition or whatever, but it isn't my tradition. I didn't grow up on the reservation like she did."

"I should cut my hair soon too," Lennox said. He tugged on a springy curl that dragged his chin. "We should go get haircuts together when I get back from my audition."

"We could go after dinner," Otto suggested. "Or before. There's a place down the road from us, and, I mean, shouldn't you get it cut and look sharp before your audition?"

"Maybe. I hadn't thought about that."

"That's what the guys on the basketball team always say. Their dads tell them to shave and get a haircut before interviews so they don't look like slobs."

"What's my long hair have to do with how well I can play a piano?"

Otto shrugged and wolfed down the rest of his snack. "Just saying."

"Whatever, ponytail."

Otto elbowed him as his phone rang.

"Come on, my mom's here."

Lennox trekked out to the parking lot after Otto. The same rusty truck from his last night at the motel, much larger and older than Will's, was sitting at the curb. Otto's mother was in the driver's seat, and a young boy was in the back behind her. He couldn't have been older than twelve, but considering Otto's size and how similar they looked he might have been six.

"Lennox, it's wonderful to see you again. How's your ankle? Your back?"

"Uh, fine."

He climbed into the cramped backseat when Otto pushed the passenger seat forward and stared at the boy across from him. Otto's nose and eyes, but a different face shape and chin. Definitely a younger brother, but Lennox couldn't recall ever being told a name.

"You've got really *big* hair."

"Shut up, Abe. You've got a really big mouth that's going to be fat in a minute."

"Rudolph, be nice to your brother. Everyone buckled up?"

After three affirmative answers, Malia drove out to the road. Abe leaned over to Lennox, his eyes still following the sway and bounce of his curls. If he cut it off, he'd certainly get a lot fewer comments about it.

"He's just mad because I glued a red nose onto him for Christmas. With Gorilla glue. It was *gr*—ow! Hey! Mom, Otto pinched me!"

"Boys, enough. I'll ground both of you all summer if I hear another word out of you before we get home." Malia smiled at Lennox in the rearview mirror. "Don't ever have more than one son, Lennox. They're a nightmare."

"I'm not having kids."

"Same," Otto said. "Not if they're like this dolt."

He aimed a slap at Abe who punched the back of Otto's seat, missed, and hit Lennox in the arm instead.

"Ouch!"

"Boys, quit!"

The rest of the ride was much calmer. Malia lectured Otto and Abe about being kinder to each other and saving the roughhousing for places outside of a moving vehicle. They pulled up to a house very similar to Will's: long and narrow, made of brick. Otto's house had a shorter driveway and was much closer to town and the road than Will's, and the garage was a covered area, an extended awning instead of an enclosed building.

Otto showed him in, and Lennox found himself in a smaller living room that opened onto an even smaller kitchen. He saw a large television along with a handful of gaming consoles, a bookcase filled with movies, and what appeared to be wood carvings.

"It's not much," Otto said. "Not like Will's. And I've got to share a room with this idiot."

Otto reached out and flicked Abe on the ear.

"I know where you sleep! I'll—"

"You'll get busy on your homework," Malia said. "You have a spelling test tomorrow and you—" She turned to Otto and eyed him sternly. "Be nice to your brother and take care of your guest. You don't have any tests until next week, correct?"

"Yeah. Come on."

Otto tugged Lennox down a narrow hallway and shoved Abe out of his way.

"Get lost. Do your homework out there."

"But my stuff's in our room!"

After several minutes of squabbling and wrestling, Malia stepped in long enough for Abe to grab his backpack and return to the living room. Otto pushed Lennox down the hallway and into a room on the right. It wasn't much larger than the office Ben used at Will's house, but it fit a bunkbed and a double-wide dresser, along with several sports equipment bags. The bottom bed was full-sized and turned in the opposite direction of the twin bed on top.

"I sure hope the bottom's yours. Mountain troll like you probably can't even get up there."

"It used to be mine until Abe outgrew his crib. Our dad built them before he fucked off."

Otto flopped down on the full bed, and Lennox joined him after another glance around the room: A few posters of athletes, one very naked woman fold-out poster covered with Post-it notes, and a beaded, feathered object hung at the window.

"What's that?"

"It's a dreamcatcher. A real one. My grandmother used to make them. I don't know a whole lot about any of that traditional stuff, honestly. Mom does, but I've always thought it was stupid. Dad was big into it like her."

"Oh. Well, what, um, tribe were they from? Is that right?"

"Ojibwe. On Mom's side. Abe's been getting really into it lately, all the stories and myths and how to make all of the stuff Mom has around the house. He's a mama's boy. A grandma's boy, too."

"I think it's pretty cool, having people to show you that kind of stuff. Heritage and all of that."

Otto grunted and pulled a magazine off the window sill and then paused.

"I guess you don't really want to look at naked girls, do you?"

A *Playboy* was dangled in front of Lennox's eyes, and he crinkled his nose. Otto sighed and tucked it under his pillow.

"You suck."

"Well, you aren't wrong. Will's dick has a great time with these lips."

Otto groaned and rolled over. With his face buried in his pillow he said, "I can't believe I'm stuck with you as a friend. How am I ever going to get a girlfriend with a gay guy hanging around me?"

"Easy. I'm hot and you're not. They'll come to get me and get you instead. You'll have even better luck if you have Will around."

"It's good, right? What you've got with him? You guys seem happy."

"I dunno. It's love. I think. That's always good, isn't it?"

Otto looked away. "Sometimes."

"Boys, dinner!"

Lennox sat up as Otto barreled out of the bedroom and down the hall. He listened to the clink of dishes and the bantering of Otto and Abe over what was clearly a very important bowl of rice.

"I get first dibs!"

"You do not!"

"Yes, I do. Otherwise you eat *all* of it!"

They went back and forth until Malia interrupted with a second bowl.

"Otto, this one is yours. Leave Abe alone."

Lennox sat there for a long time before he joined them. It was a different feeling, being at Otto's house with unfamiliar people who seemed to like him. Nobody glanced at him twice, and, despite the lack of Will, it was comfortable to be here, to feel at home somewhere he'd been immediately welcomed. Will's family was still better, but Otto's family was nice for a while.

* * *

"I can't believe you cut your hair."

Two days later and Will still couldn't stop touching Lennox's head. After dinner at Otto's they'd taken Malia's truck down the road under the guise of getting snacks, and Lennox had had his hair shaved off. Not bald and shiny, but very short. He didn't think he'd ever had his hair this short, not even at birth. Otto hadn't gone through with it. He'd been full of excuses that ranged from not wanting to irritate his mother right now to waiting until he'd officially signed up for the army in another few months.

"It looks okay, right?"

As Ben's jeep rumbled onto a new, unfamiliar highway, Will nibbled on Lennox's earlobe.

"Would I have kept you up all night if it didn't?" Will rubbed his short bristles again. Ben thumped the passenger seat.

"Stop it, guys. I'm not driving a make-out wagon. And shouldn't you be practicing?"

Lennox cringed at the reminder. They were heading to Baltimore for his audition and interview. Will had said it was a great way to start March, since they were ending it with their spring break road trip. A long list of plans had already been written down for that trip, and Lennox hadn't managed to pause long enough to understand any of them. Because today ended all of that.

Today demolished every hope Will had for him. College would sail out the window, and so too might their future together.

Their future. How had he gotten to the point of considering such a thing?

"Right, so your interview," Will said. He opened the notebook on his knees and scanned a long list that made Lennox groan.

"Do we really have to do this again?"

"We'll run through it for the whole drive if that's what it takes to get an answer out of you that doesn't involve rim jobs and rubber dicks."

Lennox grumbled and got comfortable in his seat. It was a long drive to Baltimore according to the GPS, but Will's questions would easily last until then.

"Now, what are your—"

"How long is this drive?"

Ben chuckled. "Got about three hours to go, kid. Humor him so I don't have to tie one of you to the roof."

By the time they reached the state line, Lennox's nerves were frayed, and Will was sneering.

"If you aren't going to take this seriously, then—"

"I'm going, aren't I? Can we just forget this already? I have to do the real thing in like two hours, that's bad enough without this circus."

"Will, let him breathe. You've drilled him enough."

"Right into the bed, three nights a week."

"That's enough out of you, too!"

Lennox rested his cheek against the window as the car fell silent. A towering Ferris wheel was on the coast to his right. They were crossing a large, curved bridge, and for the first time in his life he was entering a new state. Although, judging by what he could see of it, Maryland wasn't much nicer than Virginia. Neither seemed to be more than rows of houses and fields.

"Isn't that the National Harbor?"

Will leaned over to look out Lennox's window too. From up front, Ben nodded.

"Yup. We took you once. Me and your mom. You were, oh, just shy of two. It was for July Fourth. I don't remember much except how much you loved pointing out the Ferris wheel. You wanted to go up in it and then got scared when we did. Didn't make it two feet before you were bawling, and they had to reverse the ride and let your mom pass you back down to me. She went up and took some pictures of the bridge."

"This is the Woodrow Wilson, right?"

"Yup. Still have those pictures somewhere at home. Tell you what, I'll dig them out tomorrow and we'll look at them. Then Lennox can see your baby pictures."

Will and Ben chattered all the way into the city. They passed several construction zones and a river of cars, missed their exit, and got off at the next that turned them around and made the GPS angry.

"Please proceed to the route—"

"I'm *on* the route," Ben said. He slapped the little machine and it only repeated itself. To Lennox's ears, it sounded louder.

"Please proceed to the route."

"I'll show you a—"

Will's phone spoke up with directions.

"Turn left in three hundred feet."

Ben paid to park, and then they walked a few blocks to a long glass building, the convention center mentioned in the audition letter. Lennox took a deep breath as Will tried to adjust his shirt collar and the tie he'd undone on the ride.

"You need to get cleaned up and checked in," Ben said, glancing at his wristwatch.

Lennox led the way into the building and went into the first bathroom. Will tried to follow him in, but Lennox stopped him and locked himself in a stall. He didn't have to go, but all of a sudden his arms were shaking and his chest was tight. Lennox rested his back against the stall door and shut his eyes.

It would all be fine. He'd get this shitstorm over with, and then they'd be back on the road. However, being confined in a car with Will for another three hours wouldn't be fun. All Will would ask about would be his audition and the interview.

How had he ever agreed to this? Music was his greatest treasure, a memory he carried from his mother, a token of the love she'd given and so much else. Now it felt like a bargaining chip, something cheap that was being stripped from his grip.

"Lennox, do you need help with your tie?"

Will's shoes appeared on the other side of the stall door. Lennox reached out to flush and, after another moment of calming breaths, he stepped out into the main bathroom.

"What's wrong?"

Of course Will would notice. Lennox elbowed past him to the closest sink. As he washed his hands and face and ran a damp hand over his hair, Will watched him.

"You don't have to do this, you know. Not if you're just doing it for me."

"Why would I do this for you?"

Lennox scrubbed vigorously at his hands until Will's fingers gripped his shoulder.

"You do a lot of things for me," Will said. "Things I don't think you always want to, and I keep hoping you'll say something instead of letting me just figure it out and stop, but this—I can't make you do this if it's not for you."

"It's an audition for *me*. A college for *me*. How does that mean you're—"

But Will's hand squeezed his shoulder and Lennox found he couldn't finish. This, like so much else in his life, wasn't for him. Not entirely. This meant something for Lennox, but it meant something for Will, too.

"I want this for you, but that can't be the only reason. You've got to want it for yourself as well."

Lennox shut the faucet off and grabbed a few paper towels.

"I think I do. I don't know. I'd just gotten my head around the idea that I had a place to live with a lock and then you... It all happened so fast. Getting out of that motel and now all of this. Even if... What if I'm not ready? How much are you going to—"

"Hate you? Don't be ridiculous. I just want you to try. And, yeah, at first I did just think that I'd get you into a college and make your life perfect, but that's not something I can do for you. You've got to want it too. It's your choice. I can only do so much."

Will turned him around and fixed his tie. Lennox wiped his face again and leaned back against the sink. He watched Will's fingers work; over, under, crossing and knotting. In seconds, he had a perfectly knotted tie around his neck that looked ready for a photo shoot.

"I never thought music could be anything else," Lennox said. "It's always what kept me going and what kept me connected to something. I didn't think it could be stressful and scary and all of this."

Will scanned the empty bathroom before stepping forward and hugging him.

"Everything you'll ever love can be scary. Love is a lot of things, from what I've seen so far."

Lennox nodded and kissed Will's cheek before stepping away as the door opened.

"I'm learning that."

They returned to Ben and asked a man at a desk for directions to the auditions. Up an elevator to the top floor, and then two rights and a left led Lennox to a table of several people with name cards and a lot of papers. An older woman who reminded him of Karen's mother smiled at him.

"Hello, dear. Are you here to audition?"

Will nudged him forward.

"Uh, yeah."

"Last name?"

"McAvoy. Lennox McAvoy."

She shuffled through one of her piles and pulled out some stapled papers: His application, essay, and a copy of the sheet music he'd submitted a few weeks ago.

"Go ahead and check to make sure everything is right and that we've got the correct music for you."

Lennox flipped through it quickly and okayed it.

"Piano auditions are through the double doors at the end of this hall. Practice room C is open for you on the left side. Make sure you're outside the audition room a few minutes early. Good luck!"

Lennox took a deep breath and led the way to his practice room. Outside the door, Will and Ben stopped even as he entered.

"We'll wait outside, give you time to prepare and everything."

Will stepped inside the room to kiss him, and then with a final wish for luck, they turned back, and Lennox was alone. He shut the door and it was silent. A small upright piano was inside, and the walls were covered in soundproofing foam. Lennox took a seat at the piano and undid the cuffs on his shirt. The shirt belonged to Will, who hadn't worn it in several years. It fit Lennox almost perfectly, except that the sleeves were too tight around his forearms and about an inch too short.

Lennox spent ten minutes trying to play, but he was too jittery. His legs were bouncing; his fingers were shaking. So much was riding on this. If he didn't nail today, then he'd have to figure something else out. On his own.

Five minutes before his scheduled time, Lennox left his practice room and stood by the main audition door. He fixed his sleeves and adjusted his tie. This first part would be simple. Music—pressing his fingers to the keys—would be the best part.

The door opened. A girl around his age with sleek brown hair exited and an older man in a suit followed her with a clipboard in hand.

"Lennox McAvoy, two o'clock?"

"Here." Lennox gave a little wave and then added, "Sir."

"Hello, Mr. McAvoy, please follow me."

Lennox shook the offered hand, hard, the way Ben had said, and entered the audition room. He'd expected a cavernous room, maybe an auditorium or a concert hall. Instead he stepped into a room about three times the size of the practice room he'd just left. The ceiling was higher and bright with several skylights, and the floor was dark linoleum. He followed the man past a grand piano to a long table where three other people sat. A single plastic chair faced them. Lennox swallowed. All of them were old, white, and official-looking. Would they do the interview first or wait for him to fuck this up?

"Good afternoon, young man," the lady closest to him said. "What might your name be?"

"Um, Lennox McAvoy."

He bit his tongue to keep all the sarcastic remarks down. They had his information right there in front of them on those papers, why bother asking if they already knew? But Ben and Will had stressed being polite, so he bit his lip and stayed quiet.

"Well, it's lovely to meet you. I'm Dr. Peters and this is Professor Harvey, Professor Dunhak, and Dr. Arcaro." She gestured down the line and each person waved in turn. "We're all members of the piano department at Berklee and we'll be conducting your interview and audition this afternoon."

"Um, right. Er, I mean, hello."

Lennox cringed and wished he could turn away to calm himself, but the professors only chuckled and Dr. Peters smiled.

"Nervous? It's quite all right. It's natural to be nervous before an audition this important to your future. I know I was when I was in your place."

"It's not the piano that scares me."

Another professor, Professor Arcaro, Lennox thought, leaned back in his chair and nodded.

"The interview then? Shall we get that out of the way first?"

He motioned toward the only empty chair and, grudgingly, Lennox sat. It was exactly like the ones in the band room at school, only the legs were all even and the back didn't bow when he pressed his body against it.

"Now, we'll be asking you a series of questions," Dr. Peters said. "They're all very straightforward, but if you need clarification or an example, just ask, okay?"

"Okay."

And so it began. They started with music questions. Some were about music theory, others about the physical parts of the piano. As they moved on to his music education and personal history, Lennox grew nervous. He twisted his ankles one way and then the other, and finally pulled one foot up and sat on it.

"Now your essay was quite remarkable," Dr. Arcaro said. They'd been rotating questions and it was making Lennox dizzy. "You spoke a lot of your mother's influence on your early playing; did she go to Berklee?"

"No, um, I mean, I don't think she did. I'm not sure. She died. When I was young—" Lennox swallowed and took a moment, not for heartache but to bite his own tongue. Every question made it harder to not snap out something stupid, and the more closely they inquired about him, the more the feeling itched at the back of his throat. "Nobody ever talked about her after that. She was a concert pianist, and she started teaching me when I was about three. I don't know much else beyond that."

Dr. Peters took up the questions once more as the other three scribbled notes.

"Okay, we have just a few more questions, this time about your educational history. You've been expelled from a number of schools since seventh grade, and you also have a yearlong gap in your educational records. Could you please explain these circumstances to us?"

Lennox didn't catch himself in time.

"If you've got a bottle of lube—"

His interviewers stopped taking notes and looked up at him. Lennox bit down so hard on his lip he could taste blood. Ruined. Everything was finished now. They'd escort him out and never bother to send him a rejection letter. Will would be so disappointed it would open a rift between them that Lennox would never be able to cross again.

"Sorry. I... Sorry. My mouth gets away from me sometimes. I don't like to talk about that stuff. It's just hard."

"Of course," Dr. Peters said. The other three wrote more notes but continued to watch him. "Your history is very complex, from what we understand, but we would be interested to know more in your own words."

Was that all they wanted? His own explanation would be rather different from the cold sheets of paper stating his history, but Will had been adamant he have something ready to say about this just in case. Lennox hadn't done so—he'd talked himself out of that part every time—but he couldn't avoid it now.

"I... After my mom died, my dad had a lot of problems," Lennox said, his eyes on his knees. "He spent all of his time drinking while I tried to take care of my baby sister, and eventually our grandparents took us in until he got himself together. Only he didn't. We went back to Dad and I was still doing it all. Taking her to the babysitter down the street, going to school, picking her up, taking his checks from work and depositing them and then taking out enough to cover all the bills. He went to work drunk and came home that way. I guess it was too much after a while. I got expelled and our grandparents stepped in again. Lucy, my sister, did okay but I, I wasn't the grandson they wanted. Neither of us were what they wanted. I got into a lot of trouble with some stupid kids at school that kept picking on me. They didn't—" Lennox swallowed and took a deep breath. "They didn't like that I was gay, so they beat me up, and then I did the same to them and got locked up in a juvenile detention center for about a year. My grandfather got me out early and pretty much dumped me where I am now, at this motel. I'm living with my boyfriend and his parents right now. Will's the reason I'm here at all."

"Will?"

"My, um, boyfriend. This was all his idea. I didn't even think I'd graduate this year, but he's all about college and since he likes when I play he thought I could do this instead of, well, probably nothing."

He was bombing this. The expressions on each of their faces told Lennox that much. Lennox tugged at his tie and reached up to ruffle his hair, but his fingers only brushed the bristles. Cutting his hair off had been stupid. No matter how much he looked the part, he would never fit into this world.

"Okay, Lennox. I think that's everything," Dr. Peters said. She glanced down the row, and each of her colleagues nodded in turn. "We'll move on to musical exercises now. First, let's hear the piece you've prepared, okay?"

Surprised that the audition was continuing, Lennox took a minute to get to his feet and set himself up at the piano. He opened the cover, and when Dr. Arcaro approached with the sheet music he'd provided, Lennox shook his head.

"I've played it enough that I've got it memorized."

Dr. Arcaro smiled and set it on the ledge anyway. "Just in case. I know personally, I always get a little nervous and lost in an audition."

But this was the easiest part for Lennox. He never felt uncertain here. Lennox unbuttoned his sleeves and rolled them up, and then after a few plucks to make sure the piano was in good order he began. Melody flowed from his fingertips and trickled across the keys. The music swelled to fill the room, and despite its size it had great acoustics. His eyes drifted shut, and for once the music didn't appear behind his eyelids; he didn't need it. Not even his memory of the notes and the crescendos could tell him the best direction right now. Lennox was the rhythm and the heart of the song. It swept up and crashed around them, gushing like a breaking wave in all directions.

His song faded gradually, rising once more at the end before falling silent. When he opened his eyes the room was still; the sunlight had faded behind a cloud.

The four professors simply watched him. And then at once they each began to write their notes. Dr. Arcaro finished first and approached Lennox once more, this time with more sheets of music.

"Three more tasks for you," he said. "Sight-reading, ear training, and an improvisation."

Fifteen minutes later, Lennox had breezed through each task. He'd done well at all of them, if he said so himself, particularly the improvisation. As the professors scribbled their final notes, Dr. Peters spoke.

"I know earlier, when we questioned you about your goals as a future Berklee student, you didn't mention a particular direction for your major. Have you considered composition? Your improvisation was quite skilled for someone so young."

Lennox stood up and restlessly clicked his tongue ring.

Click, click, click.

"I'd never thought about it. This whole future thing is still new to me. I mean, lately I've been doing a lot of covers of stuff my boyfriend listens to while we're doing homework. Jotting down the melodies and stuff. Before now I never really had the chance to do more than play from books."

"I would consider it," she said. "You have a lot of options if you continue to play professionally. Does anyone else have any final comments or questions?"

One of the other professors raised a hand. Lennox couldn't remember her name, but she had really tall hair that reminded him of a beehive.

"What do you think you will contribute to the Berklee community?"

Lennox hesitated. Even Will hadn't been able to bullshit a good enough answer for that question. The website had talked about it, wanting each student to think long and hard about what they could bring to the school instead of just what they could take away. Nothing they'd come up with had rung true and Lennox hadn't managed to get out even their best attempt with a straight face.

"Honestly? I don't know. I could drone on and on about, like, all the experience I bring and all the stuff I've done or won or whatever everyone else is saying, but that doesn't make it true. Doesn't mean

I'll actually do it either. I'll come ready to play and to play like I'm on my last heartbeat, same as I always do. This is all I've ever had to keep me going until a few months ago, and it's all I'll have after he's gone, too. Music isn't my entire life—it's never had the chance to be—but it's always been one of the greatest parts of me. It's the last gift my mother ever gave me, and I'm never leaving it behind."

More scribbling. He could hear a faint rhythm ping-ponging back and forth between all of their pens. After a few minutes, and several nods between them, Dr. Peters turned to him and smiled.

"Do you have any questions for us, Lennox?"

Lennox shook his head.

"Okay, I'll walk you out."

He shook each of their hands, and with a few strides was back across the room and out into the cool air of the hallway. Dr. Peters called for the next person, a young woman with a short blonde bob. Lennox hurried down the hall and around the corner. He pressed himself back against the wall and unknotted his tie.

It was over. He'd only made a slight fool of himself and he hadn't been kicked out. A grin split his face for a moment before Will's voice reached his ears.

"Lennox!"

Will and Ben hurried over to him.

"How'd it go? Did you play okay? You didn't threaten to harm any of them, did you? Please tell me you aren't being sued for harassment."

"No, I'm not. It went... I dunno. It was okay, I guess. I said some stupid stuff, but I think they liked my playing. Said I should look into composing or something."

Will beamed and hugged him tightly. Ben gave him a firm pat on the back and grinned too.

"Sounds like you rocked their socks off," Ben said. "Come on. Let's grab a bite to eat and see if there's any tickets left for the game. It starts in a few hours."

"There's a baseball team in Baltimore?"

Ben shook his head ruefully as Will smacked Lennox's arm.

"We've been over the teams a *hundred* times. Baltimore has had a team for longer than Dad's been alive!"

"Don't rub that age spot too hard, Will. It's gonna start rubbing off on you soon enough."

Will stuck his tongue out at Ben as they made their way out of the building and onto the busy street. The city was much more pleasing to Lennox's senses all of a sudden: nice brick buildings, the fresh scent of the harbor breeze coming in from a few blocks away, and the sharp whip of voices echoing all around him.

Boston might be a simple, pleasant scene, so busy with people and life that he could go unnoticed until he decided to stand out. New York would be this and then some. Lennox might never get into Berklee, or he might have just stumbled his way into a college acceptance. The very idea seemed unfathomable, but for now all of that could wait. Right now he had a baseball game and dinner with his boyfriend.

⏸ twenty-one ⏵

ONE MORE GOOD SNOWSTORM GAVE Will and Lennox a few more days free from school, and Will spent all of those days planning. He found a cheap hotel in Brooklyn, bought bus tickets online for New York, then another set from New York to Boston, and then a return ride to Washington, DC at the end of the week. He made lists of places to visit and signed up for a tour of NYU's campus and then another for Sarah Lawrence, even though he hadn't received a letter from them yet.

While he was doing all of this, Lennox spent his free days playing with Oyster in the snowy backyard and trying new songs on the piano in the garage.

Spring arrived in a rush after St. Patrick's Day. After the snows all melted and the end of March suddenly blazed with spring heat, Will was through with his plans. He found Lennox shut away with Ben in the office, both of them fiddling with guitars.

"It's still out of tune," Lennox said as he twisted one of the knobs.

Will hadn't spent much time in here since Lennox had first showed him a few notes, but recently he didn't seem to find Ben and Lennox anywhere else. They spent all of their free afternoons in here, jamming and tuning, at least when Will didn't lure Lennox downstairs for more important things.

Will sat on the desk and watched them play what was clearly a dueling guitar song. They played back and forth a few more times and then laughed. Ben and Lennox were bonding at last, and that was a wonderful sight to see.

"What's up?"

Lennox set his guitar aside and stood up. He rubbed his hands over Will's thighs and wedged his hips between them as he leaned in for a soft kiss.

"Hi, hello." Will smiled and kissed him again, crossed his arms behind Lennox's head and ran a hand over the soft fuzz on Lennox's head. "Mmm—"

"That's enough, boys. You want to do that, then you take it downstairs."

Ben stood and stretched.

"I finalized and bought everything," Will said. He held Lennox's head away to stop him nuzzling his neck. "We need to be at Union Station by nine for our bus. It leaves at nine-thirty."

Lennox stepped back. "New York first, right?"

Will nodded. "I can't wait. I called Lucy and gave her the dates we'd be in Boston. Berklee has tours too, if you want to drop by and see it. She said we can sleep on their couch while we're there. Sound good?"

Lennox nodded. "I've still got some money left over from what my grandfather was putting on my card. I can pay for something. The subway or whatever."

Will agreed as they went down the hall to join Karen for dinner.

For the rest of the week leading up to spring break, Will bubbled over with excitement. At baseball practices he overthrew, and he stole more bases than he ever had in Little League. Aaron got so frustrated with how fast he threw down the signs that he hit and broke Will's face mask. He tapped his pencils instead of taking notes, and barely ate because every time he opened his mouth more facts about New York came tumbling out.

"Did you know that Central Park is more than eight hundred acres?"

"The High Line is supposed to be beautiful. Do you want to walk all of it, Lennox?"

On and on he went until he could see his friends getting bored, but he was thrilled. Lennox seemed excited too. It was such a change from before his audition that Will was sure of one thing: Lennox was going to get in to Berklee. He might be keeping all the details to himself about what had happened, but he'd been relieved afterward, and more than once Will had found him scanning the old pamphlet instead of reading for classes.

Mr. Robinette seemed more thrilled than any of them when Lennox told him about his audition. He'd said it had gone well, but obviously to Mr. Robinette's ears that sounded more like a roaring success.

They finished their last classes before spring break, and before Will knew it they were in Karen's car outside of the station in Washington, DC.

"You've got everything? Clean socks?"

"Yeah, yeah, I packed a bunch."

"Lennox, you have clean underwear, right?"

"I'm not wearing any."

"Put some on. Check the beds for bedbugs when you get to your hotel, and if you find any ask for a new room. Actually, find another hotel. Call us when you get off the bus."

"Okay, okay. Check the corners, right?"

Karen nodded and leaned over to hug Will tightly. He squeezed her back and accepted a kiss on the cheek.

"Call me. Charge your phone on the bus. Lennox, did you take the old one I gave you?"

Lennox shrugged a yes and climbed out. As he hoisted their bags out of the trunk, Karen brushed Will's hair back.

"Keep an eye on him. A boy like that could get lost in the city. And you take care of yourself too. Call us every night and every morning. Don't stay out too late, either. Oh, I love you."

They hugged again, and Will opened his door. "Love you too."

Lennox ducked his head in. "Stop being mushy and get moving. We're going to miss our bus."

Will hopped out and shut the door. "Okay, bye!"

Karen waved. Will turned into the building as she drove off. Lennox had already hoisted both of their bags over his shoulders and he was grinning, walking with a little spring in his step.

LENNOX DROPPED OFF BEFORE THEY even pulled out of the lot. He slept for the entire ride, but Will couldn't, no matter how much his eyes itched. The view was pretty boring once they left Washington, DC, but Will stayed awake to see all of it: fields and rivers, ridges, toll booths, the drool on the woman across the aisle from him. It dripped down her chin and left wet spots on the floor.

As they began to pass semis along the highway, Will pulled out his phone to check the map. He tapped Lennox on the shoulder until he woke up.

"We're almost there," Will told him. "Do you think we'll be able to see the city from the bus?"

Lennox grumbled and rubbed his eyes. "Don't care. Want sleep and food. And bathroom."

"There's one downstairs."

"Too far."

As Lennox went back to snoring softly beside him, Will leaned past him to watch the horizon. Several tall buildings appeared and Will readied his camera, but they were so close. They couldn't have crossed into Manhattan yet, could they? He checked his map again and sighed. Still in Jersey. Will leaned back and shut his eyes. Another five minutes maybe. He'd just rest and then—

"Will, wake up. Come on, we're in the tunnel thing."

"What?"

He sat up just as the bus revved up the tunnel and out into a foggy landscape. Everywhere Will looked he saw buildings. Not a strip of sky was visible. He leaned over Lennox and pressed his face right against the glass, and still all he saw was the many windows of the buildings they drove past. The bus turned off onto what must have been a side road and dropped all of them off.

Lennox seemed to fall into the rhythm of the city easily. He scooped up their bags and shuffled Will out of the way of the people who were speeding in all directions, each with a clear purpose.

"Wow, this is... Wow!"

Lennox nodded and looked around, too. "Let's find a subway station. Get to the hotel. You want to call Karen now or when we get settled?"

"Um, settled. It's kind of crowded."

He took a quick spin, and his breathing quickened. So many people. More than he'd ever seen in his life. From where he stood he couldn't even make out the street signs on either corner.

"I'm not sure where... Do you see a subway sign?"

Lennox laughed and fitted his bag over his shoulders. Then he gave Will his bag and steered him into the flow of people heading away from the bus.

"They look like they know where they're going," Lennox said as they walked. "Keep an eye out for a subway stop and we'll go from there, okay?"

"But—"

Lennox wrapped his arm around Will's waist and kissed him right on the mouth. Will tensed and glanced around, but nobody even looked at them. Will could see two older men holding hands.

"We can kiss in public," Will said.

"And hold hands."

Lennox's fingers tapped Will's forearm and Will closed his palm over them.

They grinned at each other and made their way down the street with the crowd.

A few blocks later, however, they found a subway station and Will was suddenly terrified. So many lines, so many stops, what did uptown and downtown even mean?

"I should call Karen. She can explain all of this."

"Or we can just get the unlimited card," Lennox said as he clicked buttons on the card machine. "We can see the sights at random."

"But we've got to check in at the hotel, and this bag is getting heavy—"

"Swipe. Too late. Card purchased. Here."

Lennox bought a second card for himself, checked out the map, and then pointed at the gates on the left.

"That way."

"Where does that even go?"

"Somewhere new."

"Lennox, this isn't... We need to get to the hotel."

"And what's the closest stop to the hotel?"

"I, well, I don't know," Will said, realizing this for the first time. It would have been a good idea to have looked that one up. "Let me check on the—"

"Train's coming in," Lennox said and suddenly he was on the other side of the gate. "Stopping in three, two—"

"Wait! Wait!"

Will swiped his card once, then turned it around and swiped again. The reader beeped and let him through. He stepped onto the train just as the doors started to close.

"Lennox, we don't even know where we're going," Will said as Lennox dropped down on a seat. "We could end up in New Jersey, or—"

"Subway doesn't go to Jersey. Come on, sit."

"How can I sit when we could end up lost in New York?"

"This isn't a *Home Alone* movie," Lennox said as Will sat down. "See that map?"

Will scanned the map, but it was only a twisting blob of colorful lines with minute writing.

"That map means we're lost."

"Nah, we're on the blue one. The C. It'll take us down to Brooklyn, about seven blocks from our hotel."

"How did you... You looked it up before we left!" Will punched him on the arm and glared at him. "You scared the shit out of me. I thought—"

"That I was winging it? That's for later. We've got a date with bedbugs first."

THE ELEVATOR AT THEIR HOTEL was broken. Will grumbled the entire way up the narrow staircase, while Lennox jogged ahead and then thumped back down like an elephant.

"Room's nice. Big queen bed we can fuck around on."

"It's thirteen floors up," Will said, huffing and puffing. "We're only at eight."

"No *you're* only at eight. If you'd pick up your feet, you'd be in the room already."

Will clomped along behind him as Lennox disappeared up the stairwell. By the time he reached their room, the door was wide open and Lennox had ripped the bedding up and was examining it.

"Everything looks clean. I'm not sure what bedbugs look like, though."

Will dropped his bag on the little dresser by the bed and flopped down beside Lennox. So many stairs! He'd have to take twenty laps around the school building back home to even get close to this much exercise.

"What time is it?"

"Almost three," Lennox said. "You want to just get settled and then figure out dinner? Maybe head to one of your spots so we can see how long the ride back is?"

Will agreed. They unpacked a few outfits and bathroom supplies before curling up together on the bed and checking online for a restaurant close by. But his phone kept giving him places all over New York, from the Bronx to Manhattan to Queens. Lennox tapped one at random.

"Pizza. That sound good?"

"I guess. It's not far from Times Square."

They headed out, Lennox once again navigating the subway routes and out the proper stairs. Will was helplessly lost with every twist and turn, but Lennox fit in like the city was a second skin. They ate a pie at the pizza place they'd settled on, then took another jostling subway ride up a few more stops. Even more people were on this train, and Will twitched every time someone bumped into him or stood between himself and Lennox. No seats were available, but a few stops later they got off the train and found themselves in another big crowd of people.

"There sure are a lot of people here, huh?" Lennox followed someone through an emergency exit gate, and Will stopped short.

"We shouldn't go through there," he said. But nobody paid him any mind. A dozen more people pushed through it, and not one alarm went off. Tentatively, Will followed and then they walked up more stairs to the strangest sight he'd ever seen. Night had fallen while they'd been underground, but a blaze of ultraviolet light filled the street and sky. It was as if a hundred movie screens had been set to play a dozen different films. They flashed with the lights of advertisements—cars, Broadway shows, even a cologne Will had tried once and despised—but the people provided the soundtrack of sirens, car horns, and endless chatter in a dozen or more languages.

"Wow, this is incredible."

"Come on."

Lennox took him by the arm and darted through the crowd. At the sidewalk's edge, the walk sign wasn't on, but no cars or taxis were coming so they hurried across. All evening they circled, taking pictures of the billboards and buildings they recognized. Will stopped at a few theaters to take pictures, and then Lennox convinced him to take a selfie of the two of them kissing amongst all the bright lights. A man nearby even volunteered to snap a few shots, as if that was the most normal thing in the world.

And perhaps it was for a place like New York City, where people did as they pleased in a variety of ways Will's hometown wouldn't allow them. Everyone was everywhere and in everyone's way, but nobody paid any mind to the simpler moments: to the love of two young boys alone in the world for the first time.

* * *

WILL AND LENNOX SPENT THREE days in New York City. They got lost in Central Park—twice—and toured both of Will's prospective schools. Both had been overwhelming for Will. NYU was scattered over many blocks of the city, the dorms had been minimal, and he'd gotten so turned around on the self-guided tour he'd had to sit down. Sarah Lawrence had been better. It was well north of Manhattan, which meant he'd lose the city experience he'd been so desperate to have. Yet as they climbed onto their bus bound for Boston on the morning of their fourth day, Will couldn't help but hope to give himself the distance from the city clamor that Sarah Lawrence offered.

Once they were seated together on the bus, Lennox leaned over the way he had last time and rested his head on Will's shoulder. In his hands, he held a big foam Statue of Liberty crown.

"Think I can be the queen today?"

Will took it from him and put it on. Lennox smiled.

"You're a very cute queen."

They kissed easily and then curled up together again. Only a few days in New York and they'd fallen into public intimacy with ease. Lennox held his hand as they strolled down the street; they kissed over dinner and lunch. Nothing held them back and nobody stared or said a word.

"You know," Lennox said as he kissed under Will's earlobe, "you'd make a marvelous drag queen."

Will startled at that.

"A drag queen?"

"Yeah, nice cheekbones and long lean legs."

Lennox's hands trailed over Will's thigh to his knee. They'd spent all of last night together naked and panting into each other's mouths. Before that it had been a while. Their lives had become so busy of late with classes, auditions, and planning so many things. Graduation gowns would be ready by the time they got back, along with their fourth, and final, reports.

"We can't right now," Will said, although he took Lennox's hand in his. "I doubt Lucy will care much for us doing that on her couch, either."

"Blowjobs are couch-friendly."

Will gave him a look.

"Well, the ones *I* give are. It's not my fault you don't like to swallow."

"Well, if you gave some warning—"

Someone nearby cleared their throat, and Will flushed.

"Let's listen to music," Will said as he untangled his earbuds. "You can pick first."

Lennox scrolled and scrolled as the bus traveled east and north. He picked one song, then hopped to another song after twenty seconds. Will rolled his eyes as this continued, a burst of one song and then another. Lennox crossed his legs, adjusted the front of his jeans, and clicked his tongue ring in time with each song as it began and ended.

"It's not happening," Will said after fifteen minutes of this. "I am *not* doing this on this bus."

"But Will—"

"Do you want to walk to Boston?"

Lennox frowned and changed the song one more time. He didn't speak again until the bus pulled into their stop in Boston.

"What about a bathroom break?"

Lennox nudged Will with his elbow, but Will only nodded into the crowd of people where he could see Lucy waiting for them.

"I don't think Lucy wants to wait for that."

Lennox turned and stood on his tiptoes to see to where Will was pointing. He grinned even as Lucy gave a shout of disbelief at his hair.

"What did you *do* to your head?"

Will watched them embrace and smiled. He couldn't give Lennox his sister back or a college-related future, but he could make sure he still had friendship, with both him and Lucy.

They held each other tightly until Lucy pulled away and yanked Lennox's head down to examine his hair.

"Did Will make you do this? You aren't joining the army or something insane, are you?"

Lennox shook his head, but her words held the same fear Will had expressed. Otto was joining, and while Lennox hadn't said anything beyond "no," Will had his doubts. If Berklee rejected him, well, Lennox only had so many options that didn't involve waiting, and Lennox had rarely been patient.

"I cut it before my audition. It was Otto's idea. He was too chicken to chop his off 'cause his mom would probably murder him."

"It's so short."

Lucy continued to run her hands over it as they walked down the street. She led them to a subway stop and Will groaned.

"He wasn't a fan of the subway in New York," Lennox explained. "I had to hold his hand for most of it."

"It's not *my* fault they make it so complicated," Will said as Lucy showed them how to get tickets and then led them onto a train. "There's like a billion trains going in every direction."

Lucy smiled and found them seats. "At least they aren't carpeted like in DC."

"Are they? That's stupid."

Will dropped down beside her, but Lennox only put his bag down on the seat in front of them and stayed on his feet. He enjoyed subways, clearly, and had a ball standing and swaying with the stuttering motion of the train through the tunnels. They changed trains and got out on a small block in a neighborhood with several apartment buildings.

Lucy pointed to their right.

"Berklee's that direction. About ten blocks, for some of the buildings. You're going on a tour tomorrow, right?"

Will nodded as Lennox stared down the street into the bright sunlight.

"Yeah, I'm hoping we have an easier time getting there than we did to mine. Sarah Lawrence was really far away. We had to take a real train way up north."

"We can get directions online. Come on. Kelly works 'til six, but we can meet her for dinner somewhere later."

Will followed Lucy across the road while Lennox lagged behind, his head tilted toward the sky and the tops of the buildings in the distance. It struck Will once they were inside and in an elevator—a wonderful, working elevator—that this city might be Lennox's new home in a few short months. That soon, their lives would diverge. Such a brief time together, and yet he couldn't imagine not having Lennox with him every day, or losing someone he'd grown to treasure.

Lucy's apartment was quite small. A single room housed the kitchen and living room. A small bathroom was down a very short hall, along with one small bedroom just big enough for a queen-sized bed.

"The bathroom sharing is going to suck a bit," Lucy told them as she showed them how the couch folded out. "But we're both working, so you guys should be okay once we leave for the day. There's a Subway down the street and a Starbucks on the corner. The stop we got off at will take you to most of the main spots."

"Cool."

Lennox couldn't sit still, though. He'd been bouncy for the entire trip, but now he was practically soaring to the ceiling.

"What about the museums? The ones we saw in New York were cool. What about music around here? Are there good bands? Or clubs? What about—"

Lucy whistled and waved her hands. "Slow down, man. I'll give you addresses. Come on, we'll look on the computer. Do you guys want something to eat? We can put in a movie."

Will picked the movie, a horror film he'd never heard of, while Lennox and Lucy got to work on the computer, checking out places to visit and things they could do for the two days Lennox and Will were here. Lennox picked a music hall, and decided to check out several of Berklee's other buildings in addition to those on their tour. Will wanted to see the baseball stadium and a few museums.

They spent the evening in the apartment, and when Kelly got home they all went to a little restaurant down the street. The next morning, much as in New York, Lennox led the way and Will lagged behind, feeling more and more like a country boy who needed to find a good field to hide in. Even a smaller city like Boston would take a lot of getting used to, but Lennox at least seemed to be thriving. He wove through the crowds and got on all the right trains and got them to Berklee so fast they were twenty minutes early.

"See? That was easy."

"Speak for yourself."

"Huh?"

"Nothing."

Will wandered off to find a bathroom, and then they headed up to the room where they were supposed to meet their tour guide. The room was packed with people, mostly parents with prospective students, but a few were just sets of parents looking around nervously.

"Welcome! Come on in. We'll be starting in just a few minutes."

A young woman waved them inside and handed them brochures. Will flipped through his listlessly as they found a pair of seats between two sets of parents there with their daughters. Lennox didn't open his brochure, but looked around, his jaw set.

"You okay?"

Lennox nodded and didn't say anything. The tour began with a short talk. Will was entirely out of place, being neither parent nor prospective student, but Lennox suddenly seemed to have forgotten that he was the latter. He stayed quiet, didn't participate, and hung at the back of the group as they all filed out for the campus tour.

By the third building Will could tell something was definitely wrong.

"You okay?"

"Yeah, just... I'm fine."

Lennox perked up a little after that, but Will could tell it was all for show. The buildings were nice, however. All of the music equipment looked as if it was top-of-the-line, and the recording studios were clearly state-of-the-art. Even Will, who could barely tell a guitar from a bass, could see it was a magnificent school. Lennox would have the time of his life with all he could do and learn in a place like this, and yet—

"Let's get out of here," Lennox said as the group turned to head back to where they'd begun for a meet and greet for the prospective students. "This is boring."

Will followed him as he'd done for days, but for once his anxiety wasn't about where they were going, but why. Lennox grabbed the first train that pulled into the station and they were gone. For the rest of the day, Lennox made sure they stayed busy. They tried new food and explored new streets. At one point they ended up at the river, and despite it still being very cold in Boston, Lennox kicked his boots off and poked his feet into the chilly water. When they returned from their adventures, Lucy and Kelly were back, both in baggy sweatpants and old sweaters.

"We ordered some pizza," Lucy said. "It's on the counter."

Will grabbed a few slices, but Lennox disappeared to the bathroom. The shower went on and Kelly glanced back at the door and then at Will.

"Everything okay? He looked a little rough."

Will joined them on the couch and watched the bathroom door too.

"I'm not sure. He got a little weird when we got to Berklee, and he's been acting like everything's fine, but—"

"It rarely is with him," Lucy said. "He's always had so much on his back. You want me to try?"

"No. I think this is... It's about college stuff again. And I'm the reason he's even considering it. I think I should be the one to talk to him, right?"

Kelly smiled and kissed his cheek. "You're a good little boyfriend, Will. Heart's in the right place, and the rest of you is getting there too."

"Just don't push him, okay?" Lucy stretched and stood up. "I think Berklee *is* a good choice for him, but maybe now isn't the right time. He's had it really rough for a long time."

"That's what worries me. If he doesn't go now, then when? And what's he going to do until he gets there? What if—what if he gets in trouble or takes a different path?"

"Ah. That's what this is about."

Kelly got up and hurried to their room, but Lucy stayed put.

"What?"

"You're scared he's going to find another way to be happy. One without you."

Will's insides rung like a vibrating bell.

"That isn't... He's already—"

Yet Will couldn't deny Lucy's words either. He was scared: about which college he would go to, and if his grades were okay, and if the baseball team would do well this season and then next year when almost all of their starters were gone. Will worried about how his dad would handle him leaving home for the first time and how Karen would overwork and forget to eat. His dad's health was now always at the back of his mind, and Oyster's was a growing concern too. And then he had Lennox. The boy whose only happiness was found in music and Will. For right now, at least.

"You're scared he'll find something better, but I'll tell you a secret, Will," Lucy said. "He's scared of the same thing too. Almost as much as he's scared of letting himself be happy in new ways."

Will frowned. "Any advice?"

"Yeah. Let him be happy. Encourage it, too. Don't be afraid to find happiness in your lives, even if that happiness takes you guys away from each other. You can always find a way back if you work at it."

Lucy left for their bedroom, and Will sat alone on the couch. Some of what Lucy had said made sense, but not all of it. How could he be happy if he was moving away from Lennox? How could either of them still be content with their lives—or even happier than now—if their choices took them away from each other permanently?

⏪ twenty-two ⏩

NEW YORK AND BOSTON HAD been a blast, but Lennox was also glad to get back to Leon on Saturday evening. It was warmer, for one thing, and the city got to be a lot after a while: crowds that never ended, bright lights and constant noise, rude people who knocked right into you. Lennox had loved parts of it too, like the subways and the idea of so many things in one place, like back in Richmond. Will hadn't seemed to fare so well. In fact, he'd seemed hopelessly lost from the moment they left each morning until the second they shut their hotel door again.

"How was it? Did you have fun?"

Karen took each of them into her arms in turn and messed with their hair. The gesture made Lennox rather glad he'd shaved his off. Unlike Will's, her fingers always got stuck.

"It was great," Lennox said, and Will agreed.

Yet something had sprung up between them, and Lennox couldn't place it. It had grown and grown every day they were gone, but— unlike his usual pattern—Will hadn't sat down to talk with him. They'd said almost nothing on the bus ride from Boston to Washington, DC. Part of Lennox was glad. He didn't want to talk about Berklee, about the swell inside of him as he'd walked into those beautiful, huge buildings and seen dollar signs on every brick and fixture, on every musical instrument and recording studio. A place like that was built on money, and it would charge every student more in one year than Lennox hoped to make in his lifetime.

It didn't matter if he was good or he got in on talent. He'd dig himself into a hole he'd never be able to pay his way out of.

"I knew I should have given you guys a subway talk," Karen said as Lennox followed her and Will into the kitchen. "I forgot all about it. How many times did you get lost?"

"Twice. I wouldn't really call them *lost*," Lennox said. "More like we got on those express trains and didn't realize it. Had to backtrack."

"If Lennox hadn't been there, I'd never have made it to the hotel," Will said, and he sounded rather bitter about it. "I wasn't ready for it at all."

"It takes a while to get your toes wet in New York. Well, it takes a few seconds, but it takes a while to get comfortable with it."

Will frowned as he sat at the kitchen table. Lennox joined him.

"How were the campus tours?"

"Good. NYU was huge. Sarah Lawrence was way outside the city but it was really nice. A little more my speed than NYU, I think. Berklee was nice too."

"Did you like it, Lennox?"

He nodded, because he had, but so much else went into Berklee besides liking it. Every day, he realized more went into his choices than just wanting something. Lennox had to do what was best for him in as many realms of his life as possible. Berklee meant musical opportunity beyond all of his wildest dreams, but it meant heartache too. Will would drift out of his life, and he'd bury himself in an astronomical debt he'd couldn't begin to imagine in real numbers. And he might never see his sister again if he left Virginia.

"The instruments and studios were great," Lennox said instead. "I could learn a lot there."

"And you can see yourself there?"

"Um, yeah, I think so."

"We didn't get any letters while we were gone, did we?"

Ben shook his head as he appeared with their bags and souvenirs.

"God, what did you guys buy? The Empire State Building?"

"Well, actually—"

Lennox grinned as Will dug the Empire State Building statuette out of his bag and handed it to Ben.

"We got a bunch of stuff from New York and some from Boston too."

Karen smiled. "I bet you did. Well, bring it all out while we finish up dinner."

"While *I* finish dinner," Ben said. "Last time you tried to make gnocchi you set the smoke alarms off."

"That was three years ago."

"Yeah, and I still don't trust you."

Karen sighed and joined them at the table just as Oyster pawed at the sliding glass door. She reached over and let him in and Lennox suddenly had a faceful of white fur and dog breath.

"Oh, gross!"

Oyster slobbered all over his face and hair, then whined loudly and moved on to Will. After several minutes of Will baby-talking to him, Oyster climbed onto Will's lap like a gigantic fluffy infant.

"That's my good boy," Will said, rubbing Oyster's belly. "My pretty, good boy."

"Don't get too comfortable," Lennox told Oyster. "I claimed that spot for better reasons than you could ever howl out."

"Keep it in the bedroom, guys."

Karen laughed at Ben's words and went back to asking them about their trip. The entire evening revolved around what they'd done, how they'd liked different things, what they'd eaten, and college. So much was about college these days, and Lennox's stomach churned more with every mention of it. What else could he do if he didn't go to Berklee? What choice did he have but to not go, even if they accepted him?

* * *

AFTER EASTER, LENNOX AND WILL returned to school. Walking back into the same tiny halls was surreal after strolling through the city streets for almost a week, but Lennox was rather glad to see them too. The same posters about not doing drugs and making smart decisions; the usual artwork from the art classes displayed along the back hallways; lockers with little magnets and flyers stuck on them. Familiarity was what he needed right now. Something to ground him before his hopes and dreams got too much bigger. Having Otto at his side again helped too. He didn't dream about anything ideal or ambitious. Otto lived here and was happy with continuing a simpler life in Leon after graduation in a few months. The army and then a job and a small place of his own near his family. That was all Otto was interested in, and that was all Lennox should think about too, except the family part of course. His grandparents wouldn't let him back into Lucy's life, no matter what his grandfather had said. Anything more than a simple life here was asking for struggles and pain.

"How was it? Did you guys go to any bars? Have a threesome? Is that a thing gay guys do?"

Lennox made a face and punched Otto on the arm as their classmates continued to fill the band room around them. Will had rushed back to his truck to retrieve his trombone, but Lennox didn't understand why he bothered. He'd sound better just blowing on his thumb.

"Eww, man. No. I mean, some might, but me and Will, we're a pair or whatever. We saw the sights, spent most of our time at the campuses looking around. Will didn't like the subway too much. Kept heading for the wrong train every five minutes."

"Yeah, and? Did you like Bucklee?"

"Berklee, and... I don't know. It was really cool, but I dunno. College just seems so—"

"Educational?"

"Expensive."

Otto tapped a beat out on his sneakers with his drumsticks. "Well, you know it's not my thing. I want to start my life and get away from here now. Without having to pay like a million dollars in loans and books and shit, you know? Or having to worry about *more* grades."

"Yeah, it doesn't sound like a lot of fun. Just work." Yet Lennox had always liked to learn, to be challenged by something that wasn't personal. "But in the army you've gotta worry about getting, like, shot or blown up. That's no fun either."

"Depends on what you do for them. And they pay you, train you. They've got other options besides combat. I told Mom over break. You know, for like the twentieth time, but I told her I wasn't looking to go into combat so she seemed a little better about it. She still wants me to think about college, since they'll pay for it."

"Really?"

"Uh, I think so. I've never asked. They're supposed to have a recruiter at lunch starting soon. Mrs. Martinello told me. You could ask him."

Class began and Lennox took up his place at the piano. The army was an option if that was true, but surely they'd want something in return for paying for his college. If he decided to go or even got in. More than just his life for the next twenty-odd years or whatever. They'd expect things he probably couldn't give.

But the idea of the military lingered with Lennox all day. If they would cover his tuition and board fees, then he could go to Berklee. He could do what he wanted if only for a little while. But was years of lost freedom worth a few years of happiness?

And what about Will? If he joined the military, he'd be shipped all over the country—all over the world probably—and Will would still be in New York. The military probably wouldn't like that he was gay, either, which meant Will would be left behind every time he was relocated. He'd have to hide himself and Will. That could never work.

At the end of the day, Lennox met up with Will at his locker and greeted him with their usual kiss. Will didn't have to worry about this kind of stuff. He was so sure about his plans and ready to go to New York, with or without Lennox. All he expected was for everything to work, but sometimes it didn't. For Lennox, it rarely did.

"Ready to go home? The house is ours."

His eyes alight with mischief, Will teased him with a soft kiss on his jaw. Lennox grinned too.

"Is that an offer for what I think it is?"

"If you mean, your ass and my dick, then yes." Will kissed him again, and this time his lips lingered a few seconds longer. "Come on, babe. I've got plans for you."

"Oh, look who's figured out how to flirt."

Then Will did something he'd never done before, something only Lennox had done to him. He pushed his hands into the back pockets of Lennox's jeans and squeezed. His eyes danced with excitement and just a little hint of nerves. For the last few months, Will's sexual confidence had grown exponentially, and it thrilled Lennox to see it.

"I see you've been paying attention," Lennox said as Will kissed his neck once.

"I've had a good partner to learn from. Time to take you home."

Lennox groaned as they jogged over to Will's truck and climbed into the front seat. Will drove faster than he usually did, his left hand on the steering wheel, the heel of his palm flat against the top, turning and shifting along the winding country roads home. His right hand rested on Lennox's inner thigh and his fingers rubbed light circles against his jeans. Lennox swallowed and shut his eyes, letting his mind wander for the short drive.

Will already had plans for him today. The sure way his fingers pressed and drifted lazily from his knee to the top of his thigh told Lennox that much. He never touched his cock, but Lennox was aching by the time they pulled into the driveway and unbuckled their seatbelts. This was so different from the boy he'd first met. Will hopped out, whistling.

"Come on, slowpoke. I haven't got all day."

Lennox leapt out of his side, stumbled, grabbed the side mirror on the truck and his backpack, and then face-planted in the dirt. Will's laughter was loud before the snap of the front door closing silenced it. Blushing, Lennox got gingerly to his feet and checked himself over. He had a scraped palm, but his cock was still hard and fine, and that was the most important thing right now. He followed Will into the house and had just opened his mouth to holler for him when Will appeared around the door to the kitchen and backed him up against the wall.

"Hello again."

Will's hand squeezed his hips; one finger snapped the waistband of his jeans and then slid around to his ass. Lennox whined and then bit his lip. He sounded so pathetic when he made that noise, but Will didn't seem to mind.

"You like that?" Will asked, as he placed a few wet kisses on Lennox's neck. "Oyster needs to be fed and let out, but while I'm doing that you should, you know, go downstairs. Get more comfortable, get yourself all ready for me. Sound good?"

"Yeah. Definitely."

Will smacked him on the ass when he turned away, and Lennox had to bite his lip again to stop himself from yelping out loud.

"Really? Did you just—"

"Run along, loverboy. You've got a lot to do before I join you."

It shouldn't have turned him on so much when Will took charge. Yet Will's charm and authority were so natural. He'd grown into them well over the last months. Lennox jogged downstairs, tossed his backpack aside, kicked his shoes into the corner by the closet and stripped all of his clothes off. He flung himself onto the bed and yanked open the bedside drawer. Lube, box of condoms. Lennox didn't bother opening the box. Instead he got to work with the lube, coating his fingers and warming them as he heard Will and Oyster moving around upstairs.

"You've got five minutes!"

Lennox pressed his face into the pillows and groaned. He rolled onto his side, bent one of his legs up, and began to open himself. First a tentative press in, then one finger, then a second that he scissored apart from the first. As he worked a third in, wincing and hissing as the muscle stretched too soon and burned, footsteps echoed down the stairs. A moment later, Will was at the end of the bed, his shirt already off and his belt undone.

"Looking good, babe. I really like this view."

"Yeah? I've got a better one for you."

Lennox eased his fingers out of his ass, grabbed the box of condoms and took one out. He undid Will's jeans and pulled his cock free from his boxers. Will took a shaky breath as Lennox leaned forward and ran his tongue along the underside.

"Yeah, that's definitely nicer."

"That's not what I meant," Lennox said, and for a moment he leaned in, his lips parted, just enough to convince Will that he was about to be given an intense blowjob. But just as Will's hips arched forward a few inches, Lennox shut his mouth and tore the condom wrapper open. "Still not what I meant."

"But your mouth is one of my favorite—"

Lennox rolled the condom onto Will's cock, stroked him a few times with the lube still slick on his fingers and then turned himself around on all fours, ass in the air.

Even without seeing Will, he could hear him swallow behind him.

"Well, that's also on my list. Yeah."

Lennox arched his back and sighed as Will's hands grabbed him, gently massaging his cheeks and then holding them apart.

"Fuck, you're right. That is the *best* view."

One hand left his ass, and then the head of Will's cock rubbed against his hole. They both moaned as Will pressed in. Lennox dropped to his elbows and bit down on the blankets as Will thrust all the way into him, no hesitation or worries anymore. Will's hips hit his ass and stilled.

"I swear you get tighter every... fuck."

Lennox laughed and clenched around Will again.

"You were saying?"

"I'd say that isn't fair, but— "

Lennox braced himself on the bed on all fours as Will eased his hips back and then drove them forward. As he was jolted up the bed by a second thrust, Lennox closed his eyes and bit his lip. It was wonderful to have Will inside him; it felt so good little bursts of light filled his vision and firecrackers seemed to ignite under his skin. He bit down on the blankets as Will found a steady rhythm and leaned over him so his chest met Lennox's back. One hand ran over his head as Will nipped the knot of bone at the base of Lennox's neck.

"I didn't miss your hair until right now," Will said, punctuating each word with a rough thrust. "I can't grab it and hold you in place like I did last time."

Lennox twisted the blanket more tightly with his teeth and tried not to cry out, to whimper or shout or give himself completely over to all the pulses running through him. Will seemed keener than ever to see him do just that: He seemed to want to rip him apart and watch him flutter away in the wind. Once, several months ago, Will had knocked a few whispers of what Lennox felt out of him, but that had been all he'd allowed.

"Hey, don't."

Will's hips stopped. He ran a hand over Lennox's back and then the other under him and tilted Lennox's face to the side. Even now, Lennox still had the blankets clenched between his teeth.

"You don't have to be quiet for me."

Suddenly ashamed, Lennox spit the blankets out and turned his face away.

"I'm not. I'm just not loud, okay? A silent enjoyment of your dick, that's all."

"Is that why you've been chewing on the blankets for weeks? And biting down so hard on your lip it bleeds and cracks? And why you're so tense?"

"You'd be tense too with a forearm of cock being rammed into you."

Lennox pulled his hips away from Will until Will's cock slid out. What did it matter if he didn't want to make noise? Just because his body wanted to do that didn't mean *he* did. That wasn't good sex. Good sex was hot and quick and full of his usual dirty quips and a lot of grunting and sweat. Not him crying out and babbling like a drunk toddler.

"Lennox, don't shut me out."

He sat up, wincing slightly as his ass bounced on the bed.

"I'm not. Don't be stupid. I just want to fuck, not talk."

"You're ignoring what I'm saying. Just because you don't want to be vulnerable—"

"There's nothing vulnerable about sex!"

Will scoffed and turned away. He paced once toward his desk, and then back before spinning to face Lennox.

"*Everything* about this, about us being physical together, is vulnerable." Will shook his head, paced once more and then joined Lennox on the bed. "I don't know what sex was like for you before we met, but I'm guessing it wasn't anything like what we share. But sex, for me, this is as vulnerable as it gets. I love you. I choose *you*. I am sharing every part of myself with you when we're together, and yeah, sometimes it's more about passion and heat than emotions, but I'm comfortable enough to do that too because I trust you with *all* of myself."

Lennox eyed his own cock softening between his thighs and picked at a scab on his knee. He wasn't sure what it was from, most likely a rough bout of sex, probably last week when they'd experimented in the miniscule shower at the hotel in Brooklyn. Sex was different for Will. It always had been; sex had always meant something greater to him, more than either of them could be or give alone. But Lennox couldn't fathom such a thing. Sex was a tool, a pleasure that eased the fear and loneliness and obliterated, even for just a moment, the horror of what existed around and within him.

"I've never really thought about it like that. Or... I don't know. It's just sex. It's fun. Feels good. That's enough, isn't it?"

"Not for me. Not forever."

Will leaned over, his arms crossed and elbows pressed against his knees.

"Don't you want to share that with me? Or at least get what I'm trying to say?"

Lennox slid over to him and tentatively rubbed his back.

"I don't know. I've never... Every time we do something that's new for you, I never think it's going to be anything strange for me. I've already done all of this stuff, you know? But then, every time you make it something new. And that... It scares me. I can't be that scared, Will."

"Not even with me?"

Lennox looked at him, at the strength of the trust that kept Will's eyes bright. He could get lost in that gaze, not in the gentleness of their love, but in the torrent of fear that love brought into him. Will trusted him endlessly, more than anyone ever had, and the idea of doing the same was both wondrous and horrifying. How could anyone trust another with every piece of who they were? Even the parts they couldn't yet see or understand themselves?

"I... Maybe. This is... I love you. You know that, but this—"

"Is another step in that," Will said. "Maybe it won't be today, or maybe it'll take a lot of trying until you can, but it's something I know I'm going to need eventually. And don't take that as me pressuring you, because I don't want to do that."

"I think I did more than enough of that for both of us."

"What?"

Lennox flinched at the confusion that crossed Will's face. He couldn't have forgotten how they'd met. The actions and remarks that Lennox had made had been simple to him at the time, but weren't so anymore. When they'd first met he'd been terrible to Will, so much so that he couldn't believe they were here right now, that Will hadn't just beaten him up and left him to rot on the pavement somewhere.

"When we first met, I was a little shit."

"You still are," Will said and he surprised Lennox with a short laugh. "Not a lot has changed on that front. What?"

Lennox shook his head and tried to change the expression that had clearly crossed his face. He'd changed since September, hadn't he? Hadn't he gotten less aggressive, less forceful? And he hadn't been taking advantage of Will as he'd once done.

"Nothing."

"It isn't. Tell me."

"I, I'm not still like that. I mean, in some ways, but I don't push you to do stuff or try to pressure you or get in your face anymore about sex, right? I didn't... I'm sorry I did all of that. I can't say I didn't mean to, 'cause I guess I mostly did, but I didn't mean to hurt you and I did and... Sorry. That's all."

"Oh." Will shrugged a little and uncrossed his arms. "I haven't thought about that in months, honestly. I forgave you a long time ago. We wouldn't be sitting here right now if I hadn't."

"Yeah."

Lennox nodded, but he didn't say anything else.

"Do you still think about that?"

Lennox rolled his shoulders. "Sometimes. It just hits me sometimes, I guess. That I was like that."

That I was turning into them. Just another creep from the detention center.

"Well, you've grown out of it and you're sorry and you've done a lot to make up for it, so don't feel bad—"

"No, don't try to—don't comfort me about this, all right? I fucked up. I hurt you and—sometimes I think that I'll do it again or that, that—"

"What?"

Will's hand found his and squeezed.

"That, someday, if we, if we're not... That I might do the same to someone else I care about. Or that I might start doing it to you again."

For a few minutes, Will didn't say anything. Lennox expected him to pull his hand away, stung at the very idea of Lennox moving on and dating someone else in the future if they didn't work out, and how could they possibly? But Will only held his hand, a little looser and then a little tighter.

"You won't. Not to me or anyone else," he said. "You've recognized it and you're conscious of it or we wouldn't be talking about it. You're better than how you acted; you always have been. You're a lot kinder and gentler than you let on, and you care deeply when you let yourself."

"Maybe."

He said maybe to a lot of things, didn't he? Maybe he could trust Will. Maybe he was a better person than he thought. Maybe everything the world expected him to be wasn't what he wanted anymore.

"I guess we've sort of killed the mood, haven't we?"

Will stroked his cock a few times and grinned sheepishly. It was growing soft, like Lennox's. He pulled the old condom off and trashed it.

"We can still... I want to try what you want to do," Lennox said. "Not like earlier. I mean, give me what you want to, what you think I need. Not what I always want."

"Are you sure?"

"I'll tell you if I'm not."

Will nodded and laid Lennox back on the bed. One hand ran over his stomach, up his side and then traced his ribs. Lennox shivered as Will's lips caressed his jaw.

"Relax. Shut your eyes and just breathe."

Lennox swallowed as Will's fingers continued to brush his skin, but he did as he'd been told. One breath in, one breath out. Will kissed his jaw and neck and then placed a few kisses down his chest that made Lennox curl his toes.

Click, click—

"Ah, ah, ah. None of that nervous tongue clicking."

Will's teeth nipped his bottom lip and then Lennox groaned as Will's tongue worked between his lips and drew his own out. As Will's tongue flicked at his tongue ring, his hands ran down Lennox's sides, stopped at his hips to squeeze and then rolled Lennox with him to their sides.

"Are you still ready for me?"

Lennox nodded weakly as a shiver ran through his chest like the chills he always got when he had a chest cold. Will grabbed a new condom and put it on, then lifted Lennox's right leg over his hips and rubbed his cock between Lennox's ass cheeks. He wasn't fully hard again, but he was close enough to press into Lennox a few inches. They both groaned. Will's hand guided his cock into Lennox and once he was as deep as he could go, his hands massaged Lennox's ass. He kept his hips still and kissed Lennox on his nose tip.

"Okay?"

"Duh. Like I've never had your dick this deep before."

Will smiled and kissed him once more, deeply on the lips and then along his neck and jaw.

"Relax," he said against Lennox's skin. "Let me give you what you need."

Lennox swallowed as Will's hips slowly eased back and then thrust forward. It was hardly fast enough to be a thrust, really, but it felt so good. Will's cock was a slow drag inside him, teasing and thick;

stretching him out just as he closed up again. He shivered and bit his lip, but Will wasn't having it. Will tugged Lennox's lips open with his own mouth, and a weak cry left him.

"That's it," Will said as he built that same slow, deep pace with his hips. "Tell me how good it is. Fall apart for me."

Yet he couldn't. He wouldn't let himself. He couldn't. He couldn't. He—

"Oh, fuck!"

Lennox squeezed his eyes shut. His mouth fell open as Will shifted the angle of his hips and filled him again. He didn't pause to tease him or to say anything. Will only kept up the steady rhythm of his thrusts; one hand still held Lennox's ass as the other hooked around his waist. His face pressed into Will's neck, Lennox breathed deeply and let out another tentative noise he still tried to choke down. His whimper was weak and mostly swallowed, but the quiet sound of it sent a pulse through him as Will's next thrust hit him a little harder.

Will consumed him. His mouth was fire, turning his sweat to ash on his skin, leaving blazing traces on his neck and throat. His fingernails were rivers carving deep canyons into his back, his flesh, marking every part of him anew. And his pace was the warm assurance of a sunrise, lighting his body with all the wonders he couldn't see without him. Another cry left his mouth, still choked but louder. Will hummed against his throat, nipped at his skin, ran his tongue over the same spot until Lennox called out.

"Love hearing you," Will said against his skin, his lips. "Say my name?"

Lennox shook as Will's hips knocked against him, faster now, more erratic. Will's lips continued to skim over his neck, and Lennox's cock ached between their bellies. A frenzy he'd never known coursed under his skin; his body was beyond him. His limbs tensed as they hooked around Will's chest; the heel of his raised foot pressed into Will's ass to encourage him. Everything was lost and whole, new and reunited in him.

"Will, please—I don't—Will—"

"Let go for me. Be mine for only a moment."

And he was. Truly. Colors and sounds, new tones and notes Lennox had never heard sang in him. Will's breath was a symphony on his neck and lips, a whispered promise of them as consciousness left him. Lennox was still on his side when he blinked his eyes open, but Will was no longer inside him. His limbs were heavier than wet cement and his vision was fuzzy like a television picture with a bad signal.

"Lennox?"

He gurgled like a clogged sink, then blushed as Will's giggle hit his cheeks.

"That was wonderful."

Will's voice was a little hoarse, but Lennox caught every syllable of his murmured words. He nuzzled Will's nose with his and breathed.

"I didn't break anything, did I? Or break your dick off when I came?"

Will laughed a little louder and shook his head. His smile bunched up his freckles.

"No, but I think you must have blacked out."

A finger traced Lennox's cheek, then the shell of his ear. Will's hair tickled his cheeks as he bent to kiss him.

"I love you no matter what."

Will's smile grew wider.

"Even if I go to New York and you go to Boston?"

His stomach clenched, but Lennox nodded.

"Yeah, no matter where we end up in a few months. What we have is worth the extra work, right?"

"Definitely."

⏮ twenty-three ⏭

Two days before NYU expected Will's answer to be postmarked, Will sat down with every college letter he'd received. All except Sarah Lawrence. Today's mail hadn't yet arrived, but it was April now, and no answer must mean the worst. They'd taken one look at his application and portfolio and thought he was a joke. The admissions people hadn't even bothered to consider him. Unless it arrived today.

Please arrive today.

He'd called the admissions office, of course. The day after he'd applied and then every week since. Every time they'd assured him that they had his information and that the process was proceeding as normal, but Will had his doubts. Something must have gone wrong, which meant his only real choices were the pile he'd stacked up.

Behind him, Lennox groaned and threw a pillow at the lamp, but his aim was as terrible as always. He hit Oyster in the bean bag chair on the other side of the room. Oyster yelped and raced upstairs.

"Turn that light off. It's *Saturday*. Let me sleep in unless that light means a blowjob."

"It won't with that tone. I'm sorting through my college letters."

"At—"Lennox rolled over to check the alarm clock—"six in the morning? Ugh, fuck off."

Will rolled his eyes as the other pillow was hurled across the room, and this time Lennox's aim was true. It smacked Will in the face and knocked his lamp right off the corner of his desk. The lightbulb flickered out.

"Really?"

"Go upstairs."

"You're in *my* bedroom!"

"In case you haven't noticed, I don't have a bedroom," Lennox said. "So deal with it."

He yanked the blankets up over his head and went back to sleep.

Will growled, grabbed his letters, and stomped upstairs. He slammed his door and came face to face with his dad.

"Rough morning? Bit early for a weekend. You always want to sleep 'til noon."

"I'm going over my college letters. I've gotta decide before Tuesday. And Lennox is too busy breaking *lamps*—"

"Will, it's dawn. Let him sleep in the bedroom. That's what it's for."

"But it's *my* room. I've always been able to—"

"You're sharing it now, kid. You've gotta get used to having to go elsewhere when the other person wants to sleep. College dorms are going to be like that too."

"Ugh. I like having my own room."

"Well, you probably won't for a long time now. Not with a live-in boyfriend or a college roommate or a husband someday."

Will grimaced. "We'll have our own rooms. It's going in, like, our vows. Then Lennox can sprawl out all he wants."

Ben did a double take as Will took a seat on the couch.

"You, uh, talking about marriage? Together, I mean. With Lennox?"

"Well, no," Will said. He spread out his letters on the coffee table and sorted them by locations and then school sizes. Only a few were larger schools, but NYU was one of them. All alone in its New York City stack. "We're just in love. That's what happens if you're in love. Eventually."

Ben clucked his tongue. "Not always. You've got a lot of growing up to do before you're ready to commit like that, and it's always work. Love, marriage, relationships. It's work. Constant, good work."

"We're doing that. I think we are, anyway."

"All right. Well, I've gotta get to the store. You're on your own for breakfast and lunch. Karen should be back this afternoon. They've got her working a double."

Ben left after grabbing a bagel and a cup of coffee. Will sank down into the couch and picked up the stack of Virginia letters: a few up near Washington, DC and another two in the southern part of the state. They'd all been assurance schools, backups in case all of his New York ventures failed.

But they hadn't. Not entirely. Will picked up his only return from New York and opened it.

New York University.

A school in the city he'd dreamt of but had not enjoyed as much as the area around Sarah Lawrence. The city, the rush, the floods of people, it had all been so much. Maybe too much. He was a country boy. That much had become clear during their brief trip. Without Lennox, he would have been spun around so fast he'd have landed on a subway rail and never made it home. Lennox had been his guide to the city life. To the buses and subway and the grid system of streets and avenues.

Maybe he'd buy a map. Keep it in his pocket along with one of the subway. And then circle all the stops he needed to know. Would the locals be helpful? Or he could bring a bike and get hit by a few taxis instead.

He scanned the forms to accept or reject, then tore up the rejection paper and grabbed a pen. If Sarah Lawrence didn't respond, he'd just try again if NYU didn't work out. Or check out a few other schools in the area that might have good writing programs.

By the time he'd read through and completed his acceptance sheet, Lennox had come upstairs and joined him with a big tub of cereal. Lennox never used a normal bowl if he could help it. He always took one of their Tupperware containers and dumped half the box into it and then half a gallon of milk, if he could get away with it.

"You pick a school yet?"

Will nodded.

"I'm taking the leap. NYU here I come. Just have to find a stamp and mail it."

"Great. You're going to love it in the city. You know, once you stop getting lost on the subway."

"I'm going to call you when I do."

"Can't if I'm not home."

Will folded his papers and tucked them in the provided envelope. "I wish you'd just take the extra line Karen offered. It's a cheap phone. Like ten a month. Or use the one with the pay-as-you-go plan."

Lennox only shook his head and shoved cereal into his mouth. Will left him to find a stamp in his dad's desk and then returned to the living room. Milk was all over Lennox's chin and shirt, but the tub was almost empty.

"I'm going to take it over to the post office instead of waiting. Want to go?"

"You kidding me? I got up for a snack and to see if you'd decided. It's not even nine. I'm going back to sleep."

Will kissed the top of his head and went downstairs to get dressed. Lennox followed a few minutes later and curled up on the bed under the blankets. For a moment, Will watched him wrap the blankets around himself and tuck the end under his feet.

"Later."

"I'm going to hang out with Aaron. Maybe get some doughnuts. You want some?"

"Mmm."

Will grabbed a jacket on his way out the door, but it was a warm spring morning for once. He stopped at the post office, then for a bagel and some coffee so he could text Aaron before he came by. Lennox was right. It was ridiculously early for a weekend. Aaron was awake, though. He texted back within seconds and demanded that Will get him the biggest cinnamon doughnut the shop had, and then that they spend the morning at the school field, throwing.

Will bought a dozen doughnuts, then went to meet Aaron. He shoved the box of doughnuts at him as soon as he got out of his truck, and Aaron grinned.

"Yes! I haven't had doughnuts in forever. Thanks."

Aaron tossed him a ten-dollar bill and took off down the hill for the field. Will hoisted his baseball bag out of the truck bed and followed. He'd dumped his jacket and changed into shorts when he'd stopped at home, along with—

"Man, I thought you said a dozen! There's only six in here."

"I told you half were for Lennox," Will said as they ducked into the dugout and took a seat on the bench. "I sent in my NYU acceptance."

"Really? That's awesome!"

"Thanks." Will got out his glove and a bag of balls. "What about you?"

"Probably UVA. All the scouts think I should do college first." Aaron shrugged and slid his hand into his own glove. "They asked about you too. How long we'd been teammates, if you were going to play college ball or not."

"Really? But baseball's your thing."

"Well, they asked. One of them wanted to talk to you but you'd already left. Said he'd never seen a lefty catch before."

Will's neck prickled at something in Aaron's tone. They both stood and went out onto the field to stretch, but Aaron's entire demeanor had changed. His jaw was locked and he swung his arms in circles roughly as if he was trying to fling them off.

"You all right?"

Aaron didn't say anything until they started throwing easy tosses.

"They all wanted you."

Aaron's throw smacked Will's glove, but he tossed it back without saying anything.

"One guy said he'd sign you right now to the minors. You know that? Said you called a great game and had a real level swing. Nice and quiet in the batter's box."

Will shrugged as he caught the next throw and held the ball for a little longer. "So? I've never considered making baseball a career."

"But I have!"

The words burst out of Aaron as he batted Will's throw aside with his glove.

"I've wanted this for *so long*. Ever since Little League, and all they said was to keep working and waiting. But you couldn't care less, and they'd all sign you in a heartbeat."

Aaron kicked at the grass and pulled his glove off.

"It isn't—it's not—why can't I be good enough now?"

Will took a seat on the grass. Aaron flopped down too and threw his glove aside. It landed in the dirt of the infield and left a thick cloud in its wake.

None of them were good enough, it seemed. They weren't ready for what they wanted or anything that came after their diplomas, but that time was here nevertheless.

"Your boy's got it in the bag," Aaron said suddenly. "He could play that piano with no hands, ears, and eyes and still sound like Mozart."

Will didn't say anything, but Aaron was right. Lennox had the brightest future of all. A talent unparalleled by any of their own. And yet, Will had his doubts even after all the pushing he'd done to get Lennox to try.

"Maybe. He's got his record and all of that against him. I know they always say it won't count against you, but I can't imagine it's not taken into consideration."

Aaron shrugged and ripped up a fistful of grass. He tossed each blade up into the air and watched it fall back to the ground.

"What'd he do anyway? Roxanne keeps asking."

"He—"

Should he tell Aaron? Would Lennox care if Will's friends knew? It might make things easier, so Lennox wouldn't hide when Will had them over.

"Assault and battery is the technical term, I think. These kids at his school kept harassing him for being gay. One day they took it too far. He ended up in the hospital and when he got out, well, Lennox returned the favor. One of their dads was a lawyer or something and the charges stuck."

"Even after what they did to him? That's bullshit. If they'd done something when they'd hurt *him* then—"

"Yeah, I know. It's insane, but that's what happened. Lennox got locked up with even worse people and— "

Will swallowed and caught a piece of grass Aaron tossed into the air.

"And what?"

"He doesn't talk about his time in there much. I know it was awful, but sometimes, sometimes I think, I mean, he got all of his ideas about sex while he was in there. Well, most of it. How to come on to people and act and what it should mean— "

"You think someone took advantage of him in there?"

Will shrugged and turned his gaze to home plate and the chain-link fence behind it.

"Maybe. The way he told it made it sound better than it probably was. Like a story he told to convince himself he'd wanted to do stuff. But it just sounded like excuses to me. He didn't do any of it because he *wanted* to. He just wanted to keep everyone happy and not get killed or hurt."

"Have you asked him?"

"No. I... He should tell me on his own. Or realize it on his own. I don't want to pry or force him, if it is true. That's a lot and he's already had a hell of a year as it is."

"His life is all kinds of fucked up. Well, it's better with you, right? Your dad still isn't, like, being a dick?"

"No, he's cooled off a lot. I don't know how long it'll last, but Dad's okay. Him being back at work helps."

Aaron stood up and brushed his pants off. "Come on. Let's get some real throwing in. I didn't come down here to have a heart-to-heart."

Will and Aaron threw until their arms were sore. As they packed up, Will's phone rang.

Thirty-seven missed texts from Roxanne and Natasha greeted him. He had one from Karen inquiring about dinner and another from his dad. The call was from Roxanne.

"Your girlfriend's been blowing up my phone."

"My what?" Aaron took a swig of water from his jug.

"Roxanne. She's left me almost thirty texts."

"Roxanne isn't my girlfriend."

"*Suuure.*"

"What? She *isn't*. We went out twice. It was nice, but we decided friends was better for us. I mean, we're going to be on different sides of the state in three months. Trying to start anything right now is too complicated."

"That's really smart, I guess. It shouldn't be too hard, though. Just visit on weekends, and talk on the phone or online every night."

"Yeah, for the first week maybe. But then you make your friends and get involved in whatever is happening on campus. Or in the city, for you. Going back and forth from New York to Boston isn't going to be cheap."

"Well, it's... We're going to make it work," Will said, trying to keep his voice level. "Maybe it won't be every weekend, but we'll see each other. We'll figure something out."

Aaron didn't say anything as he packed up his stuff and went to collect all the baseballs from the field. Will called Roxanne back after he'd peeled his protective equipment off and was greeted with a roar in his ear.

"Where are you? We've been sitting outside your house for almost an *hour*. Lennox is staring at us from the window and flipping us off. I think he's trying to convince Oyster to attack. Let us in already."

"I'm at school."

Natasha gave a shout of horror in the background on Roxanne's end.

"What? Why is he at school? What sort of lunatic goes to school on *Saturday?*"

"I'm with Aaron. Baseball stuff."

"Right. Whatever. Get over here. We've got popcorn and lollipops and soda and movies for a wonderful Saturday afternoon and you're *ruining* it by not being here."

"I don't remember agreeing to a movie day," Will said. The girls both howled on the other end of the phone and Aaron made a face. "What?"

"Have fun with that. I'm going home to my doofus brother and some epic ping-pong."

"Whatever."

Aaron left, and Will followed shortly, struggling to collect all of his stuff as Roxanne yapped in his ear about Lennox at the window and Oyster now at the door.

"Oyster is completely harmless and you know it," Will said. He tossed his baseball bag into the truck bed and climbed into the driver's seat. "I'm hanging up now."

"You can't leave us out here with your devil dog about to slaughter us and Lennox trying to—"

"Goodbye. Good. BYE."

Will hung up and headed for home. When he pulled into the driveway, Roxanne and Natasha were huddled in the front seat of Natasha's car and Oyster was whining at their door. He spotted Lennox watching from the window, rolling pin in hand.

"Ridiculous. All three of you."

"We are not!" Natasha gave a dinosaur-like roar and Oyster backed away from her door and hid his head under his paws. "Your boy has gone batty. Look at him!"

Will saw Lennox draw the rolling pin over his throat as if cutting it.

"He's fucking with you. Get out of the car and come watch these movies or I'll send him out to really scare you off."

"As long as your dog doesn't—"

"You have fallen asleep with Oyster drooling on you more times than I can count. Now come on, or Lennox comes out."

"I thought he already *was* out," Roxanne said.

Will snorted and grabbed his bag. As he reached the front door, Roxanne and Natasha raced up behind him, Oyster at their side, best friends again. He let the three of them in, shouted at Lennox to stop antagonizing his friends, and then returned to the mailbox to collect today's mail. It was mostly bills, several magazines for his parents, and no letter from Sarah Lawrence. He shuffled through it all as he went back inside and paused at a large envelope stuck between two magazines.

A college letter.

Had Sarah Lawrence finally answered him?

But it wasn't from Sarah Lawrence. It wasn't even for him.

The letter was from Berklee College of Music, and stamped across the front in big bold letters were two words:

Congratulations, Lennox!

Will stared at the letter, his hand trembling. Lennox had done it. He'd gotten into Berklee. They were both getting out of here.

He rushed down the hall to the living room where Natasha and Roxanne were arguing over movies.

"Well, I hate *The Last Unicorn*. We're watching *The Princess Bride* and *Texas Chainsaw Massacre* and that's final!"

Will ignored Roxanne's reply and wrapped his arms around Lennox from behind where he sat on the couch. Lennox tilted his head back and stuck his tongue out at Will.

"Why are you hugging me with mail?"

"Because one of these is for you."

Will wiggled the Berklee letter in Lennox's face and the room fell silent.

Roxanne hopped onto the couch beside Lennox and tried to pull the letter out of Will's grasp. "Is that from Berklee?"

Will nodded. "Judging by the outside, it's good news."

Lennox ripped the letter out of Will's hand and turned it over to read the words printed on it. Roxanne and Natasha gave shouts of joy and tried to hug Lennox, but he dodged them and stood up.

Will had never seen such an unreadable look on his face. It wasn't happy or scared or even angry. Lennox was blank, maybe so overcome with shock he couldn't think.

"Lennox?"

The girls glanced at each other and silently went back to their stack of movies. Will went around the couch to Lennox, but Lennox shook his head.

"I'm just going to—" He pointed his thumb over his shoulder at Will's bedroom door and then almost ran downstairs.

Will started to go after him, but then stopped at the top of the stairs. Lennox should take this moment, this victory, alone. He shut the door quietly and sat on the couch with the girls. Previews were playing on the television, but neither Roxanne nor Natasha were watching them. They each gazed first at Will's bedroom door and then at Will himself.

"You know, most people leap for joy when they get into their dream college," Roxanne said. "He looked like he was about to be sick."

Will didn't say anything.

The Princess Bride began to play, but Will couldn't focus on it. Downstairs, Lennox was opening his college acceptance letter. His dream college and yet—college had been Will's dream for him, hadn't it? After almost nine months of knowing each other, Will couldn't recall Lennox once telling him a dream he'd imagined for himself.

"I'm going to check on him."

Will went downstairs, but an eerie silence was all that greeted him. Lennox was nowhere in sight.

"Lennox?"

Will checked the bathroom, looked in his closet, and returned to his room; a trickle of fear crept down his spine. He went back upstairs and popped his head into the living room.

"Lennox didn't come through here, did he?"

Roxanne and Natasha shook their heads.

"Isn't he still downstairs?"

Will didn't answer. He took the stairs three at a time, and on the bottom step he saw what he'd dreaded. His tiny window was open and unlatched. Will stood on the stack of books piled up under the window and looked out, but all he could see was the yard. Lennox was gone, and he'd taken his letter with him.

◀ twenty-four ▶

LENNOX WASN'T SURE HOW LONG he walked. His legs were numb, his head was fuzzy, and the letter from Berklee was clutched tight in his hand, still unopened. A beat syncopated against the rhythm of his heart, a fluttering panic that grew louder and more boisterous with every step.

Berklee had accepted him.

The only school he'd tried for, had auditioned for, wanted *him*.

As a student and a musician. Somehow, he'd made it past every straight-A, two-parented, rich kid and gotten in. Was it pity?

His steps stopped at a streetlight in town, and Lennox looked around. He'd been walking at least an hour if he was here. The laundromat he'd used when he'd been on his own was just down the street, and the motel. Several cars drove past before Lennox let his feet carry him down the once-familiar street. Very little had changed; the cracked sidewalks and crumbling patches of curb looked the same; but the sights didn't tighten any knots of fear in his throat. The knots were gone, or at least different.

Would Berklee still think the best of him if they could have seen him here? Would anyone?

His own mother and father probably wouldn't have recognized him, not ten months ago, sweating in the heat of summer with a barricaded door all that kept him from the fists of tormenters. And they wouldn't recognize him now, gaunt-faced in the worn clothes he was outgrowing and with a college letter clutched in his hand.

Lennox walked until his feet ached, right past the laundromat and the motel. Everything was quiet there, and if he'd taken a picture from his last visit he could have looked at that instead. It was all the same. From the street he could even see his rickety old door swaying open and shut in the warm breeze of late spring. Beside it, Lucy's old room was shut up and dark, the curtains drawn. Even Shrimpy's pickup truck was in the lot. He kept walking before his old enemies came outside.

College was a huge step. Could he do this? How would he ever cover the expense?

"Lennox?"

He turned at the sound of his name and saw Malia Ottoman at work in the small garden she was digging in front of her house. His footsteps had carried him clear across town, all the way to Otto's house. Quickly, Lennox rolled up his letter and tucked it into his back pocket.

"Um, hi."

"Did you walk here?"

"Uh, yeah, sort of. It's a, um, nice day."

Overhead, a rumble of thunder filled the sky. Malia stood and wiped her hands on a towel she'd been kneeling on.

"I'm afraid Otto's not here right now. He had a lacrosse tournament today. He won't be back until late, but I'm just about to go in and have some lunch while this storm passes through. Do you want to join me?"

Lennox shook his head. "No, I'll just see him Monday at school. Bye."

He turned away as Malia headed inside. But Lennox stopped on the corner and went back. He took a seat on their covered porch; his letter crinkled as he sat on it. With the first fat raindrops, Malia reappeared, two plates of sandwiches in her hands. She took a seat beside him and set the second plate on his lap.

"Hope you like peanut butter and banana."

"Peanut butter and *banana?* Why would you ever—"

"My father was a huge fan. Always made me and my brothers eat it when we were growing up. A good way to get some fruit in us, he said."

"Right. That's weird."

Malia chuckled. "You know, Karen said the same thing when we first met, and then I had her over for lunch after work one day and forced her to try a fried one. She loves them."

Rain began to speckle the ground. Little rivers of topsoil and fertilizer raced down the sidewalk and over the driveway. Lennox made a face as Malia wolfed down her own sandwich. He stared at his. It looked harmless enough. He nibbled at the corner, and Malia laughed.

"Oh, no. You take the first bite right or you don't eat it at all. A nice big chunk, go on. You've gotta get the banana on the first one."

He made another face, turned the sandwich around in his hands and bit off an enormous bite. As he chewed, Malia watched him. Much to his surprise it wasn't bad, certainly good enough for another time. The smell of peanut butter and banana alone was enticing.

"Well?"

"It's good. I still like peanut butter and chocolate chips better, but this is good too."

"Peanut butter and chocolate chips?" Malia stared at him. "On *bread?*"

"Like a candy bar. It's perfection."

"I doubt that." Malia shook her head at him. "Sounds as imperfect as that letter's going to be after you finish sitting on it."

Lennox stuffed the whole sandwich into his mouth. Malia tugged on the letter until Lennox lifted his butt. Her face lit up when she unfolded it and saw the words stamped across the front.

"You got in? Lennox, that's wonderful!"

He shrugged and tried to chew the gob of sandwich in his mouth. One breath in through his nose, and then a splatter of sandwich out of his mouth.

"Stop trying to choke yourself. This is *great* news. I'm sure Will and Karen and Ben are thrilled."

Lennox swallowed what he could and worked on chewing the rest.

"I guess. Will was excited, but I dunno."

"Well, you might know if you open this."

Malia handed him the letter and took their plates inside. He heard some clinking and then the screen door squeaked open.

"You coming in or sitting out here until the rain stops?"

She held the door open and, hesitantly, Lennox followed her in. The house was the same, though the smell was different. A flowery scent filled the living room instead of food cooking and the musk of a teenager.

"Can I get you anything?"

"No. Thanks."

Malia disappeared into the kitchen. Lennox sat on the couch and listened to the sound of running water as he twirled his letter in his hands. He should open it. The surprise of getting into Berklee was already over, but the rest wasn't: the cost of all sorts of fees, and books, and probably musical instruments, and whatever else. He hooked his finger under the sealed flap, tugged, and ripped it open.

But he couldn't bring himself to pull the thick pages out. Everything was right in his hands, this future that had never even flickered in his eyes until Will, and now—

"What's it say?"

Malia sat beside him on the couch. He shoved the envelope toward her and wrung his hands between his knees. She didn't say anything, but she did pull the pages out and flip through them. It was a lot, at least ten pages of stuff. Lennox's brain ground to a halt just thinking about all the information in there, the dollar signs that preceded astronomical numbers.

After several minutes, Malia spoke.

"Do you want to read it or have me tell you?"

"I don't… It's too expensive. I'm never going to pay that kind of money back."

"Of course you can. It just takes time. I did, so can you."

"No, okay? I… Look, I spent *all* summer and the fall looking for a crappy little job around here just running a register or bagging fucking *groceries*. Do you know how many places wouldn't even let me apply?"

"No, I don't. But I can imagine. I've been there myself, and you aren't going to find that once you leave this area. Not even forty miles east. Boston is another world compared to here. So is New York City. So is most of the country and the world. Around here, people are a little less than they could be. You'll find something, whether it's working while you're in school or all the opportunities once you graduate."

"It's still so much. What if—I might get bored and fail out or—"

"You won't know unless you try, Lennox."

She handed him the papers and stood up.

"I've got to go pick Abe up from his friend's house. Let me give you a ride back to Will's, okay?"

Lennox followed her to her truck and got in. As she drove, he flipped through the papers, not reading them, but counting, wondering. After two counts of nine, he took a deep breath and read the first. The words scrambled in his brain, from the remarks about his excellence to the school's hopes for his growth and musical maturity if he chose to further his education with them. Lennox flipped to the next one as Malia rumbled to a stop in front of Will's house. It was a long list of various scholarships and explanations of what each was from and for. He just had time to think "So what?" when he turned to the third page and his jaw dropped.

"A scholarship?"

"Are you just now getting to that page?"

All of his normal sarcasm failed him. As Lennox got out and went inside, he continued to stare at the letter in his hands. Voices called out as soon as he shut the front door.

"Lennox?"

"Is he back?"

"Who *else* could it be, Dad?"

Will made it into the hallway first. Lennox glanced up and was surprised to find Will's face was redder than a cherry.

"How could you just run off like that? I thought... You're so stupid. And you didn't even open the letter before you left!"

Will yanked him into a hug, crushing the papers between them. Then he pulled back and shoved Lennox's shoulder.

"I can't *believe*—"

"I opened it."

Ben and Karen appeared next. There was no sign of Roxanne and Natasha as they all moved into the living room, but Lennox could hear the murmur of a television and voices from Will's open bedroom door.

"Congratulations, Lennox," Karen said. She hugged him as Will took a seat on the couch. "I've been hoping you'd hear good news, and this is magnificent. Both of our boys going to college, we're going out to dinner."

Lennox faltered. "Both of—"

Ben slapped him on the back as Karen let him go and grinned. "Nice job, kid. What's that letter say? Any luck with scholarships?"

Will's ears perked up at his dad's words. Lennox shuffled through the papers until he found the third one with the award.

"Yeah. I got one. I'm not sure what it all means or anything, but—"

Will was upon him again, his hug tighter and his breath warm against Lennox's ear. Carefully, Lennox wrapped his arms around him as well.

"I knew you'd get in. This is great. I'm just so... Is it weird to be proud of you?"

"A little."

"Well, I am."

Will cupped his face and leaned in for a long, slow kiss. Even as Ben cleared his throat a few feet away, Lennox relaxed his jaw and deepened their kiss. Karen hurried around behind them all.

"Shall we go somewhere fancy or somewhere more casual? We'll need reservations."

Will cleared his throat as they broke apart.

"Roxanne and Natasha are still here. How about tomorrow?"

Karen smacked her forehead. "Right. I forgot. I'm free tomorrow. Where do you want to go, Lennox? Any favorite restaurants?"

He shook his head.

"Well, we'll pick something. Maybe seafood?"

"Allergic."

"*What?*"

Will watched him in horror. "But fish! And lobster and crab and *shrimp!* You can't miss out on—"

"I can. Did you see me eat seafood in Baltimore while you stuffed your face?"

"Well, no."

"It's not a life or death allergy. Or, it wasn't when I had it as a kid. I just get all puffy and my throat and lips get itchy. Dad was so upset we couldn't have shrimp anymore. Mom banned it from the house because I kept eating it even though my face swelled."

"You *would.*"

"No seafood then."

Karen and Ben retreated into the kitchen to discuss dinner. Will sat Lennox down on the couch, but instead of sitting beside him, Will climbed onto his lap, bracketing Lennox's hips with his knees. He hooked his arms around Lennox's neck as he sat and kissed him until Lennox was warm and limp against the back of the couch.

"We're going to college," Will said against his lips. He paused to smile against Lennox's mouth and then kissed him on his nose. "We're getting out of here."

Lennox nodded, but the letter in his hand felt as if it was melting. Slick with his sweat and body heat, the letter still held so many questions, so many new worries.

"How about Italian?" Karen called from the kitchen.

Lennox made a muffled noise of agreement as Will went back to kissing him.

* * *

WILL SPENT ALL OF SUNDAY poring over the papers from Lennox's acceptance letter and looking at tuition costs online and how much he might still have to cover after the scholarship. The entire day had made Lennox's stomach turn, so by the end of band class on Monday morning, Lennox wasted no time rushing out under the guise of having to get to his next class early. He didn't explain himself to Will, but he did take the acceptance letter and stuff it under all the books at the bottom of his locker.

Karen and Ben had asked many of the same questions at dinner on Sunday. They wanted to know about fees and his scholarship and tuition and room and board. All Lennox had gathered from the scholarship was that they'd offered him some undisclosed amount of money, but he couldn't bring himself to call and ask.

He kept out of Will's sight in the halls, and when he finally saw Otto again for fifth period and lunch it was a relief. Otto would get it. He'd think college was all insane and expensive and probably pointless too.

"You look like you swallowed a bunch of gym socks," Otto said as they made their way from their classroom to lunch. "Is this about that college you got into?"

Lennox looked at him as they turned the corner and joined the line for hot lunch.

"What? You think just because she's *my* mom that she wasn't leaping for joy and telling everyone she ran into? Oh, Abe told me to give you this."

Otto punched him hard on the shoulder and said, in a very dull voice unlike his own or Abe's, "Yay go Lennox."

"Fuck off."

"What? That's what he said."

"He did not. And he doesn't sound like a morbid elephant anyway."

"Oh, morbid. Look at the college man using his college words."

The line shuffled along. Lennox grabbed a tray for himself and then smacked Otto's hand with it when he reached for his own.

"Boys, no hitting!"

The worker behind the line gave them a look, but when she turned away Otto grabbed a tray and smacked Lennox on the ass with it.

"Oh, is this your way of coming on to me? Unless you've got a foot-long dick, then—"

"Shut up. Move before the pizza's all gone."

They collected their food and paid, then went out into the lunchroom to find a seat. For once, their usual spot was taken, but Otto didn't seem to notice. Lennox was getting ready to go over and force his seat at their table when Otto made a strangled voice.

"What? You aren't choking on an imaginary dick already, are you?"

"He's *here*."

"What? Who?"

Otto pointed across the room to a little table set up beside one for the senior prom. At first, Lennox thought he meant the prom table, but nobody had so much as spoken about prom to him. Will didn't seem interested, and with the dance only a week away, Lennox didn't think much about it. But instead, Otto was pointing at the smaller table beside the prom table. A simple banner was hung on the wall behind it, advertising the various branches of the military.

Instead of fighting for their usual table, Otto hurried over to the one closest to the military recruitment table and watched the lone man behind it. The guy was in full uniform, though Lennox couldn't tell which branch he belonged to. Not the army, since it was a sharp, dark blue with lots of medals and lines of color across the breast. While Otto gazed at all of that, Lennox watched the man himself. Unless he counted the one cafeteria lady, this man was the only other black person in the room.

"I can't believe he's finally here."

Lennox snorted. The guy fixed a few stacks of pamphlets on the table.

"You sound like you're in love."

"I'm *not*. He's just… But I'm not old enough until the end of May."

"Like they care. Go over there."

Lennox started eating, but Otto didn't touch his food. After ten minutes, Lennox was finished and Otto's pizza was stone cold. He took it, and Otto didn't even notice.

"Okay, seriously? Come on."

Lennox went around the table and tugged on Otto until he stood. He shoved him all the way over to the table where the man stood and waited.

"Hello, boys. I'm Sergeant Wilkins. Can I interest you in your career options with the military?"

Lennox elbowed Otto until he spoke.

"Uh, um, yeah. I was going to, but I'm not eighteen until the end of the month."

"He's going to join," Lennox said for him. "He's been sitting over there drooling over you for the past ten minutes. Sign him up."

Sergeant Wilkins chuckled and shook Otto's entire arm.

"Which branch have you been looking at joining?"

"Uh, the um, the, er—"

"He's thinking army."

The sergeant picked up several pamphlets and handed them to Otto, who continued to stare at him as if he was a big purple leopard.

"Right," Lennox said, eyeing the many pamphlets himself. Would one of those pay for the rest of his school? Or all of it? Might this slight detour save him from decades of debt? "Well, thanks. Are you here tomorrow? He might get a few words out by then."

"Of course. I'm here all week. We'll have a representative from the army joining me on Thursday and Friday as well."

"Great. Well, see you."

"Have you considered a career in the military?"

Lennox turned at the hand on his shoulder. He bit his lip, scanned the papers, and then said the one surefire thing that would stop the questions.

"I'm gay, man. You don't want me."

Sergeant Wilkins didn't even flinch. "The military no longer discriminates based on sexual orientation, actually. To be honest, before 'Don't Ask, Don't Tell' was repealed it was pretty common for all the guys in a unit to know and accept anyone who wasn't straight."

"Oh. Right, well—"

"Have you been looking at colleges as an option?"

"I, uh, well, one. I got into a college in Boston."

Lennox hesitated as the sergeant collected a pamphlet from each stack and offered them to him. The bell rang overhead. Otto continued his dreamlike walk out of the cafeteria and down the hall. Lennox took the pamphlets but didn't look at them.

"We'll help pay the cost of college."

"Yeah?"

"Yes, sir. There are different amounts for different schools and service time, of course, but an out-of-state school is going to charge you a lot, I'm sure."

Lennox clenched the papers tighter and took a few steps backward.

"They, uh, gave me a scholarship, you know. Well, bye."

He hurried out and found Otto wandering the halls aimlessly, with the pamphlets still clasped loosely in his fist.

"Come on, you idiot. Class is back that way."

"Uh huh. Sure, I'll join. I can't wait."

"Yeah, you can."

LENNOX HID THE MILITARY PAMPHLETS in his backpack and then under Will's mattress. With no practice after school, Lennox had gone home while Will stayed for his baseball practices and games. One day after two weeks, once May had arrived with a bright burst of sunlight and hazy humidity, Lennox pulled the pamphlets from under the mattress one afternoon and read through them.

Very little of it seemed like him: directions and drills and uniforms. But the idea of going so many places, of getting to fly a plane or sail on a ship, was certainly thrilling. He'd be paid to do something dangerous; they would pay him to go to school.

Overhead, heavy footsteps announced Ben's arrival home. He hollered down and Lennox answered for Will.

"He's at baseball practice."

"You want a sandwich? I'm going to make grilled cheese!"

"Sure, thanks."

Lennox flipped through all of the pamphlets one more time before he opened Will's laptop. That Google thing Will always used would be helpful. It seemed to have the answers to everything, even Will's math homework. Sometimes it even showed the work, but Lennox had caught on to that trick after three weeks.

He opened the browser, and the first site to come up was Berklee's. Would the tuition total be listed? At least an estimate was probably available. He might even find his scholarship and how much it would give him. Lennox clicked around, went from one article to another. After about ten minutes, he was back on Google trying new search terms. Ben came down the stairs and joined him on the bed with a stack of grilled cheese sandwiches.

"Hard at work?"

Lennox shrugged. "Just looking stuff up. Berklee things. Nothing important."

"You call about that scholarship yet? Presidential Scholarship sounds important."

"I... No. I'm trying to find it online, but I suck at searching on this dumb thing."

"Here. You got your letter?"

Lennox pulled it from his backpack and let Ben read it over. But instead of reading, Ben pulled out his phone and dialed a number on one of the pages.

"No, you don't have to—"

"Yes, hello. I have a few questions about a scholarship my, uh, kid received."

"I'm not your—"

Lennox tried to grab the phone from him, but like Will, Ben was much stronger than him. One hand on his chest was enough to hold him back.

"Yes, his name's Lennox McAvoy. His letter said he's been selected to receive the Presidential Scholarship, but there wasn't any more information about it in his acceptance letter. I was just wondering if you had any information about how much of his tuition and board it might cover."

Lennox winced, shut his eyes, and stuck his fingers in his ears. But he couldn't force himself to not look. Ben's expression went from shocked to excited. He said a few more things Lennox couldn't hear and then hung up. He took one look at Lennox and yanked his fingers out of his ears.

"Get your fingers out of your ears, kid," Ben said and he was grinning so widely Lennox was sure a plane could land in his mouth. "That scholarship you got? It's given to seven kids who show the greatest musical merit and potential. And financial need."

"Well, no shit. That's what scholarships are f—"

"It's a full ride, kid. Tuition, room and board, even the fancy laptop you'll need to connect with all the recording studios and something or other. They're going to send you an information packet in the mail. They said you still need to accept your place at Berklee too."

"I—You mean they—they're going to—I don't have to—"

Lennox choked on his next words and bit his lip.

"Yeah, they're paying for it all. For all four years, well, except books, but that'll be a lot easier to cover than sixty-five thousand a year."

"So I don't have to join the army?"

"*What?* Why on *earth* would you—"

"They pay for school," Lennox said, slipping one of the pamphlets from under the bed. "That's what Otto said, and the recruiter... I was going to look it up to see what was covered by the scholarship and see if they'd cover the rest before I did anything stupid—"

"You are *not* joining the military. That is not your path. Even if it was mine and your friend's, that isn't for you, okay?"

"I know, I just—it seemed like it might—"

"Drag you the hell away from what you're actually meant to be doing. Seven kids get this scholarship a year," Ben told him, and he took him by the shoulders and shook him. "*Seven.* Out of thousands that apply and hundreds that get in, and you are one of the *best* they met. Do you understand how incredible your talent is? The kind of future you've got with music if you give this a chance?"

"I—well, I mean I'm okay and all, but I never... My mom was the concert pianist and stuff. That was her job. She was better."

"Bet she'd have some real competition from you these days," Ben said. "You are so gifted, kid. She saw that and nurtured the hell out of it while she was still around. I didn't know her, but it's clear she saw in you what she'd found inside herself and she made sure that same passion and talent wasn't left abandoned."

Lennox didn't say anything, but then Ben did something he'd never done before. He pulled Lennox into his arms and hugged him tight. The bulk of him settled around Lennox like a warm blanket. Strong and sure, and dare he think—fatherly?

"Your mom would be so damn proud of you," he said against Lennox's head. "Hell, I'm proud of you and most of the time I still feel like I barely know you. You're going to be great at that school. Just like Will is going to be at NYU."

Lennox squeezed Ben back before they broke apart. Ben cleared his throat and handed him the stack of grilled cheese sandwiches.

"Get busy on this before they get cold, all right?"

Ben stood up and went to the stairs, but at the bottom he paused.

"And for the record, that G.I. bill hardly covers anything once you get out of state or start talking big schools. About seven thousand a semester, give or take. I definitely wouldn't say it's worth it to join just for that."

"Yeah. Yeah, okay."

Lennox ate his way through all six sandwiches and then looked at the military pamphlets. It was certainly one path; might even be a good one if he didn't have music to direct his life, but it wasn't for him. This was Otto's next journey. He cleaned the pamphlets up and packed them back into his backpack. Otto could use them if he wanted, or he could take them back to the recruitment officer and tell him no. Some other kid could follow that path, but it wasn't for Lennox.

He pulled all the papers out of his Berklee acceptance letter envelope and began to fill them out.

◀ twenty-five ▶

ON MEMORIAL DAY WEEKEND, WILL sat down at the newly cleaned table on the back deck and spread out all of his college papers, awards, and a list of college expenses he'd made. Ben was at the grill, Karen was sunbathing, and Lennox—

"Cannonball!"

A wave of water washed over Karen. She yelped and then dove in after him. Oyster followed with a shrill howl and a big belly flop. Will smiled as he watched the water war begin: huge splashes, Lennox scrambling to get out of the pool before Karen caught him. Ben shut the grill and turned the temperature down a little.

"Why don't you go have some fun? Get busted for making out under the diving board or something."

"I've got to figure this out before—"

"We'll get there, Bud," Ben said. "They offered you a partial scholarship that's a little over fifteen. And I've got some saved up, mostly what was left from your mom's life insurance. That's almost another ten for each year. So that's—"

"Twenty-two a semester, so I'll have about six thousand a semester to still figure out, plus books and other expenses."

"Yeah, and we'll help. Karen and I started putting some away—"

"But that should be for vacations and your retirements—"

"We'll help. You said they've got payment plans, right? We'll do that for what we can, and see what you can get with federal aid for the rest, okay? I'm sure you'll get something since your grades have always been so good. Or maybe a little extra if you join their baseball team or something."

Will frowned. Ben, however, picked up all of his papers and notes and set them inside on the kitchen table. He returned to the grill and turned over the chicken and burgers.

"Go have fun with your boy," Ben said. "It's almost summer and in another week you'll be walking across that stage to get your diploma. I'm so proud of you. Of both of you."

Will glanced at Lennox wrestling with Oyster over a water Frisbee at the edge of the pool and smiled.

"I was wrong. All the stuff I said when he was first here, about him being a thug and using you and... I was wrong, Will. Thanks for taking his side. Sticking up for him. He's a good kid. I'm glad you've got him in your life."

"So am I."

Will got up and pulled his shirt off. "You going to join us?"

"Nah. Someone's gotta make dinner. Go give me a reason to shout at you, all right?"

Will grinned and raced over to the pool, where he jumped right at Lennox with a huge splash. They wrestled a bit as Oyster swam away and went to the stairs to get out. Karen pushed a wave of water at them as she climbed out too.

"Keep it clean, boys, or you're draining and cleaning the pool tomorrow."

"Does that mean we can piss in—*gurlgg!*"

"Will, don't drown him!"

* * *

THE REST OF THEIR THREE-DAY weekend flew by. They spent most of it by the pool, studying for their last finals and kissing until their lips ached and chapped. Roxanne and Natasha came by on Monday to play in the pool, and then Tuesday it was back to a very different school schedule. Regular classes had ended for the seniors. Instead, they rotated between exams in the cafeteria in the morning and afternoon, and then in study blocks during the lunch shifts.

Will took his last exam on Tuesday morning, then hung around to get his yearbook and see his friends one final time. A little party had been set up in the gymnasium for all of them if they chose to stay after their morning exam, so Will cleared out the last shelves and scraps of paper from his locker and went to meet Lennox.

"How'd it go?"

Lennox grunted and slammed his locker door open.

"That bad, huh?"

"It was French," Lennox said, half snarling as he stuffed the last items from his locker into his backpack. "Sounded like I was speaking in tongues or trying to exorcise the devil from the girl I had to do that monologue with. I hate French."

"Well you never have to take it again now."

"Yeah, until college."

"You could try a different language if you have to take one," Will said.

Lennox grabbed the last few papers out of his locker and a few fluttered to the floor. Will stooped to pick them up and two of them caught his eye. The first was Lennox's acceptance letter from Berklee, and the second was—

"Why do you have a Navy pamphlet?"

"Huh? Oh."

Lennox took the letter from him and shut his locker.

"It's nothing. Just something for Otto, you know?"

Lennox set off down the hall for the gymnasium, and Will followed. He was deflecting, even lying. Had Lennox joined? Was his talk of Berklee and Boston and all of those recent phone calls with Lucy and Kelly a ruse? Would Lennox lie just to give him what he hoped for Lennox to have?

"That isn't for Otto. He just joined the army, not the navy. You said you weren't thinking about this."

Will stepped into Lennox's path and blocked him in the empty hall. Up ahead he could hear the thump of music and the chatter of the other seniors spending one final afternoon together before they all went their separate ways.

"I wasn't. I mean, I did. But—"

"So you lied to me."

A flare of anger filled Will, but it went out almost at once and was replaced by a dull ache. Lennox had lied to him. He didn't trust him with the things he might want—

"I didn't. When you asked... No, don't walk away."

Lennox caught him this time and forced him to stop.

"When you asked me, I wasn't thinking about it yet, okay? It was after. Otto kept talking about it, and I hadn't figured out my scholarship yet, and I had no idea what I was doing or what might happen if Berklee was too expensive and I panicked. I figured they might pay for school if I did get in and—I don't know. It was dumb. I was scared, okay? Let's get in there before all the good food is gone."

But Will still held him back.

"Why didn't you tell me?"

Lennox faltered.

"I don't know. I guess I figured you'd freak out or think I was crazy or something. That you wouldn't want me to do it if I did decide to join."

Will's stomach dropped at his words. "I want you to do what *you* want with your life. Even if it scares the shit out of me, okay? I forced college and then Berklee on you. I was scared you'd do something rash because what I thought was good for you wasn't what you wanted."

"So was I."

Will laced their fingers together.

"Tell me next time, okay? We're boyfriends, and that means best friends, too."

Lennox nodded and pulled him into a hug. Will kissed his neck and breathed him in for just a moment before they headed into the gymnasium. They spent the afternoon with their friends, Roxanne, Aaron, Natasha, and Otto, eating and joking and, in everyone except Lennox's case, exchanging yearbooks to sign. Will passed his around last. Roxanne wrote a long gushing note on the back cover, Natasha wrote a few jokes from all their years together, Aaron talked about baseball and how they'd still need to meet up to play once in a while, and Otto drew several dicks. Then Will handed it to Lennox.

"What am I supposed to do with this?"

Will stared at him in shock. "Haven't you ever signed a yearbook?"

"No. Whose have I ever had to sign? Or been at a school long enough for that?"

"Oh. Right. Well, you can just sign it or draw stuff on your photo or whatever you want. See what everyone else did for ideas or something. I usually just jot a little note."

Lennox took the yearbook and flipped through it while Will headed down the bleachers to sit with the others. Otto had disappeared into the group of people who were starting a basketball game, but Aaron was checking baseball stats on his phone, and the girls were comparing course options for the fall.

"If I'm lucky I'll get a bunch of credits for AP scores," Roxanne was saying as Will sat down beside her. "I've already got a few from last year, but I don't know how to let them know. Do you?"

"I just called and then they had me send a copy of my scores," Natasha told her. "If I get high enough grades on this year's I'll knock out a whole semester. We all probably will if we got fours and fives."

"I won't," Will said with a weak smile. "I bombed the one for math, but I think I passed the rest. Most of my tuition and fees will be covered, and Lennox got *really* lucky."

"Yeah, he did," Roxanne said, a note of jealousy in her voice. "Wish *I* could hammer on a piano like that."

"It came at a cost," Will said, and when the girls asked what he meant, Will refused to answer.

Lennox kept Will's yearbook for the rest of the week. Wednesday was a free day, then Thursday was a brief assembly to go over parts of the graduation ceremony. Friday afternoon was a practice round of the real thing, minus caps and gowns, so Lennox and Will spent the morning lazing in bed; the house was empty, and quiet except for the click of Oyster's nails on the floor overhead.

"Can I just say, as much as I love you and all, that I'm going to be really glad to have a bed all to myself again?"

Will elbowed Lennox in the hip and tried to take back some space on the mattress. Lennox giggled and spread out farther, playfully kicking at Will until he was half off the bed.

"Whoops. Did I push you off your bed again?"

"You're a bed hog."

"And you're a space heater." Lennox pulled his shirt off and groaned, his face pressed into the blankets. "Ugh, this was great in the winter, but now—"

"If we ever have our own place we're getting two twin beds, and when we want to have sex we'll either do it somewhere naughty or push the beds together. Deal?"

"Deal. But naughty has my vote. Pushing beds together is too much pre-sex effort."

"Better to put that energy into thrusting, yeah."

Will flopped back down beside Lennox so their feet knocked together against the headboard. He kissed Lennox's shoulder and then his bicep.

"I'm going to miss this too, though. Being with you every day. It'll be weird not having you around all the time."

"You better go to clubs," Lennox said. "Shake your ass for all the men in New York and then have fun turning them down. And then tell me all about it when you're walking thirty blocks back to your dorm because you got lost on the subway and refuse to get back on it."

"I am *not*... Well, maybe."

They both laughed, and Will pulled his phone out and turned on some music. He let Lennox pick, as he almost always did these days, but it wasn't the usual jagged rhythm or even a fast or heavy one. The music was soft: gentler than a flute's high notes and easier than a string quartet. A quiet piano played, with a little static in the background as if the track hadn't been recorded in a studio. Will shut his eyes and pressed his forehead against Lennox's temple.

"You've been adding music to my phone."

"Mm hmm."

Will listened until the song ended, and then it began a second time. He opened his eyes and found Lennox watching him.

"Who was that by? It was beautiful."

"I wrote it. For you."

Lennox leaned over the side of the bed and pulled something out from under it. It was Will's yearbook. He flipped to a dog-eared page and Will found both of their photos gazing up at him, frozen in the standard tuxedos, but the boy in Lennox's photo was very different than the one lying beside him. The boy in the photo had sunken eyes, a cheap smile, and hair almost to his shoulders. So many things had changed since September, but the gift of Lennox's true smile now was his favorite. Around their pictures were musical notes, written on bars going across the top and along the sides of the page, spiraling all the way into the center between them.

"I figured it would translate a little better if I recorded it for you. I've seen you try to read music firsthand and all. So, do you like it?"

"It's—Lennox, it's wonderful. This is the *best* gift, okay? Thank you."

Will hugged him and kissed him on the cheek.

"You really like it?"

"Yeah, it's beautiful. Really. I can't believe you wrote a song for me."

"I couldn't think of any words to say," Lennox said. "But the music, it's just there. It's always there, right at the ends of my fingers."

Will rested his head against Lennox's and smiled as the song played for him. His song. A gorgeous waterfall of notes and chords and all the other terms he'd never mastered. This was the true language Lennox spoke.

"I'm so glad you got into Berklee. You're perfect for it."

"Not so sure they'll agree once I'm there."

"It's our job to shake things up," Will said. "Change the world and all of that. Even Dad says so."

"I think he might take that back in a few years."

"Years? More like a few months, knowing him."

Will stretched and sat up.

"We need to get going or we're going to be late to the graduation practice."

Lennox stayed where he was, his chin resting on the bed, stretched out with Will's phone in his hand. Soon, he'd have to say goodbye to this magnificent boy—a boy all his own—but summer had still to begin its blaze and burn out into fall. They had time together yet. Perhaps all the time in the world.

THE END

Coming Soon

Lennox and Will's story continues.

⊙ acknowledgments ⦿

THANK YOU, AZ AND BEIZY, for hanging around for all of my late night babbling text parties. You kept me on course—even though I intentionally derailed. Thanks for the encouragement. This book would have taken a very different path otherwise, and I'm glad we left the road.

To all of my friends, old and new and work-related, thank you for supporting me throughout this process and for being sources of inspiration and information. And if you read this book, don't tell me. Unless you want to see the blood vessels in my face and neck burst. Then, by all means, go ahead. The best friendships are the embarrassment-filled ones.

And to Mouthy, Mer-Mer, Brudder, and Loony Toon, you four are egg heads. I miss you terribly.

◖ about the author ◗

ZANE RILEY IS A TRANSGENDER writer who wrote his first work of fan fiction in the fourth grade. He is a recent transplant to Vancouver, Washington where he spends his time watching long-distance baseball games, hiking, and exploring the musical depths of the internet. His first novel, *Go Your Own Way*, was published by Interlude Press in 2015.

One **story**
can change **everything.**

@interlude**press**

Twitter | Facebook | Instagram | Pinterest

*For a reader's guide to **With or Without You** and book club prompts, please visit interludepress.com.*

also by
zane **riley**

Will Osborne plans to a quiet senior year, hoping that college would help him close the door on years of harassment. But transfer student Lennox McAvoy changes all of that—he's crude, flirtatious, and the most insufferable, beautiful person Will's ever met. From his ankle monitor to his dull smile, Lennox seems irredeemable. But Will soon discovers that there is more to Lennox than meets the eye.

ISBN (print) 978-1-941530-34-4 | ISBN (eBook) 978-1-941530-38-2

also from...
interlude press

What It Takes by Jude Sierra

Milo met Andrew moments after moving to Cape Cod—launching a lifelong friendship of deep bonds, secret forts and plans for the future. When Milo goes home for his father's funeral, he and Andrew finally act on their attraction—but doubtful of his worth, Milo severs ties. They meet again years later, and their long-held feelings will not be denied. Will they have what it takes to find lasting love?

ISBN (print) 978-1-941530-59-7 | ISBN (eBook) 978-1-941530-60-3

Small Wonders by Courtney Lux

A pickpocket who finds value in things others do not want, Trip Morgan becomes involved with Nate Mackey, a down-and-out Wall Street professional who looks like a child in a photograph Trip found years before. In confronting their own demons and finding value in each other, Trip and Nate may find that their relationship is a wonder of its own.

ISBN (print) 978-1-941530-45-0 | ISBN (eBook) 978-1-941530-46-7

Love Starved by Kate Fierro

At 27, Micah Geller has more money than he needs, a job he loves, a debut book coming out, and a brilliant career ahead of him. What he doesn't have is a partner to share it with—a fact that's never bothered him much.

When a moment of weakness finds him with a contact to a high-class escort specializing in fulfilling fantasies, Micah asks for only one thing. "Show me what it's like to feel loved."

ISBN (print) 978-1-941530-32-0 | ISBN (eBook) 978-1-941530-30-6

CPSIA information can be obtained
at www.ICGtesting.com
Printed in the USA
LVOW12s0310210816

501168LV00001B/2/P